I BN

1 1 0456258 4

Born in Barnsley to a French mother and an English father, Joanne Harris went on to study Modern and Medieval Languages at Cambridge. She was a teacher for 15 years, during which time she published three novels. Since then, she has written several more novels, three cookbooks and many short stories, as well as a *Doctor Who* novella for the BBC, guest episodes for the game *Zombies, Run!* and a number of musical theatre projects. Published in over 50 countries, her books have won a number of British and international awards. Harris is an honorary Fellow of St Catharine's College, Cambridge and in 2013 was awarded an MBE. She lives with her husband in a little wood in Yorkshire, where she works from a shed in her garden.

THE STRAWBERRY THIEF

Vianne Rocher has settled down. Lansquenet-sous-Tannes, the place that once rejected her, has finally become her home. With Rosette, her 'special' child, she runs her chocolate shop in the square, talks to her friends on the river, is part of the community. Even Reynaud, the priest, has become a friend. But when old Narcisse the florist dies, leaving a parcel of land to Rosette and a written confession to Reynaud, the life of the sleepy village is once more thrown into disarray. The arrival of Narcisse's relatives, the departure of an old friend and the opening of a mysterious new shop in the place of the florist's across the square all seem to herald some kind of change: a confrontation, a turbulence — even, perhaps, a murder . . .

JOANNE HARRIS

THE STRAWBERRY THIEF

Complete and Unabridged

CHARNWOOD
Leicester

First published in Great Britain in 2019 by
Orion Fiction
an imprint of The Orion Publishing Group Ltd
London

First Charnwood Edition
published 2020
by arrangement with
The Orion Publishing Group Ltd
An Hachette UK Company
London

A catalogue record for this book is available
from the British Library.

ISBN 978–1–4448–4453–5

Published by
Ulverscroft Limited
Anstey, Leicestershire

Set by Words & Graphics Ltd.
Anstey, Leicestershire
Printed and bound in Great Britain by
T. J. International Ltd., Padstow, Cornwall

This book is printed on acid-free paper

To you.
Yes, *you*.
You know who you are.

Wind

1

Friday, March 10

There's always a moment before a storm when the wind seems to change its mind. It plays at domesticity; it flirts with the blossom on the trees; it teases the rain from the dull grey clouds. This moment of playfulness is when the wind is at its cruellest and most dangerous. Not later, when the trees fall and the blossom is just blotting-paper choking the drains and rivulets. Not when houses fall like cards, and walls that you thought were firm and secure are torn away like paper.

No, the cruellest moment is always the one in which you think you *might* be safe; that maybe the wind has moved on at last; that maybe you can start building again, something that can't be blown away. That's the moment at which the wind is at its most insidious. That's the moment where grief begins. The moment of expected joy. The demon of hope in Pandora's box. The moment when the cacao bean releases its scent into the air: a scent of burning, and spices, and salt; and blood; and vanilla; and heartache.

I used to think it was simple, that art. The making of harmless indulgences. But at last I have come to learn that *no* indulgence is harmless. Francis Reynaud would be proud of me. Forty years a witch and now, at last, I have become a Puritan.

Zozie de l'Alba would have understood. Zozie, the collector of hearts, whose face still comes to me, in my dreams. Sometimes I hear her voice on the wind; the sound of her shoes on the cobbles. Sometimes I wonder where she is: whether she still thinks of me. No indulgence is harmless, she knew. Power is all that counts in the end.

The wind doesn't care. The wind doesn't judge. The wind will take whatever it can — whatever it needs — instinctively. I was like that once, you know. Seeds on the wind, taking root, seeding again before moving on. The seeds do not stay with the parent plant. They go wherever the wind goes.

Take my Anouk, now twenty-one: gone to wherever children go whenever they follow the piper. We used to be so close, she and I. We used to be inseparable. And yet I know that a child is on loan, one day to be returned to the world, to grow and to learn and to fall in love. I'd once believed she might stay here in Lansquenet-sous-Tannes; that Jeannot Drou might keep her there; that of course and the *chocolaterie*, and the promise of security. But it was Jean-Loup Rimbault, in Paris, who decided things. Jean-Loup, the boy with the hole in his heart. Did Anouk fill it? All I know is she left a hole in mine; a hole that all the chocolate in Mexico could never fill; a space in the shape of a little girl with eyes as dark as the ocean.

And now, my Rosette, sixteen years old, hears the voice of the wind, and I know how hungry she is; how wild, how wilful, how volatile. The

4

wind would take her in one gust, if she were not fastened down like a sail, if I had not taken precautions. And still the wind keeps worrying at the cords that keep us safe. Still we hear its siren call. And it smells of other places. It speaks of danger and sunlight, adventure and joy. It dances through the motes of light in shades of chilli and peppercorn. It catches at the back of the throat like unexpected laughter. And in the end it takes them all; everything you laboured for. Everything you told yourself that you could somehow take with you. And it always begins in a moment of playfulness, magic — even of joy. A moment of brightness between the clouds. A taste of sweetness; a ringing of bells.

Sometimes, even a fall of snow.

Snow

1

Saturday, March 11

It snowed today. A week into Lent, a miracle come early. At first I thought it was blossom. Blossom out of the bright blue sky, covering the pavements. But there was snow on the window-sill, and crystals in the sparkling air. It could have been an Accident. But maybe it was something more.

It hardly ever snows down here. It's hardly ever cold, not even really in winter. Not like in Paris, where sometimes the Seine used to crackle with thin black ice, and I had to wear my winter coat from Hallowe'en to Eastertime. Here in Lansquenet-sous-Tannes you get cold weather for maybe a month. Frost in December. White on the fields. And then there's the wind. The cold north wind that always brings tears to your eyes. But today, there was snow. It's a sign. Someone will be dead by dawn.

I know a story about a girl whose mother made her out of snow. The girl is supposed to stay out of the sun, but one summer's day she disobeys, and goes out to play with the others. Her mother looks for her everywhere. But all she finds are her clothes on the ground — BAM! — in a puddle of water.

Narcisse told me that story. Narcisse, who owns the flower shop. He's old now, and

9

someone else runs the shop on weekdays, but on Sundays he still comes in, and sits by the door, and watches the street, and never talks. Except sometimes to me. He says:

'We're the quiet ones, aren't we, Rosette? We don't chatter like magpies.'

That's true. While Maman makes chocolates and talks, I prefer to sit quietly, playing with my button-box or drawing in my drawing-book. When I was small, I never talked. I sang and sometimes shouted — BAM! — or made animal noises, finger-signs or bird calls. People like birds and animals. People didn't like me much, and so I didn't talk to them, not even in my shadow-voice, the one I use when I'm being someone else. Instead I went into a bird, and flew very high into the clouds. Or sometimes I was a monkey, swinging in the trees, or sometimes a dog, barking at the wind. But even then, people didn't like me; except for Maman, and Anouk, and Roux, and my best friend Jean-Philippe Bonnet. But Maman is always working now, and Anouk is in Paris with Jean-Loup, and Roux comes and goes, but never stays long, and Jean-Philippe (whose nickname is Pilou) goes to school all week in Agen, and doesn't want to play any more.

Maman says not to worry. He hasn't really changed all that much. But now he's sixteen, and the other boys would laugh at him, and tease him for playing with a girl.

I don't think that's fair. I'm *not* a girl. Sometimes I am a boy like Pilou. Sometimes I am a monkey, a dog. Sometimes I am something else. But other people are different. Other people care about these things. And of course I can't go to school. The school in Agen didn't want me. They told Maman I wouldn't fit in, or talk the way I was meant to. And then there was Bam, who wouldn't behave, and makes me shout his name — BAM! And sometimes there are Accidents.

And so now I learn what I can from books, and birds, and animals, and sometimes even people. People like Narcisse, and Roux, who never mind when I don't want to talk, or when my voice isn't a little girl's voice, but something wild and dangerous.

Maman used to tell me the story of a little girl whose voice was stolen by a witch. The witch, who was clever and devious, used the little girl's young, sweet voice to trick people into doing her will. Only the little girl's shadow could speak, but it was rarely ever sweet. Instead it only told the truth, and sometimes it was merciless. *You're like that little girl*, Maman said. *Too wise for fools to understand.*

Well, I don't know if I'm wise. But I *do* have a shadow-voice. I don't use it very often, though. People don't like hearing the truth. Even Maman prefers not to hear some of the things my shadow says. And so I stick to signing most times, or else I don't say anything. And if I feel my shadow-voice wanting to break free I shout — BAM! — and laugh and sing, and stamp my foot, the way we sometimes used to do to keep the wicked wind away.

When the snow began to fall, Maman was

working in the shop, making Easter chocolates. Rabbits and chickens and baskets of eggs. *Mendiants* and nougatines. Nipples of Venus, and apricot hearts, and bitter orange slices. All wrapped up in cellophane, and tied with coloured ribbons, and packed in boxes and sachets and bags, ready to give for Easter. I don't like chocolates very much. I like *hot* chocolate, and a chocolate croissant, but I don't want to work in a chocolate shop. Maman says everyone has something. With her it's making chocolates, and knowing which one's your favourite. With Roux, it's making bird calls and being able to fix almost anything. With me, it's drawing animals. Everyone has an animal, a shadow of their true self. Mine is Bam, a monkey. Maman is a wild cat. Roux is a fox with a bushy tail. Anouk is a rabbit called Pantoufle. Pilou is a raccoon. And Narcisse is an old black bear, with his long nose and his shuffling walk and his little eyes filled with secrets. Some people think Bam isn't real. Even Maman calls him 'Rosette's imaginary friend', especially to people like Madame Drou, who can't even see the colours. That's because Bam can be naughty. I have to watch him all the time. Sometimes I have to shout at him — BAM! — to stop him from causing an Accident.

But Maman only pretends she can't see him now. Maman doesn't want to see. She thinks it would be easier if we were like the others. But I know she still sees Bam. Just like she sees her customers' favourite kind of chocolate. Just like she sees the colours that tell you how someone is feeling. But now she tries to hide those things, to be like the other mothers. Perhaps she thinks that if she does, I'll be like the others, too.

When the snow began to fall, Maman didn't notice. She was with two ladies who were choosing chocolate animals. Ladies in spring dresses with high-heeled shoes and pastel coats. One is called Madame Montour. She doesn't live here, but I've seen her around. She goes to church on Sundays. The other one was Madame Drou, who never comes in for chocolate, but only to find out what's happening. They were talking about a boy who was fat, and wouldn't do as he was told. I don't know who the boy was. I thought of two parrots, or two pink hens, clucking and preening and fussing. And I could see Madame Montour wondering why I wasn't at school.

No-one in Lansquenet wonders why. No-one in Lansquenet is surprised that I sometimes bark, or shout, or sing: *Bam-Bam-Bam: Bam, badda-BAM!* But I could see Maman watching me. I know she worries about me. There used to be Accidents, when I was small. Things that shouldn't have happened, but did. Things that made us different. And once they tried to take me away, when I was still a baby. Someone tried to take Anouk, too, when we lived in Paris. Now Maman worries. There's no need. Nowadays, I'm careful.

I drew a rose-pink parakeet for Madame Montour, and a hen for Madame Drou. Just a few strokes for the little pink head, the beak half open in surprise. I left them there on the counter, where Maman could see, and went

13

outside. The wind was coming from the north, and there were petals on the ground, but when I stopped to look I saw that the petals were clumps of snow, whirling out of the blue spring sky like pieces of confetti.

The priest was standing outside the church, looking surprised at the falling snow. The priest's name is Francis Reynaud. I didn't like him when I first came, but now I think perhaps I do. And *Reynaud* means 'fox', which is silly, because anyone can see he's really a crow, all in black, with his sad little crooked smile. But I do like the church. I like the smell of polished wood and incense. I like the coloured window glass and the statue of Saint Francis. Reynaud says Saint Francis is the patron saint of animals, who left his life to live in the woods. I'd like to do that. I'd build myself a house in a tree, and live on nuts and strawberries. Maman and I never go to church. Once, that might have caused trouble. But Reynaud says we don't have to go. Reynaud says God sees us, and cares for us, wherever we are.

And now here comes the spinning snow, from a bright blue lantern sky. A sign — maybe even an Accident. I spread my coat like wings, and call — BAM! — to make sure he knows it isn't my fault. Reynaud smiles and waves his hand. But I can tell he doesn't see the flash of colours across the square. He doesn't hear the song of the wind, or catch the scent of burning. These are all signs. I see them all. But I can tell he doesn't know. Snow, out of a clear blue sky. Someone will be dead by dawn.

2

There she goes. How strange she is: my winter child; my changeling. Wild as an armful of birds, she flies everywhere in an instant. There is no keeping her inside, no making her sit quietly. She has never been like other girls, never like other children. Rosette is a force of nature, like the jackdaws that sit on the steeple and laugh, like a fall of unseasonal snow, like the blossom on the wind.

Women — mothers — like Joline Drou or Caro Clairmont do not understand. The dread of having a *different* child is more than they can imagine. Nearly sixteen, and still Rosette cannot speak in the normal way. To them, it makes my child a burden; pitiful; less than whole. To them, she is *Poor Rosette*, as I am *Poor Vianne* behind my back; left with that child to bring up alone, and the father so shockingly absent.

But Caro and Joline do not know how Rosette looks at me when I kiss her goodnight; or how she sings to herself in bed; or how she can draw any animal or bird, or living creature. All they see is a little girl who can never grow up, and this, they think, is the saddest thing. A little girl who can never grow up will never fall in love, or be married, or get a job, or move away to the city. A little girl who can never grow up will be a

15

burden forever, and her mother will never be able to go on that round-the-world cruise she had planned, or take up exciting new hobbies, or socialize at the country club. Instead she will be doomed to stay here, in sleepy Lansquenet-sous-Tannes; hardly the kind of place in which you'd hope to stay forever.

But I am not Caro Clairmont, or Joline Drou, or Michèle Montour. And the thought of being rooted in one place, never to be blown away, is a dream I have cherished all my life. Small dreams are all I've ever had; small dreams are all I hope for. A place in which the seeds I sow will grow into something I recognize. Clothes hanging in a wardrobe. A table, scarred with familiar marks. An armchair, moulded to my shape. Maybe even a cat by the door.

You see, I am not demanding. These things are surely achievable. And yet, whenever I think that maybe I have silenced the wind's incessant demands, it begins to blow again. The weather changes. Friends die. Children grow up and move away. Even Anouk, my summer child, with her little messages and phone calls every Sunday — unless she forgets — her eyes already alight with the thought of other places, new adventures. How strange. Anouk was always the one who *wanted* to settle down, to stay. Now her orbit has shifted, and it is *his* star she follows. It was inevitable, I know, and yet I sometimes find myself wishing, darkly wishing —

But not with Rosette. Rosette is mine. A *special* child, says Caro Clairmont, with the pious expression that so belies the genuine

16

disgust she feels. She must be a burden, thinks Caroline. A daughter who will never grow up; a child who can never be normal. She has no idea that this is precisely what makes Rosette so dear to me.

A cat crossed your path in the snow, and mewed. The Hurakan was blowing.

No. I turn away from the memory. The winter of the cat in the snow, the gilded cage, and the circle of sand. I did what had to be done, *Maman.* I did what mothers always do. I have no regrets. My child is safe. And that is all that matters.

I check my mobile phone. I have taken to carrying one since Anouk moved back to Paris. Sometimes she sends me a photograph — a little window into her life. Sometimes she sends me text messages. *Adorable blue-eyed husky outside the Metro station!* Or: *New ice cream shop at Quai des Orfèvres!* It helps to know I can speak to her, or hear from her at any time, but I try not to be demanding, or show her that I am anxious. Our phone calls are light and amusing: I tell her about my customers; she tells me about the things she has seen. Jean-Loup is studying at the Sorbonne; Anouk, who could have studied too, has taken a job in a multiplex cinema. They live together in a rented bedsit in the 10th *arrondissement.* I can imagine it perfectly: an old building, with damp in the walls and cockroaches in the bathroom, much like the cheap hotels we stayed in when Anouk was small. She could have stayed here and worked with me in the *chocolaterie.* Instead she has chosen Paris

17

— Anouk, who never wanted anything else but to live in a place like Lansquenet.

I go back into the kitchen. There are *mendiants* cooling on a sheet of greaseproof paper; little discs of chocolate, scattered with pieces of crystallized fruit; chopped almonds and pistachios; dried rose petals and gold leaf. *Mendiants* were always my favourites; so simple to make that even a child — even Anouk at five years old — was able to make them unsupervised. A sour cherry for the nose; a lemon slice for the mouth. Even her *mendiants* were smiling.

Rosette's are more complex, almost Byzantine in their design; the little pieces of crystallized fruit arranged in ingenious spirals. She plays with buttons in the same way, lining them up against skirting-boards, making intricate patterns of loops and foils across the wooden flooring. It is part of the way she sees the world; how she represents its complexities. Caro looks wise and talks about obsessive-compulsive disorder, and how common it is in those children she likes to call *special*, but there's nothing disordered about Rosette. Patterns — signs — are important.

Where has she gone this morning, so quiet and so purposeful? It is cold; the hard blue sky ringing with the frozen wind from the Russian steppes. She likes to play by the side of the Tannes, or in the fields down by Les Marauds, but most of all she likes the wood that runs alongside Narcisse's farm, a wood to which only she is allowed access, without risking the wrath of the owner.

Narcisse, who owns the flower shop opposite

the *chocolaterie*, and who supplies fruit and vegetables to markets and shops along the Tannes, is gruffly, fiercely fond of Rosette. A widower of thirty years, he has chosen to adopt her as a surrogate granddaughter. With others he is often dour to the point of rudeness. But with her he is indulgent; telling her stories, teaching her songs, which she sings without words, but with the greatest enthusiasm.

'My strawberry thief,' he calls her. 'My little bird with the secret voice.'

Well, today the little bird is off exploring the new-fallen snow. It will not last, but for now the fields are seamed in white, with the peach trees all in blossom. I wonder what Narcisse will say. Snow as late as this is a curse to fruit trees and to growing crops. Perhaps that is why his shop is still shut, even though the weekend is often the best time to sell flowers. Eleven-thirty, and the stragglers at the end of the service have all gone home to their families in the unexpected snow, their Sunday coats and berets and hats all scattered with white feathers. Even Reynaud will have gone home by now, to his little house on the *Avenue des Francs Bourgeois*, and Poitou's bakery on the square is getting ready to close for lunch. Above, the sky is blue and hard. No sign of a cloud. And yet the snow continues to fall, like thistledown on the wind. My mother would have called it a sign.

I, of course, know better.

19

3

It happened overnight, *mon père.* They found him in the morning. He hadn't been to open the shop, which he always does on a Sunday, and the girl who runs it on weekdays had gone to his house to find him there, sitting in his chair on the porch, eyes still open, cold as the grave. Of course, he was close to eighty, but even so, a sudden death always comes as a surprise, even for one to whom it should be neither a shock nor a cause for grief.

Not that Narcisse would have cared much whether I grieved for him or not. He was never a churchgoing man, and made no secret of his contempt of me and all I stand for. But his daughter, Michèle Montour, is an enthusiastic member of my congregation, even though she and her husband Michel live on the other side of Agen. They're always polite and respectful to me, though I can't say I like them very much. She is one of those women Armande Voizin used to call 'Bible groupies', all smiles in church, but cold and sour when dealing with the socially deprived.

Michel Montour is a property developer, and drives an off-road vehicle that never seems to go off-road. Both of them like money, which I suspect is why they appeared in Narcisse's life two years ago, and why they were so suddenly and graspingly attentive. Before that, Narcisse never saw them, or mentioned he had a daughter at all. And although for those two years Michèle had called every Sunday afternoon, fussed over his health, brought him chocolates, I do not think Narcisse believed her sudden show of affection. He may not have liked me very much, but he was a good judge of character. Dour, with a dry and somewhat surprising sense of humour that often came out in his dealings with the river-folk and with the little community of Les Marauds — those immigrants and transients, to whom he gave permission to camp and work and live rent-free on his land. His dealings with Michèle and Michel were drily cordial, nothing more. He was never under any illusions. The woman was after his money.

I suspect that when Michel and Michèle gain possession of that land, their interest in Lansquenet will cease. The friends they have made in the village are merely social acquaintances. Their eagerness to be part of my church — like Michèle's visits to the *chocolaterie* — was simply a means of building the right kind of profile in the village. Narcisse had made it very clear that he wanted his farm to be cared for. He wanted his flower shop to remain part of our little community. Now that Narcisse is gone, so has the need to keep up the pretence. The farm will be broken up; the shop let; the land sold off for development. This is what happens. A lifetime's work dismantled in less than the time it takes to harvest a crop.

21

Or so I had assumed, *mon père*. But Narcisse has surprised me. Of all the people he could have asked — friends, neighbours, family — to be the executor of his will, I am the one he has chosen, much to the annoyance of Michel and Michèle, who must have thought their inheritance more or less assured. However, even I did not know the details of Narcisse's will until it was read today in Agen, just after the old man's funeral. A very simple, quiet affair held at the crematorium, with as much ceremony as the short service would allow. That was what he wanted, said Michèle Montour disapprovingly. Of course, she would have preferred something more becoming to her status. Perhaps the chance to wear a new hat, to dab at her eyes with a handkerchief. Instead, her friends — the Clairmonts, the Drous — disdained the civil ceremony, and only Narcisse's friends were left — the river folk from the barges, the men and women of Les Marauds — to honour the old man's passing.

These are the people I never see in my church on Sundays: people with braided hair and tattoos; people in kurtas and hijabs. And of course, Vianne and Rosette, both of them dressed in bright colours, as if in defiance of death itself.

Roux was not there. He avoids the town, preferring to stay in Les Marauds. His boat is moored down by the old tanneries, where the river folk have their community, lighting bonfires on the bank and cooking their meals in cast-iron pots. There was a time when I might have been resistant to these visitors. I recall the man I used to be with shame. But Roux has not forgotten him, and keeps as far away as he can. Were it not for Vianne and Rosette I think he would leave the region for good. He has never had a home, or stayed in any one place for long. But he liked Narcisse, who gave him work and shelter when no-one else in Lansquenet would, and so I was surprised when he did not make an appearance.

Nor was Roux at the reading of the will. Being Roux, he only receives what mail he chooses to receive, which means that anything with an official stamp fails to arrive, or is quietly dumped in one of the bins by the edge of the Tannes. Only Michel and Michèle Montour were with me at the solicitor's office in Agen, in genteel expectation of a quietly anticipated surprise. Instead, there was stupefied silence, followed by raised voices, then by a storm of incredulous questions, all directed at me, of course, as Michel and Michèle demanded to know how I had managed to trick poor Papa into leaving a valuable asset to a man who didn't even have a bank account or a house to his name —

The solicitor's name is Ying-Ley Mak: an elegant young woman of Chinese extraction, whose perfect French and foreign name have already caused Michel and Michèle to exchange significant glances. Now they bristled indignantly, looking from priest to solicitor, solicitor to priest, in shock and growing agitation.

'Strictly speaking, the land has *not* been left to Monsieur Roux,' explained Mme Mak in her quiet voice. 'He is simply the legal trustee of Rosette Rocher, to whom your father bequeathed the land, and who is still a minor.'

'It's criminal,' said Michèle Montour. 'There must have been undue influence.'

I pointed out that over the last five years, Roux had barely seen Narcisse, except perhaps to say hello. 'Besides,' I went on, 'it isn't as if your father left you out of his will. He has left you the farmhouse; his money; most of the farmland — '

'Worthless,' said Michel Montour, 'without the adjacent woodland. Sixteen hectares of Oakland, suitable for development — not to mention the mature timber, which has significant commercial value. Why would my father-in-law leave all that to a man he barely knows? What's the story behind it? And how soon can this be overturned?'

Calmly, I explained that, as executor of Narcisse's will, I was in no position to overturn anything.

'But this isn't right!' said Michèle, her façade of gentility starting to crack. The accent she usually affects — an elongated Northern drawl — had reverted to its natural pattern of nasal inflexions and strident peaks. 'This isn't right! We're his *family*. We came here to look after him. We even joined his *church*, for God's sake — ' She paused her tirade to fix me with a suspicious gaze. 'You're really trying to tell me, *mon père*, that this is the first you've heard of this? That he never even discussed it with you?'

I assured her that Narcisse had not, and, not for the first time, it occurred to me that he would have loved this scene of growing anarchy. He would have loved my discomfort, the anger of his relatives, and the polite incomprehension of

Mme Mak, who hadn't seen any of this coming.

'He must have left documents,' said Michèle. 'Some kind of message to us, at least.'

Mme Mak said: 'Your father left a document for the attention of Père Reynaud. He makes it clear in the accompanying letter that the document in question is *only* for Père Reynaud, and no-one else.'

'But it doesn't make sense,' wailed Michèle. 'Why would Papa do this to us? To his own family?'

'I'm very sorry,' said Mme Mak. 'I'm afraid I can't discuss the details. Your father made his will very clear. The farm, except for the oak wood, to you. The shop in the village, also to you. The sixteen hectares of wood, along with any structures and contents, to be held in trust by Monsieur Roux, to pass to Mademoiselle Rocher on her twenty-first birthday.'

'What contents?' said Michèle Montour. 'Are you saying there's something more there? A structure? What kind of a structure?'

Mme Mak simply shook her head, and handed me a thick green folder, tied with pink legal tape, and labelled with my name, in ink, in the copperplate of another century.

'This was left for you,' she said. 'My client was very insistent that you should read it to the end.'

But Michèle had not abandoned the fight. 'My father would never have done this without some kind of undue influence. I demand to see that folder. You can't refuse to show it to me!'

Mme Mak shook her head. 'I'm sorry, *Madame*. Your father made it very clear that

25

no-one but Monsieur le Curé — '

'I don't care!' exclaimed Michèle. 'My father was old. His mind was gone. He had no right to do this to us, his family, who loved him.' She turned to me for support. '*Mon père*. We are not wealthy people. We have worked very hard to get where we are. We go to church. We pay our taxes. We have a son, whose special care costs us every penny we make. And now, just as the poor boy is coming into his inheritance — you understand that this isn't for us, we're only thinking of the boy — '

'A son?' I said. This was news to me. In the two years they had attended my church, I had never once heard either of them mention a son. I wanted to ask about the boy. What age was he? What were his needs? And why did his mother not use his name? But Michèle was in full flow, and could not be silenced so easily.

'Who is this Roux person, anyway? What does he want? Why isn't he here? What did my father mean by *any structures and contents*? Why would a man like my father leave sixteen hectares of land to a child?' She took a deep and quivering breath. 'And will someone please tell me: who the *hell* is Rosette Rocher?'

4

It was Reynaud who brought the news. Narcisse was gone. But I already knew. *Someone* has been up to no good. Someone caused an Accident. And now he has left me his strawberry wood, and everyone's discussing me.

They think I don't understand, but I do. It's *my* wood. My very own. And no-one will sell it, cut it down, or try to keep me from going there. I will build a house for myself, among the ferns and brambles. I will live on hazelnuts, and sorrel, and wild strawberries. And no-one will disturb me there, or laugh at all the things I do, because the wood belongs to me, and no-one else will go there. Except Pilou, and only then on extra-special occasions. And maybe, if Anouk comes home —

I miss Anouk. Not as much as Maman does, but still, it feels wrong without her. There were always three of us, standing together against the world. Anouk stayed in Paris to go to school. But that was over two years ago. She ought to have been home by now. But Jean-Loup lives in Paris, and Anouk wants to stay with him. And Maman is different in little ways; and talks too loudly, and laughs too much, and worries if I'm out on my own, and sometimes cries to herself in the night. She never makes a sound. But I know. I can smell the scent of tears, and I can feel the pull of the wind tearing at the shutters.

BAM! That wind. It never stops. It smells of smoke and spices. It comes from everywhere at once: the hot south; the beckoning east; the brooding west; the misty north. It plays among the fallen leaves; it tugs at the red rags of my hair. Sometimes it is a monkey. Sometimes, a lady with lollipop shoes. But it's never far away, and now it's getting closer. If I called it, it would blow Anouk back to Lansquenet. If I called it she would come, and Maman would be happy again —

V'là l'bon vent, v'là l'joli vent
V'là l'bon vent, ma mie m'appelle —

But sometimes there are Accidents. That's why I don't call the wind. At least, not with my shadow-voice, the one that only tells the truth. And Maman doesn't know how much I like to listen to the wind. She doesn't hear it singing to me in a voice like summertime. She doesn't know how much I want to call it in my shadow-voice, and how I have to scold it — BAM! — to bring it back under control.

Madame Clairmont thinks I have something called Tourette's Syndrome. I've heard her mention it to Maman, especially on noisy days. But Narcisse always used to say: 'Don't label the child. She's not a parcel.' And Madame Clairmont would look cross, and make her lemon-face at him, and then Narcisse would wink at me, and smile, and say in a low, gruff voice that only I could hear: 'Don't pay any attention to her. She's got a bad case of

28

Busybody Syndrome. It could kill her any day.'

That was a joke. I realize that now. There's no such thing as Busybody Syndrome. You can't die from being a gossip. Narcisse was often funny like that. You couldn't always tell if he was joking. But he was my friend, ever since that day when he caught me stealing his strawberries. I didn't know Narcisse before then. I thought he was just a grumpy old man who sometimes came into the chocolate shop. Never bought much — an apricot heart, or a single slice of cake. But Maman liked him. Roux liked him, too. And he never laughed at me, or talked to me as if I was deaf, or talked *about* me as if I didn't understand, the way Madame Clairmont always does.

I try to tell her I like to sign. Not because I'm deaf — BAM! — or because I can't talk in the regular way, but because it's safe, and neat, and doesn't get in the way of things. Madame Clairmont doesn't care. She's like a little dog, all fluff, all fuss. She makes me want to bark at her. And when she's talking to Maman, it's always in that deathbed voice. *How's poor little Rosette today? Vianne, I don't how you cope.* And Maman always answers: 'Rosette is *how* I cope, Caroline.'

Narcisse and I became good friends six summers ago, when I was nine. One day, when Pilou was at school, and I was with Bam by the riverside, I decided to explore. Going over the fields, I found a little path to a wood, surrounded by a chain-link fence and a gate with a padlock, to keep people out. I've never liked locked things. I always want to look inside. And so I did:

there was a place where the wire had pulled away from the post. Not big enough for an adult to pass, but easy enough for me to squeeze through. Bam, of course, can go anywhere. Like the wind, he goes where he wants. And there were so many places to go. Thickets of bramble. Fallen trees. Ferns, and violets, and gorse, paths all lined with soft green moss. And in the very heart of the wood, there was a clearing, with a circle of stones, and an old well in the middle, next to a big dead oak tree, and everything — fallen branches, standing stones, even the well, with its rusty pump — draped and festooned and piled knee-high with ruffles and flounces of strawberries, with blackbirds picking over the fruit, and the scent like all of summer.

It wasn't like the rest of the farm. Narcisse's farm is very neat, with everything set out in its place. A little field for sunflowers: one for cabbages; one for squash; one for Jerusalem artichokes. Apple trees to one side; peaches and plums to the other. And in the polytunnels, there were daffodils, tulips, freesias; and in season, lettuce, tomatoes, beans. All neatly planted, in rows, with nets to keep the birds from stealing them.

But here there were no nets, or polytunnels, or windmills to frighten away the birds. Just that clearing of strawberries, and the old well in the circle of stones. There was no bucket in the well. Just the broken pump, and the trough, and a grate to cover the hole, which was very deep, and not quite straight, and filled with ferns and that swampy smell. And if you put your eye to the grate, you could see a roundel of sky reflected in

30

the water, and little pink flowers growing out from between the cracks in the old stone. And there was a kind of draught coming up from under the ground, as if something was hiding there and breathing, very quietly.

After that first time, we went there a lot. Bam and I would eat our fill, sitting by that disused well, and sometimes we'd play, and run, and sing, and chase around like squirrels. Sometimes I would pretend that the circle of stones was a fairy ring, and that the well was a wishing well, that would make my dreams come true. On those days I would drop a coin or a stone or an acorn through the rusty grate, and listen for the splash they made, deep, deep down in the darkness. And I wished for a friend to play with, and for a jumbo drawing-book, and a big box of coloured pencils, the ones that come in a hundred colours, and for Anouk to come back soon, and for us to be a family again.

And then one day I got a surprise. I'd just been picking strawberries. There was juice all around my mouth, and a necklace of strawberry-leaves around my neck. I'd taken a big glass jar from the shop. I was thinking I could make some jam, and I was singing a jam-making song: *Jam-Bam-Bam, Bam, badda-jam —*

And then there came a sound from the path, something like a growling dog, and it was Narcisse, in pyjamas and boots under his old brown overcoat, glaring me from beetle brows and looking more like a bear than ever.

'What the hell are you doing here! This is private property!'

I'd never heard him shout before. I thought perhaps he was angry because I'd taken the strawberries. So I dropped the jar and ran away as fast as I could. I heard him shouting after me, sounding sorry and angry and sad, but I kept running, through the wood, and under the broken fence and along the hedge towards the river.

I didn't go back to the wood after that. I was too afraid of Narcisse. I thought that maybe his coming there had been a kind of Accident. Instead I played by Les Marauds, and kept to my side of the river, and watched the farm from behind the hedge, and saw Narcisse with his tractor.

But three days later, he came by the shop. I was under the table — *shhh!* — playing with my button-box. The doorbell rang, and I saw his boots from under the red-and-white tablecloth. He walked like a bear, very heavy and slow. I knew at once it was Narcisse. I hoped he'd only come to buy chocolates, and not to tell Maman about me playing in his private wood. So I went into a little mouse, all quiet and still. The boots came in, and stopped just by the table. I could smell the scent of them, leather and the summer soil. Then he lifted the tablecloth, and I saw a basket in his hand.

The basket was filled with strawberries.

I made a little warning sound, like a rat in a corner.

He smiled and put down the basket. I could smell the strawberries now. Then he said: 'For the strawberry thief. Take as many as you like.'

For a moment I thought that if I closed my eyes, he wouldn't be able to see me. But when I opened them again, he was still there, looking under the tablecloth with his giant beard like a bushy cloud.

'I owe you an apology,' he said in quite a gentle voice. 'I didn't mean to frighten you, or to make you run away. I hope we can be friends, you and I.'

I made a mocking blackbird call and stuck out my tongue.

'Your mother says you like to draw. I brought you this.' And he handed me a brand-new drawing-pad and a box of a hundred pencils.

I made a little excited noise, and all the cups on the table danced. Maman said; 'Rosette, be careful!' But I was too excited to stop. The fairy stones and the wishing well had sent me what I wanted. I made Bam do a victory dance, and then, on the first page of my book, I did a quick little drawing of a monkey hugging a big brown bear, and signed: *Thank you. I love them!*

Narcisse laughed. 'You're welcome. Use the wood as much as you like. It's a special kind of place, just for special people. Eat the strawberries. Climb the trees. But keep away from that old well. I don't want you falling down there.'

I gave him a nod from underneath the tablecloth.

'Promise me you'll be careful, Rosette. I want to be sure you've understood.'

'*Promise*,' I said, in my shadow-voice, to show him I was serious.

He held out his hand. 'Then we have a deal.'

Of course, I wouldn't have fallen in. I never put my weight on the grate. But I couldn't keep away from the well. I'd have to keep on dropping coins until Anouk was back again.

★ ★ ★

After that, the strawberry wood became my favourite place to go. In the summer I picked the fruit, and ran up and down the alleys of trees, and in autumn, collected acorns, and lay on my back watching the sky through the open branches. In the spring, I picked violets, and wild garlic by the riverbank. In winter I built tunnels under the barrows of brambles, and all year round I watched the well, and listened to its breathing, and sometimes, dropped a coin or a stone into the water, and whispered into the darkness.

And that's why I wasn't really surprised when Maman told me that Narcisse had left me the strawberry wood, and the circle of stones, and the wishing well. He must have meant them for me from the start. Because there's a story in that wood, a story that he wants me to know. Maman always says that stories are what keep us alive; the stories people tell us, and scatter like thistledown on the wind. And stories are all that's left of us when we're gone, she tells me, as the cold north wind sings its mournful song, over the sound of the melting snow.

I know a story about a bird that goes between the land of death and the land of the living. This bird carries messages from the dead to their loved ones. A man is mourning his dead wife. Every day, the messenger bird comes to sit on the man's window-ledge, and sings. It is a song of love and hope; a message from beyond the grave, telling him his wife loves him still, and that she is waiting. But the man, in his grief, does not understand. All he understands is loss. And so he shoots the messenger bird, to silence it forever. But the other birds have already learnt its lovely song. And so the song passes through forests and fields, and even over the ocean, until the message of undying love is sung by all the birds in the sky.

Narcisse's shop is empty today; the window all covered with newspaper. Maman says that's because ghosts can be trapped in reflections. That must be true, because when someone dies, they cover the mirrors with blankets. They sometimes stop the clocks, too, so that the dead can get into Heaven before the Devil knows the time. But Reynaud says that isn't true. He says he doesn't believe in ghosts. I sign: *What about the Holy Ghost?* But I don't think he understands. And Narcisse didn't believe in God or the Devil, or even ghosts. Do you have to *believe* in ghosts to become one? Is he nowhere now? Or is he trapped behind the glass of the flower shop window?

I think ghosts are just people with unfinished stories to tell the world. Perhaps that's why they try to come back. And perhaps I can tell Narcisse it's okay, that I'm looking after the strawberry wood, that I can finish his story. That's what I was thinking today, as I played in the strawberry wood, as I walked by the bank of the Tannes, as I looked into the wishing well, and

35

dropped a coin there in his name —

But there was no sign of him anywhere. He must be trapped behind the glass. And so, as Maman was closing up, I went across the square to see. I stood very close to the window and looked through the gaps in the paper. The shop is empty now. It was mostly dark in there, because of the papered windows. The rows of benches that used to be there to display the buckets of flowers are gone. The floor is bare boards, and nothing else. Just some flower-heads, and dust. Even the old seed calendar on the wall is gone, leaving its ghost against the faded plaster.

I pulled away from the window then, to try and see the reflections. There wasn't much more than a ribbon of glass between the sheets of newspaper. I wondered if I'd see his eyes, looking out from the shadows. But all I could see was my own face — the ghost of myself, looking back at me.

I said: 'Narcisse?'

In the window, I saw Bam, pulling naughty faces.

I didn't stop him. I needed to know. I said, a little louder: 'Narcisse?'

A tiny wind began to blow. A nothing wind, a playful wind. It smelt of spring, and thawing snow, and primroses, and promises. It blew in my ear like a playful child, it whispered like a wishing well.

I said: 'Narcisse?'

It tugged my hair. It felt like teasing fingers. Reflected in the glass I could see Bam, still pulling faces and laughing. I knew I ought to stop him before he did something bad, but now the wind was in my head, making me dizzy, making me dance —

And then, something moved. I saw someone. *Not* Narcisse, but someone else — a woman with her back to me, reflected in the window glass. A woman, or a bird, I thought — or maybe she was something of both. A lady all in black-and-white, like maybe a magpie —

I only saw her for the time it took for me to pull away, but what I saw made me think that perhaps I had seen her somewhere before —

I stepped away from the window. '*BAM!*'

I looked again. The woman was gone. Maybe she was a ghost, I thought. A ghost with an unfinished story. But now I could see something *through* the glass, something I'm sure hadn't been there before. A single, black feather, on the boards among the flower-heads and dust.

5

This morning it was sunny and bright, and Maman was making Easter things. There were eggs, and hens, and rabbits, and ducks, all in different sizes and varieties of chocolate, and Maman was decorating them with gold leaf, and hundreds and thousands, and sugar roses and candied fruit. Later she'll wrap them in cellophane, like fabulous bunches of flowers, each tied with a long curly ribbon of a different colour, and put them all on shelves at the back, as part of her annual Easter display.

This morning, Maman is happy. She got a message from Anouk today. She's coming home for Easter, instead of staying in Paris with Jean-Loup. I didn't tell her I've been dropping coins in the wishing well every day. I didn't want to spoil the surprise, or make her worry that I might fall in. And having Anouk back will be fun. We'll make all her favourite dishes. I'll show her my wood, and my wishing well. And maybe she'll like it so much that she'll stay, and we can all be together again.

But I'm still no closer to knowing the story of Narcisse and the strawberry wood. Everyone's talking about it today, asking why he left it to me. They come in to buy chocolates, but really they want to ask questions. *Why did Narcisse* leave *his* land to Rosette? *What is she going to do with it? How much do you think it's worth?* No-one seems to understand that it was a special place to him.

I helped Maman in the shop all day. Mostly because I wanted to hear what people had to say about my wood, but also to see if anyone came in or out of the flower shop. We had lots of customers. First there was Guillaume, who comes every day for hot chocolate. Then there was Madame Clairmont, and Monsieur Poitou the baker, and Madame Mahjoubi from down Les Marauds, and Madame Montour, and Madame Drou.

Madame Montour didn't say much. She didn't ask about the wood. But she watched me from her place at the table by the door, and smiled with her mouth, but not with her eyes, and talked to Maman about the snow, and didn't finish her chocolate. Madame Montour has been here before. She sometimes comes at the weekend, with Madame Clairmont, after church. But this is the first time she's called midweek. And this is the first time she's *looked* at me. I think I make her uncomfortable.

And then I forgot about Madame Montour, because Pilou was at the door. That was a surprise, because Pilou hasn't been to the shop in a while.

'*Pilou!*' I said in my shadow-voice, and Bam turned a crazy somersault. Pilou doesn't see Bam any more, and Maman gave me a warning look, and the bells on the kitchen curtain shivered and rang like icicles.

Pilou gave me a nod. He was wearing a red jumper and jeans, and carrying his satchel. He comes home from school early on Thursdays. I know. I sometimes watch him get off the bus. Sometimes he has time to play, but recently he's had too much work. His mother was with him — Joséphine, who runs the Café des Marauds — and now I could see that his face was as red as the silk sachets hanging in the doorway.

Joséphine puffed out her cheeks. 'God, what a day!' she said, sitting down on one of the chairs by the counter. 'You can't imagine how busy I've been.' She pointed at the pot of hot chocolate standing on the counter-top, and said: 'Is there any left?'

Maman smiled. 'Of course there is. And you can try my fresh *churros* — with blackcurrant *coulis* or chocolate — and tell me all the gossip.'

'*You're* the one with the gossip,' said Joséphine, taking her chocolate cup and adding whipped cream and marshmallows. 'I heard Narcisse left his farm to Rosette.'

'Not all of it,' said Maman, shaking cinnamon sugar over the freshly made *churros*. 'Just the little oak wood that runs alongside the property.'

Joséphine opened her eyes wide. 'That's incredible. Did you know? And why would he leave it to Rosette?'

Maman shrugged. 'He liked Rosette.'

'What are you going to do with it? Sell it?'

Maman shook her head. 'How could I? It belongs to her.'

At her table, Madame Montour was still watching me over her chocolate. Pilou was still

40

standing by the door, looking red-faced and impatient. I noticed he'd had his hair cut into one of those new, trendy styles.

Try the churros? I signed. *They're good.*

But Pilou only shook his head. 'Maman, we have to go. I'll be late.'

'Just a minute,' said Joséphine. 'Why don't you talk to Rosette for a while? He has some friends coming over,' she said to Maman. 'It's his girlfriend's birthday. But we have plenty of time. Sit down, Pilou. Relax a bit, for heaven's sake. Have a *churro.*'

Pilou sat down, but he didn't relax, and he didn't take a *churro.* I wondered if he was angry about something. His colours were like a bonfire. Then I wondered what Joséphine had meant by *his girlfriend's birthday.* Pilou doesn't have a girlfriend.

I made a little bird-noise and Bam made the bead curtain rattle and ring. But Pilou didn't laugh, or smile. In fact he didn't look as if he wanted to be there at all, and it made me sad. We used to be such friends, before he went off to the *lycée.* I drew him a picture of him as a cross little raccoon, sitting in front of a birthday cake.

He started to smile, then decided against it and made the impatient face again. 'Come *on,* Maman,' he said. 'We'll be late!'

Joséphine sighed. 'I'm sorry, Vianne. I'll be back another day.'

And then she got up without even finishing her chocolate, and Pilou said: 'See you, Rosette,' and set off running across the square, his satchel slung across his back. For a moment I wanted

41

him to slip on the cobbles and hurt himself, but instead I said: '*BAM!*' and turned away, and saw that Madame Montour had gone.

Maman said: 'Boys are stupid sometimes,' and poured me a cup of chocolate.

I shook my head. I was still feeling bad. And I didn't want any chocolate. I wanted to be alone, in my wood, where no-one could see or hear me. I knew Maman was trying to help, but that made me feel even worse, somehow. Maman doesn't realize I'm not a little girl any more. Sometimes I think Maman still believes that chocolate can fix anything.

6

The whole thing feels like a practical joke. On Roux, on Michèle Montour, but most of all on me, *mon père*. I know I should not speak ill of the dead, but Narcisse was always a difficult man: dry as a handful of autumn leaves; no lover of the Church, and fond of putting me at a disadvantage.

I went to find Roux at his houseboat, to explain the situation. He keeps it by the old tanneries, at the far edge of Les Marauds. That once mostly derelict part of the village of Lansquenet has become another community, mostly of immigrant families: Maghrébin and Syrian and North African and Arab. Shops, selling all kinds of food, have opened up along the Boulevard des Marauds. Shops with names like *Epicerie Bismillah* and *Supermarché Bencharki*, plus any number of tiny stands selling watermelon slices, or coconut milk, or boxes of home-made samosas, each box covered with a silken scarf of a different colour.

The scarves, I know, are a kind of code to identify the baker. Fatima al-Djerba is red: her daughter, Yasmina, is yellow. Yasmina's daughter Maya, too, has a box — her scarf is white, the samosas fat and misshapen. But Maya is only ten years old, and can therefore be forgiven.

Roux was fishing in the Tannes when I arrived, bearing the news. His red hair was pulled back in a kind of a bun, which might have looked girlish on another man, but instead made him look like a Viking on his way to ransack a monastery. He has also grown a beard, lighter than the red of his hair, and it makes him look wary and dangerous.

He listened in silence as I explained, his eyes never leaving the fishing-float bobbing in the water. Then, when I had finished, he turned to me and simply said:

'I don't want the land. Give it away.'

'I can't give it away, Roux. You're holding it in trust for Rosette. That was what Narcisse wanted, and I'm the executor of his will.'

'So, let Vianne do it,' said Roux.

I sighed. 'It's your name in the will. You're the one he wanted.'

'Why?'

'How should I know why?' I said. 'Why did he make me executor? Why did he leave the land to Rosette? Your guess is as good as mine. He just did, that's all I know.'

Roux made a harsh sound in his throat. 'The idiot. What was he thinking of?'

I didn't understand why he cared so much about not holding the land. Was it pride? Some kind of political stance? Or was it the discomfort of having to deal with officialdom, to come to an office in Agen, to sign papers in his real name —

Of course he will not tell me. He might perhaps confide in Vianne. I wonder if even *she* knows his real name, or cares about his history.

44

He has no passport, no bank account; he does not vote in elections. Roux of course is a nickname, based on the colour of his hair. He has no parents; no family that he has ever mentioned. He seems to have lived all of his life as an observer, a passer-by, moving from one town to the next whenever a place begins to seem a little too familiar. I know how that feels, although I would never think of telling Roux that. I know how it feels to exist on the outside of the group: for conversations to stop at my approach; to stand outside in a darkened street, looking in through the windows.

Of course, being a priest is a privilege that also demands certain sacrifices. A priest can never be like the rest of his congregation. He can never fall in love; never have children; never relax; never be like other men. He must never forget who he is. He must never lose sight of the fact that he is the Lord's servant. What is Roux not able to forget? What keeps him on the water?

'Narcisse wasn't his nickname, you know,' I said, to break the silence. 'It seems to have been his *Christian* name — that is, if you can call it such, with no saint or Apostle to name him after.' I always assumed his name was a joke, like calling a butcher *Jean Bon*, but apparently, his real name was Narcisse Dartigen, from Moncrabeau, along the Garonne. 'Funny, the things you learn when someone dies. Narcisse. What parent names their son Narcisse?'

Roux looked at me. I could tell he was thinking I talked too much.

'I always wondered what *your* real name was,'

45

I said, after a moment.

'Keep wondering,' said Roux.

Well, there was no point in pushing the matter. I supposed Roux would do what was necessary in his own time, at his own pace. For the present I needed to let him get used to the good news. For it *is* good news, I think. Rosette is his child, after all. Surely he must be glad that she will have this parcel of land to her name: Rosette, who may never be quite like other girls; who may never have the opportunities that Anouk will have. Surely he must be glad that she will have what he has never had. A piece of land to call her own. A place where she really belongs.

I went back home via Les Marauds, passing the samosa stand. This time I bought one of Maya's, leaving the money on the dish beside the covered box. I chose a fat pastry triangle, a purse filled with minced lamb and spices. I slipped it into a paper bag. It would do for my lunch, I thought, with a tomato salad and perhaps a tiny glass of wine. I no longer fast during Lent. I lost the habit years ago.

Maya popped her head out of the house to see who was buying her pastries. When she saw me, she gave a cry: 'Monsieur Reynaud! That's one of mine! You bought one of mine, Monsieur Reynaud!'

'Really?' I said, feigning surprise. 'They looked so beautifully made that I assumed they were Omi's.'

Maya laughed. Omi al-Djerba's samosas have become a kind of legend, all the more so because Omi — who must be ninety at least — has not done any cooking for years.

'You *knew*,' said Maya.

'Of course I knew. I came all the way here to buy one.'

Maya laughed again. Her eyes are hazel, almost green, against the warm brown of her skin. It occurred to me that one day — one day *soon* — she would be very beautiful.

'Tell me, Maya. What would you do if someone — a friend — gave you sixteen hectares of woodland?'

Maya's eyes widened. 'A wood of my own?'

I nodded.

Maya gave it some thought. 'I think I'd just sit there sometimes,' she said. 'I'd watch the animals and birds. I'd sit and think, and listen to the sound of the wind in the branches. And sometimes I would bring my friends, and play, and climb trees, and maybe build a treehouse, but mostly I'd just know it was mine, and that would be enough. Why?'

'Because,' I said, 'Narcisse has left his sixteen hectares of oak wood to Rosette, and not to his relatives.'

Maya said: 'They would cut down the trees. He knew Rosette would never do that.'

'Is that what you think?'

'Of course,' said Maya.

Perhaps she has a point, I thought, as I walked back through Les Marauds. Narcisse could be sentimental. He wanted to protect the wood. Or maybe it was simply his final way of annoying Michèle and Michel, who had borne his moods and tolerated his eccentricities, and smiled at his

47

jokes, and humoured him, and brought him little gifts — a cake, a bottle of his favourite wine — and asked after his health, and expressed concern at his aches and pains for two years, while mentally calculating the cost of a farmhouse, a shop and forty hectares.

It wouldn't have come to much, I thought, even with the woodland. The farmhouse was old and in need of work, and if it had been by the sea, or even in a place like Agen or Nérac, it might have attracted the interest of a local developer. But here, in Lansquenet-sous-Tannes, it was just another piece of land in a place where land was plentiful. As Montour had already said, the mature timber was probably the most valuable asset on the property. Without it, there was just the farm; good for growing flowers and fruit, but not what you'd call a goldmine, and the florist's shop in the square, which they would likely be able to let to another businessman.

There was no money to speak of. That, too, had come as a surprise. No shares, no savings account, not even a deposit box. Narcisse's current account had contained five or six hundred euros. And contrary to local belief that he must have had money hidden away, a search of his house had revealed nothing — no loose floorboards, no sock stuffed with cash hidden underneath the bed. Michel and Michèle must be furious that their two-year investment had yielded so little.

I was reaching the square now. The sun was almost at noon, and even though it was only March, it was warm enough to burn. Narcisse's flower shop was closed; the window covered with newspaper. There is a TO LET sign on the door. Michèle and Michel have wasted no time. An empty shop costs money. I wonder what it will become. A craft shop, perhaps, selling knick-knacks: perhaps another florist. There have always been shops in the square; Poitou's bakery; the *chocolaterie*; the shop selling graveyard supplies; the little fruit-and-vegetable stand. In any case, whatever it is, I hope it will reopen soon: an empty shop window is bad for the square, and risks being the target of vandals.

Until then, I suppose there will be the kind of speculation that always surrounds an empty shop. I remember when Vianne Rocher first moved into town all those years ago. That window, papered in orange and gold, just like a Chinese lantern. That scent of spices, and incense smoke, like something from the *Arabian Nights*. So many things have changed since then: now Vianne and I are almost friends. But how I resented that little shop, with its brightly coloured awning, and the scent of vanilla and allspice and the bitter rasp of raw cacao drifting out into the air. How I longed to step in, to taste the wares in those glass cases! Now, I tell myself, I could. But though I do not fast for Lent, chocolate still seems one indulgence too far. Maybe tomorrow, I told myself. Maybe I would call later. Maybe Vianne could give me news of what would happen to Narcisse's shop, or shed light on his reasons for leaving his oak wood to Rosette.

But I had one last thing to do before I spoke

to Vianne Rocher. One last duty to perform, before I could be easy again. I crossed the square and made for my home, still carrying Maya's samosa. I ate it with a salad, deferring the wine for the evening. And then I made a cup of tea, and, sitting in my favourite chair, prepared to read the document Narcisse had left me.

7

Dear Reynaud,

How ironic that it should be to you that I
make my confession. I never liked you. You
must know that — and yet, you were the only
one I could trust. If you are reading this, I am
dead. How strange to write those words. Unlike
you, I believe death is the end. No angels, no
trumpets, no judgement. Just the darkness.
That's good. The nightmare would be to find
all my friends and family waiting for me
beyond the veil.

I expect you'll be wondering why I made my
will as I did. My daughter Michèle will be hop-
ping mad. I never liked her, either. In fact, I
could probably count the people I have genu-
inely liked on the fingers of one hand. Roux is
one. Vianne Rocher is another. But it is
Rosette, my strawberry thief who found her
way into my heart. You'll learn why if you persist to the end of this narrative. And you will. I
know you will. These words are all that's left of
me.

But I must start earlier. The truth is like an
onion: layers of skin to be stripped away,
revealing a centre that makes you weep. My
father once said that to me. My father, the
murderer.

My head was already aching, *père*. The script was barely readable. Like a lazy schoolboy, I found myself scanning the manuscript in search of the salient details. Whom did his father murder? I suppose I will find out eventually, and yet I find it annoying to have this crucial information withheld. Even more annoying is the knowledge that in any case, I must read to the end — in spite of the migraine-inducing script and the thinly veiled insults to the Church that are likely to be scattered throughout the document. I wish I could simply put it aside, or bum it, unread, in the fireplace. But a man's last confession must be heard — even such a man as this. I took a couple of aspirin, and sat down once again to read.

But I had barely opened the folder when there came the sound of a large vehicle turning into the lane. I stood and went to the window. The Avenue des Francs Bourgeois is narrow, lined with linden trees; the tall van touched their branches as it made its way along. I recognized a removals van, and at the wheel, Michel Montour, in overalls and a baseball cap. He nodded at me as he passed, and I realized that he was heading down the hill towards Narcisse's farm.

Have he and Michèle decided to move in? It seems likely, if only because Michel used to work in the building trade. It would make sense, I told myself, to renovate the buildings before trying to sell the property. It even made sense for him to move in, to save time and to safeguard his supplies. But the size of the van suggested that the whole household was moving in — perhaps even the mysterious son, of whose existence I had only just learnt.

Perhaps I should call at the farm. I confess, *mon père*, I was tempted to go — if only to delay reading Narcisse's manuscript for a few more hours. But if the Montours were moving house, a visitor might not be welcome. Maybe I can call next week, when they have settled down. And yet it irked me that something was happening in Lansquenet without my prior knowledge. A priest should know his flock. This lapse constitutes a failure. I should have asked Vianne Rocher when I had the chance. Now, if I go, I told myself, she will know it is because I saw the removals van.

However, Joséphine Bonnet, who owns the café down the road, could certainly tell me what's happening. No-one would think twice if I called in. Everyone goes to Joséphine's. And people talk to her almost much as they talk to Vianne Rocher. She and Vianne are friends, of course, and her customers tell her things that they do not tell me in Confession. Once, this would have angered me. Now, I sometimes find myself wanting to confess to *her*.

Mea culpa. I wanted to go. The removals van was just an excuse. My head was aching, I was tired, and I was getting hungry again. One glass of wine, I told myself, and maybe a slice of the *tourteau* that Joséphine keeps behind the bar. No more than a single slice — after all, it would not do, especially not during Lent — but it would be rude to abstain, and the thought of Joséphine made me weak. I have come to realize in recent years that I am often weak, *père*, but that I rarely act on it. This is not a substitute for strength; rather, an indication of cowardice. I suspect that God is not fooled.

8

Thursday, March 16

The bar of the Café des Marauds was more crowded than I had expected. I saw a number of the older regulars — Joseph Foucasse, Louis Poireau, and the old doctor, Simon Cussonnet — but most of the people seemed young, although only one boy was known to me. That was Joséphine's son, Jean-Philippe, and I realized this was a party.

Of course. A birthday party. And there was a cake on the side of the bar, and jugs of iced punch, and lemonade. A party of adolescents, with music and cake and dancing — in fact, all the things that make me feel most ill at ease. I turned to go, but realized that Joséphine had seen me.

'Francis, you're not leaving?'

I thought she looked rather tired, her brown hair escaping from its low *chignon*. But from her lipstick and her red dress — one I hadn't seen before — I could tell she was making an effort.

'You're busy,' I said. 'I ought to go. This looks like a birthday party.'

'Yes. But the bar's still open,' she said. 'Come on in and have some cake!'

Celebrating has never come naturally to me, and I would much rather have gone home. But Joséphine brought me some wine, and some birthday cake on a flowered plate, and I sat and watched as she served her guests, fussing especially over the boy, who looked both embarrassed and tolerant. He has grown into a fine young man, with fair hair and his mother's eyes. He is already taller than Joséphine, good-looking as his father, Paul-Marie Muscat, must have been before alcoholism and hatred made him into a monster. I remember the boy playing with Rosette Rocher when they were young, but nowadays he tends to gravitate to the young people from his *lycée*, most of whom come from Agen, or from other towns and villages along the Tannes.

A pretty girl with dark-blonde hair, in jeans and a sparkly T-shirt, seemed to be taking up a good deal of his attention. She and the boy were sharing a piece of birthday cake; as I watched, they furtively held hands under the table.

'That's Pilou's girlfriend, Isabelle,' said Joséphine, seeing me watching. 'It's her sixteenth birthday today. She came to France when she was three, but she's half American.' I thought her voice sounded a little less than enthusiastic at this. Of course, Joséphine is very close to her son: more so because he is all she has. His father passed away several years ago, but he and Joséphine were estranged, and no-one — least of all Jean-Philippe Bonnet — misses him in the slightest.

'Pretty girl. Is it serious?'

'Her parents have invited him to go with them to America for the summer,' said Joséphine.

America. Joséphine found it hard enough to

let him go as far as Agen. And yet she must — as both of us know — if he is to grow into adulthood. Some parents find it easy to let their children fly the nest. Others find it impossible. I do not have to be a priest, or to have heard her confession, to know Joséphine Bonnet will find the transition harder than most.

'I sometimes envy Vianne,' she said, sitting at the table beside me.

'Really?' I was puzzled. 'Why?'

I know how close she and Vianne have been — although Joséphine no longer calls by the *chocolaterie* as regularly as once she did. I attribute this to the fact that their children are not as close as they were — or maybe it is because Joséphine is more independent nowadays.

She gave me a rather wistful smile. 'Rosette will never stop needing her,' she said. 'Anouk may move away, but Rosette will never stop being that little girl, playing with Vlad by the riverbank.' Vlad is Pilou's dog. Once they were inseparable. Now the boy is at school all day, and the dog has grown old and lazy. He spends all his time asleep by the bar, but I noticed that at the sound of his name, one ear pricked up as if in response to a half-forgotten call.

'Your son will always need you,' I said, feeling rather self-conscious. 'You're his mother.' But what do I know? My mother was always too concerned with her own affairs to care whether or not I needed her. I have no children. I never will. Most children make me uncomfortable — with the exception of Rosette Rocher and

57

Maya Mahjoubi. I half expected Joséphine to tell me to mind my own business, but instead she looked at me hopefully.

'You think so? I don't mean to interfere with his social life, but the thought of him growing up so fast — ' She lowered her voice, her eyes on the boy, who was laughing now, oblivious. 'I used to think I was different; that my boy would never be like the other boys. And it's selfish, I know. Vianne told me long ago that our children are not for us to keep, but to give away. All the same, I envy her. She'll always have her little girl.'

The cake was lemon vanilla, which I have to say surprised me. Most people buy cakes from the *chocolaterie*. I said as much, partly to diffuse the melancholy tone, but Joséphine looked furtive then, and I sensed I'd said the wrong thing.

'Pilou doesn't want to go to the shop. I called by with him, just for a minute or two, and he was like a cat on hot bricks. I think he feels guilty about Rosette.'

I shrugged. 'Boys can be awkward. I was.'

She gave a somewhat more genuine smile. 'For some reason, I can never picture you as a boy.'

Neither can I, *mon père*. My boyhood smells too much of smoke. I looked across at Jean-Philippe Bonnet, and for a moment wished that my guilt was over something as harmless as having outgrown a childhood friend.

'Rosette will make other friends,' I said.

'I hope so, Francis,' said Joséphine.

'And so will you,' I said, clumsily trying for comfort. 'You're an attractive woman. I admire your devotion to your son, but if you wanted to marry again — I mean, it would only be natural.'

She gave me an oddly reproachful look, and I remembered the woman she'd been, long ago, before Vianne Rocher blew into town. That woman had hated me — partly for my failure to curb her husband's violence, and also perhaps because I was, in many ways, a hateful man. One of the unexpected joys of the past few years has been the growing friendship we have shared; but sometimes she still makes me feel as if it is all an illusion, and that if only she knew what I *really* was, she would recoil in loathing.

'No, I don't think so,' she said. 'I've had more than enough of marriage. Paul cured me of that long ago.' She spoke with no bitterness, but with quiet finality.

I said: 'This birthday cake is good.'

'Let me bring you another piece.'

Forgive me, *mon père*. But Joséphine makes it easy for me to forget that I am a priest. It is a dangerous talent she has, and one that I should view with mistrust. To be honest, I forgot to ask about the Montours, too. She is so warm, so welcoming. She lights up the room like a fire in the hearth. And what harm is there, after all, to sit awhile in the firelight, feeling the warmth of her presence and taking comfort in her words?

9

Poor Rosette. I know how she feels. I've felt it so many times myself. The loss of a friend is hard to bear, which is why I've always tried so hard to stay aloof and not to be drawn too deeply into the lives of those around me. I have not always succeeded in this. I have lost too many friends. And she will, too, if she persists in expecting too much of their friendship.

I wish I could say something wise; something that would comfort her. 'Boys are stupid,' is hardly enough. Nor is chocolate, of course, though that is the only magic I have. She looks at the cup I have brought her, but does not drink. Instead, she stands and goes outside, face as dark as chocolate.

I call her. 'Rosette! Don't go far!'

She does not reply, but crosses the square, her red coat flapping in the wind. Where has she gone, my winter child, so silent and so self-possessed? I suspect she has gone to her wood. *Her wood.* It sounds so strange. I have never owned land, or a house, or even a pair of scissors. My professional equipment is all on loan, delivered by a firm in Marseille; the same that supplies my raw chocolate. My wooden spoons belonged to Armande; as did my copper jam-making pan. They are old and well-worn; I can feel the age in them. It is she whose hands shaped and smoothed the grip of the small utensils I use; most of them handmade by someone long dead, and scarred with the many marks of time.

I too am scarred by many marks. The thought of this reassures me. I am like the wooden spoon; the chopping-board; the table. Life has taken me and made of me something different. But what have *I* changed? What have I done to make those around me different?

It is a thought that has come to me more and more over the years. When I was young I still believed that I could make a difference. That I could change lives with nothing but kindness, and comfort, and chocolate. Now I am not so sure of this. I look at the people around me, and wonder whether, instead of helping them, I have done more harm than good. Joséphine is free of her husband, yet in spite of all of her plans she has never left Lansquenet. Guillaume is mourning the loss of the dog that replaced his old friend Charly. The Mahjoubis and the Bencharkis are still living under a shadow. And Armande — over sixteen years in her grave, and still I feel the loss of her as deeply as the loss of a limb. *She* changed *me*. But what did I do for her, except hasten her death?

When I was young, I believed that I could pass through the world like the wind through the grass, barely touching, never touched, scattering my seeds to the sky. *When I was young.* Of course I'm not old. But by the time she reached my age, my mother was already carrying the seeds of the cancer that killed her. She never knew Anouk or Rosette. She was dead by the time she was fifty.

Fifty used to sound very old. Fifty was half a century. But now it feels alarmingly close. I have closed the shutters on the morning side of the house, and opened those on the other side to watch the shadows lengthen. The shadows are still whisper-thin, and yet I can see them growing as fast as dandelions in the spring. They cannot be stopped: their seeds will be everywhere by dinnertime. My mother said you can never die as long as there's someone who needs you. If so, as long as I have Rosette, I could live forever.

I wonder what her wood is like. I have never been there — it would have been an intrusion. I'm happy for her that she has it, I think; and yet it makes me uneasy, too. What will Rosette do with a wood?

I took out my mother's Tarot pack last night, for the first time in months. The cards are so familiar now that I scarcely need to look. *Death. The Fool. The Tower. Change.* They tell me nothing I do not know. They tell me nothing about Rosette.

Maybe Narcisse left the wood to her to ensure that we stay in Lansquenet. Narcisse always liked Roux, and Roux has always stayed here against his inclination. Roux does not trust Lansquenet. Even after all this time, he prefers to live on his boat, away from the community. Sometimes he spends the night at the shop; but most of the time he leaves early, before even Rosette is awake; sleeping alone under the stars with the sounds of the river around him.

If I am to be honest, maybe I prefer it this way. Roux is uncomfortable indoors, restless as Rosette herself. If she were not here, I think he would have moved on with the river by now; moved on like the flotsam carried down the swollen Tannes. If she were not here, perhaps I too would have moved on down the river, where the wind always blows and nothing stays forever.

The florist's on the square has been let. The TO LET sign taken down, and since yesterday I see that someone has repainted the door. Once it was a sensible green: now it is bright purple — a colour that Anouk adores, but that, in Lansquenet, seems out of place: too garish, too impractical.

Who did the work? It surprises me that I did not notice. But so far, I have not seen anyone coming or going from the shop. There is no sign yet of who will be the florist's new manager. It may of course not be a florist's at all: that purple door suggests something else — a gift shop selling knick-knacks, perhaps, souvenirs for the tourists. A new shop in a village like ours always attracts attention. People are curious; they try to peer in through the papered window. But there is nothing to see as yet: no delivery van, no sign of human habitation. It could almost be me in there, the Vianne of seventeen years ago, with Anouk and her toy trumpet frightening away the ghosts. That Vianne would not have been slow to greet the newcomer, whoever they were. That Vianne would have invited them for hot chocolate, on the house. But I am more careful. I have learned. I am a different person now.

It makes me uncomfortable somehow, thinking of that other Vianne. Would she recognize herself, I wonder, if she saw me now? And what about the hole in my heart? That Anouk-shaped hole, through which the wind blows ever more insistently?

She's coming here for Easter, she says. She sent me a message this morning.

Thought we'd come over for Easter. Maybe stay for a few days. Would that be OK? Not sure what time I can get off work. I'll tell you when I know. Love, A. xxx

Of course it's okay. Does she have to ask? And yet I feel uneasy. That *we* — she means herself and Jean-Loup — makes her visit more formal than if she were dropping by on her own. And she says *come over*, not *come home*. One word makes a world of difference. *A few days.* How long does she mean? A long weekend? A week? No more. Anouk's visits are always brief, because of her job — because of Jean-Loup. And I know that Paris is good for her — that she has a world to explore — but we were always so close, she and I. It never occurred to me that she might want to explore without me.

The other Vianne would have laughed at the thought that Anouk might want to leave Lansquenet. But that other Vianne was naïve: as yet unmarked by time and events. She allowed herself to believe that maybe things could stay the same: that maybe change was avoidable. Now I begin to wonder if that other Vianne was me at all, or whether I have always been something more akin to the dark reflection of myself that I encountered in Paris: Zozie de l'Alba, the eater of lives, still alive in my memory. Where is she now? *Who* is she now? And why do I feel, after all this time, that she may still be inside me?

Mirrors

1

My father was a silent man: so silent that you sometimes almost forgot that he was there; that he was able to speak at all. He used to say that his brother had used all the words they'd had: that when they were separated at birth one got the voice, and the other the heart.

He had been one of a pair of twins. But twins had been too much of a burden for his mother, who already had four children, and his brother had gone north to a cousin in Nantes, and my father had been brought up by Tante Anna — my father's aunt, a widow whose first husband had been killed in the Great War, and who then had married her brother-in-law, only to see him dead of the flu before they could have children.

A thin, spiky woman all in black, with a silver-and-black cross in the lace at her throat and grey hair pulled so tightly back from her face that half the skin went with it. That cross of hers. I remember it well. The black part was jet, for mourning. The silver was to match her hair, because, in spite of it all, she was vain, and liked the figure she showed to the world; the elegance of it, perhaps, or the pleasing austerity. In any case, she was a Catholic by convenience, as so many people were. It would

69

not have done, in that turbulent time, to admit to having been anything else.

It never occurred to my sister and me to consider that we might be Jews. And yet I suppose we were, by birth: our mother's maiden name was Zwolaskowki, and my sister was named after her, although we called her Mimi instead; Naomi being far too cumbersome for such a little bit of a thing. It's sad that I remember the aunt better than I do my mother. But my mother died when I was four, giving birth to my sister, and the aunt — whose name had once been Hannah, but who in troubled times had learnt to spell it the way it was always pronounced — took over the mothering process with the same cool efficiency that she had done with my father. I was named Narcisse after him, which filled me with despair as a boy, but I grew into it eventually, and besides, as my father said, I could have been named for his brother, Modeste.

Will there be much more of this, père? It seems as if the old man is taunting me deliberately. There are pages and pages of this: of how the family moved; of how the brothers lost track of each other; of how the other twin, Modeste, married, but was killed by the Boche. Narcisse has a captive audience. His retaliation, perhaps, for all those dull sermons he heard as a boy. The great-aunt, I understand, was strict: forcing the siblings to church every week, while their father ran the farm that had once been the great-aunt's husband's. Forgive me, père. No more today.

Instead I shall seek out Vianne Rocher, as I meant to the other day, in the hope that she may prove more helpful than Roux on the subject of Rosette's inheritance.

The shop was empty when I arrived, except for Rosette, who was drawing. She likes to sit on the floor to draw, and on a busy day one must be careful not to step on her rows of coloured pens, chalks and pencil-crayons. Rosette is nearly sixteen years old, although she does not look it. She has the small face of a much younger child, made even smaller by the volume of her corkscrew-curly, pale red hair. She looked up as I came in, a black pencil-crayon in one hand.

A sudden icy gust of wind from the door blew my soutane up around my knees. Rosette laughed, and made an explosive sound.

'*BAM!*'

Vianne put her head around the kitchen door. 'Francis. How nice to see you. And during Lent, too.' She smiled, to let me know she did not mean it as mockery. 'Let me bring you some hot chocolate.'

I accepted the china cup, its contents dark and sweet as sin. I took a token sip, and said: 'I see Michel Montour has decided to renovate Narcisse's farm himself.'

Vianne nodded. 'They're moving in with their son, Yannick. They've put their house on the market.'

How does she know these things, *mon père*? How does she know the things I do not hear? Of course, Michel and Michèle Montour were never really part of my flock. They came for Narcisse's

71

sake, and perhaps I was too harsh in my judgement of them. If they mean to stay for good, then maybe I was wrong about their original motive for coming here.

'What do you know about the son?'

She shook her head. 'Not much. He's fifteen. He's been away at boarding school, but Michèle says it hasn't worked out. She's planning to tutor him at home. She was asking how that had worked for Rosette.'

On hearing her name, Rosette looked up and gave me a brilliant smile.

'And how *has* it worked for Rosette?' I said.

Vianne smiled. 'She's happy,' she said.

If only it were so easy, I thought. Maybe for Rosette it is. But Vianne and I know that Rosette has not had the kind of schooling she should have had. She can read and write; she can count; she has a real talent for drawing. But both of us know that this is not the kind of education a sixteen-year-old needs. But Vianne is adamant: she will not risk sending Rosette back to school. The last time was a disaster, she says. There will be no second attempt.

'She misses Narcisse,' said Vianne Rocher. 'She has so few friends now that Anouk is in Paris; now that Pilou is back at school. Narcisse was always talking to her, making her laugh, telling her stories.'

I looked at Rosette. 'Does she understand? About Narcisse's will, I mean?' It seemed unlikely; and yet at my words, Rosette cocked her head further and made a little chattering sound.

'Narcisse left some land to you,' I said, speaking slowly and carefully. 'Some woodland, near the sunflower field.'

Rosette made the chattering sound again. She sounded like a magpie. 'I don't suppose she does,' I said. 'But maybe the woodland can be sold on her behalf, and the money used to provide for her?'

'I don't think that's what Narcisse wanted,' said Vianne.

'Who knows what Narcisse wanted?' I said, perhaps more sharply than I'd intended. 'He was always a difficult man. Perhaps what he *really* wanted was to annoy his daughter and son-in-law, cause conflict and force me into a series of unpleasant encounters. While we're on the subject, perhaps you could have a word with Roux, who seems to believe he can somehow refuse to carry out his legal responsibilities — '

I saw Vianne smile, and stopped, aware that I was speaking too loudly. 'You look tired,' she said. 'Here, try one of my *mendiants*. Dark chocolate, sour cherries, and a sprinkling of coarse black pepper. They're new. Tell me what you think.'

I shook my head. 'Thank you, but I have to go. Parish duties, and so forth.'

2

Off he goes, with the sharp little nod that I used to find so forbidding. Now I know him better, and I understand that he mistrusts warmth; shies away from friendliness. Being Francis Reynaud is to be in perpetual conflict between instinct and self-discipline; resistance and abandon. I used to fear and hate him so much, in the days when Anouk was small. Now I have more sympathy. There is darkness in Reynaud, but he is not a bad man. If he were, Rosette would know. Rosette sees further than I do.

I've noticed that, since Narcisse's death, Rosette has been more withdrawn than usual. Usually she likes to help in the shop, but for the last few days she has been aloof, unreadable, even to me. I find myself searching for her thoughts, scanning her colours for a sign of something that may give me a clue as to how I may reach her, but she remains a mystery, a puzzle never to be solved.

This afternoon, while Reynaud was here, she was drawing in the book she takes almost everywhere with her. A hardback sketchbook, a gift from Anouk, in Anouk's favourite colour. I found myself admiring the way in which my daughter creates these images: the sure, economical strokes of the pen or pencil. The lines seem almost random at first, and yet each stroke has a purpose. She must get her talent from Roux, who is always so clever at making things. I always assumed that my daughters would inherit my way with chocolate, but neither Anouk nor Rosette have shown any particular interest. Rosette has her drawing; Anouk's special interests have become less clear to me over the years. Some of this is due to Jean-Loup Rimbault, a young man with ambitions and dreams, as well as a serious heart complaint that has been with him since childhood — he is often in hospital, and I some-times fear for my little Anouk, placing her own heart so firmly between his delicate fingers.

I never had relationships: I always feared their loss too much. Even Roux — so much more than a friend — is still not quite a partner. Our arrangement is one that suits us both, and if it sometimes feels a little lonely, a little strange, I tell myself it's better this way. I can concentrate on Rosette.

'What are you drawing?'

Rosette did not reply, but continued to draw, nose almost touching the paper. It was a more complicated scene than the ones she usually favours: drawn mostly in pencil, but with certain details highlighted in colour. A little girl was trotting down an overgrown path through the forest. The little girl looked like Rosette as she often draws herself — as a child of seven or eight, with mango-coloured corkscrew hair — wearing a Little Red Riding Hood cloak and carrying a basket of strawberries. Behind her, on the path, a wolf: nose to the ground, eyes shining; sleek and dark and menacing. The wolfs eyes were narrow and deceptively sleepy, and Rosette had used a bright red pencil to fill in his giant shadow, a shadow so long that it filled half the page.

Something about that picture made me feel slightly uneasy, as if it held some kind of message. Many of Rosette's pictures do, but this one seemed closer to some of the dreams I used to have when we were living in Paris. A change from Rosette's usual style. Change always makes me uneasy; it means the wind is on the move. And we have refused its call for so long. It has been years since we answered it. And yet I still hear it, calling me, its voice no longer cajoling, but openly, darkly threatening. *Thought you could hide from me, Vianne Rocher? Thought you were safe in your little house? I can take if all away. Anouk. Rosette. I'll blow your house down.*

I glanced at Rosette's picture again. I couldn't help thinking that maybe it was intended for me, a warning of something — perhaps a fear — that she could only express through art. It looks like an image from the Tarot cards left me by my mother; graphic, filled with significance, laden with secret menace.

The Hurakan was blowing.

No. My child is safe from the call of the wind.

'What's that, Rosette?' I said.

For a moment I thought she might tell me. She looked up from the drawing, her eyes meeting mine for a moment, then her gaze skipped sideways towards the newly purple door of the

76

shop that used to be a florist's, but might be almost anything —

'Rosette?'

I looked at the newly painted door; the paper across the windows. There was nothing to suggest anything strange about it. Except perhaps for the barest filament of light at the door; a smudge of something that might have been a shadow, or a reflection —

I know she's curious. I am, too. And I know she thinks we should have called round, taken the new owner a gift. But things have changed since I first arrived in Lansquenet on the skirts of the wind. Experience has taught me that it is sometimes best to be cautious. But Rosette is seldom cautious. It strikes me that perhaps she has seen something through the window. Maybe she has already met the elusive occupant —

'Did you go in there?' I said. 'Did you visit Narcisse's shop?'

Rosette does not always reply when I ask her a question. But now I thought her lack of reaction seemed a little too deliberate. She picked up a dark-blue pencil and worked at the shadows in her picture, drawing them into twisted vines of unnatural regularity.

'What kind of shop is it, Rosette? Did you see the new manager?'

Rosette never lies. But her silences are often more telling than words. She has seen *something*, I'm sure of it. Something that has troubled her. The image in her drawing; the wolf with the long red shadow, the tangle of vines — all this suggests that she is trying to make sense of something too complex to unravel in any of the usual ways. I have my chocolate, she has her art. Both are forms of divination.

'Listen, Rosette. I want you to stay away from the new shop. Don't go there alone. Don't try to look in. Wait until I'm ready. Then we can go there together, maybe take the owner some chocolates . . . '

She gave me a darkling glance.

'I know. But remember, people don't always like visitors when they're settling into a new place. Promise me you'll wait, Rosette. Don't go into that shop alone.'

She made no direct reply, but instead gave a little magpie-call, then closed her drawing-book with a snap and headed out into the street like a child into a forest.

3

Friday, March 17

I didn't tell Maman about the lady in the
window-glass. I think it's for the best. She'd only
worry, and besides, there's no reason to believe
that what I saw was an Accident. Accidents are
noisy things. Like in Paris, when I was small, and
things used to fly through the air and smash if
ever I got too upset. Those days are gone now. I
know what to do. I put my finished drawing away
and left again by the half-open door.

Reynaud's visit had made me want to go and
see my wood again. I like saying that. *My* wood.
My strawberry clearing. My path. My trees. My
fence. My wishing well. Those things are mine
now, Reynaud said. Not Roux's, not Maman's,
but mine. Mine to do what I like in. Sometimes
all I want to do is be alone; to sing, to shout, to
run about, to talk to myself in my shadow-voice.
And now I can do that whenever I want. The
wood, the clearing, and the well — they are all
mine to play with. I am no longer a trespasser. I
am the guardian of a sacred place.

That's what I was thinking as I walked across
the fields towards Narcisse's farm, and the
chain-link fence. It was late in the afternoon, but
the sun was still warm, and the birds were
singing everywhere. I didn't need to hide any
more, or crawl under the fence, but I did, out of

habit, and because I still don't have the key to the gate, and because I like it when people don't know where I am. I can do what I like when I'm here, and not worry about Accidents.

Bam went ahead. He always does; laughing and flying into the trees. I don't need to worry about him here. He's free to do whatever he wants. A flock of black birds flew up out of the trees with a sound like scattered applause. I called to them in my blackbird-voice, and ran to the strawberry clearing.

It's too early for strawberries. But the clearing is filled with their leaves and their little white flowers, like fallen stars. The wishing well was covered, too, so that only someone who knew it was there would have really noticed it. It looks like a barrow under the green; somewhere fairies or goblins might live. And there was someone already there, sitting with their back to me.

For a minute I thought of fairies or trolls. But it wasn't either of them, or even somebody special like Bam. Now I could see that it was a boy; quite a fat boy, with messy brown hair and a T-shirt a little too small for him. He was sitting on the grass, looking into the tangle of green, and even his back looked unhappy. I nearly ran away right then, but then I remembered that this was *my* wood, and that if anyone was supposed to leave, it should be the boy, who looked like a bear, sitting there in the strawberry-leaves.

I didn't want to say anything, so I made a bird-noise, like a scolding jackdaw.

The boy didn't look round, or move at all. I made, the jackdaw-call again — CRAWWK!

80

— and made the leaves of the oak trees dance. I still wasn't sure if I was cross or curious to see him there. Maybe I was a bit of both. I wondered what he was doing there. Maybe he was a traveller, wanting to spend the night in my wood. Maybe I'd let him, I told myself. Maybe he could be my secret.

'*Rwk*,' I said, in a friendlier voice.

Still the boy didn't say anything. I came a little closer. Maybe he was deaf, I thought. Maybe he was pretending. Sitting on the grass at his side, I saw he was about my age, but bigger of course, with a round pale face and small angry eyes.

'Go away,' said the boy.

I made the jackdaw noise again, more insistently this time. Jackdaws dive-bomb animals that come too close to their nests. The boy was in my place, after all. *I* certainly wasn't leaving.

'Stop making those noises,' said the boy. 'I'm sensitive. My mother says I mustn't be upset.'

I laughed. I couldn't help it. He looked so funny and cross, sitting there, telling me what not to do. If I had my pencils, I thought, I'd draw him as a brown bear, looking fat and grumpy. Instead I puffed out my cheeks and blew, and made all the leaves and branches dance. Not in a bad way but in a funny, playful way. Then I sang a little song: *Bam-bam-bam, Barn-badda-BAM!* and laughed at his expression.

The boy looked up at me. 'You're Rosette Rocher,' he said, and his voice was different. Not so cross this time, but curious. Still a bear, I thought, but not fierce. Maybe just looking for something to eat; berries, or honey, or acorns.

'I've heard about you,' said the boy.

I shrugged. Lots of people have heard about me.

'I'm Yannick,' said the boy.

I made the leaves do their dance again. It's my place: I can do what I want. I could even make him go away. But maybe I won't. He looked so sad. A sad bear with no honey.

'Why don't you say something?' said Yannick.

I shrugged again. I don't like talking. I'd rather sign, or sing, which is only one letter's difference; or chatter like a monkey, or bark like a dog. People like dogs. Me, not so much. I know that now. I didn't before. I thought that if I was a dog, the other children would like me. But they just thought I was weird, which to them is worse than anything. Even Pilou thinks I'm weird: at least he does when he's with his friends. I don't really have any friends. Except for Roux, and Anouk, and Maman, and Pilou — and Bam, of course.

Maman sometimes tells people that Bam is my invisible friend. That's not true. She can see him, and so can Anouk, and so can some other people. But Maman says it's easier than trying to tell them what Bam *really* is: and besides, what does it matter? Everyone's different. Some of us are just more different than others.

Yannick looked at me closely. His eyes aren't angry, as I'd thought; just smaller than most people's. Then he smiled, a great big, wide smile that made me laugh.

'You're funny,' he said.

I know.

'Are you deaf? Or mute, or something?'

I laughed and shook my head, and made the leaves dance and laugh with me. Yannick smiled again. He looks nice when he smiles.

'Okay. Why don't we get something to eat? I'm starving.'

All right. Where?

'I know a good place,' said Yannick. 'Come with me. I'll show you.'

I followed him.

4

My father was a gentle soul, as wary of Tante Anna as I was myself. Inarticulate by choice as well as by nature, he had learnt only the basics of reading and writing while he was at school, before being summoned to help on the farm. Tante Anna had kept his school reports; one of them for every term, all in beautiful old-fashioned script:

'Narcisse is quiet and well-behaved, but shows no natural ability.'

'Narcisse is quiet and attentive, but often mistakes the letters of the alphabet. Diligent study and practice in lettering will significantly improve his deficiencies in reading and writing.'

'Narcisse is an attentive pupil, although his speech impediment hinders him from contributing in recitation, and his continued inability to distinguish certain letters means that, once again, he is bottom of the class.'

For a long time I remained in ignorance, both of my father's dyslexia (though I never heard that word spoken until many decades after his death) and his mysterious speech impediment. In fact, it never occurred to me that my father might not be silent by choice, but might actually be afraid of speaking.

At table, he never said a word, except to

84

thank Tante Anna for the meal, which he did with the humility that some people reserve for God. He spent most of his time alone in his garden and on the farm, while Tante Anna kept the house, cooked meals and raised the children as she thought best, which was perhaps more harshly than he himself would have chosen to raise them. But Tante Anna was mistress of the farm; hers was the voice that mattered. And Tante Anna believed that children should be well-behaved and obedient, and go to church, say their prayers, and be respectful of adults.

Tante Anna noticed everything: a speck of mud on a school smock; a missing button from a shirt. And although dutiful, she was not warm: she cared for us for the good of our souls, not for the good of our childish hearts. My sister Mimi was especially troublesome. Undersized from the very start, and subject to fits and seizures, Mimi was not expected to live beyond infancy; and when she did, Tante Anna saw it more as a curse than a mercy.

Another mouth to feed, at a time when food was not always plentiful. A useless girl, at a time when girls were valued less than livestock. And to cap it all, by simply being born, she had caused the death of her mother — none of these things made Mimi's continued survival a reason for rejoicing. But against all odds, Mimi did survive — in spite of Tante Anna's outspoken belief that she was doomed from the outset. In spite of her size, her refusal to feed, her seizures, her unexplained fits of laughter, little Mimi clung to life, and grew, like the stubborn dandelion that manages to take root and flower even in the least welcoming of places. Mimi lived; a stubborn, stunted little thing that managed, in spite of everything, to try to grow towards the light.

You might have thought that caring for a younger, disabled sister would have been an unbearable chore. I was, after all, only four years old when Mimi, like an unwanted gift, was left to take my mother's place. I should have hated the pitiful thing. But somehow, I didn't hate her. Starved of affection as I was, I learnt to love my sister, first with the love that a child may give to a battered toy, or a stray dog, and then with a fierce protectiveness. It wasn't that my father was lacking in affection; it was simply that he had never learnt how to show it. As for Tante Anna, she was not given to demonstrations of weakness. She had raised my father alone; she had already buried two husbands. Whatever softness might have been in her had long ago been calcified. Now she was like that cross she wore; hard and sharp-edged and merciless. She was not a bad or cruel woman at heart, but there was no kindness in her; just a sense, of duty that she mistook for religious devotion, but which owed rather more to her pride and her fear of what the neighbours might say.

She raised me without tenderness, but in the knowledge that I would one day be a man, a worthwhile citizen. Mimi had no such potential. As a girl, she was worthless; a burden on the family. No-one would ever marry Mimi, not for any dowry. She would never learn to speak, or obey more than the simplest of instructions. She would always be subject to mysterious fits and seizures, and although she seemed perfectly content — even happy — with her lot, Tante Anna saw her as a punishment from God for some as-yet-undeclared sin, and hardened her heart accordingly.

I say all this, Reynaud, so that you may understand that my antipathy towards the Church is nothing personal. Tante Anna's religion was as cold as stone, as dry as dust; and her God never answered a single one of the prayers that I made to him.

What rubbish, *mon père*. Does he think God actually answers *prayers*? God has no time to listen to petty grievances. Did he think that God would drop everything to look into his little life? Did he hope for divine intervention every time something went wrong? You see, this is the problem, *mon père*. People take things too literally. They expect the universe to revolve around their little preoccupations. They have no sense of the scale of things, no sense of their own insignificance. So God didn't answer your prayers? Do not imagine you are alone. God doesn't *care* that you are alone, or that you are suffering. If God made the stars, then why would He care whether or not you fast for Lent, or whether you drink alcohol, or even if you live or die —

Forgive me, *père*. My patience with parishioners has never been especially great. These people seem to think that God owes them His attention. Or failing His, that I owe them mine. My sheep are such petty animals; forever bleating; forever straying. And my job is far from pastoral; it mostly consists of crowd control. Not that I can imagine doing any other; but I too have made my sacrifices. Narcisse is not the only one who has called out to God, and heard no reply.

With no other outlet, Mimi became the focus of my affection. That strange little girl, who never learnt to speak more than a dozen words, but who smiled and laughed almost constantly, was closer to me than anyone I have ever known. Perhaps that is why Rosette Rocher has come to mean so much to me. She reminds me of Mimi — or at least, Mimi as she might have been if she had not died at seven years old, cruelly and needlessly, while God's attention was turned elsewhere —

That's it, père. No more today. Every word feels like an attack — on me, on the Church, on God — and there's only so much a priest can take. This confession — if that's what it is — needs time, and he knows that, whatever my faults, I will stay until the end. But for now, I shall wander along to the farm and have a word with Michèle Montour. Maybe the elusive Yannick will be there. In any case, it will make a change.

This was what I told myself as I set off towards the farm. But Narcisse's voice followed me as I went down the *Rue des Marauds* and over the fields and alongside the wood. A very persistent voice, for one who had so little to say to me in life. But, *mon père*, I have always heard the voices of the dead best of all, perhaps because of who I am, or maybe because of the things I have done. The voices of the dead are loud, and they clamour for company.

I was never a good man. A *righteous* man, perhaps, but not good. I know this, now; too late, of course, to undo certain actions. All I can do is move forward, and try to be better than I was. *My father, the murderer.* How easily he writes those words. Whom did the father murder? I am not sure I want to know. Does the father not deserve peace? What good does it do to bring these things back into the light, things which should have been left in the dark?

Did he confess his crime, *mon père*? Was he absolved, as long ago you absolved me? Mine was a boy's trick, an accident: and besides, you said the river-rats were vermin; scum; weeds in the garden of the Lord. Mine were only the hands, you said. God's will had been working through me.

Years later, I came to understand that God had nothing to do with it. And my guilt was not for you to absolve, which is why it sometimes still weighs on me. I say *sometimes*. To be fair, there are days when I hardly think of it, and when I do, it is often as something that happened to me long ago, when I was someone different. They say the human body replaces itself every seven years. Blood cells; skin cells; bone cells. All different. I have shed my skin many times since the houseboat fire on the Tannes. I should be a new man by now. But on days like this, when the morning sun shines in a certain way on the fields; when the air is cool, and the primroses show their faces from under the hedge, the boy I once was seems very close, almost close enough to touch —

I was so lost in my thoughts, *mon père*, that I almost cried out when I saw the boy. Instead I made a strangled sound, to which the boy responded with a squawk of alarm, and Rosette, who was moments behind him as he emerged from the bushes, gave one of her mocking bird-calls.

'Rosette!' I said.

The boy gave me a look. He looked nothing like the boy I once was — being brown-haired, round-faced and somewhat on the plump side — and yet he looked thoroughly guilty. I noticed that he was carrying a two-litre jar of what looked like strawberry jam. The jar had been opened — and recently. It was now close to half empty, adorned with sticky handprints.

'Is that from Narcisse's farm?' I said. There were no other farms nearby.

The boy nodded, still looking guilty.

'Then you must be Yannick Montour.'

Once more, the boy nodded. He didn't look much like either of his parents, both of whom were slightly built, and his thin upper lip and narrow eyes gave him a somewhat petulant look. I smiled and held out my hand. 'I'm Francis Reynaud, priest of Lansquenet,' I said. 'I've heard a lot about you.'

The boy looked surprised. 'Have you?' he said.

'No, not really,' I said, and smiled. 'In fact, you're rather a mystery man. But I understand you're coming to stay?'

The boy nodded.

'Then welcome to Lansquenet-sous-Tannes.' I shook his hand, which was distinctly sticky. Rosette made her bird-sound again. It occurred to me that if I had eaten a whole litre of strawberry jam — even with the help of a friend — I would have had serious problems. Still, many things are allowed at fifteen that are no longer permissible after the age of fifty-five. Eating jam from the jar is one of them.

I said: 'I see you've met Rosette. Her mother owns the chocolate shop.'

Yannick pulled a doubtful face. 'I'm not allowed to eat chocolate,' he said, and my mind went back to another boy who was not allowed to eat chocolate. Luc Clairmont has grown into a fine young man without a trace of his childhood stutter, who visits his mother once a year and lives with his wife in Paris. If Caro had let him eat chocolate, maybe things would have been different. Who knows? These things matter to a boy.

I said: 'Sometimes, being told not to do something just makes us want it all the more. Sometimes, a little of what you crave is better than total abstinence.'

Yannick looked surprised, as the boy I once was would have looked surprised. 'I guess so,' he said. 'What's *abstinence*?'

'Something priests mention rather too much,

I'm afraid,' I said. 'Especially during Lent.'

The boy looked at me suspiciously, but seeing that I was not mocking him, smiled. When he smiles, his face lights up, and he reminds me somehow of Narcisse — not that the old man ever smiled much at me, but nevertheless, there was something. Some distant family resemblance.

My father, the murderer. Why do those words affect me so? Perhaps it has to do with the boy, who seems rather odd, perhaps even slow. Is this why his parents keep him at home? If it is, then perhaps it is good that Rosette and he seem to have made friends. Not that Rosette is exactly *slow*, but certainly she is *different*. Maybe having a friend her own age will help her develop more normally. I was about to ask Rosette what she thought of her new property when I saw Michèle Montour at the end of the lane, and heard her voice raised stridently:

'*Yannick!* What are you doing out there!'

The boy turned away, thrusting the jar of jam into my hands. 'Please! Don't tell my mother. *Please!*' Then he dived into the bushes from which he had emerged, closely followed by Rosette, whose mocking jackdaw-call I heard moving away into the wood.

A moment later, Michèle Montour was upon me. High heels, tailored trousers and a spotless white silk shirt — hardly the kind of outfit, I thought, suitable for moving house. Her face was rigid with annoyance as she looked at the jar of jam in my hands.

'Did my son take that?' she said.

A small, strategic lie, père, is preferable to exposing another soul to the sin of rage. Besides, Yannick had looked desperate.

'Ah, this?' I said, looking down at the jar. 'Er, one of my parishioners. A gift.'

'A gift?' repeated Michèle Montour.

'Well, actually, more of a sacrifice,' I said. 'You know how during Lent, some people find it hard to resist temptation. My parishioner thought it better to, er — deliver himself from — '

Michèle Montour made a derisory sound. 'My son,' she said sharply, 'is a compulsive overeater. It is a medical condition that must be strictly monitored. If unsupervised, Yannick will be happy to eat continually. This is detrimental, both to his looks and to his health, and needs to be dealt with strictly.'

'I see. It must be hard for you.'

'Mon père, you have no idea.'

'Is that why you took him out of school?'

Her lips tightened. 'My son has other — issues,' she said. 'Behavioural and social issues. My husband and I thought it better to keep him at home.'

I nodded. 'I see.'

And yes, I did see. Michèle Montour is deeply vain. Having an unsatisfactory son must irk her profoundly. So this is why she does not speak of him to her friends; why, in almost two years, I have only just seen him. I sense Michèle Montour would love to boast of her son's achievements: his prowess on the sports field; his dutiful attention to her. Instead, she must dwell on her sacrifice; the fact that she must teach him

93

at home; her patience and long-suffering in the name of motherhood. It has soured her, and yet she assumes an air of practised martyrdom when telling me about it. I know that look; I have seen it before on the face of Caroline Clairmont. I have heard that note in her voice: *Mon père, I try not to complain. Motherhood is my cross to bear, and — don't think I'm complaining, père, but no-one knows how I have suffered over the years. No-one but you, of course, mon père: I don't know what I would have done without your help.* In fact, I have done little to help but bite my tongue and listen: Caroline Clairmont uses the confessional as a means of airing her woes rather than seeking absolution. Michèle Montour has something of the same passive-aggressive style, although in Caro Clairmont's case, it comes with the kind of wan, wilting tone of voice that tests my patience to the full, and in the case of Madame Montour, it takes a distinctly combative tone.

She shot a disapproving look at the half-empty jar of jam. 'Some people — *gullible* people, *mon père* — do not believe that my son Yannick suffers from a genuine medical condition. They allow him to cajole them. Some of them even give him sweets. These people are complicit, *mon père*, in his misbehaviour. I hope that if you witness this, you will know how to intervene.'

'Of course.' I felt my face growing hot. 'Of course I will, Madame Montour.' And, head held high, I left the scene, still carrying the ridiculous jar. A mocking bird-call followed me all along the hawthorn hedge, along with the sound of

94

footsteps, one set light, the other rather less so. I pretended not to hear them, but left the jam jar on the wall at the end of the *Avenue des Francs Bourgeois*. I did not turn to investigate the sounds I heard from the hawthorn hedge, but by the time I reached the house the two-litre jar of jam was gone.

5

So that was Yannick. Now he's my friend. He's funny, and he likes to eat, and sometimes he can get upset, and he doesn't look at you when he's talking to you. It's weird who his parents turned out to be. Madame Montour doesn't like me at *all*. She only bothered to learn my name when she found out about Narcisse's will. But I like Yannick. He's nice; and he didn't laugh at me, and he has no other friends.

I get that. Making friends isn't easy when you're different. And I don't mean to be jealous when I see Pilou getting on the school bus with his friends. But he never waves to me. He should wave. He's fine with me when we're alone, but when his friends are with him — BAM! — it's like he doesn't see me.

I told Yannick. He understood. 'I used to have a friend,' he said. 'He was called Abayomi. We were the two kids at primary school who always used to get left out. Then we went to the *collège* in Marseille, and there were lots of other kids like him, but no other kids like me.'

I signed: *I get it. That sucks.*

'So, why don't you talk in the regular way? Did you have an accident?'

I shook my head. *Why bother? This works.*

Yannick shrugged. 'Fair enough. I guess if it

96

works, it works, huh?'

I smiled. You see? He understands. He doesn't think I'm weird at all.

After Yannick left, it was late. There were shadows across the square as I reached the *chocolaterie*. Maman was in the back room, still making up Easter baskets. I could hear her singing softly to herself; that song she sometimes used to sing to me when I was very small:

V'là l'bon vent, v'là l'joli vent

V'là l'bon vent, ma mie m'appelle —

I looked outside again. The shop that once was Narcisse's shop, with the newspaper on the windows, now has a sign above the door. The sign reads: *Les Illuminés*. And now I noticed something else: the paper was gone from the window.

And the door was open.

6

I didn't mean to go inside. I knew I wasn't supposed to. Just as I hadn't meant to look between the newspaper sheets and into the empty space behind. But there was something about that door that made me want to go through it. Maybe it was the colour, like plums. Purple is Anouk's favourite. Or because of the lady I'd seen in the glass the morning of the early snow. Or maybe I dreamed that. I dream a lot. Maman says dreams are a sign that the wind is changing. Perhaps it is. Perhaps this time the wind will bring something that makes her happy.

The door was half open, like an eye. I pushed it open all the way. And then I looked around the shop. It had been a florist's, with baskets and pots set out all over the wooden floor, and a long counter with cellophane sheets, and coloured ribbons, and greetings-cards, and shelves of those ceramics that you only see at funerals. Now it was different. With Narcisse, it had been full of flowers: big messy buckets of roses and great shaggy-headed chrysanthemums and sun-flowers like lions' manes and fussy little freesias. With Narcisse, it had always smelt of leaves, and soil, and greenery, and flowers. And on the floor there had always been clippings, and petals, and pieces of straw, and the pieces of dry earth that fell from Narcisse's gardening-boots.

But it wasn't a florist's any more. Now it was clean as a hospital. The floor had been polished, and there was a long purple rug in the middle of it. There were purple chairs, too, and a shiny espresso machine. At the back there was a bead curtain, where the office used to be, and in the front was a big leather chair, and lots of bright lights and mirrors. And there, in the mirror, there she was, sitting in one of the purple chairs, and wearing pointy high-heeled boots the colour of candied cherries —

It was the lady I'd seen in the window. Long hair, dark clothes, arms all covered in thick black lace; a skirt that looked like feathers. But there was no-one in the room. Only in the mirror. I looked around for the lady, but I couldn't see her anywhere.

I made a little jackdaw sound. Words seemed wrong in that mirror-place. In the mirror, the lady smiled, and the beads on the bead-curtain danced and shook —

I signed: *Who's there?*

She smiled again.

Who are you? What do you want?

The bead-curtain shook. It looked like it was laughing. And now I could hear the voice of the wind, sounding very close to me now, whispering and crooning:

What do I want? What we always want. What our kind have always craved. I want YOU, little Rosette. Most of all, what I want is you.

I stared. The curtain danced and shook. In the mirror, the lady smiled. Outside, the room was empty. Then the mirror-lady signed: *The real question is, little Rosette. What do you want?*

I turned and ran.

7

Rosette came back after five o'clock, but did not come into the kitchen. Instead she went straight upstairs, and I heard her playing with her button-box, a ritual she associates with order, comfort and relief.

Something has upset her. I can always tell; she may not speak very much, but the house reflects her emotions. From the corner of my eye, I can see Bam lurking on the stairs, a fugitive gleam in the shadows.

'Don't you want your chocolate?' She usually has a cup of hot chocolate at four o'clock, with a *croissant* or a piece of bread. Today she does not answer me, but from the kitchen I can hear the sound of buttons being moved around and around on the wooden floor. Whatever upset her, she does not want me to know. I try not to worry. I worry far too much, I know — about Rosette, about Anouk. When did that happen? I ask myself. I used to be fearless. When did I stop?

Outside the air is very still. The spring snow has melted. A vapour-trail from a plane, very high, scratches the eggshell blue of the sky. And there are crows on the roof of the church, outlined against the fading light; perched silent and still on the weathervane; strutting over the

101

cobblestones. I feel a sudden need to know what Anouk is doing, right now. Is she with Jean-Loup, perhaps, walking along the banks of the Seine? Is she shopping? Watching TV? Is she at work? Is she happy? I check my mobile phone again. Her message from yesterday is still there.

Thought we'd come over for Easter. Maybe stay for a few days. Would that be OK? Not sure what time I can get off work. I'll tell you when I know, love, A. xxx

I feel I should be happier that Anouk is coming to stay, but there is something in her tone that makes me feel uneasy. Is it a little too casual? A little too vague? It's hard to tell. And she does not give a specific date, even though she knows that I need time to make arrangements. To air out her room, to invite her friends, to make all her childhood favourites. Is she trying to say something more? Is she even coming at all?

The blue of the sky has faded now from eggshell-blue to violet. Upstairs I can still hear Rosette playing with her button-box. When I go into her bedroom I will find them arranged in complex patterns along the floorboards, under the curtains, the skirting-boards, lined up in order of colour and size. Rosette is sensitive to colours — and to other things. I would like to know what upset her, but to ask outright would be a mistake. She will tell me when — and if — she wants me to know.

I close up the *chocolaterie*. There will be no more customers today. And just as I do so, I notice that the new shop is open at last; light falls

102

from the window over the darkening cobbles. A pink neon sign — *Les Illuminés* — shines above the window.

Les Illuminés. It sounds like a chichi lighting shop. If so, it will be expensive, and I do not expect it to last very long. Lansquenet is not affluent, and the people who can afford fancy goods will buy them in Agen, or maybe even from as far as Marseille or Toulouse. I assume the Montours know the manager. Perhaps that's why they let it so fast. I briefly consider crossing the square to have a look inside. But just as I consider it, I see the neon sign switch off, and a woman's figure appear at the door, silhouetted against the light. For a moment she looks vaguely familiar, but she is too far away to see clearly. Then the light goes off, and I hear the rattle of the shutters over the window.

Such a very familiar sound. Such a familiar setting. There's certainly nothing to account for this sudden sense of unease; the feeling that someone is watching me from behind the shuttered glass. And there's something else, too, barely glimpsed against the dusk. A trace of colours around the door; a whisper of incense; a snicker of smoke; the scent of other places.

Find me. Feel me. Face me.

A challenge? It feels like a challenge. Or maybe an invitation. The pink neon sign has left a kind of after-image in the air, a kind of blur, like petrol on stone after a fall of April rain. And then there comes another memory: the sound of a pair of scarlet heels on the Paris cobblestones —

Surely not. Our kind are few. And yet I am

glad I asked Rosette not to go into the shop alone. There's something *attractive* about the place, a glamour that has nothing to do with the pretty pink sign, or the purple door. A dangerous glamour, promising much, and offering —

What do you want?

Find me. Feel me. Face me.

I watch for a time, but there is no more activity. The woman has gone back inside. Do I know her? Surely not. And still there is something about her that I find unsettling. That trace of colours in the air. Or perhaps it is simply the speed with which she has reopened the shop, so soon after the owner's death. It must be someone from out of town, I tell myself as I turn away. Anyone from the village would have waited, out of respect.

From upstairs I hear Rosette singing softly to herself. '*Vlam bam-bam. Vlam badda-bam.*' Something smells of bonfire smoke, and burning sugar, and cinnamon.

The Hurakan was blowing.

I don't know why that single phrase keeps coming back to haunt me. That phrase, and the memory of snow, and the cat, paw raised, on the doorstep —

I call: 'Do you want your hot chocolate now?'

There comes a little hooting reply. Then, Rosette's footsteps on the stairs. She glances at the window; nods.

'Did something upset you earlier?'

She shrugs. In the shadows behind her, I see a gleam of guinea-gold. I always know when Rosette is hiding something — Bam always gives

104

the game away. I can see him clearly now, grinning from the top of the stairs. Something has happened. An Accident? It has been years since the last one. Maybe she has outgrown them. I reach for her instinctively, but Rosette is unreadable; her mind a candyfloss tangle of thoughts. Try to unravel them, and she will turn on me like a weathervane.

I try for a humbler magic. 'Sprinkles on your chocolate?'

Pink marshmallows, and whipped cream. And some for my new friend. He likes pink marshmallows, too.

I pour the chocolate into her favourite cup and top it with marshmallows. Rosette drinks carefully, both hands curled around the cup.

'I'd like to meet your new friend. Perhaps you could bring him round some day.'

Will there be marshmallows?

'Of course.'

She smiles. Her eyes are clear as summertime. And yet she is hiding something, I know: I can see it in her colours. I try to put the thought aside. She will tell me, in her own time. And yet I cannot help but see Bam, in the shadows, grinning at me; or hear, in the sound of the wind, the steps of high-heeled shoes on the cobblestones . . .

8

Saturday, March 18

I do not remember the War at all. I was too young when it ended to have any clear memory of that time. But I do remember the post-war years; the bitter retaliations; the people who couldn't get served in shops. My father took no part in it; preferring his work on the farm to following village gossip. But Tante Anna was a weathervane, turning wherever the wind blew: one day refusing to speak to Madame Machin or Monsieur True; the next day complaining that Monsieur Untel had failed to greet her after church.

My father and I did not go to church. And Mimi, of course, was impossible to keep quiet in any public place. Her continuous dancing and jerking, not to mention her inappropriate laughter and the little birdlike cries she made — so like Rosette, although Mimi had none of Rosette's complexity — all these things made it better all round to keep her at home, and out of the way of the man whose daughter had died of the 'flu; of the woman whose teenage son had been shot by the Boche for making a joke; of the parents whose sons had gone to the Front and never come back; of the parents whose daughter had given birth to a Nazi's baby.

Even I could see what they thought whenever they saw my sister. Why couldn't it have been Mimi? Who would even have missed her? It wasn't fair. A useless child, a damaged child had outlived half her contemporaries. A useless, damaged, Jewish child — oh yes, we heard that once or twice. Not everyone there was as liberal as History likes to teach us, and some of them even blamed the Jews for what had happened in Germany. Those people were a minority, but I knew they existed. Some of them were our neighbours, Reynaud, and though I'm in no position to judge, I could see it in their eyes — why Mimi? Why that child, who was never one of ours?

Well, yes. Of course he is right. War is a complicated business, unsuited to the comfortable black-and-white certainties of historians. Even as a boy, I knew that virtue and villainy are largely a matter of perspective. But then, I *would* think so, *mon père*. You, of all people, must know that. I wonder, did Narcisse ever suspect who lit the fire on the riverboat? Is that why he hated me, or was it simply, as he implies, a dislike of the Catholic Church? I never told anyone. Only you, *mon père*; in tears, behind the dark screen of the confessional. And you absolved me, didn't you? You took away my burden. But absolution and forgiveness are two entirely different things. I see that, now that I am comprised entirely of different cells. The hateful act remains with me still, like the mark of God on Cain. But if absolution is not enough to

107

cleanse me of my crime, what is? And where do I go to find it?

I know. I'm aware that this manuscript is preying on my mind. But I will not abandon it. I owe that much, at least, to Narcisse, who left it to me for a reason. What that reason is, *mon père*, I currently have no idea: but now I am sure there is more to it than malice or resentment. But it is getting late, *mon père*. No more of Narcisse's story today. Today is his memorial.

It has already been a week since he died. It takes time to make arrangements. And Narcisse left no instructions for the disposal of his ashes; just a small sum to cover costs, and a reminder — *No flowers*. But he has lived in Lansquenet for longer than anyone else I know: he deserves his space in the churchyard, whatever his attitude to me. And I know Michel and Michèle will approve; a place in the churchyard — even a niche — carries a certain status. And though Narcisse was cremated — a secular ceremony, as requested — his ashes will be placed in a niche in the outer wall of the churchyard, the place marked with a metal plaque that I myself have paid for.

I know. It feels a little like pettiness, under cover of piety. But Narcisse was not a believer, and so what happens to his ashes should not be of any concern to him. It is to *me*, however — and not simply because he was the black sheep of my flock, *père*, or because I do not like to lose. Many people were fond of Narcisse: people who would like to pay their respects. This ceremony at the church will give them that opportunity.

This morning I looked for the graves of Narcisse's father and great-aunt. Neither are buried in Lansquenet — although I did find the sister's grave, hidden away beneath a yew tree, grown so broad that its skirt has engulfed a dozen graves. An hour with a pair of secateurs, and my hands were covered with those small red lesions inflicted by the toxic sap of the yew tree. But there it was: her gravestone: a stone that would have been costly, especially during the War; a sandstone crown garlanding the simple inscription. Moss and lichen have grown in the cracks, but the words are still discernible:

Naomi Dartigen: 1942 — 1949.
Now she is like all the others.

And now I try to imagine the pain that came with that inscription. Who chose it? Surely not the great-aunt, in all her hard-edged piety. The father, then? Who else was there? Certainly not the boy Narcisse, who must have been no older than eleven when his sister died. There is no mention on the stone of how the tragedy came about. But then, there are so many ways in which a child of that era could have died. I imagine Narcisse's manuscript would enlighten me: but I have read enough of that today. My eyes are beginning to blur again, and my head is aching. Perhaps I need new spectacles.

I reach for my freshly ironed *soutane*; put on a clean white collar. This is not an official event, and so I will keep it simple: no alb or chasuble for Narcisse, just the *soutane*, the collar and a stole in a subdued shade of violet. I have not gone out of my way to publicize the ceremony. The village has its own way of disseminating information; and by the time I reach the church, everyone will be waiting.

Michèle Montour delivered the urn earlier this morning. A brown plastic urn, made to look like bronze, and small enough to fit into the niche. It sits on my mantelpiece, which is otherwise bare except for a handful of pocket change and a palm cross left over from Easter. Strange, to be reading his manuscript in the company of his ashes.

And now I wonder to myself as I close the green folder; if this is Narcisse's confession to *me*, then why do *I* feel like the penitent? Why does my mind keep going back to the events of that summer, to the fire on the riverboat, to those two unfortunate people? River-folk mostly go by nicknames. Names are words of power. To know a man's name is to make a connection, and I wanted no connection with the crime. And yet I sought them out, *mon père*. I found them in the paper. Not on the front page, but on the fourth, under the news of a lightning-strike that had burned down a church in Montauban. Pierre Lupin, known as Pierrot La Marmite, and Marie-Laure 'Choupette' Dupont, his common-law wife: aged 32 and 28 respectively, both overcome by fumes on their boat. A candle left unsupervised was named as the probable cause of the blaze, though everyone knew that the couple drank; were probably blind drunk when the bedclothes had begun to burn. *At least they didn't suffer*, you said. But doesn't everyone say that? Doesn't everyone want to believe that Death is a merciful release, instead of a breathless agony of terror and confusion?

A little glass of wine, *mon père*, to steady my nerves for the service. I should not brood on these distant events. Everyone dies. God's will prevails. I only wish I still believed this as I did when you were alive. But now I have no confessor, *mon père*: no-one to tell me how to proceed — unless perhaps Narcisse himself, still watching from beyond the grave.

I pour a glass of Père Julien and raise it to the plastic urn. 'Narcisse, old friend,' I say to his dust. 'Now you are like all the others.'

9

It's Narcisse's funeral today. Well, not quite his funeral. We already had the funeral bit, at the centre in Agen. But this is a *memorial*, which means it's to *remember* Narcisse, which seems weird, because how could we forget? In any case, I had to wear a dress, a green one with little flowers on it, and Maman wore her sky-blue coat and the dress with the scalloped trim. There were a lot of people in the square when we set off. It wasn't far: just across the square and down towards the cemetery. There's a white-washed wall there, with shelves and little stone alcoves — a bit like a library for the dead. It kind of makes sense. Like Maman says, people are full of stories.

I looked around to see who was there. Maybe fifty people. Some of the old men from the *café*. And Joséphine — but not Pilou. I wondered why he wasn't there. It wasn't even a school day. Lots of people from Les Marauds — mostly women, all in black, with veils around their heads like nuns, but with them it's hard to tell if that's everyday black or funeral black. Omi was here too, with Maya. She winked at me from her raisin face. And there was Reynaud, all in black too, except for the purple thing round his neck. Not quite a scarf, not quite a shawl, but pretty. I

112

guess even he has to dress up when it's someone's funeral.

The new not-a-florist's is shut today. There's a CLOSED sign on the door, and the neon sign is off. Is it because of the funeral? I looked around to see if there was anyone unusual there. But there was no sign of anyone new. Just the Chinese lady, Ying, who smiled at me and waved her hand. And there was Yannick with his parents, his father in a charcoal suit, his mother in black lace gloves and a hat with a little spotted veil. Yannick was wearing a jacket and tie that looked a bit too small for him, and he looked hot and grumpy. I sent him a sly little gust of wind, just to make him notice me — *BAM!* He did, but just for a second. His eyes bounced off mine like pinballs.

Maman looked at me. *Stop it, Rosette.*

But he's my friend, I signed. *You know, the one who likes pink marshmallows?*

She looked surprised. 'Yannick Montour? *He's* your new friend?'

I wondered if maybe she had thought that Yannick was imaginary. It made me feel suddenly sad and cross that even Maman might be surprised when my friends turn out to be real, live people.

He was in my wood, I signed. *He's nice. He understands things.*

Maman gave Yannick a funny look, as if she was still anxious. I wanted to tell her that Yannick was nice, and not at all like his parents, but by then Reynaud had started to talk, so I couldn't say anything else. He talked about how growing things was like a kind of communion with God, and that's why Narcisse was really a Christian, even though he hated the Church. It didn't make much sense to me, and so I watched Yannick instead, and tried to make him look at me by making little stones from the path bounce against the cemetery wall. Then when Reynaud finished talking, he put the urn with the ashes on one of the shallow stone shelves, and screwed a little metal plate into the wall beneath it. There's just enough room between the wall and the footpath to plant strawberries. I'll bring some from the clearing. Narcisse would like that. I know he would.

By the time we reached the square again, the not-a-florist's was open again, and the neon sign was lit. I saw Yannick stop by the entrance, as if something new had caught his eye. There was a paper windmill, I saw, stuck in a flower pot by the door. It made a little clacking sound as it spun round and round. Rainbow colours blinked and flashed like a secret signal. I ran to catch up with Yannick, but Madame Montour gave me a look.

'Hurry up, Yannick,' she said. 'What do you think you're doing back there?'

Yannick hunched his shoulders and growled, looking more like a bear than ever. That must be what Narcisse looked like when he was a boy, I thought. Like a smaller kind of bear, shaggy brown hair and round shoulders. I bet Narcisse would be happy to know that Yannick and I are friends now. His mother didn't look happy, though. His mother looked at me like I'd stolen

114

her last pair of shoelaces.

That's my friend, I said to Maman. *Let's ask him in for chocolate.*

Maman looked at Madame Montour, then took my hand and led me away towards the chocolaterie. 'Perhaps another day, Rosette. This isn't the time for visitors.'

Why not today? Is it because his mother doesn't like me?

'I'm sure that isn't true,' she said. But I could tell she was lying.

I made a scornful sound — *Pfff!* — and Madame Montour's little black hat went spinning off across the square and into the gutter that runs along the *Avenue des Francs Bourgeois*.

'BAM!' I said, so Maman would think it wasn't my fault. She gave me a look. I gave it her back. I don't do that very often. Eyes are windows, and sometimes when you look through windows you see things you're not supposed to see. Like the lady in the glass, the one who looks like a magpie.

'Do you want some chocolate, Rosette?'

I didn't want any really, and Maman thinks chocolate's a cure for everything. But I felt bad for being cross at her, and so I smiled and nodded. Maman looked happy at that, and I felt a bit guilty. But I knew I'd feel a lot worse if I allowed her to think that her chocolate wasn't working. She's Vianne Rocher, after all. Without chocolate, what does she have?

10

Saturday, March 18

The service was good, though I say it myself. I kept it as light as I could, with as little reference to the Church as could be expected from a priest. I even managed to throw in a joke — Armande Voizin would have approved — and a ripple of amusement went through the congregation.

I have to confess, it pleased me more than perhaps it should. I am not generally known for my wit, but there is something pleasant about laughter that one has provoked. Joséphine was in the crowd: I saw her smile, and for a moment I almost forgot where I was, just as a man may be blinded by the sudden appearance of the sun.

I know. I ought to avoid her. Don't think that I am unaware of the temptation she represents. A wholly one-sided temptation, of course — my calling forbids such fantasies. But we can still be friends, I hope. In this, I see progress.

I walked home past the new shop. *Les Illuminés*, it's called. It has a vaguely clerical sound, as if it might sell funeral paraphernalia. But there are no flowers, no wreaths inside. Just a big chair, and some mirrors. I told myself I should go in, if only to greet the new owner, and to make them feel more comfortable. Lansquenet has always been a very traditional village. Strangers are not always welcome, especially in unhappy circumstances, and a visit from Monsieur le Curé ensures the approval of the more conservative element. But as I was passing the window, I glanced into the mirrors that lined two sides of the interior, and I saw someone reflected there, sitting in the big chair.

Narcisse?

It must have been a trick of the light. The chair by the window was empty. But in the mirror, there was Narcisse, just as he had been in life. I looked out into the square, to see if anyone else had seen him. But there was no-one close enough to see into the window. Then I looked inside again, and instead of Narcisse in the mirror I saw Joséphine, smiling back. But still there was no-one in the chair — and besides, I'd just *seen* Joséphine at the memorial service, dressed in her navy-blue funeral dress, though here she was wearing a tartan coat that she hasn't worn for years.

Of course it was a trick of the light. What else could it have been, *mon père?* The Catholic Church does not condone belief in ghosts. Nevertheless, it shook me, *père.* I hurried past the window. Even now I feel a discomfort, like the start of a migraine headache. How did I see Narcisse in there? I cannot read his confession. Nor can I drink my coffee. I will work in the garden instead: breathe the fresh air, pull up some weeds. And later, perhaps, when my head has cleared, I will go to *Les Illuminés,* and introduce myself to the new owner — who will be a hairdresser, perhaps, or maybe a beautician, offering half-price facials — and laugh away my foolishness and the shadows in my soul.

11

Saturday, March 18

I made the hot chocolate for Rosette, leaving the *chocolaterie* door open. Now I am certain of it: there is something odd going on in the shop across the square. It is not simply the pink neon sign, and the name — *Les Illuminés*. It is not simply the fact that children are drawn to it like bees. Since it reopened, I have not seen a single customer, delivery vehicle or workman anywhere near the place. I do not even know for sure exactly what it is selling. And yet I cannot shake the thought that something strange is happening there.

I dreamed of Zozie de l'Alba last night, for the first time in months: her direct gaze; her casual charm; the sound of her shoes on the cobblestones. I dream of Zozie, and suddenly, here comes the wind again — that playful wind that excites us both and provokes what we refer to as *Rosette's little Accidents*.

Of course, they are not accidental. They are cyclical, like the wind, and, like the wind, they determine direction. A death in the village; a new shop; a new playmate for Rosette. These things are all signs of change, as sure as the lightning-struck Tower in my mother's Tarot pack. The world around me has become an ominous forest of portents and signs. *Death.*

The Fool. The Tower. Change. And in between them all, the wind; the wind that makes us laugh and dance; the wind that Rosette rides like a bird; the wind that brings the hurricane.

Working with chocolate always helps me find the calm centre of my life. It has been with me for so long; nothing here can surprise me. This afternoon I am making pralines, and the little pan of chocolate is almost ready on the burner.

I like to make these pralines by hand. I use a ceramic container over a shallow copper pan: an unwieldy, old-fashioned method, perhaps, but the beans demand special treatment. They have travelled far, and deserve the whole of my attention. Today I am using couverture made from the *Criollo* bean: its taste is subtle, deceptive; more complex than the stronger flavours of the *Forastero;* less unpredictable than the hybrid *Trinitario.* Most of my customers will not know that I am using this rarest of cacao beans; but I prefer it, even though it may be more expensive. The tree is susceptible to disease: the yield is disappointingly low; but the species dates back to the time of the Aztecs, the Olmecs, the Maya. The hybrid *Trinitario* has all but wiped it out, and yet there are still some suppliers who deal in the ancient currency.

Nowadays I can usually tell where a bean was grown, as well as its species. These come from South America, from a small, organic farm. But for all my skill, I have never seen a flower from the *Theobroma cacao* tree, which only blooms for a single day, like something in a fairytale. I have seen photographs, of course. In them, the

119

cacao blossom looks something like a passion-flower: five-petalled and waxy, but small, like a tomato plant, and without that green and urgent scent. Cacao blossoms are scentless; keeping their spirit inside a pod roughly the shape of a human heart. Today I can feel that heart beating: a quickening inside the copper pan that will soon release a secret.

Half a degree more of heat, and the chocolate will be ready. A filter of steam rises palely from the glossy surface. Half a degree, and the chocolate will be at its most tender and pliant.

Rosette has finished her chocolate, and wandered off into the square. I feel the sudden need to look at Anouk's text message again. There is always so much to unpack from these small glimpses into her life. *Thought we'd come over for Easter.* We. That of course means Jean-Loup, as well. Not that I dislike Jean-Loup at all: but she is different when he is around; attentive to the point of anxiety. Of course she is: Jean-Loup was seriously ill during most of his childhood, and even now, is more than usually susceptible to infections and complications. Not that this seems to trouble him; but Anouk sometimes worries.

It's selfish, I know, but sometimes I wonder what would have happened if she had never met Jean-Loup. At the time I welcomed it — Anouk had *one* friend, at least — but when we moved back to Lansquenet I thought she might outgrow him. Jeannot Drou was also her friend — and he would have stayed in Lansquenet, or maybe somewhere close, like Agen, and I would have seen them every day, instead of watching from afar —

Thought we'd come over for Easter. It hurts that she does not say *come home.* Maybe she has come to see Paris as her home now. How ironic that would be, if Anouk, who for so many years dreamed of a place just like Lansquenet, a quiet place to settle down, were to become like leaves upon the wind, just as I was at her age. I finally answer.

Yes, of course! It will be wonderful to see you both!

Love, V. xxxx

I always add an extra kiss. But now that row of crosses looks like something in a graveyard, and the chocolate smells like cigarette smoke, and the wind feels as if it is blowing through the open hole in my heart.

This is what happens when I do not pay attention to the task in hand: the couverture has begun to seize, which means that I have allowed the heat to rise above 120 degrees. In a few seconds it will be like dirt; dull and thick and grainy.

Even now it can still be saved, but I must act quickly, before the chocolate loses its elasticity. I take it from the boiler and add a handful of pieces of couverture; stirring steadily until the pieces have melted evenly. The hot dry reek of cigarettes has become the scent of burning leaves; the sweet and simple bonfire scent of autumn nights by the fireside.

Try me. Taste me. Test me.

The chocolate is cooler now: the silky

consistency has returned. I return the pan to the burner. Tiny petals of steam lift from the glossy surface. They look like the ghosts of dead flowers. Scrying with chocolate is a skill that my mother never managed. It was too domestic a magic, perhaps; or maybe she simply did not trust the visions in the vapour. She preferred her Tarot cards, the images worn and familiar. But chocolate and I are old friends: we have travelled a long way, and we have always understood each other.

Try me. Taste me.

I reach through the smoke: now I can smell the heated copper of the pan; the scent of the chocolate mixture. Untreated cacao beans are red; the drink of the ancient Olmecs looked like blood mixed with water.

Test me.

I see a flock of black birds rising into a red sky: in the smoke their cries are like tiny shards of silver. Black birds are a sign of loss; that someone dear is leaving.

Narcisse? But the chocolate vapours tell the future, not the past. And now comes the scent of tobacco and cardamom from the copper pan; the heart's note of the Criollo bean, clear and persistent as memory. It smells of stories told at night around campfires and in cheap hotel rooms. It smells of brief and passionate love, of leisurely nights under strange stars. It smells of the river, and all of its paths leading to the triumphant sea; and beyond that to London, and Moscow, and Rome, and Morocco, and further beyond, to places we only ever saw in magazines, though the wind would bring us the occasional reminder of places yet to be seen, to be known, teasing and seductive.

What about Sydney? Reykjavik? Madagascar? Tokyo? Or would you prefer Bora Bora, or Tahiti, or the Azores? Come with me, follow me, trust me, and I will give you the world —

But the sly wind always lies: promising so much, and yet bringing only heartbreak. Its voice used to sound like my mother, but now it sounds like someone else: slightly drawling, humorous, a rasp at the back of the laughing throat. Why do those black birds fly, and for whom? Not Anouk. Not Rosette. I have sacrificed too much to let my daughters go with the wind. Who, then?

Find me. Feel me. Face me.

The call from the shop across the square still resonates at the back of my mind. It could almost be my own voice, the Vianne I was when Anouk was born, echoing across the years like the call of a hungry animal.

Find me. Feel me.

I banish the voice. *Tsk-tsk. Begone!* I return once again to the chocolate.

Now for the base note of the bean: a wild and bitter blackberry, like fruit picked after the turn of the year. It smells of woodland, and falling leaves, and the dark scent of winter spices. And it reminds me of something — maybe a dream, or something I saw a long time ago —

That is all the vapour shows. Those black birds. That red sky. I check the burner: it has gone out. Rather, someone has turned it off: he is standing in the doorway, watching me in

123

silence. Even now, after all these years, I am not yet used to the depth and quality of Roux's silences. This one is attentive, aware; the silence of a wild thing unsure of its reception.

'The couverture was burning,' he says.

'I had it under control.'

'Okay.'

I have not seen Roux since before Narcisse died. The business of the oak wood has kept him stubbornly distant. Even Rosette has not spoken to him, although I know Reynaud has tried. But Roux has never owned a house, or been in charge of land. He has always mistrusted these things, and the people who value them.

'I went to Narcisse's grave,' he says. 'It was too crowded earlier.'

I know why he didn't come. Roux has always hated Reynaud, for reasons I can understand. I once hoped he might soften, but Roux keeps grudges the way other people hoard possessions.

'It's good to see you again.' He smiles. I put my arms around him. He smells good: a blend of woodsmoke, oil and soap, and the ominous scent of the river.

'The chocolate,' he says.

The vapour has cooled. The chocolate is starting to harden again. Over the surface hovers a single ghostly question-mark. *What do you want, Vianne Rocher? What is it you really want?*

I banish the last of the vapour, and with it — for a time, at least — the sound of those black birds on the wind.

I close my eyes. 'The chocolate can wait.'

And yet, I find myself watching us with an air

of strange detachment; a sense of anticipated loss that cocoons every moment in spider silk. His mouth is warm on mine; his scent is warm and good and comforting: But even so, I cannot quite forget the sound of my mother's voice, and that phrase she keeps repeating; a phrase of which the meaning now seems even less clear than it did the night when my Rosette was born, and I cast the circle in the sand:

A cat crossed your path in the snow, and mewed. The Hurakan was blowing.

Smoke

1

Saturday, March 18

In spite of the disapproval of Tante Anna and her friends, Mimi was a happy child, always laughing and smiling. She loved playing in water, or even just watching the raindrops fall into a puddle or onto apiece of corrugated iron. She didn't mind getting wet, either, but would sit out in the rain for hours if she was allowed to, looking up into the sky and making those little chirping sounds.

Tanta Anna pretended to be horrified. 'You'll catch your death!' she would always say. But that was only for effect: if Mimi had caught her death of cold, I think Tante Anna might have been relieved. But in spite of her seizures and twitches, Mimi remained unaffected by colds and bronchial complaints. She was forbidden to play alone by the Tannes, and so I often went, along to watch her play in the river, or throw stones from the bank, or make little boats out of pieces of wood and drop them off the little stone bridge that separates the village from Les Marauds. Whatever might have been wrong with Mimi, she was a happy child, Reynaud. And any sibling rivalry that might have arisen between us in the case of a normal child was absent. She adored me uncritically, and I was her protector — for

Father, though fond of her in his way, lived in the shadow of Tante Anna, and was fearful of her sharp tongue.

I remember one time she caught him playing with Mimi by the barn. There was a puddle of water there, almost like a little lake, which had gathered after the rains. I was splashing in the water, wearing my big rubber boots. Father was crouching beside the pool, a patch of drying mud on each knee, showing the three-year-old Mimi how to sail a little boat out of newspaper.

'See? Like this,' said Father, pushing the little boat with a stick; making it move forward. Mimi made one of her chirping sounds. She was still young enough to sound like a baby in those days; but those were the only sounds she made. Father never minded that — he was such a quiet man — but Tante Anna was merciless. At table it was always: 'Sit straight, Naomi. Hold your fork properly. No, no — not like that.' And if Mimi got it wrong, Tante Anna would stab at the back of her hand with the tines of her own fork, so that Mimi's little hands were always covered with red spots. If Father tried to intervene, she would say: 'How will she learn if you humour her?' And then she would lean towards Mimi and say, 'Now, Naomi. Say 'fork'.' But Mimi could only make that sound — that chirping sound Tante Anna hated — and Tante Anna became convinced she was doing it to annoy her.

That day, as Tante Anna came around the corner of the barn, Mimi's voice was especially high and excited. She stamped her feet in their rubber boots; she chirped in delight at the paper boat. And then she said, very clearly: 'Boo!'

Father and I both looked at her.

'Mimi said 'boat'!' I said.

Mimi laughed.

Tante Anna's eyes went small behind the lenses of her spectacles. She was wearing that black cross of hers, and it shone in the lace around her neck. I knew that she was angry because Mimi and Father were having fun. But Father didn't see that. He was too busy hugging Mimi, who started to laugh again. I couldn't help it; I laughed too. Mimi was so funny, with her little face and enormous smile, like a slice cut out of a melon —

Tante Anna came over, her mouth compressed into a barbed-wire line.

'What is all this racket?' she said. 'I could hear you all the way from the house.'

That wasn't true. We'd made hardly any noise until just a moment before then, when Mimi said her first word. Father looked awkward. He put Mimi down. Tante Anna had very clear ideas on child-rearing, which involved men staying well away from a task entrusted by God to womankind; and children being quiet and going to church — neither of which Mimi seemed capable of doing. Seeing Tante Anna, she began to chirp and gesticulate, and splash with her boots in the water, which was just the kind of behaviour Tante Anna hated most.

I tried to divert Tante Anna with news.

131

'Mimi just said 'boat',' I said.

Tante Anna looked at me. 'Did she now?'

I nodded. I could see that my father wasn't going to say anything. He rarely did when she was around: I think he thought it was safer.

Addressing Mimi, she said: 'Very well. Let's hear you say it, shall we?'

Mimi said nothing, but chirped and stamped.

'Come on, Mimi. Your brother tells me you can say 'boat'.' Say 'boat', Naomi.'

Mimi looked at Tante Anna and twitched and chirped and stamped her feet so that brown water flew everywhere, including on Tante Anna's little boots, which were black as her cross, and as shiny.

Tante Anna looked at me. 'I think someone's been fibbing,' she said.

I shook my head. 'Father heard it too!'

Tante Anna looked at Father. 'Well?'

I turned to him eagerly, certain that this time, he would stand up to her, order her into the house — but my father simply looked away and stuttered like a schoolboy:

'M-m-maybe she d-did. I c-c-couldn't be sure.'

Tante Anna raised an eyebrow. 'You're stuttering again, Narcisse.' It occurred to me then, quite suddenly, that my father often stuttered when he spoke to Tante Anna — which was seldom; he was a quiet man — although I never remembered him doing so when he was with me. 'And people wonder why you couldn't find another wife,' said Tante Anna with contempt. 'I suppose she couldn't be choosy. She

132

needed a man in a hurry.' I knew that she was speaking of Naomi Zwolaskowki, my mother, who had died giving birth to Mimi. And in spite of it all I was curious, because my mother's name was never mentioned in the house; not by Father, or anyone, and her grave was in the Jewish cemetery over in Agen, and we never went there to lay flowers, although I knew my father wanted to.

At Tante Anna's words, however, Father seemed to harden. 'N-Naomi w-wasn't like that,' he said. 'I'll thank you n-not to s-speak of her that way.' It was the first time I'd ever seen my father stand up to Tante Anna, even in a little way. He liked things to be peaceful at home: he flinched at the first sign of conflict. And here he was, silencing Tante Anna. I felt very proud of him.

But Tante Anna was made of steel wrapped around with barbed wire. She gave my father one of her looks — pity mingled with contempt.

'You always were a fool, Narcisse,' she said. 'She saw you coming. And you obliged — you gave her a home — '

'Please,' said Father, looking at me. 'Not in front of the children.'

'The children!' echoed Tante Anna. 'The half-wit and the German brat — '

But before she could finish, my father, that quiet man who stammered at the first sign of conflict, had become a stranger. He took three great steps forwards, fists clenched, face red, angry footsteps throwing up great flags of

133

muddy water. Tante Anna stayed just where she was — dainty in her shiny boots. She looked — not frightened, exactly, but wary, like a cat faced with a big, fierce dog, but that knows just where to strike.

For a moment my father stood, facing her. Then he looked away again.

'Well,' said Tante Anna quietly. The way she said it, I wasn't sure whether it was a question or not. 'Blood talks, doesn't it? Even when the tongue is slow, blood will always find a way.'

My father looked down at his boots, which was when I began to cry. Not at Tante Anna's words — I hadn't understood their meaning at all — but at the way my father looked. He looked like a great, illiterate clod caught out in some misdemeanour.

'Well?' said Tante Anna again, and this time it was a question.

'S-so-so — ' said my father.

'So-so what?' said Tante Anna.

'So-so-s-s-s-sorry,' said my father, now shaking so hard with the effort that ripples fanned out from around his boots as if at a sudden earthquake.

'I should hope so,' said Tante Anna with her tight-lipped little smile. 'And now I think you children should come with me indoors, before Naomi catches her death. And as for you,' addressing me now, 'if you like telling stories so much, you can copy out twenty Bible verses for me, in your very best handwriting.'

That was one of Tante Anna's favourite punishments; designed both to take a long time (if

134

I happened to make a spelling mistake, I had to start the page again) and to keep me safely under her eye. As for Mimi, Tante Anna shut her up in the room we shared, and I heard her protests all afternoon — but I never heard her speak again. 'Boo' was all she managed.

The light has gone. I must have read for longer than I had intended. Strange, how the story reels me in — a story of people, most of whom were dead before I was even born. But while his story stays unfinished, Narcisse will be with me. I can almost see him now, lounging in my armchair, his eyes shining from between a cross-hatching of wrinkles. Perhaps that's why I saw him there through the florist's window. Or maybe — it is Lent, after all — I am simply suffering from low blood sugar.

A glass of brandy for Narcisse. And one for myself — *don't mind if I do*. It *is* Lent, after all. A time of spiritual reflection. Outside it is raining: the streetlight at the end of the road makes the street shine silver. I stand up to draw the curtain, and see a woman walking by. Collar winged against the rain, I can see little of her except for her shiny black raincoat and the silvery floss of her hair, but she is no-one I recognize. I tell myself that the village is filled with people I no longer recognize. For that matter, *père*, I hardly recognize myself these days. So much has changed since you were alive. So much has changed since Vianne Rocher came to Lansquenet on the wind.

Vianne Rocher. Now why did I think of *her?*

That woman looked nothing like her. And yet there was something in the way she walked; the careless turn of the head; the way the hair, all jewelled with rain, spilled from the collar of the coat. I saw her for only a moment, and yet she reminded me of Vianne, and I thought I caught a scent on the wind of burning, and woodsmoke, and gasoline.

2

Roux hardly ever stays the night. By three o'clock he was restless, already eager to be gone. I let him go, and slept until dawn, and dreamed of Roux and Anouk and Rosette all changing into a cloud of black birds, and awoke to the sound of the church bells and someone knocking at the door.

I looked out of the window. Nine-thirty — an hour before my usual Sunday opening time — and there was someone standing outside; someone I recognized from her hat, the same one she wore yesterday at Narcisse's memorial ceremony.

'Michèle, I'll be down in a minute!' I called, and, pulling on a pair of jeans and a scarlet sweater, I ran downstairs to open the door while Rosette watched from the top of the stairs, but made no effort to follow. Rosette does not like Michèle Montour — she makes no secret of the fact, although she likes the son, Yannick. But the mother is one of those pastel-clad, elegantly scornful women that Armande used to refer to as 'Bible groupies'. To be fair, I don't like her much myself, and besides, I knew what she wanted.

I opened the door. 'Michèle! I'm sorry; I overslept. Do come in and sit down. Can I offer you something to drink?'

137

Her eyes are the kind of silvery grey that reminds me of fog on the river. Her hair, which is an artful shade somewhere between silver and blonde, was knotted at the nape of her neck. From her gloves, and the hat, I guessed that she had come from church.

'Thank, you. Maybe I'll try a cup of your famous hot chocolate.'

'It might take a few minutes,' I said. 'I haven't opened the shop yet.'

'Thanks,' said Michèle. 'I'm happy to wait.'

She sat on one of the chairs by the counter in the front of the shop, and I could see her watching me as I prepared the chocolate. First, the whole milk in a copper pan, heated not quite to boiling-point. Then, the spices: nutmeg and clove, with a couple of fresh bird's-eye chillies, broken in half to release the heat. Three minutes for the chillies to infuse: then add a double handful of chopped dark chocolate pieces — *not* powder, but the chocolate that I use for my pralines — and stir until the chocolate melts. Muscovado sugar, to taste: then bring back to simmering-point and serve straightaway in a china cup, with a *langue de chat* on the side.

Michèle took the china cup and put it on the window-ledge. 'It looks delicious,' she said, but I could tell from her eyes that she hadn't come for chocolate. She played with her biscuit — her fingers are long and manicured, tipped with nails the colour of smoke. She nibbled a piece from the edge, then put it down in her saucer.

'I wondered if I might have a word,' she said, the brittle brightness of her tone belying the

138

urgency in her hands.

'About what?' But I already knew.

'It's the oak wood,' said Michèle. 'It has been part of the property since before Narcisse was born. He had no business separating it from the rest of the farm — besides which, it decreases the value of the property, in terms of access, and — '

My smile was beginning to feel a little strained. 'I'm sorry,' I said. 'But exactly what has this to do with me?'

Michèle gave me a sharp look. 'I tried to get in touch with your — er — friend, Monsieur Roux, but he seemed reluctant to — '

I tried to imagine her trying to talk to Roux. Somehow I doubted she'd even managed to locate his boat. The river-folk are loyal: they cover for each other. Any sign of an official visitor, or any unwanted attention, and everyone conveniently forgets faces, names, and mooring locations.

'Roux isn't responsible for the decision, either,' I said. 'He was named as the trustee for my daughter, Rosette.'

I saw Michèle's eyes flicker at the mention of Rosette. 'Yes, well,' she said. 'I'm sure Rosette couldn't care less about a piece of woodland. Maybe you could persuade her that it's in her interest as well as ours to return it to the property.'

I heard an indignant little crowing sound from the stairs, and knew that Rosette was listening. 'Narcisse wanted her to have the wood. It's not up to me to persuade her of anything. If later,

139

she decides to sell — '

'That child!' exclaimed Michèle. 'How can that child decide anything?' She stopped. Visibly composing herself, she went on: 'We're willing to compensate Rosette very generously. She can hardly have a use for the land, whereas if we were to develop — ' She stopped. 'There are issues of access, parking,' she said. 'It would be far easier if we could develop the site properly, without having to go around the wood.'

'I'm sorry, Michèle,' I said, and shrugged. 'I can't do what you're asking.'

Her chocolate had gone cold. I could see the skin forming on the surface of the cup and the rage rising up inside her.

'Ten thousand for the land,' she said, her lips almost rigid with contempt. 'You won't get a better offer, you know. Land isn't what you'd call scarce around here.'

'It's not my land,' I said. 'It's Rosette's. And when she is twenty-one, she will be able to consider your offer.'

'Five years!' exclaimed Michèle furiously. 'What's going to happen in five years? Is she going to miraculously grow into a normal person?' She saw my face, and lowered her voice, though she was still trembling with rage. 'I'm sorry, Vianne, but it's what everyone already knows. That child will never be normal. And ten thousand euros could go towards a fund for her — a fund for her care.' Now Michèle Montour assumed a conspiratorial expression. 'I know what it's like, you know,' she said. 'God knows, I've seen it with my own son. And from all accounts, your Rosette — '

I interrupted her. 'Thank you, Michèle. But you've heard my answer. And now, I'm afraid I must get to work. I have the shop to open.' I picked up her untouched chocolate with its half-eaten biscuit. For a moment her eyes flicked to the cup, then to the kitchen curtain, which had begun to ripple as if blown by a sharp draught.

The wind. That's all. The wind, I thought.

From the stairs, that sound again: a mocking, crowing call, like a bird — a jackdaw, perhaps — chattering at an enemy.

Michèle opened her purse and began to look inside it for change. 'You ought to consider my offer, Vianne. I only came out of courtesy. But I know Narcisse would never have left that land to your daughter if he was of sound mind. If I have to contest the will, so be it. Let's see what happens.'

For a second I thought I saw Bam, squatting balefully by her feet. Then, with a bang, the door of the shop blew open. Michèle clapped her hand to her head to stop her hat from blowing away. The wind caught a handful of notes from her purse and scattered them over the wooden floor. Michèle gave an exasperated cry and went after the money, almost knocking over her chair.

'*Bam!*'

I sent Rosette a warning glance. Her eyes were bright and challenging, like those of a small but ferocious wild animal.

Michèle had recovered the notes. Now she stood facing me, tight-lipped.

'The chocolate's on the house,' I said.

Michèle made a dismissive sound. 'You think your chocolate's so special,' she said. 'I've had far better in Marseille.'

At this, a gust of wind from outside neatly removed Michèle's little hat, and sent it flying into the square like a large insect — a beetle, perhaps — escaping into the turbulent air. She made a sound of annoyance and ran out to retrieve it. The door slammed hard on her heels.

Rosette was at the foot of the stairs, looking suspiciously innocent, drawing-pad in one hand. In it she had drawn Michèle as a predatory stork: standing on one skinny leg, handbag tucked under her wing; eyes bulging comically, as if at an elusive fish. The sketch was made up of just a few lines, and yet it managed to capture Michèle's expression perfectly.

'I told you, none of that,' I said.

Rosette grinned and waggled her head.

'I mean it. No more Accidents.'

Rosette shrugged. *I don't like her.*

'I don't like her either, Rosette, but things like that . . . ' I tried to frame it in a way that I knew she'd understand. 'We're meant to be fitting in here, not drawing attention to ourselves.'

Rosette pulled a face. *Why?*

'You know why.'

Her eyes flicked to the window, through which the new shop with its purple door seemed to shine like a beacon. I saw a shadow cross her face — a shadow, and maybe a challenge.

I reached for my everyday magic. 'What about some chocolate, Rosette? With whipped cream and marshmallows?'

For a moment the shadow lingered, like a threat glimpsed underwater. Then she relaxed and smiled. *Okay.*

I nodded, and went to fetch her cup, the one that Roux had made for her, leaving Rosette to her drawing, having seemingly forgotten the unpleasant incident. And yet, as I poured out the chocolate, as I added the cream and the sprinkles and the pink-and-white marshmallows (with a handful extra, for Bam), I couldn't help hearing that voice in my mind, as soft as approaching thunder:

For now.

3

Sunday, March 19

I don't care. I'm glad I called the wind to tease Madame Montour. Maman says I shouldn't, that it makes us look different, but guess what? I'm different already, *Maman*. There's nothing you can do about that.

I finished my hot chocolate, and picked up my drawing-pad and my pens. I slipped them into my satchel, the pink one from Paris, too small for me now, but powerful because it's old. Then I went out, and she waved me goodbye. I knew just where I was going.

I didn't tell Maman, of course. She's been trying to keep me away from the place. She says it's because the owner probably needs to settle in. I don't think she really believes that. I think she's making an excuse. And there's something about that new shop, something I need to investigate. It's not just the lady I saw in the glass, or the windmill in the flowerpot. It isn't even the purple door, or the name — *Les Illuminés*. It's the way Maman is ignoring it — or trying to make me think that she is. It's the way she keeps looking across the square when she thinks I don't notice. And there's a shimmy, a kind of gleam like sunlight reflected from water. The kind of shimmy that used to surround the door of the *chocolaterie*.

144

Doesn't she know what that means? It means that someone in that shop might be like *us*. Trying to settle into a place where people don't welcome strangers. Why doesn't she go into the shop? Why hasn't she greeted the owner? Why is she pretending that we're the same as everyone else? Pretending we're like Madame Clairmont, who makes people like us feel unwelcome?

Maybe she's afraid, I thought. After all, *I* was nervous at first. But that's not how we should behave. We're not frightened little mice, hiding away in our little house. We're adventurers. We can call the wind. We shouldn't be scared of anything. And maybe the lady in the glass is waiting to see what we're made of. After all, *she* was the one who asked me what I wanted.

And so I waved goodbye to Maman and headed off towards the fields, and when I knew she'd gone indoors, I quietly doubled back across the square to the new shop, and, opening the purple door, I smelt fresh wood, and incense and tea, and heard a little doorbell ring as the door swung shut behind me.

4

Sunday, March 19

For a minute I looked around. The shop was just as I'd seen it before: a coffee machine on a table; some purple armchairs and a rug, then that leather chair, like a hairdresser's, standing there all polished and chrome. Two of the walls were mirrors, reflecting the same things again and again. And there by the door was a big piece of some kind of woven fabric, neatly framed and under glass, with a pattern of blue leaves and vines and speckled birds and little white flowers, and everything so close and tight that it played with my eyes and made me squint. And the funny thing was, I was almost sure I'd seen that pattern somewhere before . . .

For a minute I looked at it, trying to work out the design. The leaves looked a bit like strawberry-leaves, and there were strawberries in there too, which made me think of my strawberry wood, grown dark and strange under the glass. But there were so many things in there, so many shapes and colours, that it was hard to focus. And the pattern kept repeating, so that it looked like the birds were moving; chasing each other through the leaves, and flowers, and briars, and bunches of strawberries. And then the kaleido-scope jumble resolved, and I saw someone there in the doorway between the front of the shop and

146

the back, a doorway that doesn't have a door, only a curtain of purple beads. It was the lady I'd seen in the glass, and later in the mirrors. But now she was out in the real world, watching me with curious eyes, like one of the birds in the wall-hanging, all speckled and bright-eyed and greedy.

She was tall, with very long hair that was somewhere between silver and blonde, and for a moment I thought she was young, maybe nearly as young as me. Then I saw that she was *old* — fifty at least — and that what I'd taken for a printed shirt was her long bare arms, all over tattoos, her fingers heavy with silver rings. I looked down for her shoes, but all I could see was a pair of baggy, long black trousers, with something underneath them that *looked* like feet, but I could tell weren't really feet at all.

'Hello,' said the lady. 'And who are you?'

I made a tiny jackdaw sound.

'You look a bit young to be coming in here,' said the lady with a smile, and I thought of a magpie again, always greedy for shiny things.

I shrugged and looked around. I still couldn't tell what kind of a shop it was meant to be. I looked at the framed piece of fabric and made a little enquiring noise.

The magpie lady smiled and said: 'That's one of my favourite designs. *The Strawberry Thief*, by Morris and Co. I found it in an antiques shop.'

The Strawberry Thief! I wanted to explain why that name made me want to jump up and down in surprise and excitement. But without using my shadow-voice, I knew I couldn't tell her it was a name that I knew from Narcisse, the nickname he had given me. Instead I let Bam go into the mirrors, and watched him dance and chase his tail through all the leaves and reflections. The birds (I thought they were thrushes) chased him back and forth, looking so funny that I laughed.

The lady lifted an eyebrow. There was a diamond stud in it that flashed and twinkled as she moved. 'Who's your little friend?' she said.

'*BAM!*' I said. *You can see him?*

She smiled. 'I see things. I'm an artist.'

So am I! I jumped up and down to indicate my approval. My pink satchel, slung across my back, jumped up and down with me.

'But my kind of art must be right the first time. There's no unpicking the stitches. There's no rubbing-out, no second try. If I make a mistake, then someone has to take the consequences. I have to be very careful.'

I looked at the hanging on the wall. It was even more complicated than I'd thought: the birds (I was sure they were thrushes now) chasing each other through the blue leaves; a repeating pattern of strawberries. It looked like it might be a tapestry, or maybe a curtain or bedspread. In any case, it was the only piece of art in the place.

Do you make things like that? I signed.

The magpie lady shook her head. 'I don't work with textiles.'

What, then?

She reached into the pocket of her baggy black

148

trousers and took out a thing that looked completely unlike any kind of pencil or pen I had ever seen. It looked like part of a toy gun: purple and chrome, with a sharp end. But I could see now that it was a pen. I could see where the ink was supposed to go.

'You may not ever have seen one of these,' said the lady, showing me. 'It's a very new design. Lovely to use, very quiet. Much less trauma to the skin.'

The skin?

I looked at her again, her arms all covered in tattoos. And now I knew what the special pen was for, and why she needed those mirrors. And the chair, like a dentist's chair, designed to be angled and moved around —

I put out my hand and touched her arm with an outstretched finger. The skin there was all tangles: spirals and roses and clusters of leaves. I recognized the design on the wall — the dark-blue briars, the little white flowers and the heart-shaped strawberry-leaves. But it was warm: I could feel it. I touched it with my open hand. It looked as if you ought to *feel* the texture of flowers and leaves. But really it was just smooth skin, same as anyone else's.

'You don't say much, do you? What's your name?'

I whispered: '*Rosette*,' in my shadow-voice, careful not to speak too loud.

She nodded. 'Rosette. What a pretty name. I'm Morgane. I hope we'll be friends. What kind of art do you like, Rosette?'

I looked back at my pink satchel. Normally I

wouldn't show my pictures to a stranger. But now I knew her name, and so I guess she wasn't a stranger. I took out my drawing-book, the purple one Anouk brought me from Paris. There are three hundred pages inside. Plenty of space left for new stuff.

Morgane opened it: looked at the pages one by one. She did it really slowly, looking at every drawing. A couple of times I saw her smile. She lingered for a long time over the one with the little girl, lost in the strawberry forest. It's a lot more complicated than my usual drawings, I thought. And now, looking back at the shadows there, and the briary tangles I'd drawn, I could see *The Strawberry Thief*, clear as a reflection.

Morgane didn't say anything. She turned the page and kept looking. Then at last she looked up and said: 'These are very good, you know. You have such economy of style. Such humour. This bird . . . ' she showed me a picture of Reynaud as a crow — a little drawing, just a few lines: the eyes, his beak and his *soutane*. 'That's our local *curé*, right?'

I laughed, and made Bam tumble and dance through blue reflected foliage.

'Want to see some of mine?' she said. I nodded, and she went back through the curtain into the living space beyond, and came out with an album. Inside were hundreds of photographs of different people with different tattoos.

'All of them are unique,' said Morgane. 'I never do the same design twice. And I ask my clients to think very hard about *when* and *why* they come to me. Because it can only ever be

150

once. I don't do repeat performances.'

I looked through the book of photographs. There were all kinds of people there: young and old, of all races. Some had big, elaborate tattoos. Some very simple, tiny ones. But in all of them I could see her style: dense and graphic and disciplined, like the *Strawberry Thief* on the wall, that shares my name, and managed somehow to find its way into my drawing.

And then I stopped at a photograph. A black-and-white image of a girl with a little heart tattoo. The tattoo was very simple — it looked like a single pen-stroke — and yet it was so perfect, so clean; like a piece of calligraphy. But it wasn't the tattoo that had first caught my eye. It was the girl in the picture; a girl who looked about twenty, smiling into the camera, wearing a simple white T-shirt with the sleeve rolled up to reveal the little black heart on her shoulder —

And although she'd been a lot older when we knew her in Paris, I recognized the girl with the heart. I sometimes see her in my dreams, and I know Maman dreams of her too, because I hear her in her sleep, and feel the wild wind calling me.

Morgane looked over my shoulder. 'That's an early one,' she said. 'In Paris, when I was just starting out. I remember them all, you know. Every one of my clients. And the photographs are all that I have of the art I made for them. Because art is like love. It goes feral if you keep it to yourself. Art is made to be given away, otherwise, it just rots.'

I'd never thought of it that way. I looked back

151

at that picture of Zozie de l'Alba on the page, looking so young and so innocent, her eyes all filled with dancing lights.

Who's that?

'I never asked. Just gave her what she needed.'

And that was when the little bell rang, and Maman came in through the purple door, looking angry, looking scared, with her hair all wild from the wind and her face as pale as a sheet of paper . . .

5

I saw her through the window. Her marigold hair, her vivid face — like a child in a fairytale, lost in a world of mirrors. And in the mirrors, I saw Zozie — scarlet lipstick, hair dyed blonde — watching her with hungry eyes.

I'd planned to introduce myself. To approach the woman with caution, as I might any other neighbour, with a gift of violet creams, to go with that purple awning. But seeing Rosette and Zozie inside, I threw my caution to the wind and ran in, the chocolates forgotten.

I heard a bell ring as I entered. A tiny little silvery bell, the kind that the Fool wears on his cap during the Easter procession. A rush of March wind blew in with me, and I found myself looking into the face of a woman of sixty years or so, with long ashy hair and arms that were tattoo-sleeved in charcoal and grey. She was nothing like Zozie — and yet there was something of Zozie in her: the careless smile; the keen bright eyes. I looked down quickly at her shoes — Zozie de l'Alba loved her shoes — and saw only a pair of clunky-looking things in a dark gunmetal-grey.

I said: 'Rosette. Go back to the house.'

Rosette took on a mutinous look. The purple door rattled in its frame. In the mirrors, I saw

153

Bam, grinning and pulling faces.

'Rosette, go back to the house. *Now!*'

She scowled, but obeyed, dragging her feet. Behind her, Bam pulled a dreadful face and tumbled madly in her wake.

The woman with the tattoos smiled. 'You must be Rosette's mother.'

'Vianne.'

I fought the crazy urge to ask: *And what are you calling yourself this time?* But the woman had moved to the door. Bending down rather awkwardly, she picked up the packet of violet creams. 'You dropped something.'

'How careless of me. Actually, I brought them for you.'

The woman looked at the packet, tied with a violet ribbon and a little paper flower. 'Violet creams? My favourites.'

You're lying, I thought. That charm, that comes from her like the scent of flowers picked at midnight, was darkly, sweetly provocative.

She tried a chocolate. 'Delicious,' she said. 'You must be from across the square. I've seen your shop. It's beautiful.'

'I'd been meaning to call,' I said. 'Though till now, I didn't realize you were a tattooist.'

She smiled. 'Whatever gave me away? Do sit down. Have some coffee. I can't promise it will be anything like as good as your violet creams, but it's all I have for the moment.'

I sat on one of the purple chairs positioned around the coffee machine, but made no move to pour a drink. The woman sat herself opposite. As she did, I noticed her shoes — not shoes at

154

all, but *feet*: jointed at the instep and attached to a smooth steel ankle-pin . . .

An ancient Chinese proverb goes: *Evil has no feet.* That's why temple doors have such high thresholds: to protect them from wandering demons. This newcomer too, has no feet — the irony does not escape me. I think of K'awiil, the footless Mayan god; walking on stilts of lightning, riding his serpent tail on the wind. My mother loved those legends: I found them too alien, too troubling, to be really enjoyable. And yet the wind — the *Hurakan* — has been my constant for so many years; more personal than Gaia, or Hestia, or Jesus.

She caught me looking. 'I'm sorry,' I said. *Now why did I apologize?*

She smiled again. 'I don't mind,' she said. 'I'm a transtibial amputee. I've walked with prosthetics all my life. These are my everyday feet, but I do have a more naturalistic pair, and some pretty shoes for when I feel like dressing up.'

She held out her hand. 'I'm Morgane Dubois.'

We shook. Her hands were unexpectedly warm. I felt like an impostor: a lady of the parish, welcoming the newcomer into the village. *How ridiculous*, I thought. *I don't even belong here myself.*

Morgane said: 'Have you been here long?'

I had to think about that. Time behaves differently when you stay in the same place for any length of time: the seasons turn, the grass grows, the scars on the furniture darken with time. It becomes so easy to think: *this is where I belong now*; so easy to believe in the power of roots, and shoots, and memories.

I said, 'Five years.' It made me feel strange, even to speak the words aloud. People like me do not think in years: only in days, weeks, maybe months. Years are for other people. Years are for those who do not hear the wind.

'Lucky you,' said Morgane. 'The longest I've ever stayed anywhere is nine months. After a while you just get the urge to be somewhere else, if you know what I mean.'

I had to smile. 'I think I do.'

'Besides, in the end, the work dries up. I have to follow the carnival.'

'The carnival?'

'The freakshow. The fair. The places where those who don't belong come to find out who they are.' She gave me a quizzical look over her cup of coffee. 'A tattoo reveals as much as it hides. For you, I'd recommend something small. An animal, maybe a bird — something with a heartbeat.'

'You mean — a tattoo? I'm not the type.'

'You're not a fan of body art?'

'On other people, yes,' I said. 'But I've never wanted to be marked in that way.'

Marked. What an odd choice of word, I thought. And yet it is appropriate. People like us bear no distinguishing marks. We display neither scars, nor souvenirs. Unlike Roux, whose whole body is a kind of tapestry of his life — the loves, the grief, the battles, the joys, the many, many journeys — my skin is uncharted territory. The thought of letting this woman use me — or indeed, Roux — as her canvas made me feel inexplicably cold.

'I don't think of it as marking,' she said. 'I think of it as bringing out something that has been hidden away. A secret. A confession. The Mayans tattooed their bodies, you know, in order to placate the gods. They believed that a tattoo could reveal the shape of the soul beneath the skin.'

I knew that, of course. In my line of work, I've had to learn a lot about the land of blood and chocolate. But it made me uncomfortable to hear Morgane speak so openly of the Mayans and their magic, though it suddenly occurred to me that my mother would have loved her.

'To be honest,' I said, 'I'm not sure you'll find many takers in Lansquenet. It's really quite a conservative place, compared to some of the larger towns. Can I ask why you chose it?'

She shrugged. 'No reason. Just a whim. I find that places often choose me, rather than the other way around.'

'Well, I must go,' I said.

'Thanks. If you happen to change your mind, you know where to find me.'

★   ★   ★

I went back to the *chocolaterie* filled with a profound sensation of unease. Morgane watched me from the doorway, the baggy black trousers only just hiding those troubling metal feet. Whatever the ancient Chinese believed, I have no reason to think there is evil in Morgane; and yet everything about her makes me uneasy. Her arrival, on the changing wind. The colours

157

around her doorway. The way Rosette was drawn to her in spite of my warnings to stay away. And now her talk of the Maya seems too close to be a coincidence.

For you, I'd recommend something small. An animal, maybe a bird — something with a heartbeat. What does she mean? A tattoo reveals as much as it hides. What did she see in me, I wonder, that made her draw that conclusion?

Still, she won't last long here. Lansquenet-sous-Tannes has a way of ejecting those who don't belong. I should know: I was one of them. Rumours and gossip abound here: even a whisper can be enough to make someone feel unwelcome. And there *will* be whispers, I know — whispers, and rumours are currency here. A woman of her age — and with those tattoos — she could be gone by Easter.

The thought is curiously satisfying. I think of my mother's cards again. *Death. The Fool. The Tower. Change.* Rosette is far too curious to stay away from here for long. And Anouk is coming from Paris soon; my little Anouk, who does not need another Zozie to seduce her. *Death. The Fool. The Tower. Change.* So many changes already. The images in the Tarot pack serve to focus the mind. As such, they could be anything; and yet there is power there, born of centuries-old tradition. *Death. The Fool. The Tower. Change.* Could it be that Morgane's craft is in some way related to mine? *A tattoo can reveal as much as it hides.* That sounds to me like a version of: *Try me. Taste me. Test me.*

I glance across at the purple door, closed once

more against the wind.

What did she see in me just now? *An animal, maybe a bird. Something with a heartbeat.* I can hear Rosette upstairs, sounding cross, stamping on the floorboards. I wonder, did Morgane see Bam? And if so, what else has she seen?

I go into the kitchen. The scent of cacao should be comforting, and yet somehow, it is not. *The Mayans tattooed their bodies, you know, in order to placate the gods.* If only it were that easy, I think. If only there was a way in which the shedding of blood could placate the wind.

I try to imagine anyone from Lansquenet being interested in Morgane's brand of temptation. It took them long enough to accept a *chocolaterie* opposite the church — how then could they ever accept someone like Morgane Dubois?

The blinds are drawn when I go to look again. *Maybe she has a customer,* says a little voice in my mind. *Maybe someone else has heard the siren song of that purple door. Someone who has always secretly thought of getting a tattoo. Maybe she saw them looking in. Maybe she offered them coffee and told them tales of the Maya: 'For you, an animal, maybe a bird —* '

Doesn't matter, I tell myself. She will be gone by Easter.

6

Monday, March 20

In spite of Tante Anna's unspoken contempt,
Mimi remained a happy child. I learnt to keep
her out of the way when Tante Anna was
entertaining, which she did every week, after
church, on a Wednesday afternoon; and there
was tea and petits fours, and maybe a tart from
the pâtisserie. On Wednesday afternoons,
Tante Anna's friends would wear black gloves
and talk about their work with 'the poor', as if
Mimi and I weren't wearing cut-down clothes
and hand-me-down boots with the soles worn
thin as Communion wafers. On such days the
pair of us were kept well out of the way, and
because Tanta Anna was in no position to
check what we were doing, we often took the
opportunity to escape, exploring the neighbouring woods and fields and playing in the river.

There was one place that Mimi liked best: a
place where an ancient oak tree stood next to
an old well. There was a pump beside the well,
but no-one used it any more. Instead they used
the pump that stood in the square behind the
church, the one that they use for the cemetery.
Mimi used to spend hours by that pump,
watching the water trickle into the shallow
stone trough beside the well while I pumped
the rusty handle, or dabbling her hands in the

160

muddy water and laughing like a mad thing. The well was capped with a wooden lid, screwed on to prevent accidents. Mimi knew never to climb onto that rotten circle of wood, in case it gave way and she fell. And in spite of her handicap, I was never impatient with her, or teased her as other boys might have done. I know you won't believe that, Reynaud. Patience is hardly a virtue I'd expect you to believe of me. Well, maybe my memory isn't as good as it was, or maybe it was just Mimi who managed to get the best out of me. Either way, we got along. I was a solitary boy, inattentive at school, silent and sullen of temperament. In this I was like my father, or so my aunt would tell me. There was no warmth in the comparison. I sensed that she would have liked me to be different, perhaps to be the kind of boy who helps out at church, who sings in the choir, who plans his first Holy Communion. I stoutly refused to do these things, in spite of — perhaps even because of — Tante Anna's disapproval. The priest — not your predecessor, but the man who came before him — though praising my aunt's devotion to the Church, was stern on the subject of children. But Mimi was impossible to keep quiet during services and, as I acted as her minder, I usually managed to escape them too. This meant a weekly black mark for my aunt, who resented us both accordingly. And so it went on; my childhood became an ongoing series of escapes, reprimands and punishments. Until the letter from Rennes. The letter that changed everything.

161

I had reached the mid-point of Narcisse's manuscript. I would have read further, *mon père*, were it not for a loud knock at the door. It was Michèle Montour, and from the expression on her face, I understood she had come to complain.

'*Mon père*,' she said, 'I'm afraid I was obliged to miss the service on Sunday. But I was speaking to Vianne Rocher.'

Oh. I wondered if I was expected to invite the woman in. I supposed I should; just as they say that vampires must be invited in before they can feed. 'I suppose you're very busy?' I said, hoping for an affirmative response.

'Oh, no, *mon père*,' said Michèle Montour. 'I can always make time for you.'

So much for my lukewarm welcome. 'Come in,' I said. 'I'll make coffee.'

She followed me into the drawing-room, bringing with her a powerful scent of gardenia. 'You've been reading my father's confession,' she said, squinting at the scribbled words. No doubt for a mention of her name, I told myself. Not that she would have found one, I thought. So far, Narcisse's confession extends only to the distant past.

I closed the folder. 'Confidential, I'm afraid,' I said, and, tucking it under my arm, I went to make the coffee for both of us. If I'd left her alone with it, she would have peeked. Her kind always do.

She followed me into the kitchen, bringing the scent of gardenia with her. 'The woman is impossible,' she said. 'I suppose I should have expected it.'

162

'Which woman?' I said absently, hoping she wouldn't want sugar or cream.

'Vianne Rocher, of course,' said Michèle. 'Two lumps of sugar, and cream, please, *mon père*.' It was as if the woman knew that I had neither in the house. I looked in the pocket of my coat and found two wrapped lumps of sugar taken from Joséphine's café. I do not take sugar myself, but sometimes, when I am in Les Marauds, little Maya likes to feed sugar to the horses.

'I'm afraid it will have to be milk,' I said.

'Of course, *mon père*. Lent,' said Michèle Montour, which annoyed me all the more. Michèle Montour cares no more about Lent than she does about my company: she had come to complain about Vianne Rocher, and more especially Rosette, with whom Vianne refuses to discuss the topic of Narcisse's legacy.

'I don't see why she has to be so difficult,' said Michèle. 'She can't be doing great business in that funny little shop of hers. You'd have thought she would jump at the chance to make a little money.'

I shrugged. 'Maybe she doesn't consider the land to be hers to sell,' I said.

'Irrelevant,' said Michèle. 'The child can hardly be held responsible.'

I drank my coffee and said nothing. Presumably Narcisse left Rosette the oak wood for a reason.

'I offered her a handsome sum,' went on Michèle peevishly. 'I can only assume that she believes the land will accrue in value. Maybe she thinks there is treasure buried there!'

She gave an unpleasant little laugh, and it occurred to me how often liars confess the truth while trying to say the opposite.

'But seriously, *mon père*,' she went on. 'What did he expect people to think? The wording of his will is designed to give the impression there's something more. *The sixteen hectares of wood, along with any structures and contents*,' she quoted, accurately enough to make me think that she had given the matter some thought. 'Don't tell me *that* wasn't meant to imply there's more to the place than just woodland?'

'Maybe there is,' I said, with a hint of malice. 'Narcisse was — '

'Difficult, yes,' said Michèle. 'He was a very difficult man. No-one knows how much effort we put into trying to placate him, but he never — '

'I was going to say *quixotic*.'

'Oh. That too, of course,' said Michèle, and I knew she didn't know what 'quixotic' meant. 'But that was just my father's way. He liked his little jokes. Of *course* there's nothing buried there. It's just his attempt to cause trouble. And if only that woman would see sense and sell us the land straightaway, we could dispose of the whole property so much more easily. Frankly, *mon père* — ' she lowered her voice ' — we could do with the money. Caring for Yannick has cost us almost all of our savings. You'd have thought that woman would have felt some kind of sympathy, given the fact that she too has a *special* child.' She gave the word *special* a syrupy inflexion, in contrast with her otherwise rather nasal tone.

164

I finished my coffee. 'I sympathize,' I lied. 'But what can I do?'

'You could talk to her,' said Michèle with annoying directness. 'You could get her to talk to this Roux person. He's never going to talk to me. He's already made that very clear. He wasn't even at the reading of the will. But maybe you could make them see sense. Persuade them the land is worthless. Otherwise, there'll be all kinds of talk. You know what people here are like.'

I do, indeed. I also know when someone is trying to fool me. The Montours think there is something more than oak trees in Narcisse's wood. Buried treasure? How absurd. And yet, the old man was suspicious. It would have been just like him to bury his cash in a box in the ground instead of putting it into the bank. But as for talking to Vianne, or Roux —

'I doubt it would do any good,' I said. 'And besides, I am the executor of Narcisse's will. To interfere would not be in accordance with his wishes.'

'Oh.' I saw her eyes return to the folder containing Narcisse's manuscript, which I had placed on the worktop by the kettle. 'But if there was something in there . . . ' she said. 'Something that might indicate if valuables were buried there — you'd be obliged to tell *someone*, wouldn't you? I mean, it's just an example, a silly one, but, you'd *have* to tell the solicitor, or at least inform the family — '

I sighed. 'I consider this document bound by the seal of the confessional,' I said. 'I would no more reveal it to anyone than I would reveal a confession of yours.'

'But my father wasn't even a Catholic!' protested Michèle. 'Surely, *mon père* — '

'The question is not whether *he* was, Madame Montour. *My* vows do not differentiate between believers, unbelievers — or hypocrites.'

That should have been enough. As it was, I saw her cheeks colour — with anger, rather than anything else. 'Well, it seems ridiculous to me,' she said, 'that a document that might make the difference between my son being cared for properly or being flung to the mercy of the State should have to be hidden away, on the whim of an old man who was probably not even of sound mind.'

But something she had said had alerted me. 'What do you mean, *flung to the mercy of the State*?'

Michèle Montour raised her eyes to mine. '*Mon père*,' she said, once more adopting the syrupy tone she liked to affect whenever speaking of her son's affliction. 'My husband and I will not always be able to care for Yannick ourselves. All that money, wasted on special schools and therapists, with no results, and no *gratitude*.' She dabbed at her eyes with her fingertips. 'One day, we will be gone,' she said, 'and our son will be obliged to go into an institution. That is, unless we raise the funds to enable him to be cared for.'

That surprised me a little. From what I'd seen of the Montour boy, he wasn't incapable of interacting with others, and he'd shown some ingenuity in raiding Narcisse's jam store. 'I

166

thought Yannick might be able to live independently as an adult,' I said.

She shook her head. 'Oh no, *mon père*. My son must be supervised constantly. His condition compels him to overeat to a dangerous extent, and if left to his own devices, he could be dead by the time he's thirty.'

I thought of the two-litre jar of jam and felt a little uncomfortable. 'You mentioned that before,' I said.

'Then you must understand my concern.'

I said nothing. From what I understand, there are far less drastic ways to manage the condition than institutionalization. But that was a decision for the boy's parents, I supposed. Perhaps even for the boy himself, if he could one day escape them. My mind went back to Narcisse's manuscript, and to his descriptions of Mimi. How did that loving boy become such a sour and reclusive old man? And why did his affection turn to Rosette, and not to his own daughter? I suppose I know the answer to that. Michèle is difficult to love. The irony is that if, instead of hiding her problem son away, she had brought the old man and Yannick together, Narcisse might have taken to the boy just as he had done to Rosette.

'I'm sorry,' I said. 'And I sympathize.'

'But you won't show me the folder.'

I shook my head. 'Impossible.'

'Very well,' said Michèle. 'In that case, I shall have to seek help elsewhere.' She paused, then added: 'Frankly, *mon père*, I'm disappointed that you should take the side of someone of *that* sort against a member of your congregation.'

167

'Someone of what sort?' I said.

She coloured angrily. 'You'll see. Don't think I don't see what's going on. The kind of people she calls her friends. Those Arab women from Les Marauds. Those travellers, with all the tattoos. And now, there's even one renting my shop, though if I'd known what kind of business it was, I wouldn't have given her the lease, though God knows, we need the money — '

'Wait a minute.' I was confused. 'Who are we talking about?'

She gave a humourless laugh. 'Don't you know? She said she was an artist. We thought she was opening a gallery. And now I find it's a tattoo place, and ten to one there'll be all kinds of scum hanging around there day and night, and don't tell me that Vianne Rocher wasn't the one who tipped her off that there was a shop going begging.' She dabbed a tear of rage from her eye. 'After all the work I've put into building a reputation here, now I'll be a laughing-stock. No-one will take me seriously. And unless she breaks the terms of the lease — which she might, we can only hope — she'll be there for a whole twelve months, *and* it will be a miracle if she doesn't trash the place — '

'I can see you're upset,' I said. 'But why blame Vianne Rocher for this?'

She gave a crack of laughter. 'Don't think I haven't seen them,' she said. 'Both of them as thick as thieves, mother and daughter alike. I believe the Rocher woman even brought her a welcome gift to celebrate her arrival. Well, all I can say is I hope you're comfortable with *that*

168

sort of person settling into the village. Maybe if it gets popular, you can open a sex shop next to the church, or — why not? — a *McDonald's*.'

And on that note of ultimate condemnation, she rose from her armchair and left, walking very stiffly, like a crane, or a wading bird in search of underwater prey.

7

Monday, March 20

I tried to go back to my reading, but my concentration was broken. Instead I decided to go for a walk, and maybe stop for lunch in Les Marauds, or at the café with Joséphine. But Michèle's revelation had made me curious. I did not share her outrage, but — a tattoo shop in the Place Saint-Jérôme? In Les Marauds — yes, *that* might work. Rents are low, and the river-rats are fond of tattoos and piercings. But here in the square, and under that name, which sounds like a vendor of graveyard supplies . . .

Les Illuminés. Yes, it might refer to the illumination of skin. Manuscripts in ancient times were often bound in skin, to preserve the jewelled calligraphy hiding in the pages. But that shop — so clean and bright — was not at all what I'd imagined a tattooist's to be. Though of course, to be frank, *mon père*, I had never been inside a tattooist's in my life, and therefore my expectations were entirely based on prejudice. I am not proud of my prejudices, and nowadays I try not to be as judgemental as once I was, but I have to confess that the thought of a tattooist's in front of the church appealed to me about as much as the arrival of a *chocolaterie* — and at the beginning of Lent, no less — had once appealed to my younger self.

I wondered who the owner was. If Vianne Rocher had welcomed her, then surely I must do the same? I had certainly meant to, *mon père*. The fact that I had not done so yet was a clear dereliction of duty.

And had I not seen Joséphine, reflected in the mirrors there? Could Joséphine have got a tattoo? It didn't seem like her. In fact, I could only think of one resident of Lansquenet who might welcome the presence of a tattooist, and he was already so heavily illuminated that the challenge would probably be to find a piece of unbroken skin.

The blinds were drawn when I came to the square. Those purple blinds, so like the lid of a single winking eye. But the sign on the door said *Open*, and so, with some trepidation I went inside, hearing a little bell ring as I did.

Inside it was all mirrors and chrome, just as I had glimpsed it before, with some kind of a dense pattern reflected on everything. Blue leaves, green vines and speckled birds, like some kind of old-fashioned wallpaper in an English stately home, though looking rather out of place in such an otherwise unrestricted space. Comfortable chairs around a table and a coffee machine; and one rather larger reclining chair, presumably for the process itself —

There were two people sitting on the chairs by the coffee machine. One was the woman I'd briefly glimpsed outside my house the night of the rain — I recognized her ash-blonde hair, and the angle of her jaw — wearing some kind of long garment in draped purple velvet, open at

171

the throat to reveal a pair of perfectly matched tattoos flowering from her collarbones. The other person there was Roux, looking relaxed with a cup in his hand, and wearing a sleeveless black T-shirt that showed the tattoos on his bare arms.

As soon as I entered, the smile on his face faded to a sullen blank. Roux has never liked me — for reasons both of us understand — and I have long since given up any hope of penetrating his reserve.

'Please, don't get up,' I said, as Roux made as if to rise from his chair. Addressing the woman, I said: 'I'm Francis Reynaud. We're neighbours. I just wanted to say hello.'

The woman smiled. 'Morgane Dubois.'

Roux made a sound of derision, not unlike one of Rosette's bird noises.

'Please don't go on my account,' I said, seeing him standing up. 'I didn't mean to disturb you.'

'I'm done here,' said Roux. He made a gesture of friendly dismissal at the woman, and, flinging on his jacket — a worn leather garment, sheepskin-lined, that he has worn these past twenty years and refuses to replace — he made for the door and vanished like a feral cat.

'I'm sorry,' I said to the woman. 'I hope I didn't scare away your customer.'

The woman gave a slow smile that I found unexpectedly sweet. I'd thought she was much younger than I, but now I realized that we were more or less the same age. Perhaps it is those striking tattoos that give that impression of youth; that, or the vividness of the face tucked beneath the nest of hair.

'You didn't scare him away,' she said. 'It was only the first of our meetings. I always insist on at least two before I agree to take on a job.'

'Oh.' I was a little surprised.

'Tattooing is serious business,' she said. 'A mistake can never be cleanly removed. And, however good the cover-up work, the client will always remember where the old work used to be, and feel its itch in the darkness.'

Like marks on the soul, I thought, and felt a sudden shiver of unease. Surely an inappropriate comparison, I thought. Christ erases everything.

'I'm glad you take it so seriously,' I said. 'I see so many young folk who seem to take more care over choosing their clothes than their skin art.'

She smiled again. In fact, *mon père*, the young people I had just described had been mostly on television, and something in Morgane's expression told me that she knew this perfectly well.

'I think you're unfair on young people,' she said. 'And I make sure that all of my clients are aware, both of the transaction we're making, and of what their design will mean to them.'

Transaction. An odd choice of word, I thought, invoking deals with the Devil. I wondered what it must be like to carry such a mark on the skin, and what that mark might reveal.

She indicated the pattern of leaves rising from her *décolletage*. 'Some themes are universal. Nature themes can help connect us with our world, and alter the way we perceive it.' She looked at me, suddenly serious. 'For you, *mon père*, something simple,' she said. 'Something radical and pure. Maybe something to do with fire.'

173

I flinched. 'Fire?'

She knows, mon père. A newcomer here and already, somehow, she knows. For a moment I felt sick, panicky with the certainty that she had somehow looked inside me and shone a light into the dark. Then, shrugging aside the ridiculous thought, I managed a laugh and said: 'I doubt my congregation would approve if I turned up to Mass with a flame tattoo.'

She smiled. 'Oh, you'd be surprised how many people have tattoos. They don't all choose to display them. Sometimes, a tattoo is so personal that even the family doesn't know. Some people take them to the grave.'

Like unforgiven sins, I thought.

'Would you like a drink, *mon père?* You suddenly don't look very well.'

I sat. It must have been the mirrors, but I found myself feeling nauseous. She handed me a cup of coffee before opening the blinds. The light from the street was dazzling, but my nausea abated.

'A little overwhelming in here,' I said.

'Some people find it so.' She sat opposite me on one of the chairs, and I saw that she was wearing purple boots underneath her opulent velvet. 'Feeling better?'

'Yes, thank you.' I drank. The coffee was good, stronger than I make it. 'So,' I went on, trying to take the conversation into more normal channels. 'Is there much money in tattooing?' On the whole, I imagined not. In my experience, the kind of people who want tattoos are not often people with money.

174

She smiled, as if I'd spoken my thoughts. I felt my face colour a little. 'I manage,' she said. 'I ask that my customers pay what the art is worth to *them*, rather than asking for a set fee.'

'Oh.' It sounded quite absurd. And yet the woman was serious. I was oddly reminded of Vianne Rocher, in the days of the first *chocolaterie*. I almost expected her to say: *Try me. I know your favourites.*

Absurd, of course. She is nothing like Vianne. And yet the unease she makes me feel is, strangely, very familiar. I imagine she and Vianne have already made friends: I cannot imagine Roux trusting her otherwise. Of course Roux already *has* tattoos: I imagine the decision to be more meaningful when dealing with unblemished skin.

I tried to look at Morgane's face. Unseemly to keep looking at those tattoos in her *décolletage*. And yet — speaking objectively — they are beautiful. Tendrils of stylized foliage, each tipped with three tiny flowers. It took me a moment to understand where I'd seen the design before: they are from the print by the door, that looked like English wallpaper. Looking now, I could see how cleverly one element of a more complex design had been taken and adapted to suit the tender curve of the collarbone. In spite of the clean, almost formal line, I found it unexpectedly erotic.

I raised my eyes to hers, and saw that she was smiling.

'I'm sorry,' I said. 'I didn't mean to stare.'

'It's all right,' she said. 'That was my first.'

'Your first tattoo?'

'My very first. Most tattooists start with a leg. Somewhere easy, that can be hidden away under clothing if the design goes wrong. But I had the confidence of youth. And I've always preferred working with mirrors.'

'You mean you did this work *yourself*?'

'Absolutely,' said Morgane. 'Some people use volunteers as practice. But I always thought that was dishonest. Tattooing is about honesty. I wanted my clients to know that.'

I tried to imagine the process of tattooing one's own skin using mirrors. 'Honesty,' I repeated.

'Of course. My tattoos aren't camouflage. I see them as fragments of the soul coming to the surface.'

I wasn't sure what to say to that. *Fragments of the soul.* I remembered pieces of charred and burning wood on the surface of the Tannes. Remembered the river-folk moving on, sullen and impassive.

I tried for a joke. 'Be careful. Souls are the Church's currency.'

'And the Devil's,' said Morgane. 'Everyone gets what they pay for.'

8

Maman says she doesn't want to see me talking to Morgane any more. I think if you don't want to see something, then you shouldn't go looking. Next time, we'll have to pull down the blinds, or meet somewhere in secret. Because I still want to see Morgane, and look in her book of photographs, and maybe even get a tattoo. There's something about Morgane that makes me feel I'm not a freak. As if she doesn't mind those things that make other people stare, or that Joline Drou and Caro Clairmont lower their voices when they talk about me.

Maman thinks I don't notice those things. She thinks I don't *know* how different I am. She thinks that if I'm quiet, and good, and never use my shadow-voice, then maybe I'll be like the others one day, instead of a little girl made of snow. But when I was with Morgane yesterday I didn't feel different at all. I knew Morgane wouldn't mind if I spoke to her in my shadow-voice, or if she saw Bam in the mirrors, or even if there was an Accident. She wouldn't be surprised if she knew why we had come to Lansquenet, and why Maman is sometimes afraid. And I want to know more about her now, and where she comes from, and where she's been, and what the name of her shop means, and

177

why she has *The Strawberry Thief* tattooed on her collarbones. So I was cross all morning, and wouldn't drink my chocolate, and Maman looked headachy and sad, and little things kept breaking. There was a wind, too: a sharp little wind that blew in the corners around the square, and made the shop sign dance. It wasn't exactly a *bad* wind — but it wasn't a good wind, either.

'Why don't you go see your friend Yannick?' said Maman at last, with a brittle smile. 'Maybe you could take him some chocolate.'

It was a pretty good idea, but I knew that wasn't the reason that Maman made the suggestion. She doesn't want me to visit Morgane, and she's using Yannick as an excuse. But I could tell she was restless, and I didn't want to stay in the shop. And so I took the chocolates, which were his favourites (all chocolates are), and picked up my drawing-book, and went over the fields to Yannick's house. I wanted to know if he'd seen Morgane, and what he thought of the new shop, and then I thought we could play a game, or maybe explore my strawberry wood. But when I got to the farmhouse, Yannick's mother opened the door, and looked at me in that way she has, and said Yannick was sleeping.

That was a lie. I could tell straightaway. It wasn't long after lunchtime. Why would Yannick be sleeping? And then I thought he might be ill, that maybe it was my fault, somehow, and I felt suddenly guilty. What if this was an Accident I'd caused by talking to Morgane? What if Maman was right, and I had summoned the wind without knowing it?

Yannick's mother kept looking at me, and at the little box in my hand. With her long sharp nose and her flat cold eyes, she made me think of a big ugly bird. Maybe a flamingo, I thought: ugly and out-of-proportion.

'Is that a box of *chocolates?*' she said in a high voice, as if she was talking to someone a long way away.

I didn't answer. She knew what the box was. Instead I watched Bam pull faces from behind the open door, and listened to the wind through the trees, and wished I hadn't come at all. But Yannick's mother rolled her eyes and said: '*Chocolates!*' again, in that silly high voice, then brought her face up close to mine and said, in a very different tone:

'Listen to me, Rosette Rocher. My son is a very troubled boy, and the last thing he needs is someone like you, hanging around, making things worse. So you can forget about Yannick, because he doesn't want you, or your chocolates. Do you understand me?'

I understood. I understood that Madame Montour wanted to keep me from seeing Yannick. And suddenly I didn't care if there was an Accident. I wished the wind would blow her away, and so I said in my shadow-voice:

'*Liar.*'

'So you *can* talk,' she said.

I made the sly wind tug at her skirt, so that she had to hold it down.

'Doesn't surprise me at all,' she said. 'My father may have believed in that innocent-little-girl act, but it doesn't work with me. And if you

179

think I'm going to let you take his land without a fight, you've got another think coming.'

'*My land. My wood*,' I said, and the wind blew a little stronger.

Madame Montour didn't notice. 'My father was a troubled man,' she said. 'What he left in his will confirms it. So don't start counting your money just yet. It's not too late for things to change.'

And with that she shut the door, so that Bam was left on the threshold, looking fierce and chattering. The wind blew through the hinges, and rattled the loose tiles on the roof, but Madame Montour didn't come out. I knew she was behind the door, watching through the keyhole, listening to the sound of the wind and waiting for me to go away.

And so I said: '*Bitch*,' in my shadow-voice, and tiles began to blow off the roof, one by one, like playing cards. *Two, three, fourfivesix*, they flew off into the dull grey sky, and smashed into the baked-earth ground in the yard where the henhouses were. Then I ran over the fields to my wood, and sat down by the wishing-well, and ate all of Yannick's chocolates.

But even then I felt sad somehow, and so I took out my drawing-book, and drew a picture of Madame Montour as a greedy flamingo. It made me laugh, but I still felt sad. It's not fair that Yannick's mother gets to decide who his friends should be. And she already has the farm, and the fields. Why does she want my wood as well?

'*I wish the wind would blow her away*,' I whispered into the wishing-well. '*I wish she*

180

would have an Accident, and blow away, and never come back.'

The well whispered back to me — *Never come back!* — and the wind took the whisper and blew it away. *Never come back! Never come back!* It sounded to me like the whispering voice that Omi Mahjoubi calls *waswas*: the nagging, raging voice of the wind, sometimes coaxing, sometimes mad —

I tore the drawing out of my book, and scattered the pieces into the wind. The paper fragments flew like birds over the strawberry clearing. Maybe Narcisse is in the wind, I thought. Maybe he's watching. Maman says the dead are still here, as long as someone remembers them. Maybe that's why he left me the wood. As long as the strawberries grow, he'll be here. As long as I remember.

I walked back along the river. It was raining a little now, and there were feathery little catspaws of wind on the smooth brown surface of the Tannes. Roux was burning rubbish on the bank next to where his boat was moored. The smoke was white, like feathers in a column of rising air.

He saw me and waved. I ran to him and gave him a hug. He smelt the way he sometimes does when he's slept outside, by the fire. I wish I could sleep outside sometimes. When I'm older maybe I will. I'll build a firepit in my wood, and live off nothing but strawberries.

'You should get home. It's getting late,' he said.

I wanted to be outside.

'But you know Vianne worries.'

181

That's true, I thought. She worries too much. She worries about the river. The wind. Other people. Rain. Ghosts. I'll never be afraid. Not of ghosts; not of anything. I said so to Roux, but he only smiled.

'We all think that at first,' he said. 'When you grow up, you'll understand.'

Except I'll never grow up. I've heard people say that so often. They say it like it's some kind of curse. *You're not afraid*, I told him.

He smiled again. 'You'd be surprised.'

He kissed my hair, and said: 'I hear Anouk's coming down for Easter.'

Coming down, I thought. Funny way to put it; as if Paris was a mountain. But then again, you won't hear Roux ever use the word *home*. He threw a bundle of leaves on the fire and said: 'I might move on for a while.'

Move on, he says. I get it. I know he likes to travel the river in spring, to shake the Lansquenet dust from his heels. Except that for the past six years, his boat has been moored down by Les Marauds, and I was starting to think it always would be.

He saw my expression. 'Rosette, I'd come back. I wouldn't be gone forever. But this place never suited me. Too many bigots and busybodies. And I've been here much too long. Much too long, already.'

I looked at him. I knew what this was. This was about Narcisse, and my wood, and having to be responsible. Narcisse left the land in trust, which means that Roux has to keep it for me. That means staying around for a while, at least until I'm twenty-one. But Roux doesn't like to be hemmed in. He doesn't want to have an address. He doesn't want a passport. I think if he could do without, he wouldn't even want a name. I wanted to say: *You have to stay. Narcisse left you in charge of things. If you go, then what's to stop Madame Montour from taking my wood?* But already the wind had started to change, tearing the smoke like paper, and all I dared say aloud was 'Narcisse,' and hope that Roux would understand.

He turned away. I heard him sigh. 'The old man knew what he was doing,' he said. 'He thought he could keep me in Lansquenet. Tie me down to a piece of land, the way he tied himself to his farm.' His voice was low, but I could tell how angry he was under his calm. 'What did he think would happen, *hé?* That I'd grow to love the place? That I'd give up who I am? And for what?'

I started to cry. I didn't like seeing him angry. And suddenly I could hear the wind, its jeering, persistent *waswas,* and I understood that this was my fault. I'd called it to blow Madame Montour away, and instead it was taking Roux . . .

'Rosette — ' he began.

I hate this, I said. *I hate being different like this. If I was the same as everyone else, you'd want to stay.*

'It's not your fault. I promise,' said Roux. But I could tell he was lying. The wind was all around me now, blowing smoke into my eyes. I could taste the flying ash, like dust, like sand, like powder. This is what happens, I told myself, when you try to call the wind. This is how it takes its revenge. And it takes, and it keeps on taking until *everything* is blown away . . .

I started to run. Roux was calling me back from a million miles away. But I was already halfway home, running along the bank of the Tannes. And the wind ran along beside me, wild and grey and hungry; matching me step for step, like a wolf from an evil fairytale.

9

I left the new tattooist's feeling hazy and unsettled. More time must have elapsed than I'd thought, because the shadows were lengthening. Morgane Dubois has a way of making everyday things seem portentous, so that a column of smoke or a flock of black birds were suddenly filled with significance. In the hope of restoring my equilibrium, I'd decided to make some coffee and continue with Narcisse's story. But when I got back to the cottage, the green folder was nowhere to be found.

I looked on the kitchen worktop, then at my desk, and finally by the side of the armchair that I think of as my 'reading chair'. There was my notebook; my spectacles; this morning's discarded coffee cup. But of the green folder containing Narcisse's confession, there was no sign, or clue as to where it might have gone, except for the faintest perfume, a scent of decaying gardenia —

Well, yes, *mon père*. I rarely think to lock my front door when I go out. The people of Lansquenet seldom do, except for those like Caro Clairmont, who believe that the influx of foreigners and river-gypsies down by Les Marauds has made the place more susceptible to crime. In fact, this is nonsense. There is no crime. Well, at least, hardly any, not since old François Giraudin broke his neck trying to steal lead from the church roof. Besides, what do I have, *père*, that anyone would want to steal? And yet Narcisse's confession is gone, and that scent confirms what I already suspected — that Michèle Montour is behind the theft. She could easily have done it, I thought. Waited until I went out, then doubled back and stolen the file. Who else would have done it? Who else would have cared?

I mean to call at the farmhouse, *mon père*. Confront the woman directly. And yet I suspect that if I do, her air of offended righteousness will merely serve to undermine my position still further. The woman is as hard as tacks. Beneath her gasping subservience, she has no more respect for the Church than she does for that son of hers. Why did she steal the manuscript? Surely she must know I would guess who had taken it?

Pacing to and fro, I continued to reflect on the purpose of the theft, and on my best course of action. And then it hit me like a blow. *My father, the murderer.* For some reason as yet undisclosed, Narcisse had chosen to address his confession directly to *me.* What if somewhere in it he had included some reference to that riverboat fire, more than thirty years ago?

I sat down, feeling suddenly numb. The scent of gardenia had become the scent of the riverbank at night; the ash from the bonfires; the cooking-pots; the baking stink of river-mud. It all made sense to me suddenly: Narcisse's inexplicable desire to involve me in the aftermath of his

186

death; his decision to write his confession to me; most of all, his use of the phrase: *my father, the murderer.* And now Michèle Montour has the folder, and she will read it, and I will be —

Ruined. Exposed. Condemned. Destroyed.

In a way, it is no more than I deserve. The shadow of the hateful act has already darkened so much of my life. In a way it might be a relief to see the curtains opened. I have struggled for so long under the weight of this burden. Would it not be easier to put it aside, and have done with it?

And yet, the fear of exposure is enough to make me feel cold, and to raise the fine hairs on my arms like cactus prickles. It was so long ago, *mon père.* So much has changed in me since then. I have been — well, not *redeemed*, exactly, but at least raised in the estimation of those who have come to matter to me. If they — if *she* — were to learn the truth, my life would have no meaning. Better to be dead, *mon père*, than to see her disappointment . . .

But I am being overdramatic, *père.* There is no need for panic, as yet. What must I do? To begin with, I must take back Narcisse's folder before Michèle can read it. Closely written and irksome to follow, she cannot have got very far with it. There is still time to reclaim the folder.

I pour myself a glass of wine — only for courage, *mon père*, that's all. I drink it, rather slowly, and pour myself another. I tell myself that time is short, and yet I am reluctant to move, like a hunted animal hiding in its burrow. The warmth of my hearth, the caress of the wine

187

— both conspire to lull me to sleep. But I jolt awake to a scent of smoke and, taking my coat from behind the door, I step back out into the street, where the wind is chasing the blossom from the jasmine by the door, and the red sky over the fields is filled with a murmuration of birds.

10

I ran until I was out-of-breath. It was getting late, and the sky was turning like a weathervane. The wind had dropped a little, and the clouds were outlined in pink. It was getting late, but I didn't trust myself to go home. What if the wind followed me back? What if it tried to take someone else?

I took the path along the Tannes back towards Narcisse's old farm. I still wanted to see Yannick, and find out what his mother had said. Perhaps if I went back, I thought, I could find his bedroom, and climb in through a window without his mother knowing. Or maybe, if he could get out of the house without anyone else seeing him, we could run to my wood and hide, and feed off nuts and berries.

It was getting dark by then. The sun had gone down into a tangle of purple clouds, and the rain was beginning again. There was no-one around, but then I heard a sound on the path behind me, and I hid in the hedge in case Maman or Roux had come looking for me. But it wasn't Maman, or Roux. It was Reynaud, looking cross and upset — I could see it in his colours. He was wearing a long dark overcoat, with the collar turned up against the rain, and he looked like a bad guy out of a film — a spy, or maybe a murderer.

189

I hid in the hedge until he'd gone past, and then I followed him down the lane and over the fields towards the farm, not because I wanted to, but because that was where I was going, too. I wondered what he was doing, going to the farm at that time. He doesn't like Yannick's parents. Anyone could tell you that. He ruffles his crow's feathers whenever they're around him.

It was very dark over the fields. There were no lights, except on the farm: no moon because of all the cloud. That was good, because I could watch Reynaud without being seen. I followed him all the way to the gate, and then I watched from the bushes as he went up to the front door, and knocked. After a while someone came to the door. It was Yannick's mother. I could hear her voice very clearly, sounding like some kind of bird — perhaps a shrike — with a very sharp and murderous beak.

'*Mon père*, won't you come in?'

His voice is lower, and I can't hear it so well, but I can tell he doesn't want to be there. I hear: '*One moment of your time*,' and I can tell he's furious. It isn't in his voice, but even though his back is turned, I can see his colours flare.

Her voice is high and innocent. But I can tell she's lying. Madame Montour has colours too: a kind of self-satisfied pink glow. She won't give Reynaud what he wants, whatever he says. She'll lie and lie. I listened, but I couldn't tell why Reynaud was so upset. Something about Narcisse, I think. Something about my strawberry wood. I moved a little closer then, keeping to the side of the house. I could see the yellow light from a bedroom window. Maybe Yannick's window, I thought, with the big old apple tree growing up the old stone wall. Easy to climb it and look inside. Easy for me, anyway.

I got as far as the third set of branches before reaching the window. It was Yannick's room, all right: I could tell from the clothes on the floor. Yannick wasn't there, but I could see that the window was open a crack. I got my fingers under the sash and pushed it up. I climbed inside. I'm pretty good at climbing. Anouk says that's why I'm a monkey.

His bedroom was a lot like mine, but messier, and with a big TV screen on the floor, and a Play-station plugged into it. Yannick had been playing a shooting game, but had paused it mid-frame. A blurry man was crouching down behind some rocks, with a crossbow. I could hear voices from downstairs through the little crack in the door.

Madame Montour: 'I assure you, *mon père*, I don't know what you're talking about. If some-one came into your house, I suggest you call the police. I really don't appreciate the implication that *I* was involved.' That was a lie. I could tell it was. She'd sounded exactly the same when she said Yannick was sleeping.

'Madame Montour, I'll have you know that lying to a priest is a sin.' That was Reynaud, his voice very sharp, but Yannick's mother just laughed and said:

'You're making yourself ridiculous. You admit that you left the door open. Anyone could have gone inside.'

'And stolen nothing but your father's papers? I

191

don't think so, Madame. Montour. It's too much of a coincidence that the folder should have disappeared on the very day I refused to show it to you.'

He was talking about Narcisse. I moved a little closer. I tried to look through the hinges, but I couldn't see anything.

'I find it insulting that you should believe that I would ever do any such thing.' Yannick's mother always sounds so pleased with herself when she's lying. 'I suggest you turn your attention towards those travellers, Roux and his friends, who hang around by the river all day and never seem to do any work. If there's been a theft, *mon père*, they're far more likely to be involved. And Roux, of course, has a vested interest in my father's will being upheld. Perhaps he thinks there's something more he can get his hands on.'

She was calling Roux a thief! I made an angry squirrel sound, and put my hand over my mouth. For a moment I held my breath, hoping they hadn't heard me.

Then I heard Reynaud's voice, very cold: 'Don't be absurd, Madame Montour. This has nothing to do with Roux. The papers are of no value. They're simply a collection of thoughts that Narcisse felt he had to write down. But if you know who took them, it is your duty to report the theft. I am, after all, the executor of Narcisse's will. I can delay the process if I find that something irregular has occurred.'

That set her off. 'Is that a threat? It sounds like a threat.'

'Of course not, *madame*.'

'Because a will can be overturned, especially when the person involved was old and clearly not of sound mind.'

More lies. Narcisse was perfectly sane. Or does she think that leaving the wood to me is proof of insanity? I wondered again where Yannick had gone. He couldn't have gone far, I thought. I sat down on the bed to wait. The bed was bigger than mine, and there was a furry kind of bedspread. I gave the mattress a little bounce. It was fun. I tried another one. And then my foot met something hard under the furry bedspread; something that had been left underneath — left, or maybe *hidden* there —

It was a kind of dark-green folder, tied with a piece of bright-pink tape It looked old, and there were pages inside, loose pages, written in old-fashioned handwriting. I can read pretty well from books, but this was harder to make out: there were lots of squiggles and loops, as if the person holding the pen couldn't decide if they were writing or drawing. It was pretty, but sad too, and suddenly I understood that the folder had belonged to Narcisse. Were these the documents Reynaud meant? Could Yannick have taken them?

I looked at my reflection in the darkened window. In the glass, I looked very small, sitting cross-legged on Yannick's bed. '*How did you get here?*' I whispered, softly, in my shadow-voice. Behind the glass the wind made a sound, a little crooning, encouraging sound, but I wasn't going to call it, no. I just needed a little help.

And now I could see how it happened, like a

193

shadow against the glass. I saw Yannick, playing his game: Madame Montour coming in with the folder, saying, *Keep this for me, and stay in your room.* Then as she went to answer the door, Yannick, feeling hungry, and knowing his mother was busy, creeping down the cellar stairs to check what preserves might be stored down there —

From downstairs I heard the sound of the front door closing. I knew I couldn't wait for Yannick: Madame Montour would be back soon. But Narcisse hadn't meant for her to read his papers. I knew that. And maybe there would be something about why he'd left the wood to me, maybe even something I could use to make Roux change his mind about leaving.

It wasn't really stealing, I thought. After all, Madame Montour had already stolen it from Reynaud. And so I picked up the green folder and slipped it into my backpack, then climbed out of the window again and into the branches of the tree, closing the window behind me, and slipped away into the night.

11

Reynaud, I remember that letter from Rennes. I still remember the day it arrived: the way the summer sun shone on the Tannes; the scent of petrol and smoke in the air; the solemn way the postwoman delivered the letter to my father's hand. We didn't get many letters. In fact, it was the first one I really remember. The paper, like pressed thistledown: the uniting as neat and as decorative as carving on a gravestone. Letters were usually to inform someone of a family death, and my father had no family — except for Tante Anna, of course, and his brother Modeste, who had died very early on in the war, stupidly, during an ambush, leaving his widow to run the farm and to raise their three children alone. I'd heard the story many times, mostly from Tante Anna, who liked to bask in reflected tragedy, while feeling none of the grief for herself. My father had only spoken of it once, in passing; very briefly.

'I already knew,' he had said. 'We were twins.' And that was all he would say of Modeste, the brother he had never known.

The letter was from the Mayor's office in Rennes. It informed my father of outstanding debts left unpaid by Mirabelle Dartigen, who had fled with her children some years before, leaving her farm and orchard to ruin. It warned my father that unless the money was paid by the end of the year, the farm and the land would be seized and sold to appease the debtors. Any remaining proceeds of the sale would go to the State, unless claimed by a blood relative.

Tante Anna was vocal in her disapproval. 'You're not going to go all the way to Rennes! Not with the work to be done on the farm! And what about the children? They're wild enough as it is when you're here. How do you expect me to handle them?'

But for once, my father would not retreat. 'The boy can look after Mimi,' he said (he always referred to me as 'the boy'). 'I won't be gone for more than a week.' And that was the entirety of his contribution. My aunt protested, exhorted, complained. My father was immovable. His brother's widow needed him, and even though he knew nothing about her but her name, he went to her aid as if he'd known her all his life.

Of course, those days were different. Country custom dictated that a brother, if unmarried, should wed his sibling's widow. Tante Anna told us this, with sour relish, while he was gone. 'He'll bring her back with him, mark my words,' she announced over our lowered heads. 'He never had an ounce of sense. Why should this time be different?'

I pretended not to hear. Mimi was eating green beans one by one, with her fingers. It was a childish habit that Tante Anna hated.

'Eat your food properly,' said Tante Anna,

reaching out to strike at Mimi's knuckles with the tines of her fork.

Mimi didn't say anything, but looked at Tanta Anna from under her hair. She had very curly dark hair, too thick to comb; too thick to plait. 'Cheveux de nègresse,' Tante Anna would say, which I understood to be criticism, though for what, I did not know. Mimi had stopped eating. The back of her hand was bleeding: four little pinpricks of scarlet, like strawberry seeds on the golden skin.

'She doesn't understand,' I said.

'Oh, she understands,' said Tante Anna. 'Your father may tolerate this kind of behaviour, but while you're living under my roof, you'll mind your manners, both of you.'

I looked at Mimi and willed her to pick up the fork right now, right now. Mimi looked back with her head on one side, like a baby blackbird.

'Eat your food, Naomi,' said Tante Anna in a dangerous voice. 'Eat your food like a Christian, not with your hands like a savage.'

But my sister just looked at her from underneath that bramble of hair. Then she smiled — a big, bright smile with not an ounce of malice in it, and yet Tante Anna must have seen something, something that made her swell with rage —

'Are you laughing at me?' she said.

I tried to explain that Mimi was nearly always laughing — she laughed the way a blackbird sings, without either malice or meaning — but Tante Anna wouldn't listen to me.

197

She grabbed hold of Mimi by the hair. Mimi started to struggle and scream.

I stood up, but Tante Anna froze me with a single syllable. 'No!' I remember her standing above me, with that little black cross in the lace at her throat shining in the lamplight. She looked over ten feet tall to me — a statue carved from basalt and ice, her eyes shining like the moon on the Tannes, cold and dark and menacing.

'You will finish your supper, Narcisse,' said Tante Anna, addressing me, 'and Naomi will stay in your father's room until she has learnt some manners.'

I should have spoken up for her. I tried, but at eleven, the adult world is a continent of monsters. The prospect of facing down Tante Anna in all her glacial majesty was too much for me to contemplate, so I lowered my head and tried to ignore Mimi's screams as Tante Anna bore her away upstairs towards the bedrooms.

Five minutes later, my aunt returned, looking grim and rather flushed. The key to the bedroom was in her hand, and she hung it on the key chain that she always wore at her waist. She resumed her place at table, and made a show of finishing her green beans and potatoes. Then she poured a glass of red wine and drank it rather quickly, as I tried miserably not to cry, swallowing the tasteless food in painful, swollen mouthfuls.

'There,' said Tante Anna with a smile that was sickle-thin and cheerless. 'At last, a little peace.'

I said nothing, but gave a sniff, tasting the brine at the back of my throat.

'Use your handkerchief Narcisse,' said Tante Anna, pouring herself another glass of red wine. 'If you're getting a cold, I suggest you don't go outside tomorrow.'

I said I wasn't getting a cold.

'Good,' said Tante Anna. 'Then you'll be picking strawberries. They're ripe, and I mean to make preserves to put down for the winter.'

'What about Mimi?' I said.

'Don't you worry about Mimi. That strawberry patch by the old well, under the big oak tree. That's where you'll be working this week. And if you work hard, I'll let you lick the pan when I'm done.'

This was a rare indulgence, I knew. I was supposed to be grateful. And yet the thought of Mimi alone, locked in my father's bedroom while I worked outside, was too much for me to tolerate.

'Let me take Mimi,' I said. 'I swear she'll be good. She listens to me.'

That was the wrong thing to say, of course. Tante Anna's lips compressed into a thin little wire of disapproval. 'Whether she listens to you, Narcisse, is neither here nor there,' she said. 'Your father has indulged her far more than any child deserves. He makes himself ridiculous, doting on her the way he does. Well, this time, I'm in charge. And until Naomi learns to listen to me, that bedroom door stays locked.'

I wanted to ask — why that room? Why not

199

the one we both shared? But I couldn't find the words. I know it sounds like a childish excuse, but I was afraid to argue. My father's room was forbidding. The bed, with its grey coverlet, pulled so taut that it looked like stone; the wardrobe, with its giant door and slightly distorting mirror. It had a smell, too — of floor polish mothballs and clothes that no-one ever wore. I always used to think that there were ghosts in my father's bedroom. The ghost of my mother, in the studio portrait on his mantelpiece; in her clothes, still hanging there, mothballs in the pockets.

I'd started to read at the bookmark. That's where Reynaud must have left off. I'd thought it might be legal stuff, instructions on what to do with the farm. I didn't expect a story. But that's what it was. And as soon as I got home, I'd gone to my bedroom, and opened the folder, and started to read.

Maman was worried because I was late. She asked me where I'd been, what was wrong, but I didn't tell her anything. I wanted to know more about Narcisse, and the little girl, Mimi. She's already my favourite character. I've been searching through the story for more information about her. I skip the bits about Reynaud. I know him already, and besides, he isn't a part of this. This story belongs to Narcisse — and Mimi. I want to know what happens to her. And I already *hate* Tante Anna. She's mean. I hope she dies at the end.

I fell asleep with the story open on my pillow,

and when I woke up it was morning, and some of the pages were on the floor. I got up quickly and tidied them up, and hid the green folder under my bed. It will be safe there. No-one will see. Maman never looks under the bed.

'Feeling better this morning?' said Maman, when I came down for breakfast. She was trying to sound casual, but I know when she's pretending. Her colours were all muddled and sad — the way they are when she misses Anouk. I didn't want her to be sad, so I smiled and took two *pains au chocolat*.

'You were home late last night,' she said.

I was at Yannick's, I said. And it's true, I *did* go to Yannick's house, even though he didn't see me.

'Did his mother say anything? About Narcisse, or the will, perhaps?'

I shook my head. She looked relieved.

'Well, if she says anything, let me know.'

I nodded. *Okay*. I decided not to tell her what she'd said when I took the chocolates. Or about stealing Narcisse's file. Somehow I thought that Maman wouldn't want me to read Narcisse's story. But I want to know what happens next. I want to know more about Mimi. And if there's something in the file that I can use to make Roux stay, then surely stealing it wasn't wrong. Not as wrong as calling the wind . . .

'You know, you can invite Yannick here. He can try my chocolate cake.'

I thought about that for a moment. Yannick's mother hates us. Then again, Yannick loves chocolate. It would be easy to get him to come. I

201

hope Madame Montour doesn't blame him for Narcisse's file going missing. I'll have to make it up to him if she does. In chocolate.

I smiled at Maman, and tried not to look as if I was hiding anything. Hiding isn't the same as lying, but sometimes it can feel that way. Still, I think it's best if I don't say anything to her just yet. Not about Narcisse, or Roux, or using my shadow-voice that way. I'm old enough now to make my own plans, and Maman's already anxious enough. Like Armande always used to say:

What she doesn't know won't hurt her.

Ink

1

And so, *mon père*, I have failed to retrieve Narcisse's confession. My fault, of course, yet who could have known that woman would lie so shamelessly? Mad thoughts of breaking into the house, firmly pushed aside. *Père*, is this really what I have become? And yet, if Narcisse has included any mention of that long-ago incident . . .

Incident? Really? Is that what it was?

And now his voice is in my head, as if it weren't enough to have all this on my conscience. Yes, *mon père*, Narcisse's voice, as dry as a handful of autumn leaves, and close, as close as a mouth pressed into the whispering shell of my ear. Marvellous. As if there weren't already enough ghosts in my life. I came home last night feeling hopeless and drained, and my sleep — such as it was — was filled with dark imaginings. If only I could sleep, *mon père*. Sleep and never awaken.

This morning I tried to calm my nerves by doing a little gardening. I do enjoy the ritual: the weeding, the planting, the small spring bulbs — crocus, tulip, daffodil — raising their heads above the soil in joyful resurrection. If only we did the same, *mon père*. But all we do is get older.

205

The sun was hot. I was sweating. Not in my *soutane* today, but in jeans and a long-sleeved T-shirt. The Bishop disapproves of the *soutane* in a non-clerical context. And to be fair, it's less practical when it comes to kneeling down.

My father, the murderer. It's harder to get up nowadays from that kneeling posture. It feels like more of a penitence, which I take as a good thing, but the process of weeding and planting makes it rather too much of a pleasure. I have always had difficulty reconciling pleasure with faith. Perhaps this is why Vianne Rocher has always aroused such feelings in me. It occurs to me that maybe she could help me with my predicament — but no. I cannot ask for her help. This mess is of my making.

So pray, said the little dry voice in my ear. *Isn't that what you're good at?*

Is it? I don't think so. It has been some time since I prayed, Narcisse. The sad truth is that I do not believe God is really listening. To others, perhaps, but not to me. And yet, for the first time in months, I feel in need of His presence.

There was no crucifix nearby, no altar before which to kneel. Only a bucket of weeds and a spade. And yet I found myself praying — *Please* — just that one word, like a frightened child. If asked what else I wanted to say, I might have found it impossible, but I suppose I was childishly hoping that somehow God might understand.

I used the spade to haul myself up, pushing the damp hair from my eyes. No more gardening today. I looked over the garden wall, and saw, to

206

my surprise, a round face staring through the fuchsia hedge. It was Yannick Montour whom I had already met, rather briefly, a few days before.

The voice in my ear said: *See? It works. God has answered your prayers, my son.*

'I can do without your sarcasm, thanks.'

Yannick Montour looked puzzled. 'What?'

'I'm sorry. I was just thinking aloud.' I put my hands into the small of my back, feeling the muscles crackle. 'It's nice to see you again, Yannick. Is Rosette Rocher with you?'

Shyly, Yannick shook his head. He looked awkward and a little intimidated, and I wondered if his mother had sent him to report on my movements. It would be just like her to do that, I thought. To gloat over her victory.

And then, *mon père*, I had an idea. I suppose Narcisse's voice put it there, but it leaped out at me nevertheless, radiant in its clarity. *Two can play at that*, it said. And after the strawberry jam incident, I knew exactly what weapons to use. I said:

'Do you like cake, Yannick?'

The boy's eyes opened very wide.

'Chocolate cake? Mocha cake? *Bavaroise*, with whipped cream?'

The boy seemed to glance to one side, as if to check that he was really the one I had been addressing. Then he gave a hopeful nod.

'Really? What a coincidence. I just happen to be going to the *chocolaterie* in the square. What would you say to a slice of cake? A slice of cake, and a little chat?'

He followed me without a word.

2

Rainy in Paris. I love you. A. xxxx. The extra kisses convey a kind of uneasy compensation. When Anouk was small, she would say *I love you* when she was preparing to make mischief.

I start to write: *I love you, too,* then I think better of it. Instead I send her a photograph, taken on my phone, of the church, and the whitewashed wall across the square; the almond tree outside the door blossoming against the sky. I banish the urge to gild it a little; to colour it in shades of home; to write *Come back, where you belong* in tiny, secret letters. But that is a dangerous game, I know. We do not play it any more. There is too much at stake, and the wind is a co-conspirator, promising gold and delivering nothing but handfuls of autumn leaves.

But it works, says my mother's voice. *It really works. I called you. Just the way you called Rosette —*

'No. Rosette was different.'

Of course she was. A special child. A cat crossed your path in the snow, and mewed. The Hurakan was blowing. And you were lonely and afraid, and loss was all around you —

'Stop it. Rosette wasn't stolen.' Her voice in my mind has not been this clear since before Rosette

208

was born. Rosette, my winter changeling, conceived in loss, and born from loss, and kept in fear and hiding.

All children are stolen, my mother says. We keep them close, as long as we can. But one day, the world will steal them back. That's what you said the day she was born. That's why you cast the circle in sand.

'That was only a game, Maman.' A game to keep the shadows away. And she *is* happy, isn't she? Happy as a little bird, singing from her gilded cage —

The Hurakan was blowing.

'No.'

I walk into the kitchen. The scent of chocolate is strong, strong enough to silence her voice. The scent of other places rushes in to fill the void: the ozone of the Pacific; the salt tang of the Côte d'Emeraude. I put a handful of Criollo beans into the grinder. Their scent is very far from sweet. I can smell oud, and sandalwood, and the dark scents of cumin and ambergris. Seductive, yet faintly unsavoury, like a beautiful woman with unwashed hair.

A moment in the grinder, and the beans are ready to use. Their volatile essence fills the air, freed from one form into another. *The Maya tattooed their bodies, you know, in order to placate the wind.* No, not the wind. The *gods.* The gods.

I add hot water to the beans and allow them time to percolate. Unlike coffee beans, they release an oily kind of residue. Then I add nutmeg, cardamom and chilli to make the drink

209

that the Aztecs called *xocoatl* — bitter water. That bitterness is what I need. I think of Anouk, heading home at last, and I feel the heat of the chilli scrawl a hectic path into my throat. The vapour rising from the cup makes complex patterns in the air; patterns that remind me of the wall-hanging in the tattoo shop; leaves and fronds and abstract designs sketched in sepia in the air.

The chocolate suddenly tastes too strong, too bitter for my palate. I throw away what's left in the cup, and find Roux once more standing there, a stony, patient look on his face, like that of an ancient statue.

'You should have said something.'

He shrugs, as if to convey that words have never been his currency.

'Let me make you some chocolate.'

'No thanks.'

'Okay.' I sit at the table, hoping he will join me. But Roux does not; its scars are not the familiar scars of home, and he stays there standing by the door, still with that stubborn look on his face.

At last he says: 'I checked out that place.'

I know at once which place he means. The tattoo place. *Les Illuminés.* I feign an interest I do not feel, while ignoring the growing sense of unease that spreads like a stain into the air.

'What did you think?'

He opens his shirt. A dizzy sensation of déjà vu as I see the new darkness over his heart, ringed with a new sensitivity that I know will fade with time. It is a familiar design: a serpent, with its tail in its mouth, the *ourobouros* that has existed since Egyptian times. This version is deceptively simple; a perfect, dynamic circle that looks like a piece of calligraphy. But I can see how carefully the design has been placed on the skin; the line that looks so like brushwork formed of many smaller strokes. The head of the serpent is abstract, and yet it has a personality; a kind of playful ferocity, like that of a puppy biting its tail. The shading is slightly uneven, as if executed in haste with a brush overladen with dry pigment, and it looks a little like fur, a little like black feathers. But I already know the style, distinctive as the sound of her voice, and I can see the look on her face as she worked on the design.

'Don't you like it?'

'I'm a little surprised. It's not like you to act on impulse.'

This is true. Roux thinks things out. He may not always discuss his plans, but I know that any decision he makes has been turned and turned like wood on a lathe; shaped and smoothed and finished.

'It wasn't an impulse. I talked to Morgane. Not even about her work, at first. We talked about all the places she'd been, all the people she'd met. It was nice.'

It was nice. I tried to suppress a feeling of resentment. He sounds like a man about to confess to some kind of betrayal. Some illicit liaison, or worse — some deeper, closer intimacy. I give myself an inward shake. I do not own Roux. More to the point, I do not *want* to own Roux.

211

'I've met her. She's charming,' I said. (It was true.)

He nodded. 'She reminds me of you. She has the same kind of gentle way of looking into the heart of things. Of making you see what you already know, but have been hiding from yourself.'

'And what did she make you see?' I said.

He shrugged. His eyes were filled with dancing lights. Outside, the wind made a playful sound, like a half-tamed animal that could easily turn on its keeper. I could feel my heart beating fast, in angry little shallow beats. The anger was irrational, and yet I could feel it, like the wind, getting ready to turn once more. I whispered a soothing cantrip: *Tsk-tsk, begone!*

But I already know from his face that the wind will not be placated. That look, so calm and relentless. The serpent eating itself, tail-first. We live to repeat the same mistakes, to push away the ones we love, to move on when we want to stay, to wait in silence when we should speak. In the life we have chosen to lead, loss is the only constant. Loss, that eats up everything — like the snake, even itself.

'You're leaving, aren't you?'

'Vianne, it's time.'

My voice was flat and hateful. 'Is this about Narcisse's will, and being a trustee for Rosette?'

It might be that, I told myself. Roux has never been comfortable with the idea of owning land. In Roux's world, property is dangerous; relationships even more so. In Roux's world, life is frictionless, slipping by like the river, picking

212

up flotsam and setting it down quietly, gently, further downstream.

He said, 'I'll see the solicitor. I'll make sure Rosette's all right.'

'That's not what I meant,' I said, and now my voice was a blade, its edge glinting dangerously in the light. 'Rosette doesn't need you because of the land. She needs you because you're her father.'

It was the wrong thing to say, I knew. 'Only when it suits you, Vianne. The rest of the time, I have no idea if you even want me around. You're like a bloody weathervane. Slave to every gust of wind. I never really know what you want. Tell me, Vianne. What do you want?'

I want to ask him to stay — and yet my mother's voice reminds me that this was always going to be, that everything must be paid for. I said: 'I want you to be free.'

He shrugged. 'I always was,' he said.

I think of birds against the sky, and the scent of burning chocolate. I want to tell him not to go, but there's nothing more I can say.

'It's over, isn't it?' I said.

He nodded. 'Vianne, I think it is.'

And then he was gone, like an armful of birds, out into the sunlight.

3

Wednesday, March 22

After Roux had gone I sat at the kitchen table and wept. I never cry. I *never* cry. And yet the tears kept coming, tears that fell onto the pale old wood, leaving dark splashes like fat drops of rain.

The truth is, I'd begun to think that Roux was my kitchen table. Permanent; dependable; with all the marks and scars of use, so that over the years, I came to believe that he was mine. Well, I was wrong. Nothing is mine. Everything I have is on loan. The shop. The tools. The recipes. Everything except Rosette.

I know who's to blame. Morgane Dubois. A made-up name, for certain. I should know: over the years, my names have changed like the seasons. And I have evolved an instinct for seeing through the everyday into the hidden layer beneath. But I see nothing in Morgane. Nothing but those black birds, those intertwining strawberry-leaves.

She came to us on a bad wind. I saw her in the Tarot cards and in the chocolate vapour. And while I watched from the shadows, Morgane began to ring the changes. Narcisse was the first. Roux, the second. The Pied Piper plays her tune, and heads lift; eyes shine; the air is filled with dancing spirals of confetti. The Pied Piper plays her tune, and *everyone* feels the call of the wind; the turn of the seasons; the dance of the days. It is a simple tune at first: deceptively simple; deceptively sweet. But it grows like the river, beats like blood, until it becomes a tidal wave, with Morgane Dubois riding it, oblivious to sorrow and loss; relentless and insatiable —

And the worst part is that I know I could have been just like her, without my daughters to anchor me. I could have been that inhuman thing, feeding on those around me. Is this why I fear Morgane? Because she reminds me too much of the person I could have been? The person I could *become*, if I allowed it to happen? And if I were to become someone else, could Morgane Dubois take my place?

It sounds ridiculous, put that way. And yet she and I are very alike, mirror-images of each other. Both of us have similar gifts. Both of us ring the changes. Both of us have the talent of bringing out in other people what they need to see in themselves — courage; strength; forgiveness. It is no accident, of course, that both of us are traders. Our kind were already selling our wares before the Romans invaded France; before Montségur and La Roche Aux Fées. We sold them from wagons, and on foot. We traded them for what we could. Not chocolate, in those days, but then — it was never chocolate.

And now? I used to tell myself that chocolate was gentler. A harmless kind of magic, a domesticated animal. But animals are never quite tame. A cat at night is different to a cat in daytime. A cat crossing your path at night is

215

filled with dark significance.

When I cast the circle in sand, Rosette was barely three days old. A quiet child, my little Rosette, at least until the wind changed. But the wind had been blowing at our heels for months, and there was snow in the air, and I was exhausted, and Anouk kept asking why we'd left Lansquenet. And the cat had seemed like a sign to me, and instead of singing my mother's rhyme — the one that keeps cats tame and begins: *Où va-t-i, Mistigri?* — I let the cat cross my path in the snow, and used its voice for my purpose —

They called her condition *cri-du-chat*. A genetic condition, they said, that meant my daughter would always be different from other children. That wailing, catlike cry of hers; the delicate small shape of her head; the learning and behavioural difficulties that might develop later — these were to be expected, they said, from a child with *cri-du-chat*. Some people praised my courage, little knowing my relief. My child would never be taken away. The *Hurakan* had passed us by.

But everything must be paid for. The world is in delicate balance. One child stays; the other leaves. A woman arrives; a man says goodbye. And now this very quiet but significant confrontation: the *chocolaterie* and the tattoo shop, facing each other across the square, each sending out its seductive call:

Try me, test me, taste me.

Each has its different dialect, and yet we both speak the same language, like the bells from church in the square and the *muezzin* from the mosque, each one calling the faithful to prayer: *Find me, face me, feel me.*

This batch of chocolate is ruined, of course. The reek of scorched cacao is like the smell of a fire-gutted house overrun with feral cats. Has Morgane's art ever turned on her? Has *she* ever missed her shot? The tattoo shop looks deceptively calm now, the luminous sign glowing rosily. But behind the windows, who knows? Maybe she is watching me, waiting for the next move. She knows she has made an enemy. Before Roux, I was willing to give her the benefit of the doubt. The glow around her doorway: the whispered challenges from afar. Those things might yet have been innocent; in spite of my misgivings, I might have learnt to accept her. We might even have come to be friends. But now, after this, we cannot turn back. This town cannot contain us both.

In the days before Zozie, I might not have seen the danger. I was far too trusting then. I nearly let her take me. Now I know better. Now I must face the threat without further hesitation. I have wasted too much time. She already has the upper hand. And how long will it be before Rosette hears the call from the purple door? How long will it be before she too follows the Pied Piper?

First things first. I must bring the community to my way of thinking. That means finding an entry point into her world of deception. I cannot do that by hiding away in the *chocolaterie*. I have to use my skills, the skills my mother taught me, and that I have so long tried to ignore. I must fight Morgane Dubois using her own weapons.

And maybe some that are unique to me —
learned from a lifetime on the road. Morgane
may be the Piper, but I have a song of my own; a
song that has been sung for thousands of years,
across every ocean and continent.

I go to the stove; I retrieve the pan containing
the ruined chocolate. The pan is scorched, but
not badly; a good soak should see it through.
After that —

Beware, Morgane. You thought I wasn't dangerous? That chocolate was too sweet, too soft to
rival your ink and your needles? Chocolate is an
ancient art. It comes from very far away. And
under the softness, the sweetness — it waits.
And it is bitter.

4

I have a new ally, *mon père*. I was right: Michèle Montour *did* steal the green folder from my house, and she was lying through her teeth the night I went to challenge her.

But the tale does not end there. It seems that Michèle left her son in charge of Narcisse's confession that night, but that somehow it vanished from his room, where he had left it. Michèle suspects me — as if by some miracle I might have been capable of speaking to her at the door, *and* somehow climbing up to her son's bedroom window to steal back the folder at the same time — and she has sent Yannick to discover its current location.

But Yannick has a weakness, and one that I am happy to exploit. He was mine for a mouthful of chocolate — to be fair, rather more than a mouthful, but worth every *centime* I spent on him. By the end of our conversation he had eaten four *mendiants*, two slices of *Bavaroise* and a packet of small chocolate eggs in crisp sugar shells, painted to look like hedge-sparrows' eggs, and had promised to report back — to me, rather than to his mother — if he uncovered the green folder's whereabouts.

He knows something. Of that I am sure. But I also believe he is telling me as much of the truth

219

as he can. My years as a priest have taught me how to distinguish between an overt lie and a partial truth. Yannick does not trust me enough to tell me what he suspects — not yet. But his friendship with Rosette means that he is eager to help, and — God forgive me — I am devious enough to try to exploit that weakness.

'Your mother thinks that she can use Narcisse's folder to contest the will. If she can prove he was not of sound mind, then maybe she could try to reverse his decision to leave the wood to Rosette Rocher.'

Yannick gave me a furtive look from over his slice of *Bavaroise*. 'This is really good,' he said. 'Maman doesn't let me eat cake.'

'Well, one slice can't do any harm,' I said.

'But I'm always hungry. Maman says I was born that way. I eat and eat, and I never feel full. I wish I could fast like you do.'

I smiled. 'It's overrated. Vianne could tell you a story or two.'

But Vianne Rocher did not seem to show much of an interest in talking today. To be honest, she looked preoccupied; and Rosette was out, presumably investigating her new domain. Yannick seemed disappointed in his new friend's absence, but stayed for the cake and the chocolates, eating with careful little bites, his face half hidden beneath his fringe.

He does not meet my eyes at all. In fact, he scarcely looks up from his plate, although my first impression of him as being slow has been replaced by a feeling that he is simply awkward and unused to speaking with adults. I myself have little aptitude when it comes to bonding with children, but today I received unexpected aid in the person of Maya Mahjoubi, who arrived with a little group of her peers from over the river in Les Marauds.

I saw them from across the square, looking into the tattooist's window. Then they came over to the *chocolaterie*, Maya, the youngest, leading the way. There were two boys of twelve or thirteen; a girl of about the same age, in *hijab*, and Maya, no *hijab*, and very bright and vivid in a green and orange dress.

'*Monsieur le Curé!*' she bugled, seeing me sitting with Yannick by the door. 'I thought priests didn't eat chocolate!'

I smiled, and explained that priests *sometimes* do, though I myself prefer not to indulge, especially not during Lent.

She laughed, then looked curiously at Yannick, who was looking very uncomfortable, as if afraid that his mother might come in at any moment.

'I'm Maya,' she said.

Yannick looked alarmed.

'Maya's a friend of Rosette's,' I explained.

'Me, too,' said Yannick.

Maya said: 'You're Yannick Montour. I heard about you from my Omi.'

Yannick's alarm seemed not to abate, but rather, to intensify. In a low voice, he said: 'Who's that?'

'Omi knows everything,' said Maya, laughing. 'She's basically Yoda.' Once more I found myself struck by Maya's natural confidence. Yannick, rather an awkward boy, with his small eyes and a

221

furtive look, seems less adult than she is, although she must be five years younger.

'My Omi says your parents want to take Rosette's wood from her. They want to sell it for timber. Is that true?'

Yannick gave a weary shrug, implying: *Who knows what my mother will do?*

'You won't let them, will you?' she said. 'My Omi says they're just greedy. Narcisse left the wood to Rosette, and they have no right to take it from her.'

Yannick gave me a sideways look, which I answered with a narrow smile. I said: 'The will was legally drawn up and I am in charge of its execution. Rest easy, Maya. There is absolutely no chance of anyone taking Rosette's wood away.'

Again I thought of the green folder. Until now I have only thought of it in terms of my own protection. But if Michèle Montour really thought to use it to contest the will, then Rosette and Vianne would suffer too —

All the more reason to find it, then. Put your new disciple to work.

But would Yannick's fondness for pastries be enough for him to withstand the force of his mother's personality? And was it right that I should exploit his weakness in the first place?

Maya gave a vigorous nod, which indicated that — for her, at least — the matter had been concluded. 'You should come to the shop,' she said. 'I make these amazing samosas. Even Monsieur le Curé says they're the best he's ever had. And my mother makes coconut macaroons, and really *excellent* bhajis. You should come over and try some.'

Yannick gave her a shy smile. 'Thank you. I might.'

One of the boys, Nicolas, spoke up, his eyes shining with excitement. 'I heard the new place is a tattoo shop.'

'Well, don't start getting any ideas,' I said. 'You're all far too young to get tattoos.'

A ripple went through the little group, of excitement or revolt.

'The lady says tattoos are *haram*,' Maya said. 'But we can come in and talk to her, if she's not with a customer.'

'You spoke to her?'

'She came to the shop. I like her. Her name is Morgane.'

I wasn't sure if I approved of the children hanging around that place. Nor would their parents, if they knew. There's something about the tattoo shop, something occluded and secretive. In spite of the mirrors, the colours, the lights, there's a sense of something dark. Or maybe only the guilty feel this. Maybe the darkness is mine.

I became aware of Vianne Rocher standing behind the counter. She had been busy in the back until the children entered the shop, but now I could see that she was listening attentively. Was it the name Morgane Dubois that had caught her attention? Or was it something else that made me feel that she was uneasy?

'What's it to be, then, Maya?' she said, and her voice was as friendly as always, except that I have known her for many years, and I know when

223

something is amiss. 'I have cardamom castles, and *mendiants*, and coconut truffles, and green almond crisp. Or would you prefer a *cornet-surprise*, with all kinds of different chocolate shapes — eggs, and chickens, and rabbits, and ducks, and little presents for everyone?'

The children decided to share a *cornet*. Vianne handed them the package, and they went back into the square, babbling excitedly.

Yannick said: 'I have to go. Thanks for the chocolate, Monsieur le Curé.'

I smiled. 'And so, our agreement stands? You'll tell me as soon as — you know something?'

He nodded.

'Very well, Yannick. Thank you. I hope to see you again very soon.'

'Yes,' said Vianne. 'You must come again. Rosette will be sorry to have missed you.'

5

It somehow seems very unlike Reynaud to be buying a schoolboy chocolate. Especially when the schoolboy is the son of Michèle Montour, whom I can tell he rather dislikes: Reynaud is not as good at hiding his feelings as he thinks, and his colours always betray him.

I was in the kitchen for most of their conversation, but I overheard enough to make me aware of his urgency. Yannick — or his mother — has some kind of information that Reynaud would like for himself. Something about Narcisse's will: something he cares about deeply. Maybe Narcisse revealed something in his final confession; the one Michèle Montour believes could give credence to her claim that Narcisse was unfit to decide what would become of his property. Or maybe she is still convinced that there is something yet to be found somewhere in the oak wood —

No word from Roux. I'll admit that after yesterday, I was hoping he might call. But there is no sign, either of him or of his boat, on the river this morning. Has he already gone? Or has he moved further downriver, beyond Les Marauds, out of sight from the bridge?

I looked across the Place Saint-Jérôme and saw that once more the purple blinds had been

225

pulled down in the window. *Another customer*, I thought. How does she attract them? Certainly, as far as I have seen, Morgane seldom ventures outside. And yet little Maya knows her name, which means it's all over Les Marauds. How does she do that? Does she wait until dark? And where does she find her customers?

Tattoos are haram. That's good. Les Marauds, with its largely Muslim community, will be suspicious of her. Reynaud too will take my side. Conservative enough to deplore the current trend, with a little encouragement, he could become my ally in this. A word to his congregation, and she could be *persona non grata*.

Yannick Montour had already left. Reynaud, too, was preparing to go. I saw him pull two ten-euro notes from his wallet.

'Will this be enough?'

'More than enough. Here, let me get your change.'

I took my time at the till, allowing the scent of my new batch of chocolate to filter through from the kitchen. Freshly ground *Criollo* beans; a dash of black pepper; a pinch of salt; then tamarind, vanilla and a generous measure of Armagnac.

'Nice of you to befriend Yannick,' I said. 'Rosette seems to like him. Pity about his mother, of course, but he can't be held responsible.'

Reynaud gave a guilty grin, which made him look surprisingly young. 'I don't like to speak ill of anyone — '

'Oh, do, Reynaud. *Please* do.'

He said: 'It does me no credit, of course. But people like Michèle Montour bring out the very worst in me. Do you know, she actually came to my house to demand Narcisse's confession? And when I quite naturally refused — ' He broke off the end of the sentence, and I wondered what he had meant to say.

'I can believe it,' I said with a smile. 'She's been trying to buy Rosette's wood. She offered me ten thousand euros. Then, when I refused, she threatened to contest the will.'

'She told me that, too,' admitted Reynaud.

'Perhaps you should have a word with Ying,' I said. 'You know, the solicitor? And when you do — ' I opened the door to the kitchen, allowing the scent of cacao to flow through ' — you might just ask her about the new shop.'

'The new shop?' Reynaud's eyes had already moved towards the half-open kitchen door. The volatile scent of cacao, sharpened by alcohol and spice, was tantalizing.

'The new tattooist's shop,' I said. 'I assume the Montours let it out. Pity they didn't consider the needs of the community, rather than just letting the place out to the first person who came along.'

He nodded, his eyes still on the kitchen door. 'Michèle says she was led to believe that she was letting it out to a local artist.'

'That doesn't surprise me at all,' I said. 'She probably knew she wouldn't get the lease if she told them the truth. Perhaps she has a history with her previous landlord. And now she's encouraging children to hang about the place,' I went on. 'No wonder people are talking.'

'Are they?' Reynaud looked vaguely alarmed.

227

The scent of *xocoatl* was almost overwhelming now.

'And you must be disappointed,' I said. 'After all the work you've done to bring the two halves of the village together, this must really concern you. Quite apart from the outrage from the more old-fashioned of our villagers, a tattooist's in the square is more than likely to cause another rift between us and the Muslim community.'

I was being less than subtle, I knew. But the scent of the bean was at its strongest now, and I wanted to sow what seeds I could before its charm began to wane.

'What is that you're making?' he said. 'It smells so different. So strange.'

I smiled. 'It's a new recipe. I'm hoping to perfect it by Easter.'

He shook his head as if to clear it from unpleasant dreams. 'I'll look forward to trying it then,' he said.

I handed him his change. 'Come again soon.'

'I will. Thank you, Vianne.'

And then he was gone, purposefully across the square, where the blossom from the almond tree was already starting to fall like snow.

6

Friday, March 24

Mimi stayed in the bedroom all night, I heard
her crying to get out, in a voice like a stray cat.
Tante Anna ignored her, and so did I — at
least until Tante Anna had gone to bed, after
which I crept to the bedroom door and tried to
comfort Mimi.

At first I couldn't make her hear me. She
was making too much noise. But then I
thought of pushing a note underneath the door
— Mimi couldn't read, of course, but I knew
she would see the note, and maybe come to
investigate. And so I drew a picture of myself,
in pyjamas, sitting outside the bedroom door,
with Mimi on the other side, and Tante Anna,
asleep in bed, and pushed the picture under
the door as far as I could send it.

Mimi stopped crying. I heard the sound of
her bare feet approaching on the polished floor.
Then came the whispering sound of the note as
she picked it up, and the little crowing sound
she always used to make when she laughed.

'Shh,' I said. 'It's me, Narcisse. Can you
hear me?'

The sound again.

'I can't let you out. The door's locked, and
Tante Anna has the key. But I'm here. You
don't need to cry.'

229

The crowing sound again, and a scuffle as she moved as close as she could to the door, and sat down on the polished floor.

'Are you hungry? I brought something.'

It wasn't much. One of those vitamin biscuits they used to give out to poor kids at school. But it was flat enough to fit into the gap underneath the door, and I didn't need Mimi to tell me that she hadn't had any supper. She took the biscuit, and I heard her eating it, making little dry sounds, like a cat crunching on a chicken bone.

'I'll bring you another tomorrow,' I said. 'For now, I want you to go to sleep.'

A sound of protest, which I mentally translated as: 'Don't go.'

'I won't go,' I said. 'I'll be right here. I've brought my blanket. I'll sleep on the floor. You'll be able to hear me breathing.'

A little laugh, which might have been fear, or nerves, or humour.

'It's all right, Mimi,' I told her again. 'Nothing's going to happen to you. I'll be here. I promise.'

It took me half an hour or so to make her lie down and be quiet, but eventually, she did, and much later, I too went to sleep, huddled in my blanket. It wasn't the most comfortable spot, but I slept far better there on the floor than I would have slept in my own bed, knowing Mimi was alone and afraid in our father's bedroom. Besides, I was young. The young sleep well. It is a skill we lose with age, like laughter, and innocence. In fact, I was so fast

230

asleep that when Tante Anna emerged from her room at eight and came to check on Mimi, I was still fast asleep by the bedroom door, wrapped in my blanket and dead to the world.

A cry of anger and surprise jolted me from a deep sleep. For a moment I wasn't sure where I was, or even what was happening. Then I saw Tante Anna's boots, those shiny little ankle-boots that gleamed as black as the cross at her throat, and knew that I was in trouble as deep as any I had ever known. I leaped to my feet, stammering excuses, but she stopped me with a gesture.

'Are you some kind of a dog, now, sleeping on the floor?' she said.

I started to explain once more, but Tante Anna was unstoppable.

'Did I not tell you that Naomi was to be left alone?' she said. 'How will she learn to do as she's told if you persist in indulging her?' She sighed, and I knew that her mild tone was not the sound of indulgence. 'I thought you were a reasonable child, but you're as bad as your father,' she went on. 'Very well. If you want to sleep like a dog, you can do so outside, in the yard, and take your meals like a dog, on the floor.'

At first I assumed this was more of Tante Anna's hyperbole. But, as I went down to breakfast, it soon became clear it was not.

'Where do you think you're going?' she said, as I started to sit in my usual place. 'Dogs don't eat at table. They eat from a dish on the floor.'

And she poured my milk into a chipped blue-and-white bowl that I did not recognize, and put it on the kitchen floor, with a piece of bread on the side, and said: 'There. Eat your breakfast.'

I looked at the blue-and-white bowl on the floor. For a moment I considered kicking it over. Then I remembered Mimi, still locked in the bedroom, and realized how easily Tante Anna could punish me.

'What about Mimi?' I said. 'Isn't she getting breakfast?'

'I'll check on Naomi when you're done,' said Tante Anna, pouring café-au-lait into her little porcelain cup. 'For the moment, I think she's best left alone to consider her behaviour.'

I knelt on the floor and drank my milk. I knew Tante Anna was watching. She pretended not to notice me, as she grilled a piece of bread and spread it with strawberry jam. I would have liked some jam as well, but dared not ask for any. In her present mood, Tante Anna was likely to take it out on Mimi.

I spent the day in the strawberry patch, picking strawberries for jam. The berries were small, and very sweet — perfect for the kind of preserve Tante Anna liked best — but they were difficult to pick, being so ripe that they practically disintegrated between my fingers. It took a long time for me to fill the two buckets she had sent me with, and it was late in the afternoon by the time I came back to the farm. When I did, the first thing I saw was my bed blanket on the ground by the door, and the blue-and-white bowl standing next to it. There was some kind of food in the bowl — leftovers, by the look of them, cold and unappetizing.

Tante Anna took the buckets of strawberries into the kitchen. 'No, not you,' she said sharply, when I made as if to follow her. 'You'll be sleeping in the yard, with the rest of the livestock.'

For a moment I didn't quite believe she would go through with her threat. But when she pushed me off the step and closed the door behind her, I knew that she meant to carry on until I broke. I promised myself I would not break; but looking at my blanket there on the floor by the bowl, I finally started to whimper.

Remember, Reynaud, I was very young: my father had left me in charge of Mimi; I was hungry, and tired, and my home wasn't home any more. I hoped that perhaps Tante Anna was playing a cruel trick on me; that sooner or later she'd open the door, but time passed, and night fell, and I knew she was serious.

It was summer. The night was clear and cold, but not cold enough to worry me. I'd slept outside on summer nights before, and enjoyed the experience. This was different; the yard was large, and bare, and full of shadows. The hens were in the henhouse; a stack of rabbit-hutches looked ominous in the starlight. I curled up into my blanket, keeping as close to the door as possible. I could smell the uneaten scraps in the blue-and-white bowl on the door-step. But in this light, the colours were gone. Everything was black-and-white. I lay there for

a long time, sleepless, staring at the stars.
Finally, I slept.

Well. I don't like this story at all. People are all so mean in there. Why do they have to be mean like that? I hate Tante Anna. I hate not knowing what's happening with Mimi. And I hate Narcisse's father, too, going off on business like that and leaving his children to fend for themselves. I hope Tante Anna dies soon. I hope Mimi calls the *Hurakan*, and blows her away forever.

I had to stop reading anyway, because it was time for breakfast, and Maman doesn't like me to miss breakfast. She gave me a *pain au chocolat*, and told me that she'd met Yannick, and that he'd come to the shop yesterday, and that he'd promised to come back soon. That made me feel better. I like Yannick. I'm glad he's not in trouble because I stole Narcisse's story. And Maman likes him: I can tell. She was asking all kinds of questions.

'Why doesn't Yannick go to school? He seemed a nice, polite young man.'

I shrugged. *Maybe he doesn't like school.*

'Maybe that's it.' She handed me a basket of ribbons and paper roses. 'Could you wrap these eggs for me, please? I have chocolate hens to make.'

I nodded. I like wrapping eggs. I like the crinkly cellophane and the long, curly ribbons. I like decorating the hens, too, and adding the finishing touches — beaks, eyes, combs, feathers — in a lighter grade of chocolate.

'Perhaps, the next time Yannick comes, you

234

can help plan the Easter display.'

I clapped my hands, and made Bam tumble head-over-heels across the floor. *We should ask Pilou too*, I signed.

'Maybe,' said Maman, and smiled. 'But Pilou's busy nowadays. With all his school work, and everything.'

I know what that means. It means she doesn't think he will come. But Pilou's my friend: of course he'll come. Besides, I'd like him to meet Yannick: I think they'd get on really well.

Maman said: 'We still have three weeks. There'll be a lot of planning to do. Then it'll be the holidays. Maybe Pilou will come then.'

That's true. I often forget things like that. Maybe it's because I don't go to school. Well, not officially, anyway. Maman says that my reading, my drawing, my helping out in the shop and all the things Roux teaches me are more than enough to compensate. Some people, like Joline Drou, don't agree. Joline teaches at the village school. Her son, Jeannot, sometimes comes into the *chocolaterie*, though not as much as he used to when Anouk was here. *Maybe he will visit when Anouk comes home*, I was thinking, when suddenly there he was, coming out of Morgane's shop. It's funny how that happens sometimes. You think about someone and they appear, almost like an Accident —   ·   .

I waved to him. *Hey, Jeannot!* But he was too far away to see, and so I sent the wind to shake the boughs of the almond tree, and shower him with petals. That made him look my way, and he smiled, and started to come over.

Jeannot! Come see my Easter eggs!

He understands my signing. And he doesn't laugh at me, or pull faces, or pretend not to see me, the way boys of Pilou's age sometimes do. He was wearing a band T-shirt and a denim jacket, and he looked pleased, but guilty, too, like a dog with a secret bone.

You met Morgane, I said.

He nodded.

So? I sat down at a table and beckoned him to sit down. *Have some chocolate. It's fresh. And tell me all about it.*

Jeannot sat down, but I saw how his eyes flicked towards Maman as he did. 'Don't tell my mother,' he said, and smiled, and pushed up the sleeve of his jacket.

You didn't! I said, and made Bam dance all along the countertop.

Maman looked surprised as well, but didn't say anything just then. 'I've been thinking about a tattoo for years,' said Jeannot. 'I just didn't know what I wanted. But then this shop opened and . . . ' he grinned. 'It suddenly seemed to make so much sense.'

I took a closer look at the tattoo on the inside of his wrist. It was covered in a transparent layer of some kind of protective stuff, but I could still see it clearly. It was a dandelion clock, just like the ones by the roadside; seeds blowing out into the wind. The work was detailed; delicate. And it was Morgane's style, all right: not quite realistic, and in those unnatural colours —

'Interesting design,' said Maman. 'What made you choose it?'

Jeannot shrugged. 'I guess it means I'm moving on. Going where the wind takes me. I wouldn't have thought of that design, but when she'd finished, I knew it was right. She'd done *just* what I wanted.'

'Morgane chose it for you?' said Maman.

He nodded. 'That's what she always does. She says her clients never know what they want until they have it. It's all about trust, she says. And she's right. Honestly, if I'd been left to my own devices I'd probably have ended up with a snake, or a skull, or a lightning-bolt, or something *really* lame.' He grinned and drank some more chocolate. 'Anyway, it's done now. It feels as if I've had it for years.'

It suits you, I said. *I like it!*

Maman didn't say anything.

'My mother finds out, though, she'll have a bird,' said Jeannot. 'But I'm twenty-one. Can't stay at home forever.'

Maman poured him a cup of mocha and topped it with *crème Chantilly*. Jeannot took the cup and drank. '*Mmmm*. Madame Rocher, this is marvellous.' All this time, and he hasn't learnt to call her *Mademoiselle Rocher*.

'So, you're leaving Lansquenet?' said Maman in a quiet voice.

'As soon as I can work something out. It's not that I don't like it here. But there's so much more out there, waiting to be discovered. Anouk knows that, doesn't she? She's out there, having adventures.'

Maman smiled, but I could tell she was wondering what he meant. Of course, he stays in touch with Anouk — online, and with her mobile. He even went to Paris once, but only stayed a couple of days. I know his mother didn't approve. She never really approved of Anouk.

'Adventures are overrated,' said Maman, refilling his cup. 'Once you've seen as many places as Anouk and I have, you start to realize that people are more or less the same everywhere.'

Jeannot grinned again. 'Maybe I'll believe that when I'm as old as you are,' he said. 'For now, I'm a free agent. Freedom at last!' Then he finished his chocolate and loped off into the square, looking like a happy dog, let off the leash for the first time.

When he was gone, I looked at Maman. Her colours were all over the place. I tried to tell her that Jeannot didn't *mean* to call her old; that he was just excited, but that didn't seem to convince her. Or maybe it was something else that made her colours all cloudy and dark. Maybe it was his tattoo. Maybe she didn't like it.

Don't you like his tattoo? I said.

'You keep away from that place,' she said.

But Morgane's my friend!

'She isn't your friend. You don't know anything about her. Remember what happened in Paris, last time someone pretended to be our friend?'

She's talking about Zozie, I thought. Zozie, who was in the tattoo book. For a moment I wondered if I should tell Maman about that. Then I decided maybe not. It was only a photograph, not even a colour one. Besides, Morgane isn't like her. She's nothing like Zozie at all.

238

7

Another round of confessions, *mon père*. Tedious for the most part: petty sins and everyday woes. Joline Drou is at odds with her son; Caro Clairmont broke her fast. François Pinson is *harbouring thoughts* about a lady half his age, who luckily has no idea that she is the object of an old man's infatuation. Guillaume Duplessis uses the confessional to mourn the death of his old dog; Laurent Dumont's youngest son, Pierre, thinks to shock me by claiming a string of wholly implausible felonies.

But the one confession I *do* care about continues to elude me. Narcisse's tale remains unfinished, although his voice is still in my mind; dry, and surprisingly, not unkind, though speaking with growing urgency.

Tick-tock, it whispers in my ear as I climb into the pulpit. *Tick-tock*, it says, as I lead the prayers. *Tick-tock*, it says during the sermon. *The longer that folder is out of your hands, the more dangerous it becomes. Who do you think has read it by now? Michèle Montour? Her son? Who else? Vianne Rocher? Caro Clairmont? Maybe even Joséphine?*

Michèle Montour came to church today, but did not stay for confession: from the keen look in her eye, I sense that she came to watch me.

Yannick was not with her, nor was Michel. She passed me at the church door, eyes like blades, but was silent. I can tell she wants to ask what has happened to Narcisse's folder, but it was too public a place, and besides, she does not want to give me the advantage in this battle of wits.

So, she has *not* read it yet. That means it must still be out there. My phone call to the solicitor's has yielded nothing meaningful. Mme Mak is annoyingly correct, quietly refusing to discuss anything more than my own role in executing Narcisse's will. There is very little more to do, she assures me. Maybe a few papers to sign. It is all very straightforward.

That means Michèle Montour has not yet approached the solicitor. Her threat to contest Narcisse's will must therefore be linked to the folder. All the more reason to want it back, but there is nothing more I can do. The boy Yannick is on my side. Once he has news, he will come to me. Until then, the best thing to do is nothing.

I left today fully resolved to do precisely that, *mon père*. A little light gardening, perhaps; or a walk along the Tannes. The river-rats are assembling, as they often do around Easter, staying for a couple of weeks and then moving on upriver. I saw six or seven new boats moored along down by Les Marauds: a group of people around a fire looked up at the sight of my priest's *soutane*. I recognized two of them, friends of Vianne, whom I know only as Blanche and Zézette. Blanche is a stately West African woman; Zézette, a slender young person with a shaved head and many tattoos.

'Monsieur le Curé!' Blanche called to me as I passed over the bridge. 'Come down and say hello to Saphir! We're having a birthday party!'

Saphir is Zézette's daughter. I hadn't seen her for some time: I guessed she must be twelve or thirteen. But I realized as I saw her that my reckoning was woefully out: Saphir is a young woman now, with the kind of jaw-dropping beauty that even a priest cannot fail to see.

'Eighteen on Wednesday,' said Zézette, when I ventured to inquire. 'For her birthday I got her her first tattoo! Want to take a look?'

I started to say not at all, there was nothing I wanted less, but Saphir had already pulled up the sleeve of her blouse. In the tender place between armpit and elbow I saw a cluster of pale yellow flowers with cabbage-green leaves, like a Victorian wallpaper design, or a plate from an old book of botanical illustrations. One of Morgane Dubois' designs, no doubt: as fresh against the young girl's skin as dew on one of those pale-green leaves —

'It's a primrose,' said Saphir. 'My birthday flower, according to the Revolutionary calendar.'

'Is it?' I was feeling warm: I wished I had changed out of my *soutane* before setting out on my walk — better still, I wished I had gone the other way, where I would not have met anyone.

'March the twenty-second would have been the first day of the growing month. *Germinal*, they called it. Month of bees and crocuses.'

'Did Morgane Dubois tell you that?'

Saphir nodded. 'She chose the design for me.'

'You trusted her to do that?'

'Of course,' said Saphir. 'She's an artist.'

I shrugged. I don't know much about tattoos. Still, if I were to have one, I think I'd want to control the outcome. Of course, I would never get a tattoo. The very idea is ridiculous.

Never say never, Reynaud. Tick-tock.

I shook my head, as if to remove some insect buzzing in my ear. Zézette gave me a humorous look, and handed me a wooden plate. 'Cake, Monsieur le Curé?'

'Thank you.' Of course, I could not refuse. The river-folk have a code of their own. To refuse their hospitality would have been an insult. And so I took the piece of cake — which made me think of Joséphine, and the party she'd had for Jean-Philippe's girl — and sat down on the riverbank.

The bonfire was small, contained within a ring of stones from the river. The smoke was highly scented: fir, and applewood, and wild sage. It reminded me of something; something I could not identify. Once again I wished I had taken another route home from church.

'I wondered how a tattoo shop would manage to find customers here,' I said, between two mouthfuls of cake (walnut and ginger, home-made and good).

'Oh, word gets around pretty fast,' said Zézette. 'And Morgane's *very* good. Look!' She lifted the front of her blouse to show a fresh tattoo on her midriff. 'She did this the other day, to match the one she did for Saphir.'

Once more I tried not to look, *mon père*. But the design was compelling. Another botanical

242

image, this time of a finely detailed sycamore leaf, with a twig and a couple of keys on the side, looking just ready to flutter away . . .

'It's only skin, Monsieur le Curé.' Zézette looked amused at my discomfort. 'Maybe you should get one done yourself. A crucifix. Or a holy dove. Or maybe a palm cross, for Easter.'

I shuddered. 'I don't think so.'

Saphir gave the kind of smile you see on the face of the Virgin. 'Never say never, *mon père*.'

I swallowed the last of my cake, and fled.

8

A tattoo shop in Lansquenet. I'd assumed it would never catch on. And yet, in two weeks, it seems to have infected half the village.

The problem is worse than I realized. Passing by the river today, I heard that Zézette and Saphir have new ink; that Jojo LeMollet is going next week, and Blanche is booked in for Thursday. Morgane has glamours to equal my own, and she knows her public as well as her art, spreading the word about her throughout the river community.

How could I let this happen so fast? Why did I hide away for so long? I should have acted immediately, as soon as I first suspected her. Her kind are like spring dandelions, so cheerful and sunny and harmless at first, and then suddenly, everywhere; sending their roots into every crack, invading every flower-bed. That was Zozie; this is Morgane. Her name is in the air like seeds. Even in Les Marauds, she has already made her mark. Passing by Mahjoubi's shop, I heard two woman discussing her, then, on the *Boulevard P'tit Baghdad*, two young men, at a table outside.

'They say she's amazing,' said one of them, a boy of no more than Yannick's age, with a small but hopeful-looking moustache and a *keffieh* around his shoulders. 'I wish I could get one, but

244

I'd never hear the end of it.'

The other boy nodded. 'Pilou said *he* was, but there's no way his mother'll let him.'

I stopped at the mention of Joséphine's son. Could Pilou *really* want a tattoo? Of course, he's at an age at which such a thing seems glamorous. Like smoking, or driving a motorbike, or dating an American girl. But it's a sign of how much Morgane's influence is growing here. All of the village has caught the disease: even that part of Les Marauds that considers tattooing *haram*.

Disease. I sound like Francis Reynaud. But I feel it in every nerve and cell. That dangerous charm. That sickness that spreads like a bruise under skin. I saw Roux's boat this morning, still moored down by the far end of Les Marauds, but there was no sign of him among the groups of people gathered on the riverbank, or drinking coffee on their decks. I tried not to feel too hopeful. Perhaps he means to move downstream along with the rest of the river-folk. Perhaps he's even staying until Anouk's visit is over.

This year, Easter Sunday falls on 16 April. Three weeks until Anouk's visit. Three weeks to deal with Morgane Dubois, as well as all my business. *Deal with her.* That, too, is a phrase that ought to belong to Francis Reynaud. But even as every part of me revolts against her presence, I feel a kind of lightness, too. Maybe even of righteousness.

When Zozie de l'Alba strode into my life, I thought she was there to save me. Her humour and her fearlessness made her the sister I'd never had, the friend my Anouk needed. Like

245

Morgane, she was charming. Like Morgane, perceptive. And by the time I understood the price of Zozie's friendship, she had almost consumed me; my life, my heart, my children . . .

This time, I know my enemy. This time, I know where I stand. And most of all, I have a friend in the person of Francis Reynaud, who even now is on his knees, not praying, but weeding his garden, where those yearly invaders — dandelions, ragwort, convolvulus — gleefully sink their roots into the beds so lovingly prepared for daffodils, and crocuses, and hyacinth, and peonies.

9

Monday, March 27

There are strawberries growing among my bulbs. Wild ones, seeded from God knows where, poking their pale little fingers among the tulips and crocuses. Wild strawberries are invasive; not quite as invasive as dandelions, but those little heart-shaped leaves conceal a powerful hunger for conquest, sending their runners everywhere, each one an outpost preparing itself for a future invasion.

And yet I cannot bring myself, *père*, to curb their cheery exuberance. Though more or less worthless in terms of fruit, the little white flowers and pretty leaves make excellent ground cover, keeping the thistles and ragwort at bay without suppressing my daffodils. And besides, in summer, there may be enough of the tiny red berries to put on a tart, or flavour a glassful of sweet white wine. That is, if the birds do not steal them first. They too enjoy their sweetness.

Those strawberries will creep, Reynaud, said Narcisse's voice in my mind. *Let them stay, and in a month, your beds will be nothing but strawberries.*

'There are worse things here than wild strawberries.'

'Is that so?' said a voice above me, and for a moment I wondered how Narcisse could sound

247

so like Vianne Rocher —

I looked up. She was watching me from over the garden wall, where the hedge of wild fuchsia and rosemary was already starting to flower. She was wearing a yellow blouse and a matching scarf around her hair.

'If you want them to fruit,' she went on, 'you need to take out the runners. Runners don't really want to make fruit. They just want to make more strawberry plants. Anouk used to think it was cruel, to throw all those little plants away. When we lived in Paris, I tried growing strawberries in planters. But Anouk was always going into the compost bin to rescue the strawberry runners. *They want to be with their friends*, she'd say.'

I smiled and stretched my aching back. 'Children have funny ideas,' I said.

'I used to try and explain,' said Vianne. 'The runners steal from the mother plant. They take her energy and run as far as they can away from her. *But they're babies*, she used to say. *You can't explain that to babies*.'

She laughed, a slightly mournful sound. I know she misses Anouk very much. I was suddenly reminded of Joséphine, watching Pilou with his girlfriend. *I sometimes envy Vianne*, she said. *Rosette will always need her.*

Is this parenthood, *mon père*? This perpetual sense of loss? If so, then maybe I am glad that I will never know it first-hand. And yet, I envy them that joy that I will never understand. *Mon père*, have you never wondered why priests are denied that connection? Surely a parent's love

248

for their child echoes God's love for his people? And if we cannot experience that, then how can we truly express His will?

'I heard Anouk was coming home soon,' I said.

'Yes, just for a week or so.'

'That's nice. It will give her the chance to catch up with her old friends. Is she not tempted to stay for good, and help in the *chocolaterie?*'

Vianne shrugged. 'I thought she might be, once.'

Once more I thought of Jean-Philippe Bonnet. 'I imagine when you're young, a place like Lansquenet doesn't seem very exciting.'

'Maybe that's why Morgane Dubois decided to open her business here. Maybe that's why half the village is sick with tattoo fever.'

Half of Lansquenet? That was surely hyperbole. And yet — I thought of Zézette, and Saphir. How many more of the river-folk are hiding fresh new artwork?

'Maybe the river people,' I said. 'Tattoos are part of their culture. But *our* people — surely not.'

Vianne Rocher seemed to hesitate, choosing her words carefully. 'I don't think you're aware how fast these things can spread,' she told me. 'Joline Drou's son, Jeannot, was showing Rosette his new ink just the other day.'

'Joline Drou! So *that's* why she — ' I stopped, aware that I was about to break the seal of the confessional. But this would certainly explain the tension between Joline and her son, and if Jeannot *had* got a tattoo, it was only a matter of

249

time before his friends followed the trend.

'Of course, he's twenty-one,' went on Vianne. 'He's free to make his own mistakes. But young people in Lansquenet aren't as streetwise as city kids. Jeannot has always been young for his age, young and quite impressionable. Maybe it's flattering to someone like her to be such a powerful influence: to introduce so many young people to her art for the first time. To her art, and maybe to other things.'

She was right, of course, I thought. A village like ours is susceptible to the brief but violent crazes of youth. I have seen them all before. For a month — or maybe three — all the young people are obsessed. Then the wind changes and they move on. Sometimes there is an injury — a broken ankle, a grazed knee — but most of the time there is nothing to show for the brief moment of madness. Except in the case of Morgane Dubois —

'What other things?' I said.

'Who knows? But Maya Mahjoubi and her friends hang around the place all the time. And Yannick Montour, Jean-Philippe Bonnet — even Rosette. None of them are old enough to be legitimate customers. And yet here she is, encouraging them, luring them in — why?'

I nodded, feeling slightly alarmed. I wondered what Joséphine would say if she knew her son was part of the crowd hanging around the tattoo place. Boys will be boys, I suppose, *mon père*; though I was never such a boy. And yet, although I agreed with her, it surprised me to hear Vianne Rocher speaking so eloquently against a stranger to the village. It should have pleased me; instead I felt as if our roles had somehow been inverted. After all, who was Morgane? Only a disabled woman trying to make a living. My feelings towards her on the day we met had come from my insecurity. Here, in my garden, among the bulbs, I felt more inclined to be tolerant.

'I would never have imagined *you* feeling threatened by a newcomer to the village.' I meant it as a pleasantry, but Vianne did not smile. Instead she gave me a sharp look.

'This is serious, Francis. Can't you see she's dangerous?'

Dangerous. What a baleful word, like the scent of smoke in the air. It's a word you used repeatedly, *père*, the year the river-gypsies came.

'Surely you're exaggerating,' I protested weakly.

She shook her head. 'You've felt it,' she said. 'You felt it yourself when you spoke to her. There's something unwholesome about her, Francis. I can feel it. Trust me.' She put out her hand to touch mine. '*Trust me*,' she repeated.

For a moment I felt strangely disconnected from myself. Perhaps I was light-headed from having been on my knees for so long; perhaps it was a reaction to having missed breakfast that morning. But at her touch, I felt a charge, like some kind of latent energy. I felt a sudden heat in my face; a scent of smoke in my nostrils. And haven't I felt it myself, *père*? That sense of danger around Morgane, the sense of something about to explode? *Her art, and maybe other things.* Drink, drugs, pornography? Maybe she

251

spiked my drink that day. That might explain my discomfort.

I said: 'Of course you're right, Vianne. I was hoping it wouldn't come to this. But if I need to take action, I will.'

She nodded. 'Good. What will you do?'

Good question. Where should I begin? Perhaps I should speak to Morgane. A word of warning should be enough to stress the importance of fitting in. And if not? Our folk are conservative, careful of their children. They still go to church. They would listen to me. A well-written sermon or two should bring the stray sheep back to the fold. And if not? There are other means, *mon père*. Means I would prefer not to use, but which — if she is dangerous — I will not hesitate to deploy in the protection of my flock. *Only* if she is dangerous —

'Whatever it takes,' I said at last.

After all, I have done it before.

10

My father was gone for thirteen days. Thirteen
days of Tante Anna; thirteen days that felt like
months. Four more nights I slept in the yard,
picking strawberries during the day, so that by
the end of it, my hands were stained purple
with their juice, and even the scent of them
made me gag.

During that time, I heard no sound from
Mimi in the bedroom. Several times, I tried to
climb up to my father's window, but the near-
est tree was too far away for me to climb in,
even if Mimi had known how to open the
window. As it was, I thought I saw her, just
once, from a distance, her face a motionless
white blur, looking out from the darkened
room like a plaster death mask. I tried to
attract her attention by waving to her and calling, but Mimi never moved at all, until finally I
started to doubt that I had even seen her.

On the morning of the fourth day, Tante
Anna opened the door, wearing a lace-edged
apron over her grey cambric dress, with her
black cross, as always, on a ribbon around her
throat. I watched hopefully for a sign that
Mimi and I were forgiven, and this time, as if
in answer, she smiled and gestured at me to
approach.

'How about some breakfast?' she said. 'Croissants, and butter, and strawberry jam, and maybe a bowl of café-au-lait?'

I nodded, too astonished to speak, half expecting her to laugh, and close the door in my face again. But Tante Anna simply smiled again, a smile as rare as it was unsettling.

'Come in then, Narcisse. Hurry up, before your coffee gets cold.'

I followed her inside, wondering vaguely why she hadn't told me to go and wash my hands. Even I could see that they were in dire need of washing: a combination of strawberry juice and dust and general neglect had stained them a corpse-like purple. But Tante Anna did not remark that I looked like a dirty savage, or comment when I crammed my croissant almost whole into my mouth, and suddenly I began to feel as if something bad was happening. Tante Anna never smiled, unless she was entertaining her friends. She never offered me café-au-lait, or made croissants for breakfast. And she never passed by an opportunity to criticize my deportment, or to deplore my grubby hands, or to notice my dirty clothes. For a moment my heart gave a lurch — could our father be coming home? — then I saw that Mimi's place had not been set, and the piece of croissant stuck in my throat as if it had been turned to stone.

'Where's Mimi, Tante Anna?'

Tante Anna gave that smile again, and I realized that there was nothing kind or natural about it. It was simply a meaningless flexing,

254

just as the light in her eyes had nothing to do with whatever thoughts lay within. She might have been a life-sized doll, or a plaster statuette — and with that thought came a sudden blaze of fear and understanding.

I pushed away my coffee-bowl, spilling the dregs on the tablecloth, and stood up so violently that my chair fell backwards onto the terracotta tiles.

'Where's Mimi?' I said again. 'Why isn't she here for breakfast, too?'

For a moment Tante Anna's lips tightened, and I almost hoped she would slap me, or call me ungrateful, ill-mannered, rude — anything but this tolerance that filled me with apprehension. Then she sighed, the kind of sigh that she reserved for her church friends as they discussed a neighbour's death, or the rising price offish, or the scandal of a child born crippled or out of wedlock.

'Your sister was never well,' she said, and at those words a part of my mind started to rise like a balloon and drift, untethered, into a sky that was suddenly filled with shrapnel. Below me, far below, came the voice of Tante Anna, saying: 'She had those seizures all the time. Your father knew that. So did you.'

I tried to speak, but all I could hear was a rushing of air in my ears, and the sound of the big bass drum that was my heart counting out the seconds. Baddam. Baddam. Baddam. Baddam.

Tante Anna was too far away for me to see the look in her eyes. But I could imagine it:

that look of pretend sympathy, of righteous sat-
isfaction. I said; 'No,' but from a great height,
looking down on the scene below. I knew she
was telling me Mimi was dead. But the thought
just wouldn't stay in place. It rose and rose like
a hot-air balloon, leaving everything behind.
Baddam. Baddam. Baddam.

'Liar,' I said, in a voice that seemed to come
from a thousand miles away. 'You hated Mimi.
You hated her.'

'I did not,' said Tante Anna. 'And I pray
that God forgives you for your intemperate language. Naomi was a very sick child. God took
her, in His mercy.'

Reynaud, I was only ten years old. I had no
way to process my grief. And besides, it all felt
so unreal; the rising hot-air balloon of my
thoughts, my aunt standing like a monolith,
many miles below me.

'I want to see Mimi,' I said at last, in a voice
that was shaking.

'I don't think that's a good idea,' said Tante
Anna.

I ignored her. 'I want to see Mimi,' I said,
and then she caught hold of me, her thumbs
pressing into my upper arms, and I saw the flat
light in her eyes and knew that there was something beyond the horror of Mimi's death
— something as-yet undiscovered.

'Where is she?' I said.

'In the cellar.' Tante Anna's eyes were like
silver coins. 'It's cooler there than in the
house.'

I tried to think of little Mimi, like meat on a

256

slab, in the cellar. My eyes began to sting, but with rage, the kind of helpless, hopeless rage that only a child can really know.

'How long has she been there?' I said, and now my voice was closer, as if the balloon had started to drift slowly downwards. 'How long has she been there, Tante, and why didn't you send for the priest?'

Tanta Anna shrugged. 'It's cooler down there,' she repeated, as if that were an answer. 'Now why don't you finish your breakfast?' she said, as if Mimi's death were nothing more than an interruption to our meal. 'You can try some of my strawberry jam. And then we'll walk up to the church and see Père Grégoire together.'

Once more I felt that helium-rush of unreality. How could she talk about strawberry jam? How could she talk about breakfast? Mimi was dead. She would never again play in the shallows of the Tannes. Never again give her brilliant smile, and her laugh like splashing water. Never learn to say my name, or any other word but 'boat' —

Tante Anna gave an exasperated sigh. 'For heaven's sake, finish your coffee, Narcisse, and stop making such a drama of this. You always knew Naomi wasn't a normal child. She had a lot of problems. She wasn't really meant to survive. It was a mercy things happened this way. When you're older, you'll understand.'

I heard the words, and yet my mind didn't seem to connect with them. Mimi would never grow older. Mimi would never understand. I looked at the breakfast-table: the jug of milk; the dish of fresh croissants; the big jar of jam with the long-handled spoon on the waxed linen tablecloth. I watched as Tante Anna took her place, her mouth as tight as a widow's purse, and then, instead of sitting down, I turned and ran for the cellar door.

'Narcisse!' Tante Anna's voice was sharp. But I was young, and she was slow, and I reached the stairs before her. There was a strip of opaque glass near the ceiling, bathing the room in cool blue light, and I could see a hock of smoked pork, and a couple of pheasants, not quite ripe, hanging from hooks in the ceiling. All along the walls, there were shelves of preserves in every colour imaginable; jams, jellies, pâtés, terrines, jellied meats and vegetables; pickled cabbage and salsify; brandied cherries and peaches and pears. And there, in the centre of the room, laid out on the granite countertop where Tante Anna used to prepare the meat, there was Mimi, in her nightdress, looking very small and grey, as if she had died some days before.

Behind me, the aunt descended the stairs, clattering and scolding. But I paid no attention to her. All my attention was on Mimi; the purple marks around her wrists, the dust on the soles of her bare feet —

Reynaud, I do not claim to be a man of exceptional insight. Nor was I an especially clever or insightful boy. And yet I saw it all in a brief and piercing moment of clarity. I turned and looked at Tante Anna — the cross at her

258

throat, the angry eyes, the hair pulled back in a hard grey bun . . .

I hate this story. I hate it. *BAM!* I wish I'd never taken it. It's bad enough that Narcisse died, but he was *old*, and Mimi was *young*. Young people shouldn't have to die. I slammed the folder shut — *BAM!* — and then, because I knew Maman would come into my room, I stuffed it into my satchel and ran downstairs in a rush — *Badda-bam!*

'Rosette?' Maman always knows if I'm upset. 'What happened? Where are you going?' But I couldn't tell her that, because of Mimi, and because of the wind already snapping at my heels. I couldn't bring the wind to our door. I had to lead it away, I knew, running it ragged across the fields, running it like an angry dog till it changed into a puppy again.

I didn't know where I was going at first. At any normal time I would have gone to Les Marauds to be with Roux, and we would have drunk *café-au-lait* outside by the firepit, and neither of us would have said much at all, but somehow the wind would have calmed right down. But this wasn't a normal time. I haven't seen Roux since last Monday. His boat is still here, but it's all shut up like an oyster shell, and he hasn't been to the shop, not even for hot chocolate. I wonder if he's angry at me. I wonder if I'm angry at *him*. I'm angry at lots of people these days: Roux, Pilou, Madame Montour, Maman — even Narcisse, for writing that story, for making me care about Mimi, maybe even for being dead, because none of it makes any sense and nobody knows why it happens.

And so I went to the churchyard and found Narcisse in his plastic jar, and took out his folder and threw it down, and said to him in my shadow-voice: '*Why did you pick the strawberries? You should have been looking out for Mimi. And now she's dead, and you are too, and none of it makes any sense.*'

The wind was blowing harder than ever, tearing the blossom from the trees. But no-one comes to the churchyard much, except at All Saints and Sundays. No-one was going to hear me today, except maybe the wind. I felt like crying, but I never cry.

And then someone behind me said: 'Who's Mimi?'

And there was Morgane, sitting under a big old tree, all in black, with only her hair shining in the shadows like something out of a fairytale. I was so surprised to see her that I almost forgot about being upset, and the wind gave a shiver, and then a sob, and started to die down again. Now I could see she was sitting on a very old gravestone, a grave where the weeds had been cleared away to show a sandstone garland.

She stood up and came over to me. She walks very straight, like a dancer on stilts. She picked up Narcisse's green folder and smoothed the crumpled edges. Then she opened it at the first page.

And suddenly I realized that I'd done a bad thing. I'd stolen Narcisse's story. Not by taking it back from Yannick, but by reading it myself. I

260

guess I already knew that, but seeing Morgane with it in her hands suddenly made it all clear to me. That story wasn't meant for me. I'd known it from the beginning. It was meant for Francis Reynaud, and he was supposed to read it. I wondered if Morgane would stop liking me now that she knew I was a thief. But Morgane didn't look angry. She just tied up the folder again with its piece of scarlet string. Then she smiled and said: 'Rosette, this ought to go back to Curé Reynaud. After all, it's addressed to him.'

I knew she was right. But I didn't want to go to Reynaud. He never understands what I'm saying, and besides, if I tell him what happened I might get Yannick into trouble. And I still really wanted to know what had happened to the aunt. Or did I? Now that Mimi was dead, I wasn't sure I really cared about the end of the story.

'It's up to you, Rosette,' said Morgane. 'But if you want my help, I'm here.'

I thought about that for a little while. She waited for me to decide. She has such a quiet way of looking at you and smiling, and all my bad and angry thoughts started to drift away like smoke.

'Trust me,' said Morgane.

Okay.

I watched her leave the churchyard, walking very carefully, the folder tucked under her arm. And then I went to sit for a while under the big old yew tree, and I looked at the name on the gravestone where Morgane had been sitting, and read the inscription, chiselled deep into the yellow sandstone:

Naomi Dartigen: 1942–1949
Now she is like all the others

Rats

1

Tuesday, March 28

I went to Les Marauds this morning to find Roux's boat gone from its mooring: and the rest of the travellers — Blanche, Zézette, Saphir, Mahmed — getting ready to move downstream, packing up their belongings; putting away pots and pans; picking up litter; buying supplies; kicking ashes over fires. What has prompted this exodus? I think I can guess the answer. The Pied Piper starts with the rats before moving onto the children. How many of them have come to her, in secret, behind that purple door? How many of them heard her call?

Feel me. Find me. Follow me.

Reynaud has been making an effort to help. His sermons are almost fiery. This morning, by all accounts, he spoke of corruption in our midst, but stopped short of actually naming Morgane. I need to speak to him again: the effect of our last conversation has not been as long-lasting as I would have hoped. And Reynaud is preoccupied: his thoughts are coloured with sadness and smoke. I've never found him easy to read, he's too closed for that, but nowadays he seems volatile, like paper close to combustion. Narcisse's death has shaken him in ways I do not understand. They were never friends, and yet the old man was part of his

265

childhood. Is *that* why I see the smoke? Or is it hiding something else?

Rosette has been distant, too; reluctant to help out in the *chocolaterie*, but seemingly indifferent to the flight of the river-folk. Her excitement over Narcisse's legacy, her friendship with Yannick Montour, mean that she has been unlike herself in recent days, jumping at unexpected sounds, or sometimes even no sound at all, like a cat on a windy day. And there is something else in her: something almost like anger. I do not know where it comes from. My winter child was always so sweet, so predictably erratic. But now she is stormy, impetuous; slamming doors and running upstairs, with Bam, a grinning gargoyle, pulling faces in her wake. Last night she came home with tears in her eyes and soil under her fingernails, which makes me think that she may have been planting flowers by Narcisse's grave. A harmless pastime, I tell myself, which keeps her away from the tattoo shop across the square.

As for Morgane, she remains elusive, at least as far as I am concerned. I have not seen her leave the shop once, though other people have told me she has: Guillaume has seen her twice by the church, and Joséphine saw her on market day, carrying a basket of aubergines and an armful of night-scented stocks.

'I knew her from your description,' she said, calling in this morning for a cup of mocha and an order for Easter chocolates for Pilou and his friends. 'Is it true she has no feet?'

I told her that yes, as far as I knew, Morgane

266

wore prosthetics. Joséphine looked doubtful, but said that Morgane had been wearing boots. 'I suppose they could have been,' she said. 'I didn't talk to her for long.'

She sipped her mocha, but I could see the colour rising in her face. Joséphine didn't want me to know just how long she had talked to Morgane. And there was something in her thoughts — a seam of colour; a thread of smoke — that was almost like duplicity —

'Thinking of getting a tattoo?' I said, with a humorous lilt to my voice to suggest how ridiculous it was. At the same time, I reached for her with my thoughts, and saw a ribbon of brightness; a dapple of light on foliage. An oak twig, with an acorn attached, and a couple of strong green leaves —

I felt the strength run from my legs.

'You've already got one,' I whispered.

Joséphine looked startled, and then gave an awkward kind of laugh, and coloured even further.

'Don't tell Pilou,' she said, and for a moment she looked like the woman I'd known years ago, stealing chocolates from my shop and hiding them from her husband. 'He'll never see it,' she went on. 'It's here.' She cupped her belly. 'Oak leaves, for strength and endurance. And an acorn, for Pilou, so I'll always carry him close.' She gave another of those awkward laughs. 'It's crazy, isn't it?' she said. 'I never thought I'd do something like that, but the idea wouldn't leave me alone. And then one day I just went in. She was there. I didn't know what to ask for. But once we started talking, I felt . . . '

267

'You felt as if she'd read your mind.'

Joséphine laughed. 'That's right!' she said. 'And I thought *you* were the only one.'

2

Tuesday, March 28

When she left I closed the shop and stood outside for a moment. The almond blossom from the tree has gone, to be replaced by new green shoots. It smells of spring, and mown grass, and tilled earth from the fields beyond. Now is the month of *Germinal* in the Republican calendar: the month of hyacinth, and bees, and violet, and primrose. It is also the windy month; the month of new beginnings, and I have never felt it so strongly as I feel it now: that sense of possibility; that irresistible lightness. A music seems to play in the air; the thinnest filament of sound, no more substantial than the brush of a spider's web over the tip of a dead butterfly's wing.

Find me. Feel me. Follow me.

Two can play at that game, Morgane. I send out a shimmy in the air, the scent of the Criollo bean, the scents of vanilla, burnt sugar and blood.

Try me. Taste me. Test me.

For a moment I almost thought the music halted mid-phrase. The colours in the air seem to shift, an eyebrow raised in amusement. *A challenge?* It is all the welcome I need. I walk towards the purple door. The door is ajar, as if she were somehow expecting me to call, and the blinds are closed.

269

What did I want? I hardly knew: perhaps to confront the woman at last, or to see for myself what glamours she has. I found myself at the purple door: I entered without knocking. I knew what to expect — and yet, the impact of it was no less than the first time I set foot inside: the mirrors; the lights; *The Strawberry Thief* reflected in every surface. And myself, an interloper, watching from between the leaves.

A blur of movement, reflected in the mirrors all around me. A candyfloss tangle of curly hair, dyed an extravagant purple. I turned. There was no-one else in the room. And yet, in the mirrors, I saw her again, almost close enough to touch —

'*Anouk?*'

There was no mistaking her. Purple hair, wide smile, eyes like the planet seen from space. It was Anouk behind the glass, looking so young and yet so adult. Children are always changing, dancing away through the passing years. Anouk at nine; Anouk at twelve; Anouk at twenty, and beyond —

I flicked the sign against malchance. But there was nothing to banish. I was the only one in the room. Anouk had gone. And yet I knew that Morgane had sent her to challenge me. She already knows my weakness, I thought: the weapons to use against me. I looked at myself in the mirrors: I thought my face looked pale under the lights. And all around me, there were birds, and those impossible blue leaves, and stylized, scentless flowers.

I cleared my throat, but no-one came. Morgane must have gone out, I thought. And so

I turned to go, but as I did, a stack of books caught my eye from the corner of the little table by the big tattooist's chair. They looked like photo albums. Of course, I thought. This is her work. Her archive of designs. Seized with a great curiosity, I picked up an album, opened it. As I had thought, it was filled with photographs. Some were Polaroids, faded with time, some scratched like ancient records. But all of them were of her work; of the people she has collected. Young, old, white, brown; she had them all in her album, and, moving to the most recent shots, I saw my friends and neighbours: Roux, unsmiling and shirtless and looking straight into the camera; Joséphine, grinning shyly and slightly out of focus. Jeannot Drou was there as well, and Zézette, and Blanche, and their daughter Saphir, and Jojo LeMollet, Sofia Zidane, and Nadine Poitou, and Saïd Lellouche. Even Ying, the solicitor, one hand raised to show the spray of delicate plum-blossom on her wrist. And once more, on the final page, Anouk, with her purple hair and her smile like the coming of summer —

I threw the book onto the table. It was impossible. It was a trick. Just like the trick with the mirrors. The woman had known I was coming here. She'd left me this book as a warning.

Don't mess with me, Vianne Rocher. Don't interfere with my business.

I closed the album abruptly, certain that Morgane had entered the room. I turned, but the room was still empty, speckled birds and fronds of fern reflected from every surface. I went to

271

replace the album. But as I did, I noticed a folder lying on the table. Smaller than the album, green, and tied with a length of pink legal tape, I thought I recognized it, though from where, I was uncertain. I picked it up. It opened at a bookmark — a drawing of a monkey, reading a book, and laughing.

I flicked through the rest of the folder. It was filled with loose pages. Closely handwritten, in ink that varied from light blue to rusty-black. A diary? The writing suggested another age, an age in which children were required to write on squared paper, and practise their calligraphy. And then, I suddenly realized that this was Narcisse's confession, given by Ying to Francis Reynaud at the reading of the will. How had it come into Morgane's hands? And how did a drawing of Rosette's come to be used as a bookmark?

It occurred to me that maybe all this was something to do with Michèle Montour. After all, she has made no secret of her resentment of Narcisse's will. Could she have enlisted Morgane's help to get hold of the document? And was Morgane's interest in Rosette connected to Narcisse's legacy?

In any case, I told myself, the document was no business of hers. It must go back to Francis Reynaud. I put the folder under my arm and went back out into the square. The small bell rang as I left, but nothing else marked my departure. The square, too, was mostly clear, except for a couple of children crossing over from Poitou's bakery. I moved towards the *chocolaterie* at an unobtrusive pace, opened up again, and went to

272

sit behind the counter. The folder lay on the countertop, Rosette's bookmark protruding. *Just one page*, I told myself. *Just to see if it mentions Rosette.*

I knew I was breaking a confidence. I knew the confession was meant for Reynaud. But just then all I could think about was the fact that Morgane must have read the file, at least up to the bookmarked page. And if there was information there that she could use against me or Rosette . . .

I opened the folder, and started to read.

3

Wednesday, March 29

Reynaud, it was so easy. I never even gave it a thought. I remember Tante Anna on the stairs, and Mimi on the stone slab, and the jars of preserves and pickles and jellies shining in the undersea light. Murder is that cool, blue light. Murder is like the squares on a quilt, motley and multicoloured.

I remember her looming over me from the top of the cellar steps. I remember her shiny little black boots at the level of my eyes. Without even thinking, I reached out an arm and yanked at a stockinged ankle. She gave a great cry of outrage, which turned into a wail of alarm as she toppled and started to fall. I sprang back to give space and she fell, arms outstretched, to the cellar floor and I heard the sound of wrist and collarbone breaking. There were only half a dozen steps. Not enough to kill her outright, even with luck. But then, Reynaud, I took a jar of strawberry jam from one of the shelves — a two-litre Mason jar, from the batch that Tante Anna had made that week — and before she could react, or scream, or know what I was doing, I let gravity do what I could not, and smashed it into the back of her head, taking care to use the base of the jar, which would not break under the impact.

274

I know. It sounds cold. It wasn't, Reynaud. I felt more awake than I'd ever been. Feeling awake isn't always good. But I felt as if a window had opened up into the world; a window through which I could see the truth. Perhaps that's how Adam and Eve felt, when they ate from the Tree of Knowledge. As if their world had been nothing more than a canvas, nicely painted with pastoral scenes, behind which the truth waited patiently for one of them to tear it aside.

And yet, for all these Biblical thoughts, your God had never seemed less real. Only I was real, Reynaud; and I knew I'd never be the same. Some acts are transformative. Even at eleven years old, I knew that. I'd never play by the Tannes again, or walk in the woods, or pick strawberries in quite the same way ever again, now that I was a murderer.

Tante Anna didn't die straightaway. She lasted a few minutes. Her face had gone a funny shape, and one eye had disappeared into her head. The other one just looked at me. It was blue, and very bright, and I couldn't tell if the brightness was anger, fear or hatred. She didn't say a word, though. But I could hear her breathing. And the blood was softly pooling around; staining the lace of her collar red; etching her onto the cellar stones. Finally the breathing stopped. The brightness went glassy. The blood stopped.

The jar was unbroken. It takes a lot to break the base of one of those jars. I wiped it off with my handkerchief and returned it to the shelf.

The War had mostly passed me by, but I knew enough to remember that food was a commodity never to be wasted.

It has taken me hours to read the closely written pages. I read alone, in my bedroom, late into the night, and I never stopped hearing Narcisse's voice; the voice of the Narcisse I knew, but also the voice of the boy that he had been, the one who had carried this act to his grave, and still felt the weight of it enough to want to confess it to Reynaud.

Why Reynaud, of all people? Narcisse was not a believer. He never even liked Reynaud, and yet the urge to confess to *him* was clearly too strong to resist. Why? There are answers here, I know. That is why I must keep it — at least until I have found them. I know this was not intended for me, and yet I must read it to the end. And what does Rosette know know of all this? Is she aware of the document? I want to ask her directly, but I fear she might not tell me. There's something here that links them all — Narcisse, Reynaud, Rosette, Morgane. Something about the oak wood that now belongs to my daughter. Michèle Montour already believes that there is a secret surrounding this wood. If only I can discover it —

A cat crossed your path in the snow, and mewed. The Hurakan was blowing.

That phrase. Why do I hear it so often, at night, when the world is sleeping? At first I thought it was my mother's voice; it sounds almost like her. Then I thought I recognized the

276

voice of Zozie de l'Alba. But now I think of Morgane Dubois, and the way she spoke to me when we met, the way she speaks to me even now from that shuttered window.

Feel me. Find me. Face me.

Once more I bring out my mother's cards. *Death. The Fool. The Tower. Change.* Beneath them, I draw the Three of Swords: the card of deepest sorrow. Then the Four of Disks: power. Then the Four of Staves: victory. But for whom? Morgane and I are dangerous spheres, set on an orbit to collide. One of us wants to ride the wind; the other wants to silence it. One of us wants to be deep-rooted oak; one of us wants to be dandelion seeds. And so, for my daughter's sake, and for mine: one of us will have to go.

The phone at my bedside makes a sound — a single chime, like a tiny bell. Anouk. She must be up very late. And I was so busy with Narcisse's book that I forgot to send my usual goodnight message.

Coming early. On my own. See you Friday. Got some news! A.xx

I wonder what her news may be. It sounds like change, and in my world, change is not always as exciting as my summer child would hope. Change is often dangerous; its voice too much like the voice of the wind.

I text: *Of course. See you Friday! xxx*

And yet, there's something in me that wishes she had kept to her earlier plan. I had hoped Morgane would be gone by the time Anouk arrived. Anouk is trusting. She will see no danger. She will love the purple door, painted in a colour that matches her hair. She will be fascinated by Morgane, and her metal feet, and her many tattoos. And I will be unable to stop her from hearing that whisper, that *command* —

Find me. Feel me. Follow me.

Forty-eight hours is not very long. And yet, I see what has to be done. Forty-eight hours to change the wind. To course-correct our lives, to change the cruel path of the Hurakan. Forty-eight hours, to dispel Morgane like an unseasonal fall of snow. At first it seems a hopeless task. Morgane Dubois seems impervious to my kind of persuasion. But I know someone who is not. Someone who is capable of taking all kinds of action. Someone who will understand why she cannot be tolerated. Someone who has already proved himself to be more than merely susceptible to the charm of the cocoa bean.

Try me. Taste me. Test me.

So far Francis Reynaud has not responded as well as I'd hoped to Morgane's threat. He has been weaker, more tolerant than I would have expected. His sermons have been unconvincing, dealing more with evil in general than the specific evil represented by Morgane's business. I know this because Caro Clairmont has told me about it in the shop: after one of my special chocolates, she can become quite expansive.

'Monsieur le Curé is losing his touch,' she tells me with an air of contempt. 'His sermons hardly make sense any more, and last week in the confessional, I didn't feel he was even *listening* — '

But Reynaud is the heart of Lansquenet. His influence goes far beyond that of the church-going community. With Francis Reynaud on my side, I still have a chance of victory. Even in forty-eight hours, together, we could shut her down. After all, I am still Vianne Rocher. And I know all his favourites.

4

Wednesday, March 29

Yannick Montour is avoiding me. Apparently, even the lure of cake is insufficient to make him rebel against his mother's influence. This is a disappointment, *père*. I had hoped that the missing folder would have returned to me by now. Has the boy been lying to me? Could Madame Montour still have it in her possession?

Over the past week I have prayed and suffered and sweated in equal quantity. I cannot eat; I cannot sleep; and my sermons are rambling, shameful things, unstructured and repetitive. I began yesterday's sermon with the intention of quoting Leviticus 19:28 — *Ye shall not make any cuttings in your flesh for the dead, nor print any marks upon you: I am the LORD* — and ended up speaking, for far longer than the usual weekday sermon, about the mark of Cain instead, and about how a crime is never erased, even beyond the grave.

The woman Morgane in her tattoo shop looks at me with a kind of concern — I do not know whether this is because of the content of my sermons, or if she sees my unravelling and wonders at the cause. In any case, I do not need her sympathy — or anyone's. My garden is my only release, and I take out on the wild strawberries the vengeance that I cannot direct at

280

my human tormentors.

Omi Mahjoubi, being too old to care, comments where the others dare not. 'You look ill, Monsieur le Curé,' she says as she passes my garden. 'Too many *waswas*, and not enough of my little Maya's samosas.'

She's right. I wish I could tell her so. But my confession is not for her ears. If I still believed in such things, I might take a bus, and head for Agen, and seek out another confessor. But *you* absolved me of my sin, and yet it has grown, like the strawberry plants, duplicating itself again and again, cell by dark and cancerous cell, just as I believed it was gone. Later I realized that you had not been following God's plan, but your own. That made your absolution a sham, and my repentance null and void. But now, to whom should I confess? To Père Henri Lemaître, the young priest from the neighbouring village? Perhaps to the Bishop, whose love of God comes second to his love of paperwork? The victims of my crime — Pierrot, nicknamed La Marmite, and his girl Choupette — are long gone. Even the river-folk have forgotten them. And yet, the crime itself remains. It leaves a mark that cannot be erased.

If only I could be sure the Montours had not read Narcisse's document. If only I could believe the boy when he tells me the folder just disappeared — like the answer to a prayer. But God does not answer my prayers. He means to watch me die in silence.

They passed me today as I was at work: the boy buttoned into an ill-fitting suit, as if

281

attending an interview. I tried to catch his eye, but he was with his mother and scurried away without looking at me. Madame Montour was bolder, flashing me a triumphant smile, and I noticed that she too was wearing clothes more suited to church than to shopping. A sudden suspicion came over me. Had they been to Agen? Had they been to see the solicitor?

A telephone call to Mme Mak's office proved less than satisfactory. Her secretary confirms the fact that Madame Montour had an appointment, but refuses to tell me why. Maybe she means to contest the will. This explanation — plausible though it is — does nothing to reassure me. I stop short of asking directly whether the green folder is involved. I do not want it to be known that I have lost it. I tell myself that Madame Montour's attitude may still be a bluff, an attempt to make me show my hand. I tell myself that there is still hope of the folder being returned to me, but my voice is far from convincing.

If I were someone else, I might turn to Vianne Rocher for advice. But Vianne is busy preparing for her daughter's visit, and besides, so close to Easter, the shop is always filled with customers. What can I do? I have started to take a measure of Armagnac every night, to help me sleep. But my dreams are strange, and I awake unrested, heavy-eyed and desperate. I sometimes try to tell myself this is all in my mind: that there may be no mention of what I did in the man's confession. And yet my certainty remains. Why else would he have taunted me with the words: *my father, the murderer?*

Seven days, *mon père*. Seven days. That's more than it took to make the world. Anything would be better, *mon père*, than this incessant waiting. Even death would be preferable to this calm before the storm. I do not fear death. I only fear there may be an afterlife. I keep thinking back to a poem I learnt by heart at primary school, a poem by Victor Hugo, entitled *The Conscience*. The murderer Cain, troubled by the constant presence of God's Eye, attempts to escape it. But wherever he goes, the Eye of God is always watching. At last, in despair, Cain buries himself alive, hoping to find rest in the darkness. And the last line of the poem, the one that never fails to make me shiver, goes:

But the Eye was in the tomb, and was watching Cain.

Mon père. Is this my punishment? Not to see God, but to feel His Eye on me forever? Or is it the gaze of Pierre Lupin, known as Pierrot La Marmite? Pierrot and Choupette. They sound like cartoon characters from a children's TV show. I never saw their faces. There was no photograph in the news, and yet they are very clear in my mind: the man a big, soft, ugly brute; the woman a slender thing, with tattoos.

For you, something radical and pure. Maybe something to do with fire.

Morgane knows, *mon père*. Who else has she told? Her customers are many. Does she have her equivalent of the sanctity of the confessional? Or does she whisper her secrets to every wind that passes?

5

Thursday, March 30

After I gave the file to Morgane, I did a lot of thinking. I thought about the strawberry wood, and why Narcisse wanted to leave it to me. Mostly because of Mimi, I suppose, because I reminded him of her. And I thought about her story, and how it *should* have ended, and I drew a picture of Narcisse and Mimi sailing away in Mimi's boat, and the horrible aunt being left behind, to be eaten by ducks on the riverbank.

That made me feel a bit better. Pictures tell stories as well as words do, and words aren't really my favourites. But a picture can make what happened into what *should have* happened, and that's a kind of magic you can't even make from chocolate.

I thought about Morgane, too. I think about Morgane a lot. I can tell Maman doesn't like her. She says she's a bad influence. But so many of our friends have tattoos that I really don't understand why she hates them so much. Or maybe it's just Morgane she hates. That could be it. I've heard her in the *chocolaterie*, talking to her customers. I try not to hear what she's saying, though. She's so different nowadays, all mean and spiteful and angry. Her *voice* isn't angry — but I can see the colours behind the words she's saying, and they look like Reynaud's colours now, all muddled and confused and scared. I don't like to think of Maman being scared, especially not of Morgane. Besides Maman doesn't even *know* Morgane. I'm sure if she did, she'd soon make friends. Perhaps I can help change her mind. She could really use a friend, and Morgane can make friends with *anyone* —

And so this morning, when Maman was busy with a customer, I went back to the tattoo shop. I took my book of drawings again, to show Morgane my new art. I showed her the picture of Mimi and Narcisse, and she looked at it for a long time.

'You're very good,' she said at last. 'You know, your style could easily cross over into tattoo design.'

I wasn't sure about that. I said: *It must feel weird, to draw on skin.*

She laughed at that. 'Weird? You bet it is. Rosette, tattooing's an art, and more. It's been around for millennia. The Mayans, the Egyptians, the Moche. Why did they do it? No-one knows. Maybe to placate the gods. Maybe to take on the energies of the designs they chose for themselves. But every act of creation is an act of power. It's magical: transformative. It leaves a permanent mark on the world. And isn't that really what art is for?'

She says it better than I do. But I'd already thought of that. Pictures are magic. You don't need words. And words can lie, but pictures don't.

I said: *I believe in magic.*

'Of course you do. Your mother's a witch, isn't she?'

We were having breakfast: chocolate *croissants* and coffee. The *croissants* are from Monsieur Poitou's bakery; the coffee was hot and very dark. I'm not supposed to drink coffee.

She looked at me and smiled. 'Do you think I don't know a witch when I see one?' she said. 'Scrying with chocolate, scrying with ink: there's really not much difference. Do you want to try?'

I finished my coffee. It was good. Maman says it makes me hyperactive. But Morgane drinks a lot of coffee, and *she* isn't hyperactive; in fact, she's the calmest person I know. And I love the way she talks to me — as if we were colleagues or something — and the way she always understands, even when I don't speak aloud.

'Well?' said Morgane.

'*I'm not supposed to,*' my shadow-voice said.

She raised an eyebrow. 'Why not?' she said.

'*Sometimes there are Accidents.*'

Morgane nodded and looked at me. She was smiling, but I knew that she was also serious. '*Life* is an accident,' she said. 'You can't live your life in fear. Besides, this isn't dangerous. It's only a little practice run.' She put down her empty coffee cup and handed me the tattoo machine. 'I'll show you how to use it,' she said. 'You need a steady hand, that's all; and to get a feel for the medium.'

The medium turned out to be a sheet of something like a soft white vinyl.

'It's supposed to feel like skin,' said Morgane. 'I haven't used it myself for a while, but I still like to keep some pieces around.'

I looked at the tattoo machine. It seemed like a

286

pretty simple design. I pressed the needle against the practice sheet, and made a little mark. *BAM!*

'Go ahead — don't be afraid. Try drawing something,' said Morgane.

And so I did — a monkey — taking it very slowly, keeping the needle angled just so against the piece of plastic. In the mirrors, Bam pulled a face and rolled around in the strawberry leaves.

'Let me see. Not bad,' said Morgane.

Some of the lines didn't come out quite clean.

'That's because you're not pressing down firmly enough. Try again, and be sure to keep the pressure even all the time.'

This time it was better, I thought. The line was strong, and dark, and true. The trick is keeping control of the line and going at a speed that seems much, much slower than normal. When I draw, I draw very fast, like feathers over the paper. This was like drawing in treacle. But then, your skin isn't really like paper. You're not just drawing *on* the skin: you're drawing *through*, to what's underneath.

Morgane looked at the picture. 'Good. Now look in the mirrors.'

You mean, like my reflection?

'*Reflection's* just another word for *thought.* And *drawing* just means *pulling through.* Just look, and think, and draw it through, like thread in the eye of a needle.'

I shrugged. *I'll try.*

In the mirrors, Bam chattered and danced.

'Ask your little friend to back off a bit.'

Morgane can see Bam as well as I can. One more reason to like her. I waved impatiently at

287

Bam, who stuck out his tongue, and retreated.

'Good. Now try it,' said Morgane. 'Don't think too hard. Just try to see.'

It felt odd at first, looking at the practice sheet upside-down and back-to-front. It made me feel a little sick, trying to work the perspective. My hands were everywhere, like birds pecking at canvas.

'Don't concentrate on those things,' she said. 'Don't even look at the picture. Just try to see.'

I drew a line. It looked like the bank of the river.

'That's good,' said Morgane. 'Keep going. Maybe think of someone you know. How about Monsieur le Curé?'

I smiled and drew a sad black crow, flying over the water. And then I shaded it, dark and slow, making coils of rising smoke come up from the water. I didn't look at the practice sheet, or at my hands, or even at the picture I was drawing. I just let it come, like something that had been submerged for a long, long time, rising out of the shadows and coming slowly to the surface.

When I looked up, she was smiling. Her eyes were very bright and blue.

How was that?

'Look for yourself.'

I looked at the sheet. It was better this time. The lines were steady, unbroken. But then it was a simple design, like something on a woodblock. I knew I could do better than that, but it was fine, for a first try.

I looked at the instruments by the chair. There were other attachments for the machine: special attachments for shading, different colours, stippling.

Those next, I said.

'Next time. You'd make a good tattooist, Rosette.'

That made me smile, and Bam did a dance through all the leaves and mirrors. Morgane watched and smiled too. 'I think he approves.'

I said: *I want to try on real skin.*

She smiled. 'You're keen. That's good, Rosette. But maybe some more using practice skins before you start on a human being. Besides, who would you start on?'

Me, of course, I said. *Who else?*

She laughed. 'First, more practice. Then we'll see.'

6

Thursday, March 30

I stayed until her first customer came. After that she sent me away. No-one's supposed to watch, she says. Otherwise, the magic won't work.

I'd missed lunch, but that was okay, because I'd already had four croissants, and lots of coffee with sugar and cream. I could have gone back to the *chocolaterie*, but I was still too excited about learning to be a tattooist to think about Easter chocolates, and so I put my practice skins into my pink satchel and went off to Narcisse's farm — well, I guess it's the Montour farm now — in the hope of finding Yannick. I wanted to show him my tattoo skins. I knew he'd like them as much as I do. And I still needed to explain about taking Narcisse's story. I hoped he wouldn't be upset. I hoped he would know I was making amends.

I took the path to my strawberry wood, keeping to the line of the hedge. The hedge belongs to the wood, which means that it belongs to me now. It's my responsibility. I picked up a couple of plastic bottles that had found their way into the ditch, and had a word with a couple of crows that were teasing a nesting blackbird. I didn't want to drive them away, but I want them to know *I'm* in charge now. No-one gets bullied when I'm charge. I take my responsibilities seriously.

I was checking the entrance-gap in the fence when I saw that the big gate was open. I have the key to the padlock, but I've never needed to use it. I prefer my old way in and out. I went to the gate, and looked at it, and saw that the padlock was broken. It had been cut, using something like a heavy-duty bolt-cutter, and now that I was listening, I could hear voices from inside the wood, coming from the strawberry clearing.

For a minute I didn't know what to do. I was too angry to think properly. Next to me, Bam made a horrible face, and screeched like a howler monkey. The murmur of voices stopped, as if someone had heard the scream, and then, a few seconds later, they started again: one low, the other high, like two owls calling each other.

I went through the open gate, picking up the broken padlock. I wondered who was there in my wood, and what I would do to make them leave. Yannick being there was one thing — he's my friend, after all — but that didn't mean it was okay for just anyone to come in uninvited. Besides, they had broken my padlock. That was proper trespass.

I can move pretty quietly, as long as Bam doesn't misbehave. This time he moved as quietly as a hunting tiger, eyes shining, teeth bared. I wondered what I'd do if it was thieves, or a gang of boys from Les Marauds, come into the woods to smoke and drink cheap wine from the bottle.

But it wasn't boys from Les Marauds. As I reached the strawberry clearing, I saw Madame

Montour and Yannick, not far from the old well. Yannick was carrying something that looked like a cordless vacuum cleaner. Madame Montour was wearing shiny black boots, and she made me think of Mimi's Tante Anna, with her boots and her silver cross. There was a spade sticking out of the ground next to her, and four piles of earth in the clearing that hadn't been there when I went before. It looked like a cartoon mole had been at work all over the clearing. And there was more: I could see some tools propped against my wishing-well — a hammer and a crowbar. And someone had forced off the metal grille that served as a cover to the well, and chipped off some of the stones at the lip, so that they looked like broken teeth —

I stood for a minute in silence, watching what they were doing. Yannick was passing the vacuum-cleaner thing slowly over the ground, and I realized what it was. It was a metal detector. As I kept on watching, it beeped, and Madame Montour brought over the spade and started to cut a hole in the turf —

I couldn't believe it. At first, I was too surprised even to be angry. But then the anger started to rise, and I knew I couldn't stop it. It felt like a gentle wind at first, maybe even a summer breeze, but it was warm and smelt of smoke, and I could tell it was dangerous. It's been a really long time since there was a dangerous kind of Accident, but I could tell that this time the wind could easily get away from me.

I said: '*BAM!*' as loud as I could, hoping to

bring it to heel again.

Yannick and his mother both turned. I saw Yannick's eyes open wide. The thing that looked like a vacuum cleaner fell from his hands onto the ground.

But Madame Montour wasn't surprised. Instead she made a cross tutting noise and said: 'For heaven's sake, Yannick! We haven't got all day.' She didn't look guilty, or even uncomfortable that she was trespassing, just annoyed to see me, as if I were the one who was in the wrong place.

I made a little warning sound, which was all I could manage without using bad words.

Yannick's mother gave a shrug. 'I know it's *technically* your land,' she said, 'but this is important. I mean, what good is sixteen hectares to you? Unless you mean to sell it, in which case it won't matter to you whether or not we had a peek.' She turned to Yannick. 'Don't just stand there! Pick up the metal detector. There's *something* in this clearing besides bottle tops and loose change, and we have a right to know what it is. We're his *family*, after all. He had no right to hide this from us.'

Yannick gave me a mournful look, as if to say *I'm sorry*. But I didn't have any time for that. I was feeling dizzy with anger. Little red motes danced in my eyes, like the sparks from a midsummer bonfire.

Oh, this is bad, I thought. This is bad. This is hurricane territory. I could see Bam in the oak trees, swinging madly from branch to branch, his fur like flames. It was coming.

I signed at Yannick. *You need to leave.*

'Oh, don't give me that,' said Madame Montour. 'I know you can speak when you want to. And I know what you stole from me, while I was talking to Reynaud.'

I said: '*Go away*,' in my shadow-voice. The leaves on the trees were starting to shake. The wind was growing stronger. It was only a little wind, but it was already getting cold, and I could feel the clouds drawing in, circling the clearing like water going down a drain.

Madame Montour didn't seem to notice. 'You broke into my house,' she said. 'I could report you to the police.'

I said: '*You stole Narcisse's file.*'

'I did no such thing,' said Madame Montour. 'Reynaud had no right to keep it from me. Narcisse was *my* father, not yours, and I have a right to know exactly what he left you.'

'*Please, Just go away*,' I said. '*Go away, or I'll tell Maman.*'

Yannick's mother scoffed. 'So we had a look in your private wood. It's hardly a crime to be curious. We won't be long — will we, Yannick? Just another hour or so — '

By then I was starting to feel panicky as well as furious. 'Go away. Both of you. Go away and don't come back.' And this time it *wasn't* a shadow-voice, but something that rattled the leaves like tin sheets — the voice that summons the Hurakan. Above us, the clouds were getting dark. I could feel them turning like wool onto a spindle. I knew I was causing an Accident, and yet I couldn't stop myself; at that moment I

294

didn't care if both of them were blown away.

This was *my* place, Narcisse's place. This was my private refuge. And Madame Montour had broken in, searched with a metal detector, jimmied the grate off the wishing-well, dug *holes* in the strawberry clearing. And worse, Yannick had *helped* her. I felt as I were made entirely from little red seeds, held together by heat and smoke, ready to disperse on the wind —

Yannick was looking nervous. 'Maman — ' Above him the trees were columns of smoke, their leaves like pieces of shining brass. Big drops of rain began to fall, hard and hot as pennies. 'Maman, I really think we should go.'

A branch creaked menacingly over their heads. Bam was bouncing on it, making screeching noises.

'We should *go*,' he said again, then, turning his small dark eyes to mine, said: 'It's not my fault. She made me — ' before turning and heading for home at a run, the metal detector under his arm.

'Yannick! You come back right now!' cried Madame Montour, but the rain was really coming down, though I was still dry, in the eye of it all. Above her, the tree branch creaked and swayed.

'Go now, before something bad happens,' I said, in the voice of the Hurakan, and Madame Montour gave me one of her looks and said:

'You're a dangerous lunatic. You keep away from me and my son.' Then she followed Yannick down the path, not running, not quite, but those little black heels tapped briskly against the baked-earth path, and the big branch came down just behind her — *BAM!* — in a crash of metal and firewood, and the little black heels tapped faster, until both she and Yannick were gone.

I sat down in the strawberries. My everything was shaking. But the flurry of wind was over now. The rain had stopped. The sky was blue. Even the leaves in the trees were still, though some of the new buds had been ripped off, and littered the ground like pale-green rags.

Bam was back on the ground again, his tail curled neatly around his feet. I made a reassuring noise, to tell him the danger was gone — for now. And then I took the spade that Yannick and his mother had left, and started to fill in the holes that they had dug in my clearing, and put back the torn-up strawberry plants, and stamp the loose clods back into place, so that when I'd finished, you could hardly tell where the holes had been, or that anything had changed at all.

But the wishing-well was a different matter. There was no putting back the grate, or mending the broken stones round the edge. Now you could look right into the dark, and see the circle of sky looking up, like the pupil of a great big eye, thinking its thoughts of vengeance.

7

Thursday, March 30

I barely slept at all last night. My dreams were worse than the torments of Hell. And so this morning I went to the church to pray by the feet of Saint Jérôme. It has been years since I visited the patron of our village church, but by now my need had grown so great that I was willing to consider even this solution.

A rather belated confession, *père*. I am not a great believer in the teachings of Saint Jérôme. *You* valued his work immensely, I know, and for many years I too was a disciple. But his vitriol against women, his disgust of their bodies and contempt for their minds, has latterly made me suspicious, both of his words, and even of his Vulgate translation of the Bible. I also remember how hard I prayed after the fire in Les Marauds, and how you quoted his words, *mon père:* *'Better to marry than to burn.'*

The way you said it seemed to suggest that the couple who died in the riverboat fire somehow *deserved* it for being unwed, for being asleep, perhaps for being drunk, and that I was merely the instrument of some greater intelligence. I prayed that if I were, *père*, the dreadful cup would fall from my hand; that God would return to His place in my heart; that I could be a boy again. But you made it clear that I owed God a

297

debt, a debt that could only be paid with my life, and so I exchanged my guilt for a life devoted to His service.

But you thought you could have more, says the voice that has been with me since I opened Narcisse's folder. I'd thought it was Narcisse's voice, but since then I have begun to wonder. Narcisse was a man of few words, and this voice is both fluent and articulate. *You thought you could hide behind God,* it says, as I kneel at the feet of the plaster saint. *But as time passed, you realized that God was only a shadow over the Sun, and that it was just a matter of time before you were standing in the light.*

I don't even know what that means, *père.* I used to think God *was* the light. I thought that if He could forgive me, then anything was possible.

Including your friendship with Joséphine? says the dry voice with a touch of humour. *You thought you could play the innocent in her eyes. What would she say if she knew what you did? How do you think she would look at you then?*

I know just how she would look, *mon père*: her eyes as flat as mirrors. And something hidden inside me would die, a thing that has been growing there for years, like a shoot from a hollow tree. I close my eyes and try to pray — *anything but that, please: better death and damnation than that* — but it seems absurd to expect Saint Jérôme to show me any sympathy. I am ablaze with misery: my head pounds like a hammer; my eyes and nostrils are filled with the scent of smoke.

And then I hear a sound, *père.* A soft sound of

footsteps behind me. I am no longer alone in the church; someone is standing by the door. A clammy sweat enfolds me. Have I inadvertently spoken aloud? Do I look guilty in any way? The footsteps come from the back of the church, from the region of the confessional. Perhaps someone has come to confess. I scramble to my feet; I turn, and as I do I see the door closing gently on a flash of scarlet —

Who was it? A woman, in red. But who? And why did she leave without a word?

The confessional screen has been left ajar. I move to close it, and on the bench I see a green folder, tied with a piece of bright pink clerical tape. For a moment I am unable to move. My prayer — my selfish, blasphemous prayer — has somehow, miraculously, been answered.

I pick up Narcisse's confession. My hands are trembling like aspen leaves. Is this an answer to a prayer, or a final verdict? In any case, I have to know. I cannot live without knowing for sure, even if it confirms the worst, even if it means my end. Head pounding, hands shaking, mouth dry as dust, I open the manuscript where I left off, and once again, I start to read.

8

Thursday, March 30

I spent the next three days awaiting the inevitable discovery of my crime. Raised in the eye of a Catholic storm, the whole of my upbringing based on the myths of guilt and divine justice, it simply never occurred to me that I might get away with murder.

And so, Reynaud, I waited for the eye of God to turn my way. I waited for the burden of guilt to settle onto my shoulders. But neither of those things happened. I slept dreamlessly in my little bed. I ate the eggs from Tante Anna's hens — the eggs that only she had been permitted to eat — and finished the bread that she had baked. After that, I started on one of the hams that she had put down for the winter, and fresh fruit from the orchard, and vegetables from the garden plot, and cheese from the cool pantry.

I covered Tante Anna and Mimi with two heavy rolls of tarpaulin, but even the cold of the cellar was not enough to completely halt the decay.

Once, the priest called round to ask why Tante Anna had not been to church, and I knew that this was the moment at which my crime would be discovered. But I told him she had a migraine (Tante Anna was prone to

300

migraines), and that she was lying down in her room, and to my surprise, the priest went away, and when he returned, my father was home, and his authority had been restored.

I'll admit, I hadn't given a great deal of thought to what I would tell my father. I had never been prone to wild tales, and besides, the bodies in the cellar told their own gruesome story. He arrived late one night — a Thursday, I think — with a satchel of papers and photographs, and found me asleep, with the lamp still on, and the door to my bedroom open. Tante Anna would never have allowed either of those things, of course: but Tante Anna's reign was over.

If my father had given me time to think, perhaps I might have tried to lie. As it was, he barely had time to ask why Mimi's bed was empty, and the whole sorry story came pouring out — the blue-and-white dish; the strawberries; the locked door and the Mason jar. It sounded absurd when I told him — 'Mimi's dead. I killed Tante Anna' — and yet my father stayed very calm, as calm as the plaster Jesus that hung above Tante Anna's bed, listening in a silence that might have seemed forbidding if he had not taken my hand in his, and held it very tightly.

'Show me,' he said. And so I led him to the cellar, and showed him the rolls of tarpaulin. He looked underneath, his face very still, and then he said: 'I need to think,' and sat down on the slab by Mimi, and lit a skinny cigarette, and smoked it very slowly, cupping it inside his

301

palm in the way that the War had taught him to.

I'd never thought of my father as any kind of thinker before. In fact, I'd often heard Tante Anna call him an oaf and an imbecile. But that quiet passivity had always hidden a deeper core. The doggedness that had sent him in search of his twin brother's widow now turned itself to my predicament, which quietly, and without reproach, had now become our predicament.

'I'm sorry,' I said, when my father looked up. It seemed the proper thing to say. And yet I still felt no remorse, nothing but grief for poor Mimi, and sorrow for my father, and fear that I would be guillotined, or maybe shot like a traitor.

He looked at me. 'Sorry won't fix this,' he said. 'We have to think of a story.'

And so I sat on the cellar floor, like a schoolchild waiting for storytime, and listened to my father as he lit another cigarette, and paced between the hanging hams and shelves of strawberry preserves, and sometimes spoke, as if to himself, in that soft, reflective voice. In all my life I'd never heard my father speak as fluently as he did to me that night. Now he did, as if the death of Tante Anna had released him from the spell that had kept him silent all his life.

'I used to stutter badly,' he said. 'I stuttered almost from infancy. Anna used to correct me. She used every possible method but one. Sympathy was beyond her. Patience was impossible.

Her methods were ridicule and blame, so that every time I opened my mouth seemed like a declaration of war. I used to imagine her as a hen, pecking at the words on my tongue. I often wondered if my brother had the same impediment. If he did, they cured him of it. But I had Tante Anna. I stayed mute.'

He smiled and blew smoke into the air. In the light of the oil lamp it gave him a golden nimbus, like a saint's.

'I had to go north, you understand,' he said. 'It was essential. Not because of the widow, but because the widow remembered him. My brother. The twin I never knew, taken away in infancy.' He crushed out the cigarette under his heel. 'Narcisse and Modeste. What old-fashioned names. Someone's idea of a joke, perhaps. I was named for the beautiful boy who pined for himself in the looking-glass. He was Modeste, the quiet one. The one who sacrificed himself. That made us opposites, he and I, reflections of each other.'

I listened in fascination to the tale my father told. I didn't understand it all, but I was old enough to know that this story wasn't meant for me. It was my father's confession, Reynaud — one that no priest would ever hear — and as he went on, I understood that it was also his way of saying goodbye.

Another confession. The father, this time. Must I also give *him* absolution? It seems there is absolution for all, except of course for me, *mon père* — I must carry my guilt forever. Does absolution even work once the person is dead? Or is it up to God after that? Wasn't it *always* up to God? And if so, how can anyone ever be sure if they have been forgiven? I turned the page, and read on:

'My brother's widow had been on the run since the very end of the War. Something to do with the Nazis. Black market trading; maybe more. Village talk. I didn't ask. I traced her to Nantes eventually. She was living in a boarding-house with her three children, taking in sewing work. She was ill. Her legs didn't work. She'd had to leave her farm behind. I introduced myself, but neither my name nor my brother's seemed to mean anything to her. I later found out that he had changed his Christian name when he was a child. I didn't blame him. I might even have done the same, if Tante Anna had allowed it.'

My father ground out his cigarette on the floor where my aunt's blood had spilled. 'Talking makes you thirsty,' he said, sounding surprised. 'I didn't know. I'm not used to talking so much.' He went to the shelves of bottles and jars; selected a bottle of cider. I still remember the sound of the popping cork, festive in that place of death. There was foam at the bottle's mouth; the ghosts of past summers gilded the air.

'I did what I could. I paid off her debts. I owed that to my brother. In return she gave me an old album of photographs. Pictures of my brother's life. His childhood. His adopted life. He looks very like me, but younger, now, brave

in his army uniform. He enlisted early on, and
died on his very first outing. He was thirty.
Older than most. Another year, and he might
have missed the draft altogether.'

My father took another drink straight from
the bottle, and belched. Then he looked back
at Tante Anna lying under her tarpaulin, and
gave a twisted smile, as if even now he was
aware of her silent disapproval. He raised the
bottle in what looked like an ironic toast, and
went on:

'Narcisse, you might have wondered why I
never joined the army. The fact is, I wanted to.
I tried, but my age was already against me.
Besides, the stammer I'd had since childhood
made it hard for me to communicate. I tried
several times — I even wrote a letter to the
Commissaire — but every time I presented
myself my voice refused to function.

Tante Anna was jubilant. 'I always knew you
were weak,' she said. 'You can't even die for
your country. Imagine being such a worthless
thing that even dying's beyond you.'

He managed her voice so convincingly that I
was almost alarmed, Reynaud. It was as if she
had crawled into his mouth, and was using his
voice as a medium.

'I'd been living with her for twenty-nine
years,' my father went on. 'God only knows
why she took me in, but she was never a
mother to me. In her eyes, I would never grow
up: I would always be that boy, the boy who'd
never quite been a son. But then I met Naomi.
I met your mother, and everything changed.'

305

Ah, that old tale again, *père*. Love is transformative. Love redeems. I've heard this story so many times, from hopeful women with broken teeth; from hopeful men in denial. *Love changes everything. Love made me a better person.* This is the dream they are sold, *mon père.* This is their hope of salvation. And yet, the world still turns, with all its burden of sin and misery. Love changed Narcisse's father, he says; and yet he stayed at Tante Anna's farm, to bear the brunt of her ridicule. Love crosses continents, and yet he never left his village until murder forced him to do so.

My father paused for a moment, and smiled. 'Until then I hadn't realized how much one person can change someone's life. But Naomi did. She did, somehow. Naomi saw me. Heard me, even when I was silent. She came to us just before the War, with a group of Polish refugees. She was nineteen. I was twenty-five. She went to live with a Jewish family down the Boulevard de Marauds. She came to the farm in summer, to help with the picking and harvesting. In those days the farm was very hard work. We had fields of maize and wheat, three orchards, a vineyard, a strawberry field, as well as potatoes, onions, cabbages, parsnips, beans and Jerusalem artichokes. We needed to bring in labour, and Naomi and the others were there. We got to be friends. She was funny and kind. One day I asked her to marry me.'

My father finished his cider. I could tell that in his mind, he was far away from the cellar;

the slab; the thing under the tarpaulin. His face was animated; his eyes were bright and shining with the past.

'Of course, Tante Anna protested. A Jewess! A foreigner! Was I mad? I must have been, because for once she did not change my decision. I married Naomi quietly, in a synagogue in Agen, and she came to live with us on the farm. Of course, Tante Anna hated her. But she needed me there, and besides, Naomi was at my side. I know you don't remember her much, Narcisse, but your mother was very strong. Stronger than anyone I've known; strong and sweet as peach liqueur.'

I tried to remember my mother, Reynaud. You read all kinds of stories in which children remember their mothers by a lullaby, a certain word, a certain scent or feeling. But all I could remember was the photograph by my father's bed: the single wedding photograph, taken by a man in Agen eighteen months before I was born. My father, clumsy in his suit, with a smile as broad as a tractor grille; my mother, small and unremarkable, her dark hair half hidden under a light-coloured hat. Mimi, with her small features, looked a little like her. It made me sad I couldn't remember anything about her, and so I simply said; 'I know,' and hoped he would be satisfied.

My father sat silent for a while next to the body of Mimi. His smile had faded, and I knew that he was back in the present day.

'Tante Anna delivered Mimi, you know,' he said, putting down the empty cider bottle. 'You

307

were born in hospital — delivered by a midwife — but by the time Mimi was born, Agen was occupied territory, and even in the villages, things had got too dangerous. Rather than risk attracting attention, Tante Anna delivered the baby herself — and your mother bled to death because we couldn't save her.'

'I didn't know,' I said.

He shrugged. 'You were too young to understand.'

And now, I thought, I'm a murderer. What a journey I had made, from motherless child to this. What a journey — well, Reynaud, you should know. You made it, too.

And here it comes. I knew it would, once the story neared its end. My hand began to tremble. My head was like a live grenade. This was what I'd been waiting for: the few incriminating lines that make the difference between Heaven and Hell. I wanted to read them, and yet my mind seemed incapable of reading the words. The looping script danced in front of my eyes like the patterns of Morgane's tapestry. In spite of the space around me I felt completely unable to move —

And then, once more, I heard the sound of the church door opening. Freed of my paralysis, I quickly closed the folder and hid it underneath my pew. Absurd, I know; and yet I could not rid myself of the idea that anyone who set eyes on it would instantly know its secrets. I turned, and saw Vianne Rocher standing by the confessional. She was wearing a bright red coat, and in the greenish light of the church, she looked peculiarly out of place. She never attends services. I have seen her here, in Saint Jerôme's, maybe twice in twenty years. I stood to greet her. She walked down the aisle and I saw that she was holding a silver box, tied with a long red ribbon.

'I hope I'm not disturbing you.'

'Of course not.' It was not quite a lie. I confess I felt a certain relief at this surprise interruption. My head was aching, my vision was blurred with the effort of reading the script, and I realized that I had left my spectacles at home.

'I thought you might like something sweet,' she said. 'You've been looking a little tired lately.'

I had to laugh. 'A little,' I said.

'Easter's a busy time for us all.'

If only she knew, I told myself. If only my business was like hers: my concerns as sweet and harmless as wondering how many chocolate hens or *cornets-surprise* to put on display.

'I've been trying something new. Something a little more potent than the usual truffles and *mendiants*.' She handed me the silver box. 'I thought you could try one out for me. Tell me if the recipe works.'

I took the box. It was very small and light, and yet I could smell what was inside — complex and heavy with spices.

'But it's Lent,' I said.

'Not for long,' said Vianne. 'Besides, this is research, not greed. I need to test your palate.'

I opened the box. A single chocolate, perfectly round, topped with a circle of scarlet glaze and polished to an impossible shine. How does she

309

get them so shiny? I thought. And why do I think it looks like an eye?

'Go on. Try it, Francis,' she said.

I hesitated. I could smell the rich dark scent — she uses only the finest beans, shipped from a plantation off the west coast of Africa — the chocolate infused with spices, the names of which sound like islands in a vanished archipelago. She tells me their names — *Tonka. Vanilla. Saffron. Clove. Green ginger. Cardamom. Pink peppercorn.* I have never travelled, *père*, and yet those names take me elsewhere, to undiscovered islands, where even the stars are different.

I pick up the chocolate. It is perfectly round, a marble between my fingers. I used to play with marbles once, long ago, when I was a boy. I used to put them to my eye and turn them round and round, to see the colours winding through the glass. I put the chocolate, whole, in my mouth. The red glaze tastes of strawberries. But the heart is dark and soft, and smells of autumn, ripe and sweet; of peaches fallen to the ground and apples baked in cinnamon. And as the taste of it fills my mouth and begins to deliver its subtleties, it tastes of oak and tamarind, metal and molasses. And once more I am by the Tannes, breathing the scent of smoke and soil, and I want to tell her everything, I want her to hear my confession —

'I found Narcisse's document at the new tattoo place,' she said. 'I thought maybe you should have it back. Don't worry, I haven't read it,' she added, as she saw me flinch. 'I only saw enough to know what it was.'

310

My mouth was on fire. '*She* had it?' I said.

'I suppose she must have taken it,' said Vianne Rocher. 'I don't know why.'

I reached for Narcisse's confession and held the folder tight to my chest. 'Did she read it?' I said.

Vianne shrugged. 'I wouldn't put it past her,' she said. 'Perhaps she's working for Michèle Montour.'

I looked at her.

'Oh yes,' she said. 'I know, about that. I guessed when you brought Yannick to my shop. Michèle has been making trouble since she first arrived in Lansquenet. And now it looks as if Morgane has been helping her all along. I knew there was a reason Michèle rented the shop out so quickly. They've been working together to undermine you — to undermine us both, Francis — '

My aching head was spinning now. The taste of chocolate was like being buried alive in sweetness.

'She has to go, Francis,' said Vianne. 'Whatever it takes, she has to go.'

I nodded. She was right, of course. I'd been so concerned about the Montours that I had forgotten about Morgane. Now I saw it clearly. It was she who had taken Narcisse's file — doubtless on Michèle's instructions. She must have been spying on me from the start, finding out my weaknesses. But she had made a big mistake in assuming I was helpless. I suddenly felt a tremendous surge of energy rush through me. My headache was gone. Instead I felt a new

311

confidence, a certainty that I had not felt since I started to read Narcisse's confession. What had I been so afraid of? I thought. Why had I been so slow to see that *I* was the one in authority?

'Absolutely right,' I said. 'I'll deal with the woman myself. *Today.*' I handed back the silver box which had contained the chocolate.

'Was it good?' said Vianne Rocher.

I nodded. 'Very good,' I said. 'I don't know what you put in there, but really, I feel like a new man.'

She smiled. 'I thought you would,' she said.

I followed her out into the light.

9

I hate Yannick. I hate him. *BAM!* Pretending to be my friend, and then sneaking behind my back like that. The rain had become just ordinary rain, whispering through the leaf canopy, and I was still there in the clearing, sitting on the rim of the well, face turned up towards the sky. I can scream here if I like. I can sing and dance and run. So I screamed in the voice of an angry bird, and then in the voice of a wildcat, until my throat was sore with it, and my eyes were red and burning.

How dare they? How dare they? It's *my* wood. *My* place. Mimi's place. Perhaps it's really because of Mimi that I was so angry with Yannick. This wood is all that's left of her. That's why Narcisse left it to me. He knew I'd look after it. After *her*. Because I'm like her. He knew that. I'm not like all the others.

I miss Pilou. I wish he was here. He'll come back from school at four tonight, and get off the bus, and see his friends, and not think about me. Maman says that boys can be stupid, sometimes. But Pilou was never stupid. We used to have such a good time playing with Vlad by the river. I don't think he's really changed. If we talked, I think I could make him understand.

But I *don't* talk. That's the problem. Only in my shadow-voice, and that can sometimes be

313

dangerous. I won't use my shadow-voice with Pilou. You never know what might happen. An Accident with Mme Montour, or with Yannick, that's one thing. But with Pilou, an Accident would be worse. Maybe much worse. But then, Pilou isn't like Yannick. If I told him what had happened, I know Pilou would understand.

I was thinking all this as I sat in my wood, listening to the ticking and tapping of the raindrops in the leaves. I was sheltered by the trees, and the rain made everything smell of earth, and green, and there were little insects that crawled up to the tips of the blades of grass and hung there like droplets, sensing the rain. I decided to wait for Pilou to come home, and then to tell him about Yannick, and Narcisse, and Mimi. He'd understand. I knew he would.

I waited until I heard the church clock tower strike four. Pilou's bus gets in at ten past. Then I ran up to the bus stop on the Boulevard des Marauds, and waited for Pilou to get out. At first I didn't see him at all. He was walking with a girl. I wouldn't have noticed her, either, except that she was wearing his jumper. It was a brown one I recognized, and it was much too big for her. I ran up to them both and hugged Pilou. The girl in the jumper gave me a look.

'Rosette!' He didn't sound very happy. 'What are you doing here?'

I had to laugh. *I live here, Pilou.* I jerked my chin at the girl. *Who's that?*

Pilou looked back at the girl, who was still looking at me. 'Isabelle, you go ahead,' he told her. 'Let me sort this, and I'll join you.'

314

Let me sort this. I didn't like the way he talked about me as if I were an unexpected chore. I made a mocking blackbird noise, but I wasn't feeling too chirpy.

The girl gave me another look. *BAM!* She was a kind of leggy girl, the kind of girl that looks good even when she's wearing an old brown jumper of Pilou's that's at least two sizes too big for her. I promised myself to draw her as soon as I got a chance — maybe as a gazelle, which rhymes with her name, and suits her, with her long eyelashes and skinny legs.

'Don't be long,' she said, and smiled at Pilou and gave him a little pat on the arm. It wasn't much, but I can tell a lot from what people say without words, and that little pat looked a lot like: *He's mine.*

I waited till she was out of the way. She walked as if she was wearing couture instead of a ratty brown jumper that Vlad sometimes uses to sleep on. I jerked my head at the place she had been.

Who's that? And why is she wearing your clothes?

He sighed. 'She was cold. That's Isabelle. My girlfriend.'

I laughed. It was laughable. Then I remembered Joséphine saying something about Pilou's girlfriend. At the time I hadn't believed it. Pilou doesn't *have* girlfriends. Pilou's like me: he thinks that that kind of thing is totally ridiculous.

Pilou made a face. 'Don't do that, Rosette. I'm serious. *We're* serious.'

I shrugged. *What does that even mean?*

'It means I grew up. It means that I might

315

want something more than this village for the rest of my life. Her parents have invited me to their place in New York. *New York*, Rosette! In my whole life I've never even been to Marseille. My mother's always saying how she wanted to see the world. But she never did. She just stayed here. To run her stupid little *café*.'

I wanted to say: *But there's Lansquenet. There's a whole world of things to discover right here. You haven't even seen my wood. There are little anemones growing under the oak trees. There are blackbirds, and in a month the floor will be thick with wild strawberries. They used to be cultivated, but mostly they've gone wild. That's fine, though. When they're wild, strawberries are sweeter. You could help me pick them some day. We could make wild strawberry jam. You could bring Vlad. He'd like that. Remember in the old days? When you and I and Vlad would play at building dams by the river? Those were good days. Those were the very best days. You can't believe that growing up, and seeing New York, and having a girlfriend, could ever compete with the days we used to have —* '

But all I said, in my shadow-voice, was: 'Vlad,' and it sounded strange and sad.

Pilou sighed. 'Oh, Rosette,' he said. 'I know you'll never understand. We'll always be friends, but Isabelle — ' His eyes light up when he speaks her name. He lowered his voice and looked around, but the bus had gone, and the other kids had all gone home. The street was bare. 'Don't tell anyone,' he said. 'We're in love. We even got matching tattoos.'

316

I looked up. *You did?*

He grinned at me. 'My mother will never notice,' he said. But *look —* '

And he opened his fingers and showed me, in the space between his index and middle fingers, a tiny, five-petaled flower, pale blue, with a speck of sun at its heart —

'It's a forget-me-not,' he said. 'She's got one too, in the same place. She hides hers under a friendship ring. That's why we got the tattoos. It means we're going to get married some day.'

I made a raucous jackdaw sound. But I didn't feel like laughing at all. Pilou, married? Pilou, gone away to some place like New York or Marseille?

But you're only sixteen, I said.

He shrugged. 'So what? My mother was married at eighteen.'

Yes, and look at what happened to her.

I don't think he understood what I'd said. Instead he looked at me in that way that somehow reminds me of Madame Clairmont — as if he wasn't nearly my age, but older, so much older.

I said: *Is that why you're avoiding me? Because of Isabelle?*

He shrugged. 'Rosette, I have to go,' he said. 'Isabelle's a bit jealous of you. She knows we're only friends, but she kind of wishes she and I had grown up together, like we did.'

Except I never grew up, I said, and made Bam turn a somersault. But either Pilou didn't see, or he was too busy thinking of her.

'Boys are so stupid,' I told him, using my

317

shadow-voice this time, but he was already starting to run, running after Isabelle like a stupid, eager dog trying to catch up with a deer. It would have made a good drawing, I thought. But somehow I didn't want to draw. Instead I thought of Vlad, and felt a kind of little hole in my heart, as if something had punctured there, and air was suddenly rushing through.

'*Boys are so stupid*,' I said again, even though there was no-one to hear, and I felt the wind stir, just like a dog sitting up to attention, and knew that I could call it, perhaps even make it take Isabelle —

But that wouldn't change anything. Pilou said it himself. He grew up. If not Isabelle, then someone else. Some other girl. People move on. They make other friends. They grow. They change. They go away.

But not me, I thought. I don't change. I'm not like all the others. I'm the Snow Child, who isn't allowed to play with her friends in the sun. Because if I do, then one day they'll find my clothes abandoned on the ground, and nothing left of me at all, except for a puddle of water . . .

10

I waited until dark, *mon père*. I thought it might give me a better chance of finding the Dubois woman alone. Not that she has opening hours, so even then I could not be sure if she would have a customer. As it happened, she did not: the door was ajar, and I came in, having knocked and received no reply.

The tattoo parlour was empty. A faint thread of incense in the air; a scent of frangipani. I personally do not enjoy the scent of incense. Even church incense seems too rich, too potent to be holy. When I was a boy, I would admire the great silver censer in the church, and breathe in the smoke, and imagine myself swinging it over the heads of the people. I liked the frankincense in those days: it made my head spin rather pleasantly. Later, I realized that I had been slightly intoxicated. Power intoxicates, of course. You know that already.

'Hello?' I said. 'Madame Dubois?'

I sensed a movement beside me. Turning, I thought I saw Roux, reflected in the opposite wall. That was a surprise — I'd thought the tattoo shop empty, and besides, I'd heard he was leaving. And yet here he was, watching me from beneath his curtain of hair. I blinked, and there was no-one. More of Morgane's illusions. I know

319

them now, I told myself. They have no power over me. Turning back, I saw that the mirror was now nothing more than birds and leaves, and myself, like a child in a forest, and the slowly rotating fan of the smoke.

'Madame Dubois?' I was aware that my voice was sharper than I'd intended. But seeing Roux in the mirror like that had made me lose my composure. I sounded rattled, lost to myself, and just at that moment Morgane came in from the room at the back of the shop, looking cool and elegant in a long dress of heavy dark silk, holding a tumbler in one hand.

'It's *Mademoiselle* Dubois,' she said. 'But maybe you should call me Morgane.'

I nodded, knowing I never would. Formality comes with the *soutane*; and like the *soutane*, it serves as defence.

'Perhaps you'd like a drink,' she said. 'At this time in the evening, I like to change from green tea to something a little more potent.'

I shook my head. 'No, thank you.'

She smiled. 'Then I hope you don't mind if I do. This is a margarita. It's the one thing I can make in the kitchen.' She sipped her drink, looking both young and old with her long pale hair and her many tattoos. Is her hair blonde, or silver-grey? Even now, it's hard to tell. And her dress? Is it blue, or purple, or green? Either way, it is reflective, shining like oil on water. She might be Vianne's age, or her mother's: she moves from one to the other as I see her from different angles. Of course, those mirrors do not help: it's hard to see things as they are.

I indicated Narcisse's file, which I was carrying under my arm. 'I hear you were in possession of this,' I said. 'Madame Dubois, would you care to explain?'

She looked at the file. She seemed unsurprised. That was disappointing; I'd hoped for some kind of sign, however small, that I'd shaken her composure. But she was flawless, unshakeable: standing there in her watered silk like a figure from a Victorian painting. Her prosthetic feet were invisible under the floor-length fabric, and she moved so languidly that I could almost have believed that she was floating over the ground like a ghost, or a will-o'-the-wisp. And yet there is nothing insubstantial about her. If anything, she is heavier than average. She stands very straight, very sure of herself And it is I who feel weak in her presence, as if the smallest wind could blow me away.

'Are you sure you don't want a drink?'

'Maybe just a small one,' I say.

She smiled and stepped behind the curtain, returning almost straightaway with an ice-filled jug and a glass. 'The folder doesn't matter,' she said. Her tone made it into a statement. 'There's something else you need. I can tell.'

I shook my head and sipped my drink. The taste of lime was fresh and strong, masking the strength of the alcohol. I wondered if I hadn't made a mistake in challenging her openly. But it was too late to back away now. A warmth had begun to radiate from the pit of my stomach; a warmth that fanned out fingers of heat across my temples and my neck.

'Did you take the folder?' I said.

She smiled. 'Not exactly. It came to me. I thought maybe you'd want it back.'

'Did you read it?'

She sipped her drink. 'Does that matter?'

The fingers of heat had reached my face. 'Did you read it?' I said again.

'No, I didn't read it, Francis. But I can tell it's important to you.'

'A man's last words are sacrosanct,' I said. 'It was Narcisse's legacy.'

She gave her little half-smile again, as if contemplating mysteries. 'Narcisse. I hear so much about him,' she said. 'If I believed in ghosts, I might be tempted to think that he was still here, watching us.'

I made a dismissive sound, to imply that I was above superstition. Of course, it could be argued that if Catholics believe in the *Holy* Ghost, that tacitly implies a belief in the unholy kind. Morgane went on:

'Did you know that people used to believe that the soul of a dead person could be trapped in a mirror? That's why so many old people here still drape the mirrors after a death, and stop the clocks, to give the deceased time to reach Heaven before the Devil finds out they're dead.'

I looked over her shoulder, left bare to expose a wreath of strawberry-leaves. In the mirrors, I saw myself, caught in a thicket of blue leaves and brown. The mirrors are positioned to project that tapestry everywhere: the effect is like a tower of cards, endlessly reflecting those wholly unnatural flowers and birds, that wholly impossible foliage.

Suddenly I realized how much I hated *The Strawberry Thief*: its regimented patterns, its drab and relentless colours.

'My God, how can you bear it?' I said.

'We all see what we need to see. Some see freedom; others, constraint. Some see their loved ones; others, their death.'

Death. Once more I thought I smelt smoke; heard the sound of voices far across the burning river. I wondered: if I stay here, would I see Pierrot and Choupette, hand-in-hand, like the Babes in the Wood, looking out from the undergrowth?

'What about Roux? What did he see?'

'I don't discuss my clients.'

'No. Of course not.' Once more I smelt smoke; watery and bitter. 'He doesn't like me much,' I said. 'I don't think he really likes anyone here, except for Vianne, and Joséphine. Maybe that's why he's been so difficult about holding the land in trust for Rosette. Maybe he feels as if the trust is somehow forcing him to stay here. Although you'd think a man like that would be grateful for the chance to be part of a community like ours.'

Morgane poured another drink. 'He already has a community.'

'The river-rats?' I had to laugh. 'No-one *chooses* that lifestyle. Moving from village to village, picking fruit, doing odd jobs? It's all right when you're in your twenties, perhaps, but the man has a daughter who needs him. He needs to grow up and take responsibility instead of playing pirates on the river.'

Morgane smiled. 'Perhaps,' she said. 'But

323

everyone has a story.' She sipped her drink and turned away to look into the mirrors. 'Years ago, in Lansquenet, when you were still a boy, Francis, there was a terrible fire on the Tannes. It was summer, the river was low, the boats packed together like bales of hay. And like bales of hay, they burned, one after the other. There could have been more casualties. As it was, two people died. A couple, asleep on their houseboat. Roux was six years old at the time. He'd crept outside to sleep on the bank, disobeying his parents. And later, after they were dead, he blamed himself for not being there.' She smiled again. 'Of course, that's absurd. You and I know who's really to blame.'

I put down my glass, very slowly. My head was spinning like the stars. I felt like a moth impaled on a collector's needle. I said in a shaky voice: 'I thought you didn't discuss your clients.'

'I wasn't discussing *him*,' she said. 'One more drink, Francis, for the road?'

I nodded. My mind was in pieces. Was *this* why I had seen him today? Was this why he hated me? Could Roux be the child of Pierrot and Choupette, come back to avenge them? And now the memory of the fire returns to me like a hurricane. The scent of smoke across the Tannes; the fat dank reek of river mud; the desperate cries of the child on the bank. No wonder he hates me. Even if he does *not* know, instinct must have alerted him. But what can I do? The past is dead. I am a different person. Every cell in my body has changed — except for the knowledge I carry within, the cancer that still keeps growing.

We all see what we need to see. Some see freedom; others, constraint. Some see their loved ones; others, their death.

Is *this* what she sees in me? Is this what Roux sees in me? And if so, how can I possibly hope to escape the Eye of God?

I moved to the chair at the back of the room. I heard the chime of ice cubes. In the mirrors, a thousand deep, a dozen different versions of me converged slowly into one. I rolled up my sleeve and laid my head back onto the leather headrest.

'Are you sure you want this?' she said.

I nodded. 'Will it hurt?'

She smiled. 'It may hurt a little,' she said. 'But then, Francis, doesn't everything?'

11

First, the circle in the sand, ringed with coloured candles. Red for desire; blue for calm; green for growth; pink for love. And black, for midnight workings, for secrets unspoken, tales untold.

I saw him leave after midnight. Walking very slowly, his livid colours distressing the air. Somehow, she has broken Reynaud. In spite of his courage, in spite of his rage, in spite of the power I gave him. All I have left to fight her now is the magic of the last resort, the magic I swore I would never deploy, the magic that calls the *Hurakan*.

My mother always told me that there was magic in stories. Stories tell us who we are, and who we were, and hope to be. Stories give a shape to our lives, an underlying narrative. And sometimes, stories allow us to tell those things that cannot be spoken — secrets even to ourselves — outside the conventions of fairytale.

I know a story about a child whose voice could summon the Hurakan. Her mother loved her very much, but the girl was very wild, and the mother was afraid that one day the wind would hear her call, and take her away. And so, she cast a magic spell, with sand and smoke and starlight. She bound it with the cry of a cat that crossed her path in the falling snow, and cast it over the

326

sleeping child, so that when she awoke, her voice was gone, leaving only the cry of the cat in its place.

Robbed of her voice, the daughter could not be like other children. She could not call the wind, nor could she ever grow like other girls. And at this the mother was glad, because it meant her daughter would stay by her side always and forever. But she never told anyone how the child had lost her voice. She listened to the cry of the cat, and knew that the wind had passed them by.

Of course it wasn't *quite* like that. My mother's paraphernalia — the sand, the cards, the candles — were only there for colour and show; theatrical props, designed to make a tale into a ritual. The *real* magic was something else; something less conspicuous. Something driven by despair. Something driven by desire.

A cat crossed your path in the snow, and mewed. The Hurakan was blowing.

Understand that I was afraid. I've been afraid since Anouk was born. To be a mother is to know love and loss in equal parts. And Anouk was already growing so fast; reaching out towards the world with such a voracious appetite. I'd always known I would lose her one day: the question was never *whether* I would, but rather to *whom* I would lose her. To Zozie, of the lollipop shoes? Or to Jean-Loup Rimbault?

But Rosette — Rosette might be different. I hoped that I could keep her. And so I cast the circle in sand, and summoned the *Hurakan* to my will —

Across the square, a single pane reflects the light in my window. Morgane, too, is awake tonight. Maybe she senses activity. Maybe she too has a circle in sand, and candles to light against me.

The sand is from a beach, far away, where Mother and I once spent the night. Spread it onto the floorboards into a mystic spiral. Ehecatl, the god of wind, was represented by a spiral: the Aztecs used a conch shell, sliced to reveal the spiral inside, as part of his secret rituals.

Vl'à l'bon vent, v'là l'joli vent —

Of course I mean no harm to her. All I want is for her to leave. Red for desire; blue for calm; green for growth; pink for love. Tomorrow — or rather, *today*, I suppose — Anouk will come, without Jean-Loup. This makes me happy — not that I dislike Jean-Loup, but I prefer to see Anouk without him. Anouk is different when he is around. She laughs; she smiles in a different way. His presence alters the way she moves, makes her oddly self-conscious. And there is always concern there; concern because Jean-Loup was ill for such a great part of his childhood; concern because to Jean-Loup Rimbault, even a cold may be dangerous, and the smallest infection could bring about another stay in hospital.

Why is she coming without him now? She said she had news. Have they broken up? The thought of it fills me with absurd hope, like wine into a broken glass. Outside, the voice of the wind becomes the growl of a sleeping tiger.

328

Vl'à l'bon vent, v'là l'joli vent —
Vl'à l'bon vent, ma mie m'appelle —
Red for desire; blue for calm. *A cat crossed your path in the snow, and mewed.* In the window across the square, I see a glimpse of shadow. Is Morgane looking out at me? Perhaps she is. There's no way to tell. I can hear the sound of the leaves in the almond tree in the square. The wind is rising. The night is ablaze. Is she aware of my presence now?

Find me. Feel me. Follow me.

I don't think so. A tremor runs through the dark electric air. A scent of bitter chocolate mixed with ozone accompanies it. I can feel the clouds gathering now; stitched through with incipient lightning. Whatever she has, what glamours, what tricks, *this* will overwhelm them. This is a magic that *always* works — although it must be paid for.

The light across the square goes out. It is nearly three in the morning. The candles are starting to gutter: the one that goes out first will be the one that determines the outcome. Red for desire. Blue for calm. Green for growth. Pink for love. And black — black as the eye of the storm, the centre of the spiral. The black candle gutters: the *Hurakan* stirs.

Vl'à l'bon vent, v'là l'joli vent —
Find me. Feel me. Follow me.

12

Friday, March 31

I have been awake all night. Sleep, *mon père*, is impossible. My pounding heart refuses to return to any normal rhythm. My arm feels grazed and painful beneath its protective film of plastic. Underneath, the skin looks inflamed, a shapeless blur of colours. What is it meant to be, *mon père?* A lightning-bolt? A pillar of smoke? The Eye of God?

'Be patient,' she says. 'Sometimes the skin takes a day or two to heal.'

What have I done? What have I done? A madness must have possessed me. I remember being in the tattoo shop, drinking cocktails with Morgane. I remember sitting in the chair and feeling the needles on my skin. I cannot blame this on drunkenness. In fact, I feel perfectly sober. And yet I cannot sleep, but lie restless as the wind outside rises from an ominous hum to the howl of an angry woman, screaming through the tattered clouds.

Now it is almost dawn, and I know that sleep is no longer an option. And so instead I try to read to the end of Narcisse's manuscript. But now that the suspense is gone — now Morgane knows my secret — I have no urge to continue. Whatever happens, I must confess. I cannot let an innocent man live with a guilt that belongs to me. And once I have confessed to Roux, all eyes will be upon me. And so I sit and wait for dawn, and feel the scorched mark on my arm; the symbol beneath the plastic patch, glimpsed only through the mirrors.

'How do you know what people want?' I ask her, eyes closed, in the chair.

'I don't give my customers what they *want*,' replies Morgane, and I can tell from the tone of her voice that she is smiling. 'I only give them what they *need*.' And then I feel the needle graze its slow, reflective path through my skin, and I surrender myself to the sound of the chirping of metal songbirds.

'I know a story,' she tells me, 'about a boy who had a secret. The secret was so heavy that the boy could barely carry it. And even as he grew, so did the terrible weight he was carrying, until at last it became so great that he was sure the rest of the world must see it. And so the man the boy had become grew up crooked and solitary. He pushed away his friends, in the fear that they might learn his secret. And as time passed, the secret grew from heavy to unbearable, and still the man chose to carry it, because it was all he had ever known.'

Face it, *père*, she had me there. No-one else has ever come close. I keep my eyes shut, and pretend to sleep, and follow the path of the needle over my arm, hoping to be able to tell what kind of design she has chosen.

'This man,' she goes on,' was no plaster saint. Neither was he all bad. But he was a creature of absolutes, and he was unable to compromise. As

331

long as he carried the secret, he thought, it would never be part of him, and no-one else would judge him for the terrible thing the boy had done.'

I open my eyes for a moment. I see myself, on the ceiling, with Morgane, in the mirror, surrounded by leaves, and speckled birds, and strawberries.

'And then one day the man met a witch,' says Morgane in her smiling voice. 'The witch told the man that if he paid her in gold, she would change his terrible secret into a fruit, and that if he ate it, he would be free of his lifelong burden. And so the man paid the witch in gold, and ate the fruit she gave him. It tasted sour, and the man was suddenly afraid that it might have been poison. All night he was feverish; tossing and turning in his bed; and all night he went over the witch's words, which now in his delirium, seemed increasingly sinister.

'Well, if I am to die,' said the man, 'at least I can do so honestly.' And he flung open his windows and doors, and from his bed of fever and pain he cried out his secret to the wind. And the sly wind carried it far and wide, so that everyone heard it. Some were shocked. Some, angry. But most of the people who heard it felt pity for the man who had spent his life alone with his secret. And they came to his bedside, one by one, bringing flowers, and food, and forgiveness.

'The dying man closed his eyes, and slept. And when he awoke, his fever was gone, and so had his terrible burden. All that remained of his

332

secret was a handful of seeds from the magical fruit. And so he planted the seeds, and watched to see what kind of a tree would grow. But when it did, he found that it was only an ordinary apple tree, with fruit that was hard, and a little sour, and only good for birds to eat. And the man began to realize that maybe — just maybe — the woman he'd *thought* was a witch was merely a traveller passing through, with a handful of fruit to sell, and an original sales approach.'

What does that story even mean? Why did I not ask Morgane? Perhaps I was a little drunk last night, though this morning I remember it perfectly. My skin under the plastic sheet burns and itches like nettle rash. I look at the clock. Six thirty-five. I make a fresh pot of coffee. I drink far too much coffee, *père*: it interferes with my sleep. And yet I find it clears my head, at least as a temporary measure.

Another hour or so and it will be time to prepare for this morning's Mass. I must be sober for that, *père*. Perhaps a walk, to clear my head. I choose the riverside path. It smells of rain and wild garlic. It must have been a big storm last night; the trees have been stripped of their blossom. It is still too early for smoke from the chimneys of the riverboats. I do not see Roux's boat among the dozen or so that are moored by the bridge. I wonder if he has already moved on — and I am slightly alarmed by the surge of helpless relief that comes with the thought.

Then I see it, moored downstream. A shimmer of smoke from the chimney tells me that the man

333

is awake. But I still have a Mass to perform, confessions to take, a flock to tend. I tell myself that I will speak to him this afternoon. I cannot help but look at this day as if it were my last day on earth — tomorrow, everything will change.

Reaching the Place Saint Jérôme, I see, without surprise, that the tattoo shop is closed. The shutters are drawn; even the sign has been taken down from over the door. Of course, her customers do not come early in the morning. Like myself, they prefer to come to her under cover of darkness. Perhaps I will see her after Mass — if only to demand the meaning of that story. But now I see a piece of paper taped to the door: a single sheet of stiff white paper, marked with two stark words in black —

TO LET.

The Piper

1

Friday, March 31

I awoke to the sound of church bells, and the morning light casting its jigsaw-puzzle of leaves over the whitewashed bedroom wall. The sky was blue after the rain; a scent of damp soil and greenery. Rosette was already gone, leaving a drawing of a bird in flight tacked to the open kitchen door and an apple core on the table. So, she has had breakfast, at least. One less thing to worry about.

I opened the shop, knowing that there was little chance of business. Few people choose to buy sweets during Mass. Afterwards, depending on the content of the sermon, some may affect to wander my way, and come in as if by accident. Meanwhile, I made preparations for Anouk's arrival. I always keep her room ready, in case she should drop by unannounced, but today I also changed the sheets to match the violets by the bed, and placed her old stuffed rabbit on the pillow next to her nightdress, although she has long since outgrown him, and will smile at my sentimentality.

I leave the window open awhile. The air is sweet with birdsong. I am already planning what to make for dinner when she arrives — late and tired, without Jean-Loup, and bearing news. What kind of news? Is she coming home to stay?

337

Looking out across the square, the tattoo shop is silent. No sign of movement from within: no sign of a customer. I force myself to ignore it, though I am longing to look through the blinds. Everything feels clean today, clean and fresh after the rain, and the only sign of last night's storm is the blossom that lines the cobblestones, lying thick as snow on the ground.

There is a note pinned to the door. I cannot read it from where I am. The bells ring for Mass, and now the congregation drifts away, blowing like fallen leaves across the square, some heading for the churchyard, some for the Poitou bakery. Someone stops by the handwritten sign, someone wearing a tartan coat. It's Joséphine. I know her walk. But I haven't seen that coat for a while, and she doesn't normally go to church.

She stops to read the sign on the door. Turns to call someone over. It's one of her waitresses from the café, Marie-Ange Lucas. I know her well. Coffee creams are her favourites, and she eats them with a sullen look, as if she were hoping they were something else. Marie-Ange, too, has her back to me now, but I did catch a glimpse of her profile. She looks almost excited, her pale hands fluttering like birds. And now Joline Drou steps over, making it a threesome. Joséphine tries to peer between the shutters at the window. Joline does the same; shielding her eyes to try to see beyond the reflections in the glass.

Something must have happened, then. She turns once more to the other two. Joline's quarrel with Caro Clairmont must still be ongoing: never would she otherwise deign to talk to Joséphine.

Try me. Taste me. Test me.

I send a tiny suggestion their way; accompanied by the mingled scents of hot sugar, nutmeg, vanilla and cream, with the dark rasp of the Criollo bean underpinning everything, like a handful of minor chords under a lighter melody.

Try me. Taste me.

And of course they come to me, as they always come to me. Joséphine comes first, then Joline, then Marie-Ange with her sullen mouth and her bright and envious eyes.

'Morgane's gone!' said Joséphine. 'I looked through the blinds, there's nothing there!'

Joline nodded. 'The sign says TO LET. She must have left during the night. How did she *do* that? The furnishings — all those mirrors, her gear — how did she move it all so fast?'

'And *why* would she move?' said Marie-Ange. 'I was going to get a tattoo. I was thinking, a pair of angel wings? Or maybe a star. Do you think she's really gone?'

I hid a smile. 'Who knows?' I said. 'Perhaps we'll learn more later.'

They were not the only ones to notice Morgane's disappearance. Over a dozen customers commented on the sign on the door — including Guillaume Duplessis, who uses his daily walk to collect all kinds of information.

'Madame Rocher, it's a mystery.' After all these years, he still prefers to call me *Madame Rocher*. 'In with the wind, out with the wind, she almost reminds me of someone else, who blew in

339

on the wind of the carnival.'

I shrugged. 'Do you think? We're nothing alike.'

'Oh, I don't know, Madame Rocher. I spoke to her at length, you know. I found her very approachable. We spoke about old Charly, and Patch, and how hard it is to let a friend go.'

Guillaume has been without his dog for a little over three months. Several people have offered to find him another dog, but he says that at his age, he's too old to accept the responsibility.

'What would happen when I died?' he says with his customary earnestness. 'How could I be sure the dog was cared for properly when I was gone? And besides, dogs are faithful. He'd miss me. He'd pine.'

How like Guillaume, I thought, to put the feelings of an imaginary dog before his own need and loneliness.

'But Morgane Dubois showed me how I could keep them with me always,' he said. 'I was very nervous at first. But when I saw the work she'd done for other people, I knew I could trust her judgement.'

'Not you too?' I said, amazed.

'You think I'm too old for that kind of thing. I'll admit, I thought that too. But then I thought, if not now, when?' And he rolled up the sleeve of his shirt to reveal a linear design of two dogs in a basket. It was a simple, striking design, and yet somehow the artist had managed to capture the spirit of both dogs: the boisterousness of the Jack Russell; the rather mournful expression of his elderly predecessor. And there was something in the style that somehow I thought I recognized —

I thought back to the bookmark; the one with the yellow monkey. That tattoo is not Morgane's usual style. It has none of the stifling intricacy of Morgane's other designs. Has Rosette shared her art with Morgane? It seems only too likely. And if so, what else has she shared with her?

2

Friday, March 31

Last night I dreamed about Morgane. Or maybe it was Maman. In my dream I couldn't tell the difference. Maman-Morgane was wearing red shoes, and had regular feet, like everyone else.

She said: 'Rosette, I'm moving on. My time here is nearly over. You can follow me if you like, but there's something you'll have to do before I can take you with me.'

I looked at her. *'What do I have to do?'*

Maman-Morgane said: 'Cut off your feet. Use this. It hardly hurts at all.' And she handed me her tattoo pen. I saw that I was already barefoot. And with the pen, I drew a dotted line around my ankles and wrote the words: CUT HERE on my calf.

'See?' said Morgane. 'Now you're free.'

'Free?' I said. 'But I wanted to be just like all the others.' And in my dream I realized that I wasn't using my shadow-voice, but a voice I'd never heard before. And it sounded so strange and so wonderful that I stopped talking and just looked at her.

'That's your *real* voice,' said Morgane. 'The one you lost when you were born. But now you can have it back — as long as you leave your feet behind.'

'But how will I walk without any feet?'

342

She laughed, and said: 'You won't need to. You'll *fly*.'

Then I awoke, and it was still dark, and the wind was making a keening sound. And above it, I could hear Maman singing softly in her room:

Vl'à l'bon vent, v'là l'joli vent —

Vl'à l'bon vent, ma mie m'appelle —

It's an old song she used to sing to me when I was a baby. She sang it to Anouk as well; but I know that with me it was different. She used it to sing us both to sleep, but with me, it was more than a lullaby. It was a story, a magic spell — sometimes even a warning.

It starts with the wind, calling to a lady, thinking about her love. And in the song she calls the wind *the good wind, the pretty wind*, because she doesn't want to go, because she has to flatter the wind to keep it under her control. And her love is calling her, and the wind is calling her too, and you know that the wind is stronger than love; stronger, maybe, than anything.

That's just the chorus. There are verses, too: verses that tell the story, but it's not a very nice story at all, even though it's a lullaby. It's about a girl who keeps three ducks in a little pond by her house. Two are black and one is white. The King's son, out hunting, aims at a black duck, but shoots the white one by mistake, and as it dies gold falls from its beak, and diamonds from its eyes. Its white feathers blow away on the wind, and three mysterious ladies gather them all to make a bed for the girl and her mother to sleep in forever.

I never liked those verses much. I was sad for the poor white duck, in spite of the gold and diamonds. And the ladies sounded too much like the Kindly Ones, or the Norns, or the Fates, and the feather bed sounded nice at first, but sleeping forever is scary. Sleeping forever sounds like death, or like Sleeping Beauty's curse. But would the King's son awaken me? Or would I sleep forever?

Maman used to tell me that it was a song about sacrifice, and how when you give up something you love, you can get something even better. But I don't think the girl wanted diamonds. All she wanted was for her ducks to be safe and happy.

'*But ducks sometimes fly away*,' Maman said, and that's when I remembered my dream, and wondered why she was singing that song, all alone in her bedroom.

And so, very quietly, I climbed out of bed and went to the door. My bedroom is up a little ladder, like a crow's-nest on a boat, and the ladder sometimes creaks a bit, but I'm very good at being quiet. I climbed down very slowly, making sure to keep my weight steady as I moved from rung to rung, and I hardly made any noise.

Maman was still singing, in that very soft voice, like a shadow-voice, that she only uses when she sings that song. Her bedroom door was open a crack. She never closes it all the way. I could see a bar of yellow light reaching across the landing. I put my eye to the crack, and saw some candles burning, and a spiral of sand on the boards, all set out in a circle —

I know what that means. I don't need the sound of the wind in the trees to tell me. The spiral is the symbol of Ehecatl, the wind god. Is she trying to cause an Accident? Perhaps she felt the *Hurakan*, and she's trying to flatter it back to sleep. Or perhaps she wants to call it herself — but who can she be calling it *for*?

I watched Maman for a long time, but all she did was sit and sing. Not just the chorus, but all the verses too, over and over and over again. Through the crack in the door I could smell candle-wax and incense. Something rich and creamy, like pink cedar or white sandalwood. It made me feel sleepy. I lay on the floor, and listened to the rising wind and the sound of Maman singing.

Outside, the wind was singing too. I could hear it in the wires. Its voice was soft but powerful, purring like a tiger. And then I must have fallen asleep, because I had another dream, this time about the ducks on the pond, and the King's son, and the feather bed, and the three ladies gathering duck down.

'Must we sleep forever?' I said in my new, non-shadow voice.

Maman looked up from her circle and said in a voice that reminded me of Morgane:

'*Sometimes, children fly away. We do what we can to keep them.*'

I woke again to find myself back in my own bed, which isn't made of feathers at all, but of something sensible, with springs, and the crows were shouting; *War! War!* and chasing each other across the sky.

Maman always tells me that dreams are lessons in disguise. I got up very quietly and picked up my pink satchel. It was pretty early, and Maman was still sleeping. I didn't want to tell her my dream, because then she'd know I spied on her. I thought perhaps I could ask Morgane what she thought my dream meant. Morgane knows a lot about dreams. She says that stories, and pictures, and dreams are all just part of a river that goes through every world there is, and that everyone dips in from time to time.

But when I went to the tattoo shop, it was shut, and the blinds were drawn, and there was a TO LET sign on the door.

TO LET? Has she left without me? And why? *Is this why Maman called the wind?*

I pressed my face against the glass to look through the slats in the blinds. The room was bare. No *Strawberry Thief*; no mirrors; no chairs. Only some sheets of newspaper on the bare floorboards, and something in the corner —

I couldn't quite see what it was because of reflections in the glass. But it looked like a box, a shoebox perhaps, left behind in the shadows. I tried to look closer, but there was no way to escape those reflections. And then I thought I saw something move, something inside the darkened room, and I felt a sudden leap of hope. Was she still there? Was she hiding from me?

I ran back to the door and knocked. I knocked as hard as I could, but no-one came to answer. So then I tried the door again, and whispered in my shadow-voice:

'*Open up. I want to come in.*'

346

And at that the door swung open, even though I knew it was locked, and there came the ringing of a bell that wasn't hanging there any more . . .

3

Friday, March 31

Knowledge is a burden, Reynaud. It weighs as heavily as guilt. I suppose you must know that already, taking confessions as you do; absolving others of their sin while holding yours as close as a child. And like a child it grows, just as mine grew to fill my entire life. I never told anyone, you know. Not my wife, nor my family. My wife Eloise was a good soul, but she wouldn't have understood. As for Michèle and her husband — well. Need I say more? Of course it's my fault. I let poor Eloise spoil her. Michèle was all the love she had, and what should have helped her blossom and thrive made her mean and stunted instead. I blame myself. I was distant. I knew it even then, and yet we cannot stop ourselves from repeating the patterns of childhood. A strawberry, planted in different soil, will still grow into a strawberry. We may wish for peaches, or gages, or pears. But our nature is predetermined. That's why I wrote this for you, Reynaud. Because, in spite of our differences, we have at least this much in common. Both of us are damaged. But you at least will never have children.

When my father had finished his tale, we carried Tante Anna's body outside. We used the wheelbarrow to take her down the path to

348

the copse of trees that stood to one side of the strawberry field. We didn't discuss it, but neither of us wanted her body next to the house. Then we dropped her into the well — an old well that ran nice and deep, right down to the seam of clay. We didn't say anything as we worked. We didn't even say a prayer. Then we covered over the well with its wooden lid, and went to bed, and I slept like an animal, dreamless, until my father awoke me at ten o'clock, with news that the priest was on his way.

For a moment, panic clawed at me. But my father simply smiled and said:

'I thought of a story.'

Even after my long walk, I could not eat breakfast this morning. Nor could I concentrate on Mass. I mouthed the old familiar words without a thought to their meaning, feeling nothing but the itch of Morgane's needle on my skin, and the greater itch that came with the terrible news of Roux's parentage.

Confession was worse. I wanted to scream with impatience as time after time my people came to confess their little sins — of pride, of rage, of gluttony. I wanted to confess to *them* — *I was the one! I lit the fire that killed two people in Les Marauds!* And at the same time I wanted to laugh, to weep, to tear my hair — and yet I forced myself to sit in silence behind the confessional screen, itching and stinging and burning. Narcisse's green file sat next to me. More unfinished business. Six more pages of script remain. Then I will be free of him.

For a last day on Earth, *mon père*, it could have been more inspiring. There should have been something more than this round of daily chores and duties. I wanted there to be *meaning*. I am facing the unthinkable. But everyone else is still the same: Caro Clairmont and Joline Drou, watching each other over the pews; Guillaume Duplessis on his morning walk, for the first time without his dead dog's lead. Over at Poitou's bakery, there is a line of people. In Les Marauds, there will be the smell of frying spices and chai; the sound of children's voices at play. If I died today, how soon would I be forgotten? And who would mourn a man like me — a hypocrite, a murderer?

I must see Roux today, I know. It is my duty to confess, and yet, like a child, I keep putting it off. Like the remaining pages of Narcisse's confession, it feels like a foreign border, beyond which lies nothing but chaos. I dropped into the *chocolaterie* — hoping perhaps that Vianne might have some miracle cure for my trouble — and found her in excellent spirits, arranging flowers in a vase, and singing softly to herself.

She smiled at me as I came in with the green file under my arm. 'I've just made some hot chocolate,' she said. 'Can I tempt you?'

I wanted to say yes. But my stomach was filled with barbed wire, and my head was pounding.

'Yes, I know. It's Lent,' said Vianne. 'But sometimes you really have to allow yourself a little indulgence.' She nodded towards the tattoo shop. 'I hear our friend moved out last night.'

I nodded. 'So it would seem.'

She placed the vase on a table. 'Perhaps she couldn't afford the rent. Or maybe she realized she just didn't fit. Either way, it's for the best. The village can go back to normal now.' She paused and looked at me. 'I thought I saw you leaving her place. Quite late, around midnight. Did she say anything to you?'

I shook my head. The design on my arm felt luminous, as if she should be able to see it through my sleeve and the plastic patch. I did not say what I had been doing at midnight at the tattoo shop, but I sensed her curiosity, and behind it, her concern. It was that — her concern for me — that I found unbearable. I wished I could confide in her. I wished more than anything in the world that I could sit at a table, and drink a cup of hot chocolate, and tell her all my troubles. But when she knows my secret, *père*, she too will turn from me in disgust. How could she not? How could anyone? And so I said nothing, and tried to smile, and left with a sense of quiet despair and went in search of Joséphine. I know. She and Roux are old friends. I cannot expect absolution from her. And yet I wanted to see her. One more time, before the news of what I did was all over town. One last moment of peace, before everything changes.

But when I arrived at the Café des Marauds, I found only Marie-Ange in charge. Joséphine had gone out, she said. She had not said when she would be back. No last moment, then. No reprieve. My duty was inescapable. I had to find Roux, and confess to him. After that — by tomorrow all this will belong to a world in which

351

I am not. I wonder, did Narcisse ever think: *What will things be like when I am gone?* Did it trouble him at all? Or was he glad to be rid of the weight of his lifelong burden?

Turning towards Les Marauds, I became aware that I was still carrying Narcisse's folder. Six closely written pages remained. Ten minutes more would finish it. Story told, confession done. At last, I will be free of him.

4

It was dark inside the shop. BAM! Of course, I thought: the blinds are down. It smelt very faintly of incense, and the damp smell of an empty house. It was a smell that made me think that no-one had been there for a long time.

In the corner I could see Bam, looking small and faded. And there was the box, with its cardboard lid, left by the door like a present. Written in capitals on the lid was just one word: ROSETTE. I opened it. And inside there was a bundle of tattooist's practice sheets, and Morgane's tattoo pen, and an ink cup, and a power pack, and a bottle of tattoo ink in a kind of charcoal grey. There was no note, no message, just the tattoo kit, the ink, the cup and the pile of practice sheets.

I thought of my dream, and the dream-Morgane telling me to cut off my feet. It wasn't really a scary dream, even though it might have been. It must have been a message, I thought; and I took the contents of the box and put them in my satchel, and quietly left the empty shop and took the riverside path to my wood. I wanted to think, and that's the place where I can think best, surrounded by trees, and quiet, with my wishing-well and only the birds for company.

Out in the countryside you could see the

damage from last night's big storm. Torn-off leaves covered the ground like sheaves of shredded paper. A big tree had fallen — not one of mine, but one of the big aspens on the Rue des Francs Bourgeois. And the sky was a strange kind of almost-pink, all clouded over with tumbling birds. No damage that I could see in my wood, except for a half-dozen patches of earth, where Yannick and his mother had been digging, and of course, the metal grate and the stones they'd taken from the well.

I found a dry place to sit, cross-legged, on a piece of discarded stone. Bam came to sit right next to me, quiet for a change, and dim. There were so many thoughts running through my mind: so many things to untangle. My mother saying, in Morgane's voice:

Sometimes children fly away. We do what we can to keep them.

And then the circle in the sand, and the song, that she uses to talk to the wind.

What did you do last night, Maman? Did you send Morgane away? Did you do it to keep me safe?

I ought to ask her. I know that. But Maman sometimes lies to me. She does it because she loves me, the way so many grown-ups do. She does it because she's afraid. I know. I can see her colours.

What are you afraid of Maman?

I know a way of finding out. I could use my shadow-voice; the one that always tells the truth. There's no-one to hear me in my wood; no-one to stop me from finding out. And I could use my

354

drawing-book, to help me see more clearly. Just like Morgane taught me to do with the tattoo ink and the mirrors.

I took out my book and my pencil-case. I always carry them with me. I rested the book on the side of the well. I thought perhaps the well could be my mirror, although I couldn't see much down there. But the well was full of whispers, friendly and encouraging. And so I began to draw, and as I drew I hummed the wind-song — *Bam bam bammm — bam badda-bammm* — not loud enough for an Accident, but just enough to get into the mood.

At first I drew a lake, with ducks, and a little girl and her mother standing watching the ducks on the bank. The little girl looked a bit like me, and the mother looked a lot like Maman, with her black hair and red dress. There were some trees in the distance, and I thought they might be my wood, so I drew Bam in the branches, perched there like a golden bird.

I stopped to have a look. Not bad. So then, I sang the words to the song, in my shadow-voice that never lies, and I felt the wind prick up its ears like an animal scenting rain:

'*V'là l'bon vent, v'là l'joli vent*
V'là l'bon vent, ma mie m'appelle,
V'là l'bon vent, v'là l'joli vent
V'là l'bon vent, ma mie m'attend.'

Above me, in the oak trees, I thought I felt a stirring. It might have been a gust of wind, or squirrels in the branches. And so I went on to the verse, the one about the ducks on the pond.

'*Derrière chez nous y'a un étang . . .*'

355

Above me, that stirring of wind again, like something alive in the treetops. And in the wishing-well I heard the echo of my voice as I sang, broken into pieces like reflections on a mirror lake.

Then I sang the next verse, the one about the King's son, and the one about the white duck with gold and diamonds in its beak, and the one about the three ladies gathering feathers for a bed —

Now the wind was getting strong. I could hear its voice in the well, sighing and moaning and whispering. *What do you want, Rosette?* it said. *Tell me, What do you really want?*

And so I summoned my shadow-voice and looked into the wishing-well. It was dark in there, and smelt of stagnant water, ferns, and weeds, and things that only bloom at night. And I said:

'*Why am I different? Why did I not grow, like Pilou? Why do I see the things I see? Why am I not like the others?*'

And then, all of a sudden, I *knew*.

I knew what last night's dream had meant, and why Maman had called the wind, and why I am so different, and why she's afraid of Accidents. And then I said in that *other* voice, the voice I recognized from my dream:

'*You* did it, didn't you, Maman? You did it to stop me flying away.'

And the voice from the well, the voice that sounds like my shadow-voice, and never lies, came back at me in a thousand whispers and reflections:

Yes.

5

Friday, March 31

The priest of Lansquenet at the time was a very old man called Père Matthieu. He had known both World Wars, and what he had heard from the shadows of the confessional had given him a distant gaze, as if perpetually watching for a ship on the horizon. He had already known that my father had gone to Rennes on family business, and my father's story played on that. I listened as he explained to the priest how he had been away for the week, and had returned to find his son and his daughter shut up in their room, and Tante Anna nowhere to be found.

'She was harsh with the children,' he said. 'She would often lock them indoors if they were unruly or thoughtless. But this time, I knew something was wrong. When I opened the door of the room, I found my son barely conscious, and my daughter — ' Here his eyes filled with tears. 'My daughter was prone to seizures, mon père. She must have been dead for quite some time. At first I thought my son was dead, too. He hadn't eaten or drunk for days.'

It was a simple lie; simple enough for the priest to believe it. This one listened in silence to the tale, eyes narrowed against an invisible sun. And my father was convincing. His grief was certainly unfaked. When he had finished his story, the priest rose from his armchair by the hearth and said: 'Where do you think your aunt could have gone?'

My father raised his hands helplessly. 'All I can think is that she must have come to harm in some way. She would never have left the children locked up without food for so long. Maybe she collapsed somewhere, or fell into the river. I was going to ask for your help to organize a search for her.'

Lansquenet has always been a close-knit little community. Once the story was known, our friends and neighbours came out in force to help. My father led the searches. We searched the riverbank, the woods, the area around the farm. Some of the men used hunting-dogs, but Tante Anna's scent was everywhere, and the disused well by the copse of trees went unseen and undisturbed.

I don't know who it was, Reynaud, who first mentioned the river-folk. Even in those days they were there, though the War had been hard on the gypsies. Now, they had come out of hiding once more, moving up and downriver with the changing of the seasons. A band of them had moored their boats in the shallows of Les Marauds, down by the old tanneries — in those days still open, and reeking. You have to understand, Reynaud. I was a child, just as you were when you did what you did. Traumatized by the death of Mimi, and by my terrible deed. Terrified of discovery; sleeping little, eating

less, my head filled with imaginings. The idea
that someone else might take the blame, and
carry it far away from me — downriver, even to
the sea — was wildly, darkly appealing. And so,
on my father's suggestion, I helped to plant a
suspicion in the minds of my neighbours and
friends. I'd seen a man, a stranger, I said,
hanging about the farm at night, just before
Tante Anna disappeared.

'What kind of a man?'

'A tall man, dark, with a scar on his face.'

I'd taken the description from one of the
books I'd read at school. I had no idea that I'd
just described one of the river-gypsies. But the
folk of Lansquenet needed no further encouragement. The thought that Tante Anna might
have been the victim of a prowler was far more
plausible than the truth that was right there
under their noses.

They arrested the man, a Greek by birth,
whose name was Yannis Vasiliou. Sixty-two; a
loner with a murky reputation. It was said that
during the War he'd worked for the black
market. He had a violent history, he'd served
five years in jail for assault, during which time
he'd gained the scar that did so much to con-
demn him. He pleaded innocence, of course;
but a search of his houseboat revealed a cache
of stolen goods — nothing from our farm, but
more than enough to confirm their suspicions
that he had murdered Tante Anna when she
had surprised him prowling about, and that he
had disposed of the body in the hope of avert-
ing suspicion. A court in Agen found him

guilty, and he was guillotined in Toulouse, where so many people had suffered the same fate at the hands of the Germans.

My father was never the same again. He never spoke of the Vasiliou case, although he kept a box full of clippings at the back of his wardrobe. His stutter returned, worse than ever, until I could barely remember his voice, and the image of that night grew dim and distant in my memory. He sent me off to school in Agen until my sixteenth birthday: most of my fellows were country boys, forced to board because they lived too far to travel to school every day. I saw my father only during the school holidays, and he was often busy then, leaving me to my own devices. He had created a new project, which took up a great deal of his time: he had taken to ordering and planting hundreds of oak saplings around the copse by the side of the cornfield. He'd hired a group of the river-folk to run the farm on his behalf, and he devoted much of his time to this mysterious new project. Everyone had a different theory about it. The most popular was that my father was trying to create the perfect conditions for truffles. Truffles love oak woodland, and there was far more money there than in wheat or sunflowers. The second, almost as popular, explanation was that my father had gone mad. Certainly, since Mimi's death, he had never been the same. He had become increasingly withdrawn; he only ever seemed to speak to the river-folk who worked his farm. And oak trees take decades to grow — even if he were lucky enough to encourage truffles to grow on the site, it would surely not be in his lifetime. And yet he persisted: planting more than ten thousand trees — some from acorns, some saplings — in the eight years between Mimi's death and his own.

By the time I finished school he was even more distant than he'd been when Tante Anna was alive. His project took up all his time, although it was still less clear to me now precisely what he was doing. His project — you could not call it a wood — stretched all the way to the bank of the Tannes, except for the little odd-shaped clearing that had once been a field of strawberries. In the clearing was the well in which we had buried Tante Anna, now blocked with a solid metal grate sunk into the concrete. At first I thought that maybe my father had wanted to keep the strawberry field, but as time went on and he made no attempt to cultivate or pick the fruit, I realized that strawberries were not a part of his design.

Left to my own devices, I ran a little wild. I drank. There was a girl in the village, a pretty girl, Eloise Goujon. I got her pregnant when I was eighteen and she was nearly twenty-one. We married in the village church, under her grandfather's watchful eye. My father was there, but he barely spoke, barely joined in the celebrations. I remember him saying to me, just after the ceremony:

'I want you to keep the oak wood, Narcisse. For Mimi's sake, and for your own children, when you have them.' And he put his arms

361

around me for the first time since I'd been a boy, and whispered:

'Love is the thing that only God sees.'

At the time I wondered if he was drunk. He certainly smelt of wine, although I had not seen him drinking. But in the ten years after Mimi's death, my father had scarcely spoken a sentence without stuttering. Mimi's name had not passed his lips since the funeral. As for the reference to God — my father was no Catholic. He never went to church any more, he never read the Bible. Nor was he drawn to Judaism, in spite of Naomi's influence. As far as he was concerned, the God of the Torah was no kinder than the God who had sacrificed his son for the sake of a stolen apple. But it was the last thing I recall my father ever saying to me.

Six months after that, he died, leaving the farm to me and Eloise. The village curé — a young man, newly appointed after the death of père Matthieu — agreed to turn a blind eye to the circumstances. My father had made a confession, his first in over twenty years. Of course, the young priest did not reveal exactly what he had told him. But when my father hanged himself from a beam in the cellar, it was the priest who let it be known that old Dartigen had died of a fall — not quite a lie, but enough to ensure a decent funeral. There was no note. No diary. But at the back of his wardrobe I found the clippings relating to the death of Yannis Vasiliou, carefully stored in a shoebox, the lid marked in red ink: MURDERER.

That word, Reynaud. That dreadful word. For ten years it had remained unspoken between us. Now it glared from the lid of the box; accusing; condemnatory. I took it as a message from the man who had never forgiven me. And why should he? I was the one who should have saved Mimi. I was the one who sacrificed a stranger to protect myself. Worse still, I was the one who left him to carry the burden of memory, while I went on with my life, as if I were somehow entitled to all the things he'd forsaken —

I burnt the shoebox in the hearth, along with all its contents. I never told Eloise about the Vasiliou affair, or Tante Anna, or any of it. She was a kind, unimaginative girl, raised by her grandparents during the War. All she wanted was a home, and children, and a family. I gave her all that — but most of myself I kept hidden away from her. My father died when his burden became too hard for him to carry. I have carried mine until now. I tended it, and watched it grow. In sixty years my father's trees have grown into an oak wood. I never really understood why he needed to plant them, but I'd always felt close to him there, as if the trees had somehow kept a part of his spirit with them.

Trees are very forgiving, Reynaud. They give their shade equally to the living and the dead. Innocence and guilt are nothing to them. I'm not going to tell you my spirit is there, but if I believed in spirits, it might be. In any case, I'm leaving it to Rosette. She will enjoy it, just as Mimi would have loved it, if she had lived.

Roux's boat was moored under the trees, some way downriver from Les Marauds. The air was mellow with midges and the scent of blossom from the bank. A filament of hyacinth smoke arose from the boat's little chimney. I sat down on the river-bank, as best as I could in my bulky *soutane*, and pulled off the clerical collar. For a moment I closed my eyes, listening to the small sounds of the river; the whispering of leaves in the trees; noticing the sharp scent of the reeds; the distant rise and fall of voices from the *Boulevard des Marauds*. There were bees in the canopy overhead, and a scent of something burning. I opened my eyes, and I saw the door to the houseboat standing open, and a man standing on the deck — a man with red hair and a wary look.

'Funny place to sit,' said Roux.

I took a breath. 'I was waiting for you.'

'That so?' His voice was warier still.

'I have something to confess.'

6

Friday, March 31

Confession is good for the soul, they say. I wouldn't know. My soul is dark. Dark as a stained-glass window in a place where no-one prays. I was a lonely child. A boy without any friends, and a family held together by the appearances of faith. My father was an alcoholic: he prayed to the Lord on Sundays, and on weekdays drank half a bottle of whisky per day, plus wine with meals; as well as *apéritif* and *digestif* and *café-cognac* at breakfast. My mother took comfort where she could in the arms of various different men. The only stable point in my life was the church, where Monsieur le Curé would talk to me as if I were a man of his own age, instead of a boy of seven or eight, and where I could enjoy peace and sanctity away from the taunts and jibes of my peers, and my mother's perpetual rages.

Monsieur le Curé was neither a patient man nor an especially kind one. He had been ambitious, once, though his hopes of high office had died. Rumours of a previous post, somewhere in the north of France, which he had left, very suddenly, suggested some earlier scandal, but to me he seemed the image of what a priest was meant to be: hard as oak; upstanding and strong; impervious to weakness.

It was Monsieur le Curé who encouraged me to give up reading novels and to study the words of Saint Augustine. It was he who comforted me when the other boys were unkind, and told me I was better than they because I knew how to suffer. He told me I was destined for greater things than village life, and guided me towards the Church as a potential vocation. It was he who taught me that congregations are like sheep: they need a fierce dog to keep them in check, if they are not to fall to the wolf. And it was he who taught me that bringing order from chaos is the Church's primary task, that even kindness can be misplaced, and that God's law is paramount.

I'm not saying this to be forgiven. In fact, I'm not really *saying* it at all. The words that I try to express to Roux are poor, chaotic sentences; nothing like the carefully chosen words of Narcisse's confession. Monsieur le Curé would have been dismayed at my inarticulacy. But words are not enough to say everything I need to confess. Words are feeble things in the face of the man whose life I stole.

Roux, I killed your parents.

There can be no excuse, I know. My age; the fact that I had thought the houseboats were unoccupied; the fact that I had been brainwashed into believing my actions were righteous. None of that excuses the fact that *I* was the one who lit the fire that caused the death of two people. Just a little fire, on the bank; and yet it grew into a blaze. And though I confessed, and was absolved by Monsieur le Curé himself, that absolution was not his to give, nor mine to claim.

I know that now. I've always known. Perhaps that was why I hated you, and all the river-people. Not because of what they are, but because of what I did. And because of what I did, I have been cut off from other people. Perhaps that's why I hated *them*, too, with all their foolish friendships. I thought myself purer, harder than they — hard as a diamond, wrought in fire — but all the time I envied them. I would have given everything just to erase that one mistake.

I do not mean to imply that because I suffered, I should be absolved. I understand that nothing can change what I did that summer. But after reading Narcisse's file, I see that there's one thing I can do. I can tell *you*. I can confess to the one other person whose life has been marked by what I did.

I'm not asking for your forgiveness. I simply want you to know how much I regret what I have done. I have no excuse. I am a coward and a murderer. Morgane said you blamed yourself for the death of your parents. But you were a child. You were innocent. I am here to claim what's mine. See, the mark of Cain on my arm, there for everyone to see —

The words poured out of me like blood, and all I can see now is his face; his eyes as grey as the ocean. I could hope for no sympathy, only the hatred I deserve. I rolled up my sleeve, revealing the patch that covered my still-blurry tattoo — and at that moment, behind him, standing by the galley door, I saw someone else. It was Joséphine.

She was wearing jeans, and a top I liked — blue, with yellow flowers. Her hair was tied up, and tendrils of soft brown hair blew across her face. *You said you wanted to see her*, said Narcisse's dry and pitiless voice. *Well, you got your wish, mon père. Prayers do get answered, after all.*

She must have been in the galley, I thought. She must have heard every word I spoke. For a moment, I stood there in silence, aware of every detail. The wind, the small sounds of the Tannes, the scent of fallen blossom. Inside me, there was a silence deeper than the ocean.

Finally, she knows, I thought. And I have no-one to blame but myself. This was always going to be: I had always known she would find out. Childish of me to imagine that I could hold onto something good in the deluge of my life. Even more so to believe that I might earn forgiveness.

From deep underwater, I heard her voice. Her words came to me from so far away that all I could hear was a rushing sound, like something in a diving-bell. My vision was blurred; my stomach ached; my feet were a thousand miles away. I stumbled down the riverside path, not knowing where I was going; simply aware that I needed to be gone from that place immediately. Someone called after me. I did not turn. There was nothing to turn for. I ran along the side of the Tannes, finally leaving them behind, along with the sound of the river. I skirted the houses along the *Rue des Marauds*, and cut across the ploughed fields, and found myself on the small dirt path leading to Narcisse's oak wood.

This is the place, I told myself. This is where I will end my life, among the flowering strawberries that I will not live to see ripen. Like the man in the story, I hope that death can somehow redeem me. I do not pray, except to the dark and blasphemous hope that perhaps at last I can disappear, evaporate into the air and not be remembered by anyone —

7

Friday, March 31

I know the story of a girl whose voice was stolen by a witch. Oh, she wasn't a wicked witch; only a sad and frightened one. All she had was her children: a summer child and a winter child, both of them born wild and full of life and curiosity. And the wind, the jealous wind, would blow around the witch's house, calling them, calling her, reminding her that magic comes at a price that must be paid one day, in full.

But the witch had known the wind all her life. And she thought that perhaps she could cheat it, and be like the other mothers, and live in a quiet village somewhere, with only the kind of magic that can be hidden away in chocolate.

And so she stole the little girl's voice, and sacrificed it to the wind, so that only the little girl's shadow could speak. And thus, she kept her daughter safe, so that only in dreams could she fly away —

But now I am awake, *Maman*. I know there are no Accidents. Only the wind, reminding us of what we owe for being who we are. Only the magic that lives in us all, and reaches out to everyone. You can't keep a child like a duck on a lake, wings clipped to fool the wind. The wind is only fooled for a time, and when it returns, it comes with all the force and rage of the *Hurakan*.

And now the wind is blowing again, and I can hear its voice, a voice that could be anyone: Morgane Dubois, or Vianne Rocher, or even Zozie de l'Alba . . .

Or it could be mine. *I* have a voice. It's just that I've never used it much. I thought it wasn't safe to use. I thought it didn't belong to me. But now I can claim my voice again. I can use it. I know how.

Above me, in the trees, the wind is beginning to misbehave. I can hear it taunting me from deep inside the wishing well. I know what it wants. I tell it. 'BAM! *I'm* in charge now.'

I know what I want to do first. I find a new page in my drawing-book. I draw Narcisse's farmhouse. Yannick and his mother are outside; I draw her with a flamingo head, Yannick as a sad brown bear. I know how to do the voices, too. All those bird and animal-calls will come in useful after all.

Yannick is shouting. '*It's not fair! You never let me have any friends!*'

His mother sounds cross and shrill, like the wind. '*That's not true, Yannick,*' she says. '*I want you to have normal friends, not —* '

'What?'

I know she means me. Yannick's voice is almost a roar: a bear defending his honey. I almost laugh aloud at the thought, but I don't want to excite the wind.

'*Normal?*' he says. '*You mean not like me?*'

'*You're not a freak, Yannick,*' she says. '*You're just going through a phase. If only you could make an effort, I'm sure —* '

'*I've made an effort,*' says Yannick. '*But underneath, I'm always me. It's like you're ashamed of me, Maman. Hiding me away like this. Pretending I'm an invalid. Pretending I'm going to be better someday. Thinking I'll be different.*'

'*But Yannick —* ' says his mother, and now she sounds ready to cry. I feel a little sorry for her. She's his mother, after all. She only wants the best for him. '*Yannick,*' she says. '*You're my only son. All I want is to see you happy.*'

'*Then let me be myself,*' he says. '*I've always been the way I am. I'm never going to be different. And from now on I'm going to choose my own friends, and go my own way, be a freak if I want to. That's how I'll be happy, Maman.*'

He's right, of course. There's nothing wrong with being a freak. Freaks are extraordinary. That's what we are, Yannick and me. We are extraordinary. Oh, and one more thing, Yannick. '*I want you to leave Rosette alone. No more talk about her wood. No more digging for treasure. Okay?*'

The wind gives a rebellious moan. I silence it with a gesture. I draw a picture of Madame Montour giving Yannick a pot of honey. Then I turn the page. The voices stop. And in the lull that follows, I hear the sound of footsteps on the path, and someone comes into the clearing. It's Reynaud. He looks terrible. I duck down by the side of the well and crawl into the bushes to hide. Reynaud doesn't see me. I don't think he sees anything.

What is he doing here? This is *my* wood. That

makes him a trespasser. Priests are supposed to know better than that. Don't they say: *forgive us our trespasses?* But there's something wrong with Reynaud; his colours are wild and ugly and mad, and he's talking to himself in a low voice a bit like my shadow-voice, in broken phrases that don't make sense. I hear *mon père*, and *confession*, and *river-rats*, and *Joséphine*. Then he walks up to the well and looks inside, and whispers something. I don't catch the words, but it sends the echoes from the well flying out like a cloud of moths.

I hope he didn't make a wish. I'm afraid if he did, it might come true.

8

It was late in the afternoon, and I was making truffles. My back was turned, but I knew my daughter at once from the sound of her breathing.

'Anouk.'

She was by the window, and her face was to the light. She has dyed her hair again — pink this time, like candyfloss — and although it suits her, I wonder why she needs to change its colour so often. She is, and always was, beautiful, her dark eyes like the edge of the sky. Her hair is candyfloss-curly and already growing dark at the roots. The pink makes her skin look paler; bleaches her of her nectarine glow. I sometimes wonder if she is trying to make herself different from me.

'Maman.' She hugs me clumsily; she feels as if she has lost weight. Anouk at nine was sturdy, puppyish and full of fun. Now she is like an armful of birds, delicate and ready to fly.

'It's good to see you.'

'You, too.'

There's something else that's new, I see: a shimmy in her colours. Anouk was always easy to read, but as she grows older, her colours have changed; shifting, growing more complex. I want to ask about her news, but I know she will tell

374

me in her own time.

'Do you want some hot chocolate?'

She nods. She has not drunk hot chocolate more than three times since she was a child. So this means something important; perhaps even something unsettling. I know not to ask her about it just yet: let the chocolate do its work.

I pour the drink into Anouk's cup, the one that no-one else uses. It smells of damp earth after the rain, and cardamom, and sandalwood, and fresh green tea scented with rose. She always liked the scent of rose, and now, though she seldom drinks it, I always include a splash of rosewater in the Chantilly topping.

She drinks in careful little sips, knowing the bitter drink's potency. As the quiet air settles into a new shape around her, I send out tiny tendrils, a questioning of her colours; a lullaby murmur that croons to itself:

Try me. Tell me. Trust me.

She puts down the cup. From behind her I think I see a sudden quick flash of grey. Another reminder of childhood — I have not seen Pantoufle for years. It almost feels as if Anouk is seeking out a previous self, perhaps in the hope of finding a line of communication —

'How's Jean-Loup?'

She smiles at his name. 'He's fine.' A pause. 'He's found a job.'

'Already?' Jean-Loup is still in his final year of study. He still has examinations to take. 'What kind of job?'

Her eyes are bright. 'It's his dream job, working with a wildlife group. He sent them samples of his work, his photographs, his writing. They want him to fly out in July. He's terribly excited.'

'Fly out? Somewhere in Europe?'

She looks at me and shakes her head. 'New Zealand. Then Australia.'

Australia? 'How long for?'

'A year, to begin with. Then, if it works — '

A year. To begin with. 'And after that?'

She shrugged. 'It depends. I don't really know.'

My head is spinning. 'It makes no sense. Surely there must be photographers in the southern hemisphere. And what about his condition? His heart?'

'Maman, they're a charity. They're progressive about hiring.'

'That wasn't what I meant, Anouk.' I tried to find the right words, but forming them was like seizing smoke. My own heart was beginning to lurch; there was a kind of buzz in my ears, and once more I thought of my mother, in the few months before she died; the feverish look and sound of her as she huddled against me on the bed of some anonymous boarding-house or hotel room, with the air conditioning making that same distant buzzing sound, and my mother saying:

'What about it, *chérie*? I've never seen the Southern Cross. What about Australia? New Zealand? The Whitsunday Islands?'

My mother carried maps in her head the way I carried recipes. Both impossible, of course: those distant lands as exotic as the spicy *tagines* and *laksas* and *callaloo* that I had only seen in books, or in the menus of restaurants that we could never afford to try. And still she kept making plans, even when she could hardly walk: the Virgin Islands, Tahiti, Bora Bora, Fiji. Never mind that she was sick, that we were down to our last centime; that we were living on what I could earn from day to day, waitressing. That defiant spark in her eye — that's what I saw in Anouk now.

'What I meant,' I said, 'is it — safe?'

Anouk gave me a bright look that was curiously adult. 'You can't always be safe,' she said. 'Jean-Loup's lived with that all his life. He knows he could die tomorrow, or he could live to be eighty. No-one knows. That's why he wants to see the world. Not in a month; not in a year. But *now*. Because now's all there is.'

'And what about you?' I could bear it no more. I already knew the answer.

'I'm going with him.'

How could she not? The child is in love. She can't leave him. Love, that eater of hearts, that wind that sweeps away everything we build.

'Australia?' I said.

Anouk, whose only wish as a child had been to stay in a place like Lansquenet. Everything was going numb. I felt like the survivor of some tremendous explosion: my retinas still stamped with the blast; my eardrums ringing with the tinnitus of shock.

'Australia?' I repeated.

'Only for a year, at first. There's Skype, and FaceTime, and email, and — please. Please, Maman. Please don't cry.'

377

'Of course not. It will be an adventure.'

She nodded. 'We got married,' she said. 'Last week, in Paris, at the *mairie du dixième arrondissement*. We wanted to do it quietly. No-one was there, except for two witnesses we'd only just met.' She paused, set down the chocolate cup, and now I could see the tears in her eyes. 'Tell me you're not sad, Maman. Tell me you can be happy for us.'

There's always a moment after a storm when the wind settles into a gender routine. It plays at domesticity: it flirts with the clouds in the ringing blue sky; it tugs at the trees like a playful child, promising once more to be good. But this moment of playfulness is when the wind is at its worst. Later, when the promise has been broken like so many before, we tell ourselves: *never again*. And then, when we think it has taken all that it can possibly take, that tiny thread of hope returns, that this time, maybe *this time* —

I hug her very tight. I say: 'Of course I can. I love you, Nanou. If you're happy, I'm happy.'

'We took some pictures. Want to see?'

I smile at her. 'Of course I do.'

The photographs are in a book, a second-hand album no doubt bought on the *Marché aux Puces*. On the cover, a picture of old Montmartre in its heyday, faded by time; a sky the colour of memories. Inside, she is wearing jeans; a flower crown on her candyfloss curls holding a strip of veil that flies in the wind like a pirate flag. Paper confetti, like blossom, like snow, like the confetti that flew on the day that we came on the wind of the carnival.

I hear my mother's voice in my mind. *Children are only on loan*, it says. *One day, we have to give them back*. My mother never gave me back. My mother chose to leave me instead. I wonder if Anouk will hear *my* voice at the back of her mind. Or will she simply move away into a different orbit?

Her smile in the pictures looks different: a smile that only Jean-Loup sees. Of course, the two of them could not afford a professional photographer. It occurs to me that Jean-Loup will soon *be* a professional photographer. The boy with the jigsaw heart and my child now interlocked together. Are they not too young? Perhaps. But wasn't *I* too young for a child? And how much older do I feel, twenty-one years later?

I turn the page. Here are some shots of both of them together. Jean-Loup looks taller than I remember; taller, more handsome and much more assured. The awkward teenager I knew has become a fine young man. Beside him, Anouk is a blur; illuminated with laughter and joy. None of these pictures are posed, but I sense the eye of a professional. And then I see a familiar face, half turned away from the camera, her silvery hair caught in movement, cutting into the air like a scythe —

The world stops turning for a beat. Everything begins to fly off.

'Who's that?' I manage to ask.

'Oh, that's the tattooist. She was one of our witnesses. We thought it would be cool to get wedding tattoos instead of rings.'

And now she shows me her wrist, and I feel

the world come away at the edges. Everything is burning; the sky is ripped apart like paper. A wild rose, as pale as young love, its petals barely unfolding, sends its tendrils down her wrist. The pattern is strangely familiar; its pastel colours shadowing the soft blue veins of her inner arm.

'Do you like it?'

'It's beautiful.' I do not even have to lie.

'I'm glad,' says Anouk, hugging me. 'I feel like I've had it forever.'

9

The well in which Narcisse and his father disposed of Tante Anna still stands, in a clearing in the wood. There is a little path from the gate, which leads to the location. I wonder vaguely why Narcisse chose to maintain the burial site — in his place I would have preferred to fill in the well and allow the brambles to cover it. Instead, Narcisse has chosen to make a clearing around the well, a clearing that is overrun with furrows and wreaths of wild strawberries.

But someone has been here recently. Earth has been turned over in several parts of the clearing. I suspect Michèle Montour, with her talk of buried treasure. And there are footprints in the grass, and an area next to the well where someone has spent a considerable time.

Rosette? A discarded pencil suggests that I am probably right. It occurs to me that if I die here, the child will probably find me. That would not be a good thing. I have no wish to do more harm. All I want is to disappear and never be seen again by anyone.

Surprisingly, this simple plan is riddled with complications. I cannot hang myself from a tree, for fear of Rosette finding my corpse. An overdose of pills at my home would mean someone — the neighbours, perhaps — having to report the signs of something decomposing next door. Leaping into the Tannes might work, but I am an excellent swimmer, *père*, and besides, the thought of little Maya or one of her friends discovering me on the riverbank makes me feel quite nauseous. The same applies to leaping from the church tower, or under a train. A suicide leaves so much work for other people to do, *père*. So much potential for doing harm; so many duties unfulfilled.

By now I suppose Roux and Joséphine will have spread the news around Lansquenet. Everything I thought I had — my reputation, my flock, my life — held up to contempt and scorn. Everyone will know that the man who claimed to guide them was no more than an imposter. Caro Clairmont and her cronies, who courted me for my status. Poitou, the baker. Joline Drou. Ying-Ley Mak. The Bencharkis. The river folk. The sullen waitress from the café. The postman. The Bishop. Vianne Rocher. Omi Al-Djerba. Little Maya.

And Joséphine — my *Joséphine*, whispers the blasphemous voice in my mind. Words that I could never say, even before my confession. Now, of course, they will never be said. That, I suppose, should be a relief. She knows that I am a murderer, but at least she will never know *that*.

I look into the open well. The hole looks deep, and smells of rain and vegetation gone to rot. I think of Cain, trying to hide from the Eye of God. I wonder if the drop would be far enough to kill me, or whether I would slowly drown, like a rat in a vat of rainwater. I am afraid to die, *mon père*. And yet I am also afraid to live. Maybe I always was, *mon père*. Maybe that is my tragedy.

Suddenly, it occurs to me that I have not yet seen my tattoo. The skin beneath the plastic patch is still inflamed and sensitive. But did Morgane not need me to see the image she designed for me? Is there not some message there that I am meant to understand?

I push up the sleeve of my *soutane* and gently remove the protective patch. The air feels good against my skin, cool and reassuring. I look for the mark of Cain — the Eye, the flame, the bolt of lightning — but there is nothing. No design. Just an area of skin a little more sensitive than the rest, like a patch of sunburn . . .

What's this? Is it a joke? A trick?

I inspect the whole of my arm. Nothing there. The blur of violent colours I'd seen is as absent as Morgane herself. But there was a tattoo. There must have been. I saw it. I *felt* it. I spoke aloud.

'There *was* a tattoo. I know there was.'

My words come back at me from the well, broken into pieces.

And then, once more, I think of the tale of the man who had lived all his life with a secret so dark that only death could absolve it. Was this how she had tricked me into declaring my own secret? Is this the punchline to a joke of which I am the target?

The man in her story was saved, of course. Confession released him from his sin. But it will not release me from mine. Roux cannot absolve me. My whole life has been a series of bitter jokes, of terrible mistakes. Everything that has happened over the years has led me to this.

There is a piece of scrap metal by the side of the old well. I drop it into the cool damp air, and listen for the splash. It comes after a long time, from far away into the dark. Looking down, I can just make out the faded silver disc of the sky reflected in the distant depths. And now from the throat of the well I can almost hear the sound of voices; high, like those of children at play. A trick of the well's acoustics, perhaps. It reminds me of the tale of the Pied Piper, and how with his music he lured the children of Hamelin underground. Only two children, one lame, one blind, escaped, but spent the rest of their lives dreaming of what might have happened if they had been like the others.

As for the man behind it all, who would not pay the piper his due, he drowned himself in the river, or hid himself underground, like Cain, depending on the version you read.

I realize that I have lost the green folder containing Narcisse's confession. I must have dropped it, I suppose, somewhere by the riverside. But there can be no going back. Whatever else happens, my path ends here. My duty to Narcisse is done.

Now I must pay the rest of my debt, the one I owe the Almighty. An eye for an eye. A life for a life. Time to pay the piper.

10

And now I know what the *Hurakan* has taken in place of Morgane Dubois, and the world falls down like a tower of cards, like the Tower in my mother's pack, spilling the pieces of my life among the truffles and nougatines.

Anouk is going away. My Anouk. This moment I have feared so long. A stolen child myself I know that, at heart, *all* children are stolen. They run with the hare, they melt with the snow, they follow the Pied Piper. And sometimes they blow away like confetti on the wind —

Anouk went up to her room to unpack, leaving me to make dinner. Something quick and simple, I thought: a salad of ripe tomatoes, served with baked goat's cheese, fresh bread and a dish of fat brown olives. I managed to hide my anxiety until she had left the room, but my hands were shaking as I cut up the tomatoes. A little oil, some sea salt, shallots, a handful of fresh basil. Food is the thing that unites us all, that brings us back together. Food is the thing we can provide when there is nothing else we can do. That's why we serve it at funerals. To remind us that Life always goes on.

The church clock rings six-thirty. It's late. Rosette should surely be back by now. The shop across the square looks dead: there is no sign of movement. I tell myself that Morgane has left town — silently, unobtrusively, as I might have done twenty years ago, answering the call of the wind. But I do not believe it. I suspect she still has one surprise to bring out of her bag of tricks. One more, final turn of the card.

The goat's cheese is almost ready. Upstairs, I hear the shower running. Rosette should be here: she knows Anouk has come to visit from Paris. Could Morgane have taken her? No. And yet the fear remains in my mind, coiled tight as a worm in a cherry. The lights are all out in the tattoo shop, and yet there's something that catches my eye in the darkened window. Maybe a reflection. But then I see a golden blur at the edge of the window —

I turn off the oven and go to the door. To check will take two minutes, no more. Anouk is in the shower, and there is no-one else around. I cross the square at a run, and peer into the shuttered window. There are no mirrors inside; no sign of any human activity. And yet I sense a presence there; something that gleams in the shadows like the golden trail of a mythical beast —

I move to the door. I start to knock. But the door is already open. The catch must be broken, or maybe Morgane forgot to lock it on her way out. It pushes open into the scent of violet and tuberose.

Rosette is sitting on the floor, in the last late bar of sunlight. Around her, spread out on the boards, there are sheets from her sketch-pad, and pencils, and colours, and something else

386

— a tattoo kit, with a pen and a cup and something like a power-supply.

She does not look up when I come in, but says in a strange, but very clear voice: 'I've been waiting for you, Maman.'

It's a voice I've never heard before. Low, like the sound of waves on a beach, and though strange, it's not quite unfamiliar. I've heard something like it before, in dreams, and on the wind of the carnival, and in between the boats on the Seine, and through the leaves of autumn trees. It's not unlike my mother's voice, or mine, or maybe even Anouk's — but to hear it now, after all this time, from Rosette, makes me shiver.

'You're talking,' I say. 'How can that be?'

She looks at me without smiling. Her eyes are like a hatful of stars. 'Is it true, what you did?' she says, and now I can hear the voice of the wind, speaking through my daughter. 'Is it true you stole my voice, so you could keep me with you?'

For a moment I contemplate lying to my daughter. But there is no point, not now that she knows. My daughters are not like other girls. My daughters see more than other girls see. My daughters are children of the wind, and only the wind can claim them.

'I wanted to keep you safe, Rosette. I love you.'

'Love is never safe.'

She smiles. It might be Anouk speaking. First Anouk, and now Rosette. The wind has taken everything. She indicates the drawings spread out on the dusty wooden floor. I see a drawing of a lake, with ducks, and a hidden hunter. Morgane's tattoo pen is by her side, plugged into its power pack.

'What are you doing with that?'

She shrugs. 'I've been learning to use it.'

'What for?'

'Because it's a kind of magic,' she says. 'Ancient people all over the world tattooed their bodies to honour the gods. Some believed that a tattoo could reveal the shape of the soul.'

They are almost Morgane's words, and the voice is almost Morgane's voice, or mine, or Anouk's, or my mother's. It strikes me that our voices have *always* been very similar. We are the daughters of the wind: the wind blows through us, like it or not.

'Where's Morgane?' I say.

'She's gone.'

'Why did she leave you her instruments?'

She looks at me. Her eyes are dark as the cloudline of an oncoming storm. 'Because I see things. We all do. We see the thing that others need. Sometimes we even give it to them. Let me show you what I can do.'

I sit down next to her on the floor. I want to tell her so many things. But now I am the one with no voice, and the wind is tearing me apart, scattering me like feathers.

'Don't cry, Maman,' says Rosette.

I'm not crying. I never cry. How easily power passes from one generation to another. Yesterday, Rosette was my child; today, in an instant, I am hers. I put my head on her shoulder and close my eyes. I want to sleep. I want to sleep in a feather bed until the end of everything.

'What do you want to show me?' I say.

Rosette puts a hand on my hair. 'Later, Maman. Be patient. Right now, I want to tell you a story.'

The Crow

1

I know a story about a sad boy who was turned into a crow. He was not really a bad boy, but badness and sadness are two black birds that always fly together. And as his sadness grew, so did his conviction that he was bad, and undeserving of anything. And, little by little, it turned the boy into a harsh and raucous bird, feeding on carrion, mocking the weak, envying their happiness.

Narcisse told me that story, of course. He told me so many stories. Stories of a girl like me: stories of a wicked witch. Now I know that the girl was Mimi, and the witch was Tante Anna. And stories of a sad crow, who I think was Francis Reynaud.

The crow had a deep, dark secret. It was even darker than the secret that had turned him into a crow in the first place. And he carried this secret with him, softly and sadly, wherever he went, in the form of a single pale feather, hidden away under his wing. No-one saw it but the crow. And yet it made him different. It made him long for the boy he had been. It made him long for sweeter things. And it made him long for love, though love was forever out of reach.

He was standing on the lip, looking into the darkness. He'd picked up a piece of metal from the ground; now he dropped it into the well, and I heard the splash from deep underground. I watched from the bushes, not knowing quite what to do or to say, Narcisse had warned me about that old well, how deep it was, how dangerous. And I still couldn't quite believe what Reynaud was thinking of doing . . .

I made a little magpie noise from my hiding-place behind the trees. Reynaud didn't hear it. The wind was quiet as a sleeping mouse. I knew I needed something more. But would Reynaud listen to me? Or would my appearance make him fall?

I summoned my new, commanding voice and stepped out into the clearing.

I said: 'It's me, Monsieur le Curé. I can forgive your trespasses. But you have to get down from there.'

For a second, I thought Reynaud might jump. He turned, and wobbled on the lip of the well. His eyes were wide as windows. I came a little closer. Now I was by the side of the well. I looked up at Reynaud and said: 'Come down from there. You'll fall.'

He looked at me. I could tell he wasn't really sure if I was there or not. He said:

'Rosette Rocher? Is that you?'

I nodded.

'But you can talk.'

'Of course I can. Now please, come down.'

He shook his head.

I tried to read his colours again. Reynaud has never been easy. There's so much background noise in him — nothing's ever simple. But now he was nothing but pain and regret — swirling purples and crimson and black — and I realized that if I had been even a minute later, he would have jumped into the well, and died there in the darkness.

'You don't want to jump,' I said.

He laughed. It wasn't a happy laugh. 'I have the mark of Cain,' he said. 'You want to know what it looks like?' And he pushed up the sleeve of his soutane and showed me a patch of pink skin on his arm. 'She gave me this, to help me,' he said. 'She said it was what I needed.' Then he gave that laugh again, that sounded like something breaking.

'You mean Morgane?'

He nodded. 'She said it would reveal something. Something that I needed to know. But when I looked, there was nothing there. But I can still feel it. The mark of Cain. And now — '

I took his hand. 'Get down.'

'You don't know what I did, Rosette. If you knew, you'd hate me.'

I wondered. I didn't think that was true. You don't just suddenly hate someone, even when they've done something bad. It's like Yannick, trespassing in my wood. Or Pilou, avoiding me because of his silly girlfriend. People sometimes do bad things. It doesn't make them bad people. But I could hear footsteps on the path, and I knew what that meant. It meant I didn't have much time before someone interrupted us.

'Get down, Monsieur le Curé,' I said. 'No-one hates you. Not even — '

And then there came the rustling sound of someone entering the clearing, and I saw Roux and Joséphine standing on the strawberry path.

Reynaud gave a tiny moan, and I felt him pull away from me. And so I grabbed at his *soutane* and dragged him backwards as hard as I could, so that he lost his balance and fell into the grass and the strawberries.

Roux was carrying Narcisse's file. Joséphine was holding his hand. Roux's colours were angry and confused; Joséphine's were frightened and soft. She ran over to Reynaud, who was sitting in the grass where he'd fallen, his face in his hands.

'Are you all right, Francis? Are you hurt?'

Reynaud didn't say anything. He just sat there in the grass, looking like he wanted to die.

'Why did you run?' she went on. 'We looked for you for ages. And then we found your folder, where you'd dropped it on the path, and followed you here. What's going on?'

'I'm sorry,' he said. He sounded like a baby crow, fallen too early from the nest. You try to save them, help them to fly, but mostly they just die of fright.

'What were you trying to do?' she said. 'You could have fallen and killed yourself.'

Reynaud still wouldn't look at her. 'I already told you,' he whispered. 'I already told you what I did.'

'You told us a nonsense story,' said Roux in a voice that sounded harsh, but which I knew was just concerned. 'Something about my parents dying in a fire on the Tannes? Reynaud, my parents live in Marseille. They're fine. They never even had a boat. And wasn't that fire on the Tannes decades ago? That is, if it happened at all?'

'It happened. I was there,' said Reynaud. 'I was the one who lit the fire. Two people died. Their names were Pierre Lupin and — '

Roux interrupted. 'And when was that? It was years ago. You must have been a child, Reynaud. You can't have meant to hurt anyone. Children do stupid things all the time. Why bring it up now? The world moves on. And what could possibly have made you think those people were my parents?'

'Morgane Dubois told me,' he said.

Roux looked more confused than ever.

'She gave me a tattoo,' said Reynaud. 'She told me it would help me. But there's nothing here.' He showed them his arm. 'Nothing to see but emptiness.'

Joséphine put her hand on his forehead. 'You're running a fever, Francis,' she said. 'You need to see a doctor, not a tattooist. Come on.' She held out her hand to him. 'Come with me. We'll take you to Dr Cussonet. He'll give you something to calm you down.'

'I don't need to calm down,' said Reynaud. 'No-one can give me what I need.'

'I think I can,' I said.

Roux and Joséphine looked surprised. 'You're not signing,' said Joséphine.

'I found my voice,' I told them. 'And I think I can help Monsieur le Curé find the thing he's looking for.'

'How?' said Reynaud.

I opened my pink satchel again and took out Morgane's tattooing kit. 'She gave it to me. I've been practising.'

For a long time he looked at the kit. Put out his hand to touch the chrome. I could tell he didn't think any of this was really happening. Roux and Joséphine stood by, looking like children lost in a wood. When I have time I'll draw them as a fox and a big-eyed rabbit, looking down at a baby crow. Then I saw Reynaud's colours shift towards something less sad and fraught. There was still a lot of grey in there, but I was starting to understand there might be something I could do.

'You wanted to see the truth,' I said. 'And now, what do you have to lose?'

For a moment I thought he wouldn't have the nerve.

Then he nodded. 'Do it,' he said.

2

And that was my first tattoo, *Maman*. It felt nothing like the practice sheets, but I kept the line. It was easy. The ink was grey, like the skyline of Paris on a cloudy day. I used the patch of skin that Morgane had already prepared for me. The skin was still tender, but it was right. I already knew what he needed. Roux and Joséphine sat by the well and watched me from a distance. I didn't want them looking at me as I worked. I closed my eyes. I've always seen things better that way.

Scrying with ink is easier than scrying with mirrors, or chocolate. At least it's easier for me. The ink was cloudy-grey, like smoke, like something burning under the skin. I pushed, and felt resistance. I pushed a little harder. Now I could almost smell the smoke. It smelt of dead leaves and petrol. Then I saw a string of big black birds flying over a river. It was the Tannes; I could see it now, grey as the rising smoke. The river was on fire, I knew, and I could fly above the hard mud flats and see the riverboats stranded there. Then I saw a dark shape standing on the riverbank.

I knew at once who *that* was. Monsieur le Curé, of course, his eyes as grey as river-stones. Monsieur le Curé, whose mark has been all over this story from the start, standing there in his black robe, surrounded by his birds of malchance.

Reynaud flinched. I opened my eyes and wiped the fine droplets of blood from his arm. 'Are you okay?'

He nodded.

'Morgane told you a story,' I said. 'Now let me tell you another.'

I know a story about a boy who was really a crow in disguise. This boy liked to watch the gypsies as they passed by in their caravans, and the river-boats that they liked to paint in bright and rainbow colours. He loved to hear their music as they played beside the riverbank, and watched, round-eyed as they sang and danced, and worked their secret magic. But the gypsies never noticed him, or asked him to sit by their campfires, and the boy grew increasingly angry, and swore that one day he would be avenged.

The boy grew up to be a priest: a black crow with a raucous voice. And he befriended boys who were lonely and awkward and angry and sad, and turned them into crows like himself and sent them after the gypsies. The flock of crows did all they could to frustrate the travelling folk. They carried rumours and stories and lies. They told dark tales of corruption. And when War came, and the gypsies were rounded up and taken away, the priest and his flock of crows rejoiced in the knowledge that they were righteous.

Time passed. The priest grew old. His flock of crows deserted him. Except for one, a sad young boy who was not like the others. And the old man taught the boy all he knew; poured all his rage and hatred into the boy's receptive ears; to turn him into a crow, like himself. And when one day the gypsies returned, he sent the boy out in the form of a crow to bring disaster to their camp, and rubbed his hands in rejoicing.

For a moment I opened my eyes again. Reynaud was standing rigidly, his head turned away from the needle. The design was nearly half finished; the lines as soft as eiderdown.

But the boy was not yet fully a crow. At the last moment, he felt afraid. He lit a little fire on the bank near where the riverboats were moored, but did not stay behind to observe. Instead he ran, and the fire went out, leaving nothing but scarred grass.

But the old man was watching him. Through his telescope, he saw that his disciple had failed. And when night fell, he went to the place where the boy had lit the fire, and set fire to the boats himself and watched them burn from his hiding-place. And when the morning came, and the boy came running to him with news, the priest — perhaps to punish him — allowed the frightened boy to believe that it was he who committed the crime.

I felt Reynaud flinch again.

'Shh,' I said. 'I've nearly finished.'

And though he too became a crow, a single pale feather set the boy apart from all the others. The pale feather marked him as different. Throughout his life he had tried to become just as his mentor had wanted, but time after time he failed in his task, weakening at just the wrong moment. Every time the travellers came, he failed to do what he set out to do, and finally he understood that he would never truly be a crow because of that one pale feather.

And so he resolved to pluck it out, and be like all the others. But the more he did so, the paler the single feather grew back, until all the other crows saw it, and drew away, knowing that he was not one of them. The crow who had once been a boy took this as a sign of his guilt, not knowing that it was the opposite. Until one day a girl came along — a young girl of the travelling folk. And she told him a story about a boy who grew up to think he was a crow, because an old enchanter had put him under an evil spell. And at last, when he came to realize that he had never been a crow, he shed his feathers one by one to reveal the man he had always been —

I opened my eyes. It was finished. There was hardly any blood. 'Do you want to look now?'

Reynaud nodded. His eyes were wet. And at last his colours had started to change — the muddy greys and dismal browns shifting to something like the dawn. 'Your story,' he said.

'Not *mine*,' I said. 'Yours.'

3

That child is not my daughter, I thought. She *looks* exactly like Rosette, big dark eyes and mango hair, but her voice is that of a stranger. Or maybe not a stranger: her voice is that of Morgane Dubois, and of Zozie de l'Alba, and of the *Hurakan*, and I know that I cannot keep her safe, or even keep her, ever again.

I know a story, she tells me. Then she tells me about Reynaud, and scrying in the tattoo ink. I feel surprise at my surprise. My daughter has skills. I knew that, of course. But the depth of her vision is something that I had not really recognized. She was always good at drawing, even when she was a child. I'd thought that talent came from Roux. Maybe that's why I overlooked it for so long. But now I realize that all the time, Rosette was speaking through her art; showing us the things she saw, silently, in colours.

'I'm glad you were able to help Reynaud,' I said. 'I tried, but I couldn't.'

'He needed more than chocolate.' There was no harshness in her voice, and yet I felt it in the place where only our children can reach us.

And who will give me what I need? I did not speak aloud, and yet I knew Rosette had heard me. I even knew what she would say next, in that strange new voice of hers, which is also the voice of my mother, and of Zozie, and of Morgane, and of everything and everyone that returns to remind me that life is on loan, and that all the things we find on the way — lovers, children, happiness — have to be given back in the end. But instead she turned to me and said:

'Morgane left something, else, *Maman*. Here. Come see.'

Rosette stood up. I was stiff from sitting on the floorboards, and she held out her hand to help me up. Thus, with a gesture, the balance of power shifts from mother to daughter, without either one even noticing; and the world shifts imperceptibly on its axis and settles back into its new position. *Change*.

'Here. In the back room,' said Rosette.

I looked back at the tattoo kit lying on the wooden floor. I could see the last of the light shining through the slats in the blinds. The room smelt of sawdust, and incense, and ink, and the ghosts of flowers long dead, and I already knew what was coming. I'd seen it before in my mother's cards. *Death. The Tower. Change. The Fool.*

I followed her into the back room — a room I had never seen before, not even in Narcisse's day. It was very like the back of the *chocolaterie*, but with ancient wooden work surfaces instead of my worn granite ones, and it was perfectly clean and bare — except for something standing there on the counter by the door. Two things, in fact; a matched pair: gleaming darkly in the light that filtered through the window. It was

404

Morgane's prosthetic feet, now looking nothing like feet at all, but more like an ugly pair of shoes out of an ugly fairytale, left for someone else to wear, while their owner took wing and flew away —

I gazed at them stupidly. 'Her feet. Why did she leave her feet behind?'

Rosette shook her head. 'Maybe she didn't need them,' she said. 'Or maybe it was a message.' And she told me about a dream she'd had, a dream in which Morgane had told her to cut off her feet so she could fly . . .

And *now* I knew what she was going to say. *Death, The Fool. The Tower. Change.* The cards never lie. They simply say the things we know, deep down, to be true. That everything in life is on loan, and must be given back in the end. Roux. Anouk. And now Rosette, now that she has found her voice, she too will be moving on. Nothing — no-one — can stop her now. She is like the strawberry runners growing away from the parent plant, hungry for new soil, hungry for change. If left unchecked, the strawberry plants will reclaim their wildness; their leaves growing small; their tiny fruit sweet and shrunken. *Change. The Tower. Death. The Fool.* Fool to think I could hold her back. Fool to think that Morgane Dubois was my only enemy.

She looks at me. 'Maman, it's time.'

'Yes, I know.' My changeling. You have grown so brave and sweet, curious and powerful. I will miss you, but I know that you too must move on. I tried to keep you. I was wrong. Children are not ours to keep, but ours to give to the future.

405

I roll up my sleeve to the elbow. The inside of my wrist is a paler shade of brown. There are veins here, blue as a bruise, a scar from some long-ago accident. I am marked in so many ways: stretch marks on my belly and hips; scars on my knees and knuckles. Marks from the sun on my arms and face; still pale, but growing darker. Wrinkles in my forehead; laughter lines around my eyes. Like the table in the *chocolaterie*, I bear the blemishes of time. I do not begrudge this. It means I have lived. It means that I have lived well.

But now, I will have another mark. One that my daughter will give me. Here, on the inside of my wrist, between the blue vein and the scar. It will remind me that I have a child, somewhere in the universe. What will it be? A flying bird? A blue sail, heading out to sea? Blossom on the wind? A golden monkey? A broken heart?

There is an old chair under the counter. Perhaps it was there before Morgane. Rosette pulls it out for me. 'Sit down. You'll be more comfortable here than on the floor.' She's right, of course. The floor is too hard for me to sit still for long enough. Rosette goes into the front of the shop; comes out with her tattooing kit. Changes the nib on the tattoo pen. Plugs it into the power pack. It makes a tiny droning sound, like the buzz of a leafcutter bee.

'Are you ready, *Maman*?' she says.

Yes. No. Always. Never.

'It's all right, *Maman*. This won't take long.'

Sixteen years. I close my eyes. I do not ask if it will hurt. Instead I concentrate on the sound; the tiny drone of the leafcutter bee. I think of Anouk at six years old, and of Rosette, and Pantoufle, and Bam. I think of Roux, and the way he smiled, the day I first saw him on the Tannes. I think of my mother's face before the cancer made its mark on her. My mother was younger than I am now when she died. I have outgrown her. And yet she is still with me, just as my daughters will always be with me, however far they go. Perhaps this is what Rosette means when she tells me she knows what I need.

The needles are almost painless. Even Narcisse's abandoned old chair I find surprisingly comfortable. Eyes closed, I realize how tired I am; how tired I have been for months, maybe years. I hear the drone of the leafcutter bee, and remember my mother's stories, stories that started with the words: *I know a tale the bees used to tell* . . .

I realize that the humming has stopped. I open my eyes. She has finished. I want to look down at my finished tattoo, but just at that moment a doorbell rings — a doorbell that has already gone, along with its shadowy owner — and someone comes into the front of the shop.

I know those footsteps very well. Light as a fox on the floorboards; red as a fox in the evening light. 'I thought I'd find you here,' he says.

'I thought you were gone.'

He shrugs. 'Not yet.'

And outside, I hear the sound of the wind, the good north wind, the dancing wind, whispering in my mother's voice: *See, Vianne? Everything returns.*

407

4

I walked home by the side of the Tannes, watching the last of the sunset. The lights on the river were starting to burn; the lanterns on the riverboats, the soft lights at the windows. It smelt of woodsmoke, and spices, and oil, and the good smells of cooking from the Boulevard P'tit Baghdad. And yet something is different. It took me some time to understand. And then, suddenly I realized. The scent of smoke on the river no longer seems to trouble me.

So this is absolution, *mon père*. This is what innocence feels like. After all these years, at last, I have put aside my burden. Rosette Rocher has healed me. She made me look inside myself, and showed me what I needed to see. I am not guilty of lighting the fire. You did that yourself, *mon père*. You did it in order to own me, to keep me forever by your side. I ought to hate you. And yet I do not. You must have been so unhappy. Maybe you even loved me, in your bitter, twisted way. And I kept you close to me all these years, like a secret too terrible to confess, but now I can let you go at last. You too can be finally free.

I mean to destroy Narcisse's file. As soon as I get home, I thought, I will burn it in my fireplace. He too deserves absolution, the chance to be remembered kindly. And after all, he was

408

only a child when he committed the deed that has followed him to the grave, shrivelling every relationship, every dream he dared to dream. Narcisse deserves forgiveness too, and under my breath I murmur the prayer of absolution. Someone like the Bishop might balk at my bending the Church's rules in this way, but our Saviour was a breaker of rules. I like to think He'd understand.

Opening Narcisse's green file, I realized there was still a page that in my haste, I'd left unread. Folded right at the back of the script, I'd almost missed it completely. Now I unfolded the single sheet, and, in the afterglow of the sun and the lights shining over the river, I read Narcisse's final words, then closed his confession one last time, and headed for the Café des Marauds. One last toast to old Narcisse. And if *she* joins me — well, we'll see. One thing at a time, Reynaud.

One summer, when I was still a young man, an ancient biplane landed in one of the fields that I'd left fallow that year. The pilot was selling rides, and already a dozen people were watching and waiting by the gate.

'Are you the owner?' the pilot asked, pulling off her flying-helmet. She was a young brown-skinned woman with curly hair and a smile that shone like half the sun.

I said I was.

'If you let me use your field, I'll give you a ride for free,' she said.

I was a little unsure at first. But I'd never been in a plane, although I'd seen enough of

409

them, scratching the sky far overhead. I imagined looking down on the farm, on the village, on my land, and I agreed, if only to have that view to keep forever in my mind.

I'll admit it, Reynaud: it was a little frightening. But the view was as marvellous as I'd hoped, and the sound of the wind was exhilarating, and if I had believed in God, I might have felt his eye on me as I watched my world unroll below me like a bolt of cloth. There was the farm, and the sunflower fields, and my truck the size of a sugar cube, and the little scatter of people there, faces turned up to the sky.

And then I saw it. My father's wood: thick by then with twenty years' growth, but still not fully mature. A half-grown wood of oak trees around that little clearing, which, with my new perspective, I could see made the shape of a heart.

I stared down at the clearing. The heart was unmistakeable; tapered at the base with the strawberry field in the centre; a stand of trees to form the cleft. How long had it taken my father, I thought, to plan the formation, to plant out the trees? How many calculations had he made to create this God's-eye view? I thought of the years I had been at school; the years I had felt his absence. I remembered the contempt I'd felt at his little hobby. And finally I understood what he'd tried to say to me on the night of my wedding.

'Love is the thing that only God sees.'

I'd wondered at the time what he meant. My

410

father seldom spoke of love; rarely showed affection. Perhaps that was Tante Anna's influence, or maybe the few words he'd had were all spent on Naomi. But here it was at last, I saw: the heart-shaped meadow in the wood, a silent testament to grief; a last, enduring promise.

Love is the thing that only God sees. I suppose you'd say that's because he sees into our hearts. Well, if he ever looks in mine, he'll see no more than I've told you. Confession may be good for the soul. But love is even better. Love redeems us even when we think ourselves irredeemable. I never really loved my wife — not in the way that she deserved. My children and I were never close. Perhaps that was my fault, after all. But Mimi — yes, I loved Mimi. And I loved Rosette Rocher, who was so very like her. One day I hope Rosette will see the heart-shaped meadow in the wood, and know that love surrounds her, whether she can see it or not. And you, Reynaud. I hope one day you can feel what only God sees, but which grows from the hearts of people like us: the flawed; the scarred; the broken I hope you find it one day, Reynaud. Till then, look after Rosette for me. Make sure she knows my story. Tell her to take care of my wood. And keep picking the strawberries.

All Fools

1

Saturday, April 1

All Fools' Day, and the *chocolaterie* is filled with comings and goings. My chocolate fish are best-sellers today, each with its hand-painted sibling, lovingly designed by Rosette, which, according to All Fool's Day tradition, must be furtively pinned onto the unsuspecting back of a friend, to be worn all day, unless someone kindly points it out. I have already seen my paper fish on the backs of children in the square, as well as on some of their relatives, including old Mahjoubi, whose pretended ignorance of the joke sent his granddaughter Maya into an ecstasy of giggling.

Today my customers are filled with questions and curiosity. The Montours are leaving, I hear; apparently they have already found a buyer for the farmhouse. Yannick Montour told me as he came in to buy his chocolate fish. And Monsieur le Curé was actually heard *laughing aloud* in church today — a sound hitherto unknown among the people of Lansquenet.

Joline Drou — who always sits in the pew at the front — thought she saw something on his arm through the half-open vestry door. *Something like a tattoo*, she says, in the breathy tone of voice she adopts when speaking of something scandalous.

'Not Monsieur le Curé!' says Caro, who has

been sporting a paper fish, pinned to the back of her jacket since Mass. I suspect that the trickster is Joline herself, or maybe Pilou, or even Roux, who has been in the tattoo shop all morning, helping Rosette move her things in.

Yes, she is a little young. And yet she is not moving far. But a tattooist needs space to work, and the rent is quite affordable. Anouk is strangely unsurprised: she says she always knew Rosette was not made to work with chocolate. 'She's too volatile,' she says. 'She doesn't have the discipline.'

I had to laugh at that. That Anouk, barely twenty-one, newly married and about to fly across the world, should know more than I do about it — and yet, there is a wisdom in them both, and a fearless determination.

I had that once. Today I think that maybe I could find it again, like something I thought lost forever, brought back with the rising tide. *Everything returns.*

'Do you want some help?' said Anouk, watching me bring out the big glass jars of raisins and cherries and sprinkles and nuts to decorate the *mendiants.*

I smiled. 'Of course. My favourites.'

It has been a long time since Anouk wanted to help me make chocolates. Now she does, as a child might play with her favourite toys for one last time before putting them aside for ever. Almonds, candied lemon peel, fat black cherries, green cardamom, and a sprinkle of edible gold to highlight the rich dark chocolate. Once sold by travellers door-to-door, these are kings and queens of the road, gilded, glossy and glorious.

'I made mine into faces,' she said.

I smiled at her. 'You always did.'

Death. The Fool. The Tower. Change. This time, *I* have been the fool. I have feared the wind for so long; I have hidden away from the truth. Now it feels as if the sky has cleared after a storm. The roof of my house has been torn away, and yet the sun is shining. My children have grown up at last, and now instead of loss, I feel a strange kind of *potential*.

Anything could happen, Vianne, says my mother's voice in my mind. *Death. The Fool. The Tower. Change. The wheel keeps turning, turning until everything comes round again.* From across the square, I could see the door of the shop. It was open. There was someone at the door, carefully stripping away the purple paint with a blowtorch and a palette knife. His face was turned away from me, but I would know him anywhere: the tattooed spirals on his arms; the red hair tied back in a knot.

Roux tells me that Rosette prefers to choose her own decoration. Yellow, maybe pink, she says. Roux has promised to stay and help. I deliberately did not ask *how* long he was staying. Maybe a week. Maybe a year. As Anouk would probably say, now is all that matters.

'You look different,' said Anouk.

'Different?'

'It suits you.'

Rosette's design is a simple one, drawn on the inside of my wrist. A strawberry runner, the little trefoil no larger than a clover leaf, flanked with a tiny wild strawberry and a five-petaled flower. It still feels a little sensitive, but, as Anouk would probably tell me, that means I am still alive.

I know a story about a woman who knew what people needed. Her gift was to look into their hearts and find the thing that was missing. And yet, when it came to her own heart, the woman was strangely powerless. And every time she used her gift, she felt a piece of herself disappear, and it made her sad and frightened. And she clung to the pieces of her heart like handfuls of leaves against the wind, but the more she clung, the more the wind would scream and blow and threaten.

And then, one day a stranger came to this woman's village. A stranger like herself, with a gift for finding out peoples' secrets, for teasing out their deep desires and most hidden terrors. The stranger was fearless, elusive, and strong, and the use of her gifts, far from weakening her, only made her stronger.

This made the woman uneasy, and she tried to confront the stranger. But for everything she tried to do, the stranger seemed to surpass her, until at last she called the wind, commanding it to do its worst. All night long, the wind screamed and blew. And when it was done, the stranger had gone, blown away into the dark.

And yet the woman was still afraid. Although the stranger had gone, her voice, the sound of her footsteps, the scent of her remained, as if somehow she *herself* had been displaced, and the wind had found its way into the spaces inside her, and blown the heart of her clean away.

But little by little, the voice of the wind started to talk to the woman. It told her everything returns, that if you set free what you love it comes back like the turning tide. And finally she understood that she had only been fighting herself. There was no mysterious stranger, no shadowy adversary. *Hers* had been the voice of the wind: raging, scolding, hectoring. And now that it was calm again, she understood that she was free. Free to go or to stay as she chose: free to use her gifts as she chose; free to love without fear of loss.

I put my arms around Anouk and gave her a kiss.

'Good work,' I said. 'Now how about a cup of chocolate, to celebrate?'

She nodded. 'Let me make it.'

Of course. She knows the recipe. Straight from the Criollo bean, sweetened with cane syrup and vanilla and spices and topped with a spoonful of whipped cream and a dash of red chilli. She makes it as well as I ever did, perhaps even better. She pours a cup for each of us. I reach out a hand; she stops me.

'Wait.'

Smiling, she reaches behind my back. I feel the tiny tug of the pin as she removes the paper fish. Her laughter is warm, and I feel it like sunshine on my dappled skin.

'Rosette?'

She shakes her head and grins. Her eyes are filled with mischief. I feel a surge of joy at the world, because my daughters are in it.

I kiss her again. 'You got me,' I say. 'Now, what

about that chocolate?'

It is my recipe, and yet it is not quite familiar. A little less sugar, a little more vanilla, or cardamom, or maybe turmeric. In any case, it is sweet and good, and it smells of other places, of wonderful things to discover. But it also smells of home; of the scent of fig leaves in the sun, and Armande's peaches cooking. It smells of moonlight on the Tannes, and the scent of Roux's tattooed skin against mine. It smells of the past and the future, and suddenly I realize that I am no longer afraid of anything that future may bring. The hole in the world has somehow been filled. I am whole again, and free.

'This tastes different,' I say. 'What did you change?'

'Trade secret.' She smiles.

And then I see it in the air; a shimmy so pale and fleeting that it was almost invisible. My summer child has skills of her own, skills that are different to mine or Rosette's. Where will they take her? Where will she go? What winds, what oceans will she ride? What lives will she change forever?

I finished the chocolate. 'It's very good. Even better than mine, I think.'

'Of course it is. I made it,' said Anouk. 'Mine was always better.'

She handed me one of the finished *mendiants*. A fat black cherry for the nose; a candied lemon slice for the mouth. She had made all her chocolates into little faces. Features added in gold leaf; almonds, raisins, poppy seeds. All of the chocolates different, all of them marked with her signature:

Love me. Feed me. Free me —
And all of the chocolates were smiling.

Acknowledgements

It takes a whole village to raise a book. Some books can even build villages — at least in the minds of their readers. This is the fourth book in this series of interconnected tales about the village of Lansquenet-sous-Tannes, which has been built on foundations laid in place over twenty years by many, many editors, copy-editors, cover artists, publicists, booksellers, book reps, bloggers and readers, without whom I would never have had the chance to return to the world of *Chocolat*. All of them deserve credit, although to name them all is impossible. You know who you are, though. You did this. I have not forgotten you.

But for this particular book, I owe heartfelt thanks to all the excellent folk at Orion; to editors Gillian Redfearn and Clare Hey; to copy-editor Sally Partington; to Jon Wood; to Charlotte Abrams-Simpson for her marvellous cover design[1]; to publicist Rebecca Gray and marketer Lynsey Sutherland; sales people Jennifer Wilson, Jo Carpenter and Rachael Hum; MD Katie Espiner and Executive Publisher Sarah Benton; and to all the booksellers, bloggers and reps who have worked to keep my books on the shelves. Thanks also to my agent, Peter Robinson, and to my friend Christopher Fowler, who was there from the very

[1] Orion edition

start. And of course to Kevin and Anouchka, who were *before* it started, and without whom I might never have put pen to paper at all.

The final debt, as always, is to you, the reader, whoever you are: new arrival to the party, or old friend at the reunion. Stories don't live in a vacuum; they need an audience to survive. Thank you for your attention, and for those who are old friends in this world, thank you for your loyalty. I made this for you. I hope you like it.

We do hope that you have enjoyed reading this large print book.

Did you know that all of our titles are available for purchase?

We publish a wide range of high quality large print books including:
**Romances, Mysteries, Classics
General Fiction
Non Fiction and Westerns**

Special interest titles available in large print are:
**The Little Oxford Dictionary
Music Book
Song Book
Hymn Book
Service Book**

Also available from us courtesy of Oxford University Press:
**Young Readers' Dictionary
(large print edition)
Young Readers' Thesaurus
(large print edition)**

For further information or a free brochure, please contact us at:
**Ulverscroft Large Print Books Ltd.,
The Green, Bradgate Road, Anstey,
Leicester, LE7 7FU, England.
Tel:** (00 44) 0116 236 4325
Fax: (00 44) 0116 234 0205